THE KEYS TO THE STREET

THE KEYS TO THE STREET

A NOVEL OF SUSPENSE

RUTH RENDELL

Doubleday Canada Limited

Canadian Cataloguing in Publication Data

Rendell, Ruth, 1930-

The keys to the street

ISBN 0-385-25598-5

I. Title

PR6068.E63K49 1996 823'.914 C96-930572-9

Design by Leonard Henderson

Printed and bound in the United States of America

Published in Canada by
Doubleday Canada Limited
105 Bond Street
Toronto, Ontario
M5B 1Y3

For Don

THE *K*EYS
TO THE *S*TREET

I ron spikes surmount each of the gates into the park, twenty-seven of them on some, eighteen or eleven on others. For the most part the park itself is surrounded by thorn hedges, but thousands of feet of spiked railings still remain. Some of these spikes are blunted, as on those enclosing the gardens of Gloucester Gate, some are ornamented, and some take a bend in the middle. On the tall railings outside one of the villas the spikes have clawlike protuberances, six on each, curved and sharp as talons. A certain terrace has spikes on pillars, splaying out and blossoming like thorn trees. If you started counting spikes in the region of the park and its surroundings you could reach millions. They go well with the Georgian architecture.

By night the park is closed to people. Of the living creatures that remain within its confines, most are zoo animals and waterfowl. The spiked gates open every morning of the year at six and close every evening at dusk, which is at four-thirty in winter but not until nine-thirty in May. Its 464 acres of land fill a circle. Inside the ring of streets that surrounds it lies another ring and within this, widely separated, the equilateral triangle of the London Zoo, the lake with its three arms and four islands, and around the ornamental gardens a road that on the map looks like a wheel with two projecting spokes.

The park is deserted by night. That is, the intention is that it should be deserted. The park police patrol between dusk and dawn, paying special attention to the restaurant areas that make likely shelters and to the park residences, the villas, the expensive properties, and Winfield House, where the American ambassador lives. No vagrant could sleep undisturbed under the lee of the pavilions or the bandstand, but the police cannot search everywhere every night. The canal bank remains as a place of concealment amid the wide green spaces and, in summer, the long grass under the trees.

To the north of the park, beyond the zoo and Albert Road, lie Primrose Hill and St. John's Wood; here are St. John's Wood church, Lords Cricket Ground, and, turning south eastward, the Central London Mosque. Park Road runs down toward Baker Street and Sherlock Holmes by way of the London Business School and St. Cyprian's Church, Anglo-Catholic, white and gold inside and scented with incense. The Marylebone Road, the Planetarium, Madame Tussaud's waxworks—most popular of all London's tourist attractions, more visited than the Tower and Buckingham Palace—the Royal Academy of Music, Park Crescent and Park Square with their secret gardens and the tunnel passing under the road that links them. And so the park is encircled, here by Albany Street, running from Great Portland Street station due north, as straight as a Roman road, to meet Albert Road and Gloucester Avenue. The streets of Primrose Hill form a shape like a tennis racket and Gloucester Avenue is its handle. There are railings everywhere, their spikes straight and pointed, twisted at a right angle or ornate and blunted.

· · ·

Albany Street is not leafy and sequestered like almost every other in the vicinity of the park, but wide, gray, without trees. Barracks fill much of one side, but beyond the other side of it lie the grandest and most lavish of the terraces, Cambridge, Chester, and Cumberland, with their colonnades, their pediments, their statuary, and their wealthy occupants. Beyond the other side the area quickly becomes less respectable, though it has a long way to go before sinking to the level of Somers Town between Euston and St. Pancras stations. From one of these streets, near St. James's Gardens, a young man was walking across Munster Square, heading for Albany Street.

The name everyone called him by was Hob, the three letters of which were the initials of his two given names and his surname. Apart from this, the feature that distinguished him from his contemporaries was the size of his head. His body was solid and thickset but his head still looked too big for it. When he reached fifty, if he ever did, his jowls would be down on his shoulders. His fair hair was cut an inch long all over his big head and gleamed in the yellowish chemical light. It was an unusual combination, that of fair hair and brown eyes. His eyes were a curious textured brown, like chocolate mousse, and the pupils were sometimes as big as a cat's and sometimes the size of a full stop on a keyboard.

Hob had a job to do, for which he had just been paid half his fee of fifty pounds. That is, he had been paid twenty-five pounds. This he intended to put with everything else—he had to buy what he needed before he could do anything at all. Often he wished he were a woman, because for women making money was quick and, as far as he could see, easy. One of the first things he remembered hearing from a grown-up—it was an uncle, his mother's boyfriend—was that every woman is sitting on a fortune.

He was in a state. That was how he put it to himself, the phrase he always used for his present condition. One of his stepsisters had described her panic attacks to him and in her description he recognized his own state. But his was longer-lasting and somehow *bigger*. It took in the whole world. It made him afraid of everything he could see and hear and just as frightened of what he couldn't see and of silence. As the state intensified, a huge bubble of fear like a glass ball enclosed him so that he wanted to beat and thrash at its curved walls. Sometimes he did, even out in the street like this, and people crossed the road to avoid this madman who punched at the empty air.

The state had not yet reached this level. Nor did he yet have pain or nausea. But beyond walking to his destination, up this long, wide gray street where at present there were no people to avoid him or to stare, he could have done nothing, certainly not the job for which he had received half the fee. Walking became mechanical. Even in a state he sometimes thought he could have walked forever, on and on, over the dark lawns, the green peak, the hills of north London, to the fields and woods far beyond.

But walking miles would be unnecessary. Gupta or Carl or Lew would be on the other side of the Cumberland Gate, where the Chinese trees were. He walked through the wells and alleys and up the slope at Cumberland Terrace. His shadow was a lumbering black cutout on wrinkled cobbles. Lights shone up on walls and behind cascades of leaves.

The Outer Circle, so busy by day, was deserted at night and no single car was parked on its gleaming surface. The great terraces, palaces in woodland, slept heavily behind dark foliage, and though many of their eyes were shuttered, some were alive with orange light. Lamps were lit along the pavements as far as he could see in each direction. The spaces between them were filled with shiny darkness. He crossed the road. The Cumberland Gate was locked and had been for nearly three hours.

The railing of which the gate was made was topped with iron spikes, eighteen on each gate. When he was well—the term he used for his condition when not in a state—he would have thought nothing of climbing the gate. Now he scrambled over it like an old man with an old man's caution and fear of puncturing flesh and breaking bones. On the other side an expanse of half dark lay, gray lawn, pale paths, black trees, spindly black Chinese trees that made him think of scorpions.

The police patrolled in cars, on foot, on bicycles, sometimes with dogs. It was a principle of his, and of Carl's, that they cannot ever be everywhere. Mostly they were not where he was or Carl was. He walked into the trees. He meant not to make a sound but when a young scorpion leapt off its parent's back and grew wings and turned into a pterodactyl—it was a pigeon flying from a treetop—he let out a cry of fear.

A hand came from behind and went over his mouth. He wasn't afraid, he knew who it was.

Gupta said,

"Are you crazy?"

"I'm not well."

Even in the dark he could see Gupta's bloody teeth when he spoke. They looked as if he'd been chomping on raw steak, but in fact it was betel he chewed. All the money Hob had was exchanged for what Gupta produced, a plastic bag holding a small block of something like a white pebble but rough and irregular, not smoothed by the sea. Not for the first time he thought of his strength and Gupta's frailty and of the other white stones in the yogurt carton, enough to keep him well for a long time. But it was no use. Retribution would be swift. He'd carried out some of it for them, so he knew. They'd start by breaking his legs. He doubted if he would even get beyond the first thump of his fist into Gupta's skinny belly.

It was strange, he had stopped trying to understand it, the state was so awful, so why did he want to prolong it? He always did. That uncle—or one of them—would have said it was like banging your head against a wall, it was so good when you stopped. But that wasn't quite how he felt; rather, as if the pain and the state, the panic and the total meaningless of everything, became pleasure when he knew he had the means of ending them. The state became almost enjoyable and he walked inside his glass bubble, rolling his head and mouthing something like a smile.

If he headed for Chester Road and the Inner Circle he would be bound to encounter the police, so he turned back.. But instead of climbing the Cumberland Gate once more, he kept close along the dark grass under the hedge, aware now that he was cold. The night was cold as nights in April are. The sweat that kept on breaking out on his face and chest dried cold and salty. He could taste the salt when he licked his dry upper lip.

Soon, if the state were too long prolonged, trembling would start and the sick feeling and the great weakness as if he were aging years in as many minutes. It was a matter of striking the happy medium. Again he climbed a spiked railing, this time at the Gloucester Gate, and this time it was harder, he was an even older man with worse arthritis and more frightened bones.

He got over the gate and waited at the lights at the top of Albany Street. Some seconds, a whole minute probably, passed before he understood that the lights had changed from red to green and back to red again. A solitary car stopped and waited. He went across, holding on to the wall of the bridge now, just another drunk to passersby, turning clumsily into Park Village East and pushing open the gate into the ruined garden.

They were doing up the house that loomed above him in darkness. Its windows were gone, leaving black pits. The builders' materials lay in heaps, timber, bricks, a ladder. He nearly blundered into a concrete mixer, a thing like a great pale zoo animal with heavy backside and tiny stupid head. Down the slope, black but with the gleam of water in its depths, lay the Grotto. He scrambled down, scratching his hands on brambles, trying to avoid the coils of barbed wire. There, at the bottom, his seat on the coping lit by a thin shaft from a lamp on the bridge, he shivered and hunched his body before feeling in the pocket of his jacket for his materials.

They were kept in a red velvet drawstring bag, the kind of thing a box containing a ring or necklace is put into in a jeweler's shop. He had found it in a waste bin in York Terrace, where the rubbish is of high quality. From the bag he took first another find, the metal rose from a galvanized iron watering can, then a tin lid that by chance— he had searched for quite a long time—exactly fitted over the rim of the rose, the screwtop from a vodka bottle with *Purveyors to the Imperial Russian Court* and the dates *1887–1917* printed on it in red. He pulled out a drinking straw still in its plastic wrapping he had helped himself to from the counter at the refreshment place near the Broad Walk, and a cigarette lighter.

First he took the white crystalline substance he had bought from Gupta between finger and thumb. His hand was shaking but that didn't matter, as all he had to do was crumble the substance up. He dropped it through the neck of the rose onto its perforated base. Then he screwed the vodka cap, into which he had bored two holes about a centimeter apart, onto the neck. He removed the drinking straw from its wrapping, cut it in half with nail scissors, and inserted the two halves to a length of about three centimeters into the holes. It was just light enough to see to do this, but he could have done it in pitch darkness.

Having checked by feel that the straw halves were inserted to the correct length, very important this, he struck the cigarette lighter and set the flame to the perforations on which the rock rested. The second it caught he closed the lid over the base of the rose, took the straws into his mouth, and drew in a deep inhalation. At this, the first draw, he always made a noise. It was a sound of joy, of orgasmic happiness, but to others it would have seemed like a groan of despair.

No one heard him. There was no one to hear. When educating him to work for them, Lew had told him jumbo took just ten seconds to reach the brain. He told him it would change him from one kind of person into another kind and he had been right. Hob grunted his satisfaction. A car passed along the bridge and the trees shook a little. The state began to recede like something evil in a dream being sucked away out of a door. It struggled as it went, but the door closed and clouds of warmth filled its space, and sweet singing and hope. He closed his eyes. Once, when he first used the watering can rose, he had simply turned it upside down and inhaled through the perforations, but he found you wasted a lot that way. Waste was a crime.

After a while he removed the vodka cap from the neck of the rose, shook out the rose and the lid, put them back into the jewel bag, and threw the straws away into the bushes. He had begun to feel strong and immensely happy. That was just the start.

Traffic was at its lightest, no heavy lorries or containers, only private cars. There are always some private cars. There are always people in Camden High Street, no matter what the hour. After midnight, for a while, London throbs softly but it still throbs. Chemical lamps color the darkness greenish-white and dull orange, and the traffic lights change from green to amber to red to amber again and to green silently and often to an empty street. At such a place, where the lights changed to no purpose to a deserted roadway, he crossed to Albert Road, to Parkway. When he was well he was a different person and he walked springily.

The different person, the person who was not in a state, was a joker, facetious, a user of peculiar slang. Everything made him laugh. He was strong, he could do anything, he could certainly do the job for which he had received half-payment. The watch he had often nearly sold but had not yet sold told him it was twelve minutes past one.

The mark was due to arrive in London on the nine twenty-five train from Shrewsbury, which comes into Euston Station at one-fourteen. Euston was less than a mile away, the nearest of all the London stations. If the train was on time and a taxi was waiting, he had just enough time to make it to St. Mark's Crescent—nice time, in fact. A mark living in St. Mark's Crescent was something else to make him laugh, and he did so, but quietly, to himself.

He walked up Gloucester Avenue, took the fork into Regent's Park Road and up the fork to the right. The park was invisible, though lying only a few yards behind the tree-shaded walls. Dark shadows and leaves that scarcely rustled. Dustbins awaiting emptying; a cat that padded as silently as the place was silent, listened, froze, smelled or intuited him, and streaked, quick as a weasel, over the wall.

Lights were on in the houses, but not many. There were no lights on any floor of the house that was his destination. It had a dingy front garden, thick with weed bushes. He knew some of these were brambles because they caught on his clothes as he dropped down among them. A briar tugged at the back of his hand, scratching and puckering, making a zip fastener of blood on the skin.

It was so quiet that he heard the taxi when it was still in Regent's Park Road. He felt very calm and happy, wishing only that he had someone to talk to and clown with, maybe put on his hit-man act, talking like a TV actor. The taxi turned the corner and pulled up outside the garden where he was. Its light shone right on him, into his eyes. He kept as low down as he could get. He heard the exchange.

"Take three."

"Thanks very much, guv."

The gate opened. The taxi started, moved, began to turn. If the driver had waited till the front door came open he didn't know what he'd have done. A suitcase was pushed in onto the path and the gate closed behind it and its owner with a soft click. The lights of the taxi dwindled, disappeared, and the throb of its engine faded.

He stood up and used his bare hands, first his hands, then his feet. One over the mouth from behind, a stranglehold armlock to bring him down, and when he was on the ground, the kicking. Not enough to kill or permanently disable but enough to injure, break a couple of the mark's ribs, maybe not improve the future prospects of his spleen. Some dental work would probably also be needed.

He enjoyed it. He admired himself for doing it so well, particularly his skill in doing it in silence. Long practice and the use of his hands had ensured not a sound escaped from that mouth out of which blood now trickled in a thin stream. He knelt down. There was nothing in his brief about robbing the man, but when you came to think of it the fee was laughable. He was entitled. He put his hand inside the jacket, felt in the pocket, and found a wallet. Credit cards were no use to him, there was only one thing he wanted to buy and neither Carl nor Gupta would take Visa. Ten pounds, twenty and another twenty . . . Joy began to fill the spaces of his body with warmth. Eighty pounds. He stuffed it into his pocket alongside the red velvet bag.

Then, because he liked a joke and was feeling cheerful, he opened the suitcase and took a look inside. Not surprisingly, it was full of clothes. The surprise was that they were women's, mostly women's underwear. It now came back to him that he had heard there was something funny about the mark, though he'd half forgotten what.

He set about hanging the stuff on the bushes, red silk bikini pants, French knickers, a black bra, a black lace nightie. It looked as if a couple of girls were camping there and had done their washing before they kipped down for the night. Whatever the name of the black see-through thing was, a sort of all-in-one with a fastening in the crotch, he didn't know, but he draped it over the gate and dropped a couple of suspender belts on the mark's recumbent body.

The faint groaning coming from that half-open mouth meant it was dangerous to remain any longer. He left the garden, licking the blood off the scratch on the back of his hand, walking fast, going in the opposite direction this time, toward Primrose Hill. His spirits had begun to sink. Lew had told him about the ten-second effect but said nothing about depression coming back half an hour later. It was too late now. Gupta would no longer be among the Chinese trees, but Carl or Lew might be on the Hill or the Macclesfield Bridge. He headed that way, his gains in his pocket.

"Jumbo, jumbo," muttered Hob, and then he sang it to keep his spirits up. "Jumbo, jumbo . . ."

2

The letter came the day she left. There was a postcard from her grandmother, a bill for water, and this letter in a brown envelope with the Harvest Trust logo that looked like a scarlet mushroom, but was not of course that, was something quite other than that. She postponed opening it. Her grandmother's post-card was from a place called Jokkmokk in the north of Sweden. It said, *Dear Mary, I shall be back in London next Thursday, by which time you will be settled in Park Village. Will phone. Surprising heat here and midnight sun. Much love. . . .*

"I'll want a check for your half of the water," Alistair said, very sour and cross, truculent with resentment.

Mary said nothing about having paid all the electricity bill her-self. He had got hold of the other envelope and was looking at the red logo.

"May I have my letter, please?"

He handed it to her reluctantly. "They want more, I suppose."

"Very unlikely." She was trying to keep everything she said to him brief, civil, equable. The rows were in the past. "It will just be the update. They keep in touch."

"I hope it's to say he's dead," said Alistair viciously.

It was hard to stay calm in the face of this. "Please don't say that."

"It would be the best and ultimate way to show you how you've wasted your time and rubbished your body."

"I'm going to finish packing," she said.

He followed her into the bedroom. There were two open suitcases on the bed, one half-filled with her clothes. She put the letter and the postcard on top of a blue T-shirt and laid her trouser suit, folded with tissue, on top of that. A week had gone by since she had slept in that bed with him. He slept in it and she had the sofa-bed in the living room. It was easier that way, if her aim was a quiet life for what was left of it for the two of them together. She found her checkbook in a drawer and wrote him a check for half the water rate.

A nod, no smile, no thanks, and he had put it in his pocket. "If you hadn't this plushy place to go to you wouldn't be going, would you? If it was a furnished room, for instance? Or back to grandma?"

"We've been through all that, Alistair."

"And when they come back from this protracted holiday—what then? When they kick you out of glitzville? You'll come back here and say you've made a mistake and can you have your old bed back."

"Perhaps, though I don't think so. This is supposed to be a separation."

"A *trial* separation."

"If you like." Why did she always weaken, compromise? "We may both feel differently after four months."

"You'll allow for that, will you? That *I* may feel differently. That I may no longer want to marry you? That's going now, you know, that's been on the wane ever since you deceived me over that harvest thing I'm not supposed to mention. Since you deliberately made yourself ill for nothing, for no more than to get on a feel-good high, to be a martyr, to have 'done some good in this world'—wasn't that the phrase?"

"Not used by me," she said, and she felt her temper going, slipping away, a ball dropped on a slope, running downhill. She made a grab at it, hung on. "I never said any of those things, never." Thank God, I never married you, she thought. Things could be worse, I could have married you.

She closed the lid of the suitcase, started filling the other. He watched her, his upper lip slightly curled back, an animal's expression she had never seen when first they knew each other. "If my grandmother phones, will you give her this number? I'm sure she has it but just in case."

She had written it down along with the address: Charlotte Cottage, Park Village West, Regent's Park, London NW1.

"Cottage!" he said.

"The house was thought small when it was first built."

"Pretentious," he said. "A sort of Petit Trianon."

"It's near my work," she said. "I can walk to work from there." As if that was why she was doing it, as if proximity to the museum was her reason.

He had an uncanny way of intuiting these things, of picking up on a weakening. His face changed and he wheedled. He had never wheedled when first they met. "You'll ask me over, won't you? Come to that, there's no reason why I shouldn't move in there too."

"There is a reason," she said quietly. Her temper was back with her. It had never had much independence, was almost incapable of getting lost, a timid thing like its owner, not much good at standing up for itself. She fastened the second suitcase, picked up her bag, put it down again to get into her jacket. "There are quite a few reasons, Alistair, but there isn't any point in talking about it."

"You don't seriously believe I'd ever—" he hesitated, looking for a word, a silly word perhaps, a baby word, something that reduced violence to play "—smack," he said, "smack you again, do you?"

Yes, she did. Not that there had been much of that, but there had been enough. Enough to change her from the woman, typical, normal, who says, *He wouldn't hit me twice,* who says of abused women, *Why do they stay?* to the half-accepting kind, the it-was-only-once kind, even the kind who says, *He was provoked beyond bearing.* Except that now she wasn't staying or accepting or bearing but getting out.

He stood in the doorway, between her and the hall, and she had to pass him. What was I thinking of, she asked herself then and there, what was I thinking of, staying for even five minutes with a man who frightens me? An unreasonable man who thinks he owns me, body and soul?

She took a suitcase in each hand and walked by him, every muscle tense, her breath held. Instead of stepping back, he stood his ground and she had to push past him. He didn't touch her with his hands. Once, she remembered, he had stuck out a foot and tripped her up. That had been in the early Harvest days, when he first found out. He had extended a foot and sent her sprawling and said when she picked herself up, "That wasn't me, that was your bones, you've weakened your bones, you've made yourself into an old woman."

But he didn't touch her. "Alistair, good-bye," she said, a safe distance from him.

He put out a hand, then both hands, his head a little on one side. "Kiss?"

And if he seized hold of her, struck her face with one hand, then the other, shook her, threw her to the floor, used his fists . . . ? He had never done anything like that, nothing on that scale, but she found herself shaking her head. She opened the front door. Outside by the lift someone was waiting. Thank God . . . Alistair said, in his old warm voice, "Good-bye, darling. Keep in touch," but whether it was for her benefit or the listener at the lift she couldn't tell.

She had forgotten to call for a cab to take her to the tube. She lugged the suitcases round the corner, to a point invisible from any window in the flat, and sat on the low wall in front of the estate agent's, waiting for a taxi to come.

•   •   •

Devonshire Street was the farthest south any of Bean's dogs lived. This was Ruby the beagle. The next one was Boris the borzoi in Park Crescent, rich dogs both of them, well-fed, with top-grade veterinary insurance, sleek and proud and indulged. But all Bean's dogs were like that or they wouldn't have been his dogs. It would have been unthinkable for him to walk a cross-breed or a mongrel.

With Boris and Ruby on the double leash, he made his way down the slope that leads to the Nursemaids' Tunnel. This passage connects Park Crescent Gardens on the southern side with Park Square to the north. It passes above the Jubilee line of the Underground and under the Marylebone Road. By day and night the traffic here is heavy, thundering westward to the Westway, the M40, and eastward to Euston and King's Cross. It never really ceases, not even at three and four in the morning, but in the early mornings and the late afternoons, the times when Bean took his dogs out, it was heaviest. *Boom-boom-boom* it went above the tunnel roof, shaking this subterranean lane whose brownish walls and damp stone floor were lit by natural light from the open entrances at each end.

Crossing the road by the other possible means was difficult at any time. The green prancing man was lit up for almost too short a time to get to the island and thence to the other side when you had two dogs with you, both inclined to stop for a sniff without warning. As a resident of the Crown Estates, Bean had his own key to the gardens and hence the tunnel. It was once used by nannies and their young charges and as a place of assignation for lovers. Bean doubted if anybody much used it now but him.

His route was carefully organized so that the most athletic dogs had the longest run and the small short-legged ones the shortest. He started with the beagle at three forty-five, the borzoi five minutes later, and proceeded to pick up Charlie the golden retriever in St. Andrew's Place and Marietta the chocolate poodle in Cumberland Terrace, marching them through the terrace passages and out into Albany Street.

It was a sunny afternoon in late April, not warm but with a chilly wind blowing clouds across the blue face of the sky. The trees were in tender spring leaf and flowers were coming out in window boxes. Bean, at seventy, was a strong, spry, though small man who looked fifty-five from a little way away. Applying, back in 1986, for the last employment he was ever to have, he had given his age as forty-nine and been believed. By design he dressed young, but not absurdly so. Though possessing several of the late Maurice Clitheroe's suits, all altered to fit him, well-pressed blue jeans, a roll-necked sweater, and a blue padded jacket were his winter attire. Ne'er cast a clout till May be out, they said, and April wasn't out yet. His hair he had always kept militarily short, but these days he shaved his head to achieve a dense whitish stubble.

Bean stipulated that he wouldn't take old dogs or fat dogs or dogs with health problems. Six was his maximum number, never to include dogs the law required to be muzzled. Making a pretty good living at what he did, much more than a supplement to the retirement pension, he had quite a lot of rules, had to be strict, as he explained to a Mrs. Goldsworthy in Albany Street, whose scottie he was taking out for the first time.

"Seven days' notice of the dog going away on its holidays, madam," he said to her, "and a month for termination of contract. Except in a case of illness, naturally. And if anyone else or your good self takes the animal walkies that's as well as not instead of, if you take my meaning."

"Oh, yes, of course."

"So this is McBride, is it? Game little dogs, scotties, but a bit short in the leg, so he'll come in for the medium-scale run along with Lady Blackburn-Norris's shih tzu." Bean dropped names unashamedly. It was good for business. "We'll see you in three quarters of an hour, then."

Bean (in his own words) was as fit as a fiddle from all that walking, the old ticker as good as one thirty years younger, and he strode up the long straight street at four miles an hour. He was a vegetarian and it was only on Friday nights that he drank a drop of anything stronger than Coke. Health-conscious and regarding the streets merely as exercise equipment for himself and "his" dogs, he was unaware of the history of the place and its architecture, nor of the park itself. He noticed little of that distinguished building of the sixties, Lasdun's Royal College of Physicians, and never noticed that the point at which he crossed the road was outside the Danish Church of St. Katharine's, a not entirely successful copy of King's College chapel in Cambridge.

The crescent called Park Village West, and also called, especially by those who live there, the most beautiful street in London, debouches from Albany Street at the Camden Town end. Albany Street is a much frequented thoroughfare, free of heavy traffic only by night and on Sunday mornings, but Park Village West is a little haven of peace and rustic charm. It is something like a cross between a country lane and a cathedral close and in the springtime it smells of flowering trees and narcissi and wallflowers.

Bean and his dogs turned in there under the overhanging trees. "Disarming villas," these 1840-ish houses have been called, "masterpieces of the Nash school." Each one stands alone in its embowering garden and each one is different with its own style of classical ornament, blank windows, storied urns, imperatorial busts, Della Robbia medallions, gazebos, weathervanes, and garages disguised as temples to Olympian gods.

The house where his next call was to be made was separated from the pavement first by a spacious front garden, then by a low wall, freshly painted and with CHARLOTTE COTTAGE incised in its stucco. Bean secured the handle of his leash to a gatepost, and bidding his charges sit quietly, went into the garden and up the path. Last petals were falling from red tulips, baring their sooty calixes. Pansies and auriculas were out and the laburnam soon would be. A clematis with flat blooms like dull blue satin spread its tendrils across the creamy, faintly glossy facade of the house. Fluted columns stood on either side of the blue front door, supporting a pediment with Nash's gods and goddesses disporting themselves in creamy relief on a blue ground. A downstairs window was open and a woman of about Bean's age or older put her head out.

"Is that the time?" she said. "I wouldn't have put it at a minute after three."

"It's four-sixteen, Lady Blackburn-Norris," said Bean in his invariably polite way, for good manners cost you nothing. She retreated and after a few seconds opened the front door, carrying the shih tzu, the chrysanthemum dog. Gushi's coat of golden fronds, petallike and flopping into his eyes, resembled his owner's strawberry-blond hair, her fringe restrained by a pair of blue-framed mirror sunglasses.

"Whatever is that beagle doing to the borzoi?"

"Best ignore it, madam," said Bean. If she didn't know by this time, he wasn't in the business of telling her. He took the shih tzu from her and as he was attaching a free branch of the leash to its collar, fending off Ruby's overtures, a taxi came round the corner and drew up outside Charlotte Cottage.

The young woman who got out of it, and lugged out two suitcases from the seat next to the driver, must be the Blackburn-Norris's house-sitter. She looked very young to Bean, though he admitted that the greater part of the population looked young to him, and he could no longer tell whether someone was eighteen or thirty. This woman—girl, he thought—had an appearance of fragility, as if the wind could blow her away. She was slim and for some reason made him think of a lily, long-necked, white-skinned, and very fair. Not the sort to take Gushi out for long walks herself by the looks of her, and that was all to the good.

He nodded and said good afternoon. He could see that many would have called her attractive, even beautiful, but she held no attraction for him. What he had known of sex, particularly in later years, had seemed to him at best grotesque and at worst frightening. When Maurice Clitheroe died he put all thoughts of it away forever with a sigh of something stronger than relief. It crossed his mind to help the young lady up the path with her cases, crossed it and fled. His hands were full with the dogs. Besides, she shouldn't bring heavy suitcases with her if she couldn't handle them herself and if she tipped him it would be the average woman's ludicrous offering, twenty pee or at most fifty.

By this time the dogs were straining and pulling, impatient to be off, anxious for the real outing to begin. He crossed the street and the Outer Circle, taking them into the park by the Gloucester Gate, and on the broad expanse of green south of the zoo he unfastened the leashes and let them run free.

In the distance the woman who exercised a dozen dogs, but behaved more like a nanny with her charges, was playing ball with three labradors and a boxer. Bean gave her one of his looks but she was much too far away to see.

. . .

"We are starting out in Brazil," said Lady Blackburn-Norris, "then on to Costa Rica and Mexico. California after that, Utah for the great national parks or whatever they call them, and then on to New England. We shall be back by September, shan't we, darling?"

Her husband had a face and figure very much like the borzoi Mary had seen at the gate, even to the spindly legs, bent shoulders, and anteater's proboscis of a nose.

"If it hasn't killed us," he said. "I expect we seem far too ancient to you, Miss Jago, to be doing this at all. And you would be right. I am eighty-two and the madam is seventy-nine."

"My grandmother is older and she still travels a lot," Mary said.

"Oh, dear Frederica! If only she were coming with us! But she's still in Sweden and apparently she has a long-standing engagement to go with the Trattons to Crete next month. I can't tell you how grateful we are to her, Miss Jago, for bringing us you. Without someone really reliable in the house we couldn't be going away at all, could we, darling?"

Sir Stewart Blackburn-Norris said in his dry restrained way that indeed they could not. Frequently, in the past weeks, he had entertained murderous thoughts toward his wife's best friend Frederica Jago for making this protracted trip of theirs possible. Notifying the police was all very well and they had a dog—if Gushi could be called a dog—but nothing equaled *someone in the house.* Without *someone in the house* even his wife would have thought twice about going. Of course he didn't want to go. With his intimates he made no secret of it. He wanted to stay here, to stroll down to his club in Brook Street every morning and lunch there; every afternoon to take a cab back to Park Square for a chat with his friend, the director of the Crown Estates, in his sanctum, a templelike building next to the Nursemaids' Tunnel entrance; to go on eating his dinner at Odette's three times a week, at Odin's three times a week, and at the Mumtaz on Sundays.

"It was not to be," he said aloud but didn't explain when Frederica's granddaughter looked enquiringly at him.

He showed her how to work the heating and his wife showed her how to work the VCR, they gave her the list of useful phone numbers and indispensable services. She was instructed on no account to take Gushi out between eight and nine in the morning or four-fifteen and five-fifteen in the afternoon, Bean would do that, but she could take him out at other times if she—and he—felt like it and had the strength.

"I doubt if I will," said Mary. "I'll be at work during the day."

"Oh, yes, you work, don't you?" said Sir Stewart as if he had just about heard of women pursuing this freakish course, as if maybe one in a thousand did so due to esoteric pressures or rare idiosyncrasy. "At that Sherlock Holmes place in Baker Street, wasn't it?"

Mary laughed. "No, no. Not Sherlock Holmes. Irene Adler. I work at the Irene Adler Museum in Charles Lane." She thought the name might mean something to them but it evidently didn't. "That's St. John's Wood. I can walk to work from here."

Sir Stewart insisted on looking it up in his Geographer's London Atlas. He was calculating the distance, deciding perhaps whether it might be too far for her to walk, too far for *anyone* to walk, let alone someone as fragile-looking as she, when Bean came back with the dog. Introductions were made and Bean said,

"I'll see you at eight-fifteen A.M. then, miss."

No one had ever called her "miss" before. It made her feel like the daughter of the house in a Victorian novel. Fondled and spoken to nicely, Gushi launched himself at her, licking and snuggling, settling into her arms like a bunch of chrysanthemums.

"Get down, bloody dog," said Sir Stewart.

Mary said, "Why Gushi? I mean, where does the name come from?"

"Gushi Khan ruled Tibet in the seventeeth century, didn't he, darling?"

"God only knows," said Sir Stewart. "His first owner named him. I'd have called him Sam."

Mary wandered through the rooms while the Blackburn-Norrises put the final touches to their packing. It was a pretty house, comfortable and elegant, furnished charmingly yet indistinguishably from the interiors of a thousand houses and flats that bordered on the park. Chintz, velvet, Wilton, Chinese porcelain, Georgian silver, poppy heads and peacock feathers, button-back chairs, chaise longues, rent tables, Hope chairs, and one that might have been a Duncan Phyfe. She knew about these things, sometimes hoped wistfully for something different, to come upon an interior that might surprise or delight. One day, no doubt, she would have a house of her own to furnish.

There were shutters at the windows and these would help with security. No lace curtains hid the lattices or obscured the view. She stood looking out on the garden with its pergolas, and its ornamental pond, and beyond it to the green space that divides the two segments of the village. At this time of the year trees and shrubs were luxuriant, flowering creepers sprawling across every wall and height, brickwork hidden under a complicated leafy tapestry, so that nothing could be seen that might not have been in the depths of countryside. If skyscraping towers were somewhere out there, the trees clothed in fresh green and jade and golden-green hid them. Aircraft trails that scored broken white lines across the blue sky might have been streaks of cirrus.

In the garden a white lilac thrust its spires of blossom between those of a late forsythia and the snowy net of a spirea. For some reason, the beauty of it added to her sudden, unexpected loneliness. It was a long time since she had lived alone and in half an hour she would be quite solitary. Except, of course, for Gushi, but Mary was not one of those who find the companionship of an animal equal to that of human beings. She stroked the dog's head, for the thought seemed a shade treacherous.

The taxi came early. Mary opened the door to the driver. The Blackburn-Norrises were still upstairs. Sir Stewart, as soon as he heard voices, began shouting for the driver to come up and lend a hand with the cases. Five minutes of chaos ensued, the driver arguing and grumbling about his back, Lady Blackburn-Norris fluttering in circles and suddenly, surprisingly, kissing Mary good-bye, Sir Stewart inexplicably choosing this final moment to tell her how the window locks worked.

They went. The dog had gone to sleep. Mary continued to look out of the window until long after the taxi had disappeared. It was very quiet, silent as the country, and though she strained to listen she could hear nothing of the throb and hum of London. Alistair came into her mind and she thought of what it meant to be afraid of someone you had once loved and admired. He would very likely phone this evening. She wondered what would happen if she failed to answer it, if she let it ring, and the caller was a friend of the Blackburn-Norrises.

The idea of speaking to Alistair was suddenly very terrible. Perhaps she could go out for a walk or go to the cinema. There was a cinema by Baker Street Station and another one in Baker Street itself. Wouldn't it be irresponsible to leave the house and the dog immediately she had got here? She went upstairs and began to unpack.

Her bedroom looked out over the garden and the gardens of Park Village East and across the railway line to Mornington Crescent. A gas balloon, segmented red and yellow, floated up in the sky over Euston Station. She emptied the first case and hung things up in a mahogany wardrobe with claw feet. The clothes on the top of the second case went into drawers. She lifted out the trouser suit. Underneath were the postcard from Jokkmokk and the letter from the Harvest Trust.

Mary sat on the bed and looked at the envelope in her hands for a few moments before opening it. This was normal for her with letters from the trust. She wanted to know and she dreaded to know, so she always hesitated like this, bracing herself, being prepared. Could you prepare? Wouldn't the worst thing, the thing she dreaded, be a shock, however much she anticipated it?

Alistair had said he hoped the man she knew only as "Oliver" was dead. No doubt he had not absolutely meant that, he was illogical, unreasonable, about everything to do with the donation, but "Oliver" might be dead, this letter might be telling her so.

When had she last heard? She thought back. Before Christmas, October or November, more than six months. But that, of course, was normal, the way things should be. She had asked the trust to supply information after three months, after six, nine, twelve, and eighteen months. It must now be more than eighteen months, nearer twenty, since the harvest was taken.

He might be dead. The success rate was only twenty to fifty percent. In fact, he was rather more likely to be dead than alive. Prepared, or as near prepared as she was likely to be, she opened the envelope quickly, tearing at the flap with her thumbnail.

The letter was from the Harvest Trust's donor welfare officer. It reminded her that she had "requested anonymity be relaxed after one year and a half if all continued to go well." Therefore, subject to her consent, her name and address would be supplied to "Oliver" and his, with his consent, to her. Or, having obtained "Oliver's" address, she might go ahead and make contact with him herself. It was advisable for the parties to correspond with each other before arranging a meeting. The donor welfare officer would be happy to assist in every possible way. She hoped "Helen" would consult her if she had any problems, and she signed herself, Deborah Cox.

Mary read it again. She had been given something to occupy her first evening.

3

I rene Adler, adventuress, beauty, one-time mistress of the king of Bohemia, resided, according to Conan Doyle, at Briony Lodge, Serpentine Avenue, St. John's Wood. But this is fiction and the only street in London to be designated Serpentine is in West Two not West Eight, so the founders of the museum that bears her name had to be content with a house in a turning off St. John's Wood High Street.

It holds no memorabilia of her. How could it? The only woman that Sherlock Holmes ever loved—or at least, admired—appears in one single story. No sooner had he set eyes on her than she had married Mr. Norton, leaving nothing behind but a photograph of herself for Holmes to treasure. But the objects in the museum are the kind of things she might have possessed: a collection of late-nineteenth- and early-twentieth-century dresses, Pre-Raphaelite paintings, numberless exercises in the *art nouveau,* furniture of the kind with which the Blackburn-Norrises furnished their house, jewelry in silver and jet, pinchbeck, cairngorms, and moonstones, a few treasured copies of the "Yellow Book," Swinburne, Watts-Dunton, a great many Beardsley drawings, and a first edition of *Zuleika Dobson.*

Mary Jago's introduction to it was soon after she left art school and set up her own business, restoring costumes. It had not been lucrative, but it brought her into contact with Dorothea Borwick, who ran the Irene Adler and who later offered her a partnership. For the museum, largely ignored by Londoners, was a success with tourists, particularly Americans. Sometimes Mary and Dorothea even had to restrict admittance, roping off the entrance for half an hour, their hearts gladdened by the sight of a queue forming and extending round the corner into St. John's Wood Terrace.

Dorothea never came in on Mondays, just as Mary never did on Saturdays, and when she got there it was still only twenty past nine and Stacey, who sat at the ticket office and served in the shop, had not yet arrived. Mary had left Charlotte Cottage as soon as the dog-walker had brought Gushi back. She was uncertain as to the where-abouts of a pillar box in which to post her letter to the Harvest Trust, but she had found one at once, at the point where Park Village West debouched from Albany Street.

A good deal of thought and careful deliberation had preceded the writing of that letter. It had taken up most of the evening, causing her to give up ideas about a visit to the cinema. Did she, for instance, want the Harvest Trust to have her new address? Was there any point when it was only temporary? The Blackburn-Norrises would be back by early September and then, unless she felt very differently, unless she was utterly changed and had decided to go back to Alistair, she must find a place of her own. But the reply to this letter would be very important, the revealing at last of "Oliver's" identity. She almost decided to phone instead, but would they tell her on the phone? Of course not, she might be anyone, an investigative journalist, a spy, no one at the trust would recognize her voice. Back to the letter, then, the blank sheet of paper on which she had not even yet written an address. If she put Chatsworth Road, Willesden, now that she no longer lived there, would Alistair send the trust's reply on to her? Or would he take pleasure in destroying it?

The simplest plan would be to head the paper with her grand-mother's address. She had a key to the house and, besides, Frederica would be home in a day or two. After this letter from the trust, there would very likely be no more, for information about his condition would come to her straight from "Oliver." She wrote *c/o Mrs. F. M. Jago* in the top right-hand corner, Lamballe House, Belsize Park

Gardens, London NW3. The substance of the letter was to ask for "Oliver's" real name and his home address.

This way it would be out of Alistair's reach. In the past year and a half he had become angrier and more resentful of what she had done, not less so. In some curious way he had seemed to want revenge on this man he had never seen and she had never seen, whose only offense had been to suffer from acute myeloid leukemia. As she walked across the park, crossing the Broad Walk, and took the path that runs along the southern boundary of the zoo, she thought once more of Alistair's inexplicable behavior. She thought of how her action had seemed to change him and turn him into an unreasonable and at times cruel man.

The Harvest Trust had recommended a discussion with one's family before the decision to be a donor was finally taken. Alistair and her grandmother were her family, she had no other, but while her grandmother had been supportive once she'd conquered her original anxiety, from Alistair she had had nothing but anger, incredulity, rejection.

The trust's very name had provoked shudders. He seemed to have a gift for picking out from its literature every point that might be construed as ominous.

"A harvest, they call it a harvest what they do. Doesn't that tell you something? They're harvesting the marrow out of your bones."

And then, "They insure you for a quarter of a million pounds. Look, it says so here. Do you think they'd do that if it weren't dangerous?"

"I'm young and healthy," she had said. "They wouldn't take me if I weren't suitable. I just look fragile but I'm not."

And that was before she had been asked to give the donation, when she had only put her name on the register. To give in to him, to what was after all a quite unreasonable demand, she had felt would be weak and positively wrong. She knew that she belonged in the victim type, the quiet gentle person, usually female, who yields for the sake of peace, who placates and smiles and who, of course, brings out the worst in the bully. It was a casting, a role, she had lately been setting out to resist. But when the trust came back to her with a potential recipient and asked her to attend the center for a medical examination, she had not been able to stand up for herself.

She said nothing to Alistair. She went for the medical in her lunch hour. Of course, she still intended to tell him. Ironically, if things had been going badly for them she might have told him, she might have been made stronger by adversity, but their relationship was in a successful and happy period—why spoil it? Just the same, she meant to tell him well in advance of the harvest date. She would have to tell him, she knew that.

The bank sent him to Hong Kong. He was to be away a week and it was during that week that the donation was to be made. Donors should be met, it was advised, on leaving the hospital and accompanied home. She would have to do without that, or she would have to do without Alistair. Dorothea would meet her, Dorothea was discreet and would say nothing. Perhaps Alistair need never know. Whatever advances she had made, she had by then reverted to type, and telling herself she was a coward and a fool made no difference.

Mary relived all this as she walked through the park to the Monkey Gate, over the canal bridge and into Charlbert Street. It had been a day like this, sunny and breezy, but autumn not spring, when she went to the hospital for the harvest collection. The only risk, contrary to what Alistair suggested, was that associated with general anesthetic, the same as if undergoing any operation. She was "out" for about two hours, during which time they took a liter of marrow and blood, or five percent of the total in her body.

Coming round, she had felt at first excitement. It was done, she had done it. She had been able to do it, use her own good health to repair someone else's ill health, to mend nature's mistake. If she had done nothing much up till now, no good deeds, if she did none in the years to come, she had performed this one act to justify her existence.

To no one on earth would she actually have said those words; to Dorothea when she came in to visit she made light of it, saying it was nothing, a breeze. But in her heart she experienced a deep satisfaction. Even if it failed, if the transplant was useless, she would have tried, she would have done what all philosophies and all religions told us we were here to do: love our neighbor and with positive intent.

This emotional high was not long enduring. The words she had used, though silent and unspoken, now embarrassed her. She came back swiftly to practical things. Dorothea accompanied her home in a taxi, made a meal, and shared it with her, telling her to take it easy, not to come back to the museum till the following week. Mary had been tired and a little stiff but otherwise well. She ate three meals a day, went for gentle walks, took the iron pills prescribed for her, and waited for Alistair to come home.

It was something she had never been able to account for, to explain to herself, why she had not once looked at the place on her body from which the harvest had been taken. She knew precisely where it was, the cavity of the hip, the iliac crest. It would have been normal surely, natural, to have studied these punctures on the smooth pale skin, even though she had been assured they would not leave a scar. Some revulsion, if not regret—never that—must have kept her eyes from the spot while she undressed, while she took a shower. Some unwillingness to see what altruism had done to a body that was perfect, without a blemish?

Alistair saw the marks. He saw them when they made love and the bedroom was flooded with autumn sunshine, soft golden light falling on her nakedness, her whiteness and its single flaw . . .

.   .   .

The first-comers made straight for the shop where Stacey sold them calendars and postcards of Lily Langtry and Eleanora Duse, leather-bound reissues of the novels of Ada Leverson, painted fans, beaded bags, batik, appliqué work, and very expensive mock-Fortuny Knossos scarves. Mary set to work in the hat room, mending a silk brim, reattaching black ostrich feathers. "A crab shelled in whalebone" was Aldous Huxley's description of the Edwardian lady, and he called her plumed hat "a French funeral of the first class." There were more than twenty such hats in this room, all huge gâteau-like confections, pearly white, rose pink, blue, yellow, black, festooned with roses, ribbons, feathers. On one wall was a *Vogue* cartoon from 1909 of a tiny woman wearing a hat as big as an umbrella on whose brim sat a rabbit gobbling up a cabbage.

When she was in here or in the corset room, Mary often thought Irene Adler's incursions into male attire—as when she whispers "good evening" to Holmes in Baker Street—entirely understandable. The crab in whalebone could have known comfort only in bed at night, never by day in the S-shaped whalebone stays, the buckled and webbed bodices, the crustaceous layers, and those furbelowed cartwheel hats. Other pictures on the walls showed Edwardian women attempting to mount stairs, board trams, and manage their hats on windy days.

The first visitors began wandering through and Mary put her work aside. The Americans asked the most questions and there was a preponderance of Americans. She had expected a quiet slack day, as Monday usually was, failing to take into account that the tourist season was approaching its height.

"How did they handle those trailing skirts in the rain?" someone asked. It was a stock question and one she could scarcely answer.

"What about ordinary women?" was another. It was asked more and more often. "What did the poor do? The ones who couldn't afford maids to dress them and cabs to ride in? How did they manage?"

And always, "Who was Irene Adler?"

They sold more copies of the Sherlock Holmes story *A Scandal in Bohemia* (Irene as crab in whalebone on the front cover and in jacket and breeches on the back) than all the catalogs and brochures put together. A favorite place was the facsimile of Irene's drawing room, as it must have been at Briony Lodge, with the secret panel by the fireplace where the compromising photograph was kept hidden, open for all to see the secret spring. Gustav Klimt had not painted her, for he was real and she was fiction, but the mock-Klimt portrait of Irene in sequins and pearls posed against a gold-leaf screen, framed in narrow gilded wood, went back to hang on the walls of many a Midwest condo. Business was too brisk at lunchtime for Mary to leave the museum. It even looked at one point during the afternoon as if admission would have to be restricted for half an hour. But the crowd dwindled as five approached, by which time the shop had run out of calendars and Knossos scarves and Stacey was on the phone to the sales rep. Mary worried a little about Charlotte Cottage. Would Bean have let himself in satisfactorily at four-fifteen, found Gushi, and by now have brought him back? Would he have secured the front door behind him?

She considered taking a taxi back, for she had had one good walk that day. But the sun was still shining and the wind had dropped, and once she had entered the park she forgot about a reluctance to walk, she forgot about Charlotte Cottage and Gushi, and turned southward across the broad open space. Strange, how seldom she had come in here at all while she lived in Willesden, and, though working at the museum, had scarcely ever crossed the canal or even set foot south of Prince Albert Road.

Taking the path that leads down to the boating lake, she noticed for the first time how open the park was, how relatively treeless in its center, a great plain of green fringed with the towers and landmarks of London, the gold dome of the mosque, the slender column of the minaret beside it, the art deco edifice of the Abbey National in Baker Street, the Post Office Tower, and, behind her, the Mappin Terraces of the zoo. There were trees on the north bank of the lake and at its shallow rim a cluster of waterfowl, pochards and mandarins and a black swan, squabbling over the spilled slices from a cut loaf.

She crossed the Long Bridge and paused for a while to look at the heron perched on one of the island trees. It should have been possible to turn left and head for the Cumberland Gate, but there was no way through.

She was learning that this was characteristic of the park, perhaps inevitable in a design based on a circle within a circle that were not concentric. Paths seldom led where you thought they would, and it was very easy, especially in this vicinity, to take what you thought were all the right directions yet find yourself heading back for the zoo and St. John's Wood. Through the Looking Glass was what it was like, the bit where Alice notices that the path that seems to lead straight to the garden does not and is afraid of going back through the glass into the old room. I, at any rate, shall not go back to the old room, the old life, Mary thought, and with that she came out into the Inner Circle by the Open Air Theatre.

It was a short distance from there, through the golden gates and along Chester Road, to the Broad Walk. The new fountains were playing. Flowers spilled over the rims of the lion tazzas and the Roman vases. The flowerbeds, formal rectangles that flanked the wide path, were filled with polyanthus in bloom, with pansies and yellow jonquils. All the way along, from Park Square to Chester Road, and up beyond where there were no flowers but only trees and a certain wildness, seats faced each other, most of them occupied by two or three people. But on the seat nearest to the point where the road crossed the Broad Walk a man was sitting alone.

People of his sort always did sit alone, unless another of their kind joined them. No one would choose to sit on the same seat as he. Mary, approaching along the path from the west, sought about in her mind as she had often done before, for the right word for him. Dosser? Street person? Street sleeper? Not beggar, he wasn't begging. Not tramp, that was from her grandmother's time. Perhaps there was no word and perhaps there should be none.

He was reading. That made him different, set him apart. He seemed oblivious to everything and everyone, concentrating on his book. The barrow that contained his possessions rested against the metal arm of the seat. From the rag tied round his neck to the boots on his feet, his clothes were well-worn denim, rumpled wool, and threadbare polyester. He wore a dark-colored quilted jerkin. His hair was dark, the thick bushy beard that covered the greater part of his face iron-gray. She thought she had seen him somewhere before without being able to remember where. It was his hands that recalled this previous sighting or meeting. They were long, narrow, beautiful hands, sun-browned but smooth, and on the left one was a gold wedding ring.

He looked up as she passed and for a moment, infinitesimal, fleeting, their eyes met. His were blue, a strong sea-blue. He lowered his eyes almost immediately to his book and turned the page in a precise controlled movement. Trying to remember where she had seen him that first time—in Baker Street? Outside Madame Tussaud's? But she hardly ever went that way—Mary walked along the path where the gingko trees grow, the Chinese Maidenhair trees, toward the Cumberland Gate. Had he asked her for money? Had he perhaps been selling the *Big Issue*?

At the sound of her key in the lock, Gushi made three sharp barks. She called his name and he came running. If he was tired from his walk he gave no sign of it. She squatted down and he jumped into her arms, nestling there and burying his chrysanthemum face in her neck and shoulder.

• • •

Mary Jago may have failed to remember where she had previously seen Roman Ashton, but he had no trouble in placing her. She was the young woman who, arriving two hours earlier than usual at the museum in Charles Lane, had come upon him waking up on the doorstep. Irene Adler, the place was called. It had a glass-covered porch outside its front door that extended to the pavement across a small forecourt. For several nights he had slept there, dry and secluded, but he never went back after she had discovered him.

"I'm so sorry," she had said, not wanting to step over him, also perhaps afraid. A great many people were afraid of them, himself and his kind. "I woke you up. I didn't know anyone was sleeping here."

It was a principle of his not to speak to the "public," to speak only to his fellows, though that had its own problems, its own guilt. There was no reason for him to speak to people, he had no need to beg and never did, so if they addressed him he merely nodded or shrugged or gave no sign of having heard them. This delicate-looking slender girl, fair and somewhat fey-like, merited more than that. She had spoken to him as politely as if he had been a respectable householder. So he nodded, got to his feet, and rolled up his bedding in a quick, deft movement, stepping aside to let her pass.

"Sorry about that," he said. "I'm going."

She must have heard it as a mutter, a low growl. She was not to know those were the first words he had uttered to anyone apart from the street sleepers for a year. The first sentence to escape him since he had closed up his house and taken to the outdoors. And now he had seen her again. For a moment he thought she was going to speak to him and he wondered what reply to make, if any, whether to be as he once had been, a pleasant, courteous, easy-going sort of man, or as he now was, forbidding, grave, dour. But she had not spoken, she had not recognized him. It was just as well. Conversation with ordinary people was not for him; they spoke different languages.

For a little while he continued to read *Dead Souls,* or tried to read it, but the doings of Chichikov no longer held his attention. He had been distracted, not so much by the sight of the pale fair-haired girl with the swinging stride as by the emotion and the reflections thinking back to that earlier time had evoked.

He put the book into his buggy, a wooden barrow with four

wheels and a handle like the shaft of a spade, and, pushing it ahead of him, began ambling along one of the paths in a westerly direction. He had no clear idea where he was going, a common state for him to be in, for one of the benefits of his condition was perfect freedom.

It was a warm, still afternoon and this he enjoyed after the winds of the past weeks, the cold spring, the long damp winter. If happiness was denied him forever, was something exclusively for others, he could feel pleasure and that sometimes more intensely and sensuously than those who lived under roofs and slept in beds. His appreciation of the sun on his face and the soft balmy air was luxurious and profound. It almost made him smile.

Another of his principles was never to make plans during the afternoon or evening as to where he would sleep that night, for to do so was to abrogate that freedom, and freedom was all he had. Everything else had been taken away or he had taken it away himself. He would give some thought to his night's "lodging" when it was dark and the streets were empty, the cars had gone, the pubs had closed, and those like himself came into their own.

He crossed over York Bridge and entered the sequestered part of the park on the southern shore of the lake. On the seats along here his fellows were often to be found, Effie with her bundles wrapped in green plastic, or Dill, who would be accompanied by his dog but encumbered by so little, a nylon backpack, a couple of coats tied round his middle by their sleeves; but there was no one today. He knew Dill could live that way because he mostly had a bed in the Marylebone Road shelter or the one in the Edgware Road, something Roman's guilt and sense of being always a phony and a fake would never allow him to have. After all, how many of those others had possessed a house of their own, possessed it, sold it, and banked the money?

For much of each day Roman lived in the past. And this was deliberate, a purposeful exploration of the time of his happiness, a reliving. Sometimes this dreaming occupied him for several hours on end as he walked across the park and the streets that made a net-work like the weaving of a nest around its center. He would select a particular happening from that past and enter it again, as it might be the birth of one of his children and the things he said to Sally and she to him, or even earlier to his first meeting with Sally at university.

Once he had been quite unable to do this, had been afraid to do it, more than afraid, terrified. The sight of that delicate fair girl re-minded him that when they first encountered each other had been the time of his beginning this process of recall. Walking away from her, his bedding in the buggy, he had thought that speaking to an ordinary person, a dweller in the world he had left, should serve as a sign for him, and there and then he decided to put an end to the time of denial. Total change, absolute alteration of circumstances, utter abandonment of the past—all these had served their purpose. Now it was time to move on and take the plunge into pain. He would rip the scar tissue off the wound and lay a cold probe against the rawness. He had nothing to lose. It had to be done and now was the time to begin.

He had begun by a kind of meditation, his eyes on his wedding ring, the symbol of what had been and what was lost. Since then, in this world he had chosen for himself, both unreal and more real than any reality he had ever known, he had re-experienced every day his lovely history, a chapter of it or part of a chapter, and it did not heal the pain or come near healing it. But something else was happening. He was more aware than he had ever been of what it was to be a human being and it was as if, in all his joyous and contented days, he had never really known this before. And self-pity, so rebellious and consuming, was utterly gone. He had become unaccommodated man, perhaps even what those existentialists said man should be, free, suffering, alone, and in control of his own destiny.

Now he chose for his excursion into the past a holiday he and Sally and Elizabeth had had in Crete. It was ten years before, almost exactly ten years. Elizabeth had been four or five. They had chosen

May for the wildflowers that cover the island with blossom at that time and because the sun was warm but not yet hot. He chiefly remembered from that holiday the color of the sea, the blue of Elizabeth's eyes, the languor and the sweet idleness and his and Sally's lovemaking, the best since their honeymoon. They had been the young ardent lovers of seven years before and in those two weeks Daniel had been conceived. With a pain that made him gasp, Roman remembered their bed and waking in the morning naked, uncovered by bedclothes, and Sally naked beside him. Like gods they were, discovered by the morning light.

As he left the park by the Clarence Gate, he found himself able to summon up from that past time the things they had said to each other and even the expression in Sally's eyes, the tranquillity and sometimes the passion. He remembered walking on the beach with his daughter and carrying her because the sand was too hot on the soles of her small tender feet. "Daddy, Daddy," she had said, lifting up one foot, "my soul is burning!" Or that was what it sounded like and they laughed, he and Sally, for what did he know then of burning souls and hellish torment?

Across Gloucester Place he walked and into the hinterland of Marylebone Station, where the shabby streets make so extreme a contrast with Nash's palatial terraces. He took the steps down into Boston Place and through Blandford Square into Harewood Avenue. The sight of a corner shop reminded him that he must buy food for his supper. Sometime or other it must be done, but shops were always open till all hours in these streets. He came into Lisson Grove and turned south, conjuring Elizabeth's face in his mind, its innocence and its rapture, and as sometimes happened, the tears came into his eyes and fell down his cheeks.

Other people took no notice. They expected him to be different from them, demented, drug-crazy, drunk, ungoverned, mad. It was because of these things that he was where he was and they were where they were. Only Pharaoh, leaning against the door of a shop closed for the night, eyed him with some feeling of kinship and, holding out the bottle from which he had been drinking, said, "Here, mate, want a sup?"

Roman had long ago ceased to worry about catching things from drinking out of other people's bottles and, though he didn't want it, God knows what it was, he accepted and took a swig. Rioja and meths, he thought. Wiping his mouth on his sleeve, the way he had learned from Dill and Effie, he sat down on the stone step and looked up at Pharaoh. He never stopped hoping to see some change in the man's face, some improvement. By that he meant that madness would be less evident there, that the slipping away of sanity would have halted so that something human still remained, some kindly light in the feral bloodshot eyes, some relaxing of the mouth so that the lips were neither curled back nor sucked together in a whitened rigidity.

But there was no change and the sign of humanity Pharaoh had given in offering a drink to a man in tears, was a rare happening. Soon even that would cease. He squatted down and thrust his haunted face into Roman's, his black beard that he streaked with dark blue dye into Roman's beard.

"Have you got a key for me?" he said.

Roman shook his head. Anyone who looked more closely at Pharaoh—no one ever looked closely—would have seen the hundreds of keys that hung round him, strung there on the rope that served him as a belt, pinned to his clothes with safety pins, brass and steel and chrome, Yale keys and Banhams, front door keys and backdoor keys, keys for opening suitcases and keys for locking padlocks. From the irregular bulges in his clothes Roman suspected his pockets too were filled with keys. He clinked and rattled when he walked, shuffling in and out of doorways, going where his voices sent him in search of the ultimate key.

Where did they come from? Whose had they been? Pharaoh never said and Roman never asked.

"The keys of the kingdom," Pharaoh said.

His black eyes rolled. When he looked about him he made jerky startled movements. One of his voices told him that when Christ said, "I will give unto thee the keys of the kingdom of heaven," it was an actual bunch of keys that He handed to Peter. These were lost, had been lost for two thousand years, but it was Pharaoh's mission to find them. He speculated constantly as to their nature and appearance.

"They'll be made of gold, won't they? Purest gold? Only gold'd unlock the gates of heaven."

Pharaoh should not be here at all, an outsider, on the street, but in the kind of place that had no existence these days, a place that was comfortable and clean and civilized, where he could have some dignity, where caring people would look after him and doctors well versed in the tragedy of his existence would put him on a regimen of drugs. Roman had no idea whether he was autistic or schizophrenic or mentally handicapped. He preferred the word "mad" to all these because he knew that he too was mad and that being mad was a prerequisite of what he had done in becoming an outsider.

Patting Pharaoh on the shoulder—from which the man with the blue-streaked beard started back, recoiling and snarling like a wildcat poked with a stick—Roman got up and continued on his course toward the Marylebone Road and across it back into Gloucester Place. It amused him to reflect that being addressed by Pharaoh would once have alarmed him very much. He would have been frightened, though not admitted it, would have pretended not to hear. And to have entered into a conversation with such a creature would have been unthinkable. He was such a creature himself now, or not far off.

Turning into Crawford Street, he waited before crossing the road for the red and white food delivery van to pass. What would Express Tikka and Pizza say if he phoned from a call box and asked for a delivery of Chicken Masala to the third seat on the left going up the

Broad Walk from Chester Road? A verbal equivalent, he supposed, of the look he got in the sandwich bar where he asked for cheese and pickle.

They looked askance, but they served him. It was his accent, Roman knew, it made them think that maybe they were wrong, that this was no dosser but an eccentric, an absentminded professor who forgot to have baths. He would have lost his accent if he could, but his attempts to do so sounded like grotesque parodies. Tomorrow, he was reminded, he had better have an all-over wash, in a public convenience somewhere. Keeping clean, or avoiding utter filthiness, was one of the grimmer problems the outsider faced, and one that no insider ever took into account.

Turning into Old Quebec Street, wondering where to settle down and eat his supper, he came under the windows of Talisman, the environmentalist publishers. He wore no watch but told the time by the state of the light and traffic and the movement of people, and he guessed it was seven. The staff, such as it was, would have gone home an hour ago. To the front door Talisman's logo of a lyre-tree leaf was attached with its name and that of its editor-in-chief, Tom Outram. Once his name had been there too, but that, like so much in his old life, was water under the bridge, flowing into the sea of his memories.

4

N
o one but Alistair would phone so early. Urgency was always implicit in phone calls made before nine in the morning.

Bean had called and collected Gushi. It was half past eight. Mary thought she knew who her caller must be and she hesitated before picking up the receiver. But there was always her grandmother to think of. Her grandmother was strong and healthy but very old.

"How are you settling in?"

He had never spoken to her like that before. It was the phrase of an elderly parent delivered in a tone that was solicitous but querulous, too, and aggrieved. She tried to sound brisk and cheerful.

"Fine," she said. "I'm all right. It's nice here. I've been walking a lot."

As soon as she had said it she knew it was an unwise thing to say, for he immediately countered by telling her not to overdo things. She was not strong, she was a fragile creature. He managed, without putting this into words, to imply that by her irresponsible and thoughtless conduct she had put her health in jeopardy.

"When am I to be allowed to come and see you?"

"Alistair," she said, "we're having a separation, remember?"

"A *trial* separation."

She tried again. "I have left you. We're apart. We've discussed it, we decided. My coming here was to mark the beginning of our separation."

"Oh, come on," he said, "that's just a figure of speech. The mistake was mine in giving any of that stuff credence. Absence makes the heart grow fonder, that's the real reason, isn't it?"

Hers or his? There was no need to ask. He implied that being parted from him would increase her affection for him. Affection—that lukewarm word. Even of that she felt very little. If you were like her, receptive, anxious to please—euphemisms, she told herself, for passive and ingratiating—you found it hard to understand how anyone thought love could be won by bullying. He set about bullying her now.

"You can't escape me so easily, you know, Mary. I'm not the kind of man to wreck two people's lives for a woman's whim. Haven't I proved in the past that I know what's best for us?"

She should have refuted that, but she feared the storm that would ensue. She had left him, hadn't she? That great step had been taken, she need not learn to fight him. She told him she was in a hurry and must go.

"All right. I know that tone of voice. There's no getting a word out of you when you've decided to sulk. You'll soon get over that. I'll be over very soon."

As if she had invited him . . .

"No," she managed to say. "Please, no." The effort of refusing always made her tired, as if she really was the delicate creature she looked.

"I'll drop in one evening," he said as if she hadn't spoken. "I'll take you out somewhere."

Mary went back into the kitchen and poured herself a second cup of coffee. It was going to be harder getting away from him than she had thought. The strength of will she hoped she was learning would be needed, but what of the strength that women can never acquire? She would never come near to matching him physically. Like stigmata appearing at certain triggers, her face suddenly stung from the blow on the cheek he had given her when he saw those puncture marks. She looked in the mirror and saw the flush that bloomed there, brighter on the right side than the left. Alistair was left-handed.

They had been making love. He drew away from her and, extending his right hand, touched those marks with the tips of his fingers.

"What's that?" he said. The tone told her he knew. "Scorpion bit you? Poison ivy? Barbed wire?"

There is something terrible about the mood of lovemaking, so tender, languorous, exciting in that uniquely warm and breathless way, being broken by a harsh voice, sarcasm, barely suppressed rage. Nothing comes so quickly as sexual desire and nothing ebbs so fast as sexual willingness. It was like feeling cold water poured over her body.

She turned her face away. "The bone-marrow harvest," she said. "I told you I meant to do it."

"You deceived me," he said and, taking hold of her face in an iron grip with fingers that dug, struck her cheek with the flat of his hand, the hardest blow she had ever received. Until then, the *only* blow.

It was not quite a beating up he gave her. You could hardly call a slap on the face, a shaking, another slap, a pulling upright, and a throwing to the ground, beating someone up. She had crawled away and shut herself in the bathroom. Her cheek was bruised the next day and she had bruised her leg when she fell.

He apologized to her, he crawled, he didn't know what had come over him, only that it never would again. Predictably, he showed the other aspect of the bully's character. It was this wretched temperament of his, he excused himself, his love of physical perfection, his worship of the ideal.

"You're so perfect, I can't bear to think of your body assailed, plundered." He was almost crying. "I can't bear to think of all that beauty endangered."

Except by him, she thought later, except by him. He had touched her bruised cheek with tears in his eyes. . . .

Still, that would never happen again. None of it would happen, it was all over. She had left and, under another roof, could withstand any onslaught. Upstairs she dabbed at her cheek with pale powder, as if it were still red and marked by Alistair's hand. Her eyes had that panicky look he had lately induced in them, but as she made herself breathe deeply, her face smoothed and grew calmer, her shoulders relaxed. Gushi was brought back just as she was leaving. She showed him his freshly filled water bowl, gave him a quick caress, and, running now, caught up with Bean and his troop on the corner of Albany Street: Boris the borzoi, Charlie the golden retriever, Marietta the chocolate poodle, McBride the scottie. Only Ruby the beagle was absent.

"Gone on her holidays to Ilfracombe," said Bean. He had a camera on a strap round his neck, like a tourist. "She'll be missing the park. Them hounds need a lot of exercise."

"Won't she be able to run on the beach?"

He never answered questions. She wondered why she bothered to ask. Bean countered questions with a statement or a question of his own as competently as any politician trained to do this on television. Sometimes his statements were relevant, sometimes not.

"A hound can run twenty miles and think nothing of it," he said.

She felt like saying, but can hounds think? Instead, she remarked on Bean's expertise in the handling of so many dogs. He nodded, accepting the praise as his due, and said in the tone that sounded disparaging, though probably was not, "I'll say good-bye then, Miss. We mustn't detain you."

"Good-bye."

"Mind how you cross the road. The traffic's very treacherous in these parts."

Had he once been a butler? Perhaps. His manner was that of a superior upper servant—well, a superior upper servant in a film of the fifties. Her experience of the real thing was nonexistent. The grandparents who had brought her up, though by no means poor, had only run to a cleaner who had come in twice a week. She took the lower path, the one that runs close up against the fence of the Abika Paul Memorial Gardens, the better to see the cattle and deer.

Her grandmother had sometimes brought her in here as a child, had once taken her to the zoo with a friend who lived in Primrose Hill. A sheltered childhood and youth it had been, she supposed. Her grandparents had been discreetly wealthy, what they called "comfortably off." Such strange expressions, "comfortably off," "well off"—off what? Off the poverty line, the breadline?

Their income had never been mentioned, money never talked about. Even now she had no idea how much Frederica had, even if she was rich or genteelly poor. Alistair had shown an interest, but her grandmother had never been forthcoming to Alistair, had never liked him. If she had agreed with Alistair in anything it had been over the bone marrow donation, and her opposition had been mild compared to his, had been no more than a fear of "unnecessary" anesthesia and a conviction, despite all evidence to the contrary, that Mary must be as vulnerable as she looked.

People were a mixture of subtle contrasts. Malleable, weak, diffident she might be, but she had gone ahead with her resolution. She had persisted. It's a man, the trust had told her, twenty-two years old, suffering from acute myeloid leukemia. The donation would take place in this country, they said, but they had not told her whether the recipient was British or of some other nationality.

After the transplant they gave him the card she had written to him and they gave her the letter he had written to her. Both were unsealed, both had been scrutinized to make sure identification of either donor or recipient was impossible. His name was Oliver, but they smiled when they said it, making clear this was a pseudonym. Her name, that she was told to put on the card, was Helen, and they had told him she was twenty-eight and in perfect health. She had chosen "Helen" because it was her dead mother's name and she wondered why he had picked "Oliver" or if it had been chosen for him.

She had not known what to write on the card, so had done no more than call him "Dear Oliver," wish him a speedy recovery, and sign herself, "Yours sincerely, Helen." It was rather ridiculous. What could it mean to him? His letter to her was typed, not very expertly. It was formal, lifeless. "Dear Helen, I want to thank you for what you have done for me," but ended as if emotion had broken through, "In undying thankfulness, Oliver," and she wondered that they hadn't demurred at that, that most unfortunate word, for he very likely would die, in spite of the donation; he was rather more likely to die than to live.

Then came the updates from Oliver's transplant center. He was well at three months and at six. There was a delay, she heard nothing for six months and was sure he was ill again, was dying, then the nine-month report and the twelve-month came simultaneously. Oliver continued well. She kept the updates away from Alistair but inadvertently let out that Oliver was thriving.

Alistair claimed to have seen a decline in her own health since the donation and a fading of her looks. She told him she was perfectly well, she looked just the same. Her grandmother, in spite of earlier opposition, had remarked on her appearance. Perhaps it was bringing Frederica into it that had set him off. He had taken hold of her by the shoulders.

"You need some sense shaken into you," he had said, and had proceeded to shake her, gently at first, then with a kind of frenzy. She had fallen against a table, dislodging a glass vase, which had broken and cut her leg. He had had to take her to the hospital, to the emergency room, and when her leg had been stitched and strapped up, had wept all over her, bemoaning the loss of her beauty, the draining away of her "life-blood."

"Why did you make that stupid sacrifice? Why did you destroy your health and your looks? Now you can see what it's led to."

It was the beginning of the end. Some of the worst of it for Mary was the realization of her own poor judgment. How could she have loved him or even have thought she loved him? Why hadn't she detected this behavior in him before? And then there came back to her the slight unease she had always felt when he seemed to judge people by their physical appearance. She met his mother and found this aging woman doing the same thing. Like Sir Walter Elliot in *Persuasion,* Marina Winter remarked constantly on the propensity of those around her "to lose something of their personableness when they cease to be quite young," and made irrelevant comments on "freckles, and a projecting tooth, and a clumsy wrist."

Discovering where this trait in Alistair had come from went some way to excusing it in Mary's eyes, but later on she came to wonder how it would be if they stayed together and when she too aged and began to lose her looks. Would he call her a dog as she had once or twice been shocked to hear him describe an older woman? Would everything else she was, her closeness to him, the sexual life they enjoyed, the gentle tranquillity she knew was hers, her skills as a craftswoman, would all this go for nothing when lines came on her face and gravity pulled her earthward?

She had found out sooner than she expected. He punished physical diminution, not with words but with blows. Remembering, she felt the blood mount into the cheek where he had struck her. She felt it settle there and burn the skin.

5

W ith Gushi in her lap, Frederica Jago said, "Where will you go when the Blackburn-Norrises come back?" And without waiting for an answer, "Come back and live with me."

Mary laughed. "That's a rash invitation. I might take you up on it."

"It's your home, my dear. Where else would it be natural for you to go?"

"To a place of my own."

"Of course my house is much bigger, but it's not in the same league as this one. But what is, when you come to think of it? Still, you would have the run of it and you'd often have it to yourself. You know I'm always away."

It was true. While Mrs. Jago's husband was alive they had never set foot west of Cornwall or east of Suffolk, for Lucian Jago had a fear of flying and a tendency to seasickness. Since his death and Mary's departure, if she had not wandered the earth, she had taken every available package tour, to India, to Tashkent and Samarkand, the rose-red city of Petra, up the Yangtse and down the Nile, California, New England. Lately, as she passed eighty, she had restricted her traveling to Europe, forsaking the travel agent's recommendation and visiting out-of-the-way places.

She was a small, thin, pretty woman, bird-faced with a crest of white wavy hair and her granddaughter's green eyes, and indeed very much as Mary would one day be, her bones more apparent than her flesh, the shape of her body still uncannily like a young girl's.

Having arrived at Charlotte Cottage in a taxi with a gift for Mary from Lapland and a bottle of champagne, she renewed her friendship with Gushi. She had brought him a dog-chewing bar, which she assured him was made from reindeer skin, and, feeling for it in her bag, brought it out first and then an envelope.

"I nearly forgot. This came for you."

Mary took it. "I was going to ask, but I thought it would be too soon."

"Too soon for what?" Frederica gave Gushi the chewing bar and he rolled on his back on the carpet, grasping it in his paws and growling. "What is it? More about your bone marrow man?"

"I hope it's his name and address." She hesitated, as she had done with the trust's last communication, turning the envelope in her hands, looking at the logo, the stamp, the postmark. "I shall know at last. It's rather daunting."

"Don't be daunted. Would you like me to open it?"

"No. No, I don't think so."

"My darling Mary, you don't have to open it in my presence. I shan't be offended. Keep it till I've gone."

Mary shook her head. "I'm going to open it now."

It would, after all, be only a name. An ordinary sort of name, probably, and a number and a street anywhere in the country, in a city or a town or a village. She had been told it was in the British Isles, that was all.

There was no need, this time, for preparation, for bracing herself. Timidity was ridiculous when the contents of this envelope could not possibly contain any threat. Frederica handed her a paper knife from the desk, ivory handled, with a long thin blade. She had probably seen the Blackburn-Norrises use it. Mary slit along the top of the flap and took out the enclosure. The letter was short.

Dear Ms. Jago,

We note that you have not asked us to pass your own name and address on to "Oliver" and therefore assume you will do this yourself. He is now willing to be identified. His name is Leo Nash and his address Flat 24, Redferry House, Plangent Road, London NW1. I should like to take this opportunity of wishing you a pleasant and rewarding meeting with Mr. Nash.

Yours sincerely,
Deborah Cox

Mary read it aloud. She said, "How very strange. Plangent Road can't be far from here. It's North-west One like this is."

"Maybe, but it's not much like this," Frederica said dryly. "It's Somers Town. And you know nothing else about him? Nothing except that he's twenty-three and male?"

"Twenty-four by now," said Mary. "Do you know, all these months I've longed to meet him, and now I can I don't know whether I want to or not. It's a mistake to meet people in these circumstances, isn't it? One's always disappointed."

"These circumstances aren't within my experience, Mary. I don't know. It's old-fashioned to say this but I am old-fashioned. It would be unnatural if I wasn't."

"Say what?"

"I was going to say, I *am* saying, that it's best to meet people through being introduced by your friends or family. Or at work perhaps, only I've never been to work, so I can't say. This young man owes you a lot, he is under a great obligation to you, and that isn't the best basis for a friendship."

"A friendship!" said Mary. "He may not even answer my letter. If he feels he's under an obligation he probably won't want to meet me."

"Is it true that we dislike those who have done us a service?"

Frederica asked. "If so, the greater the service perhaps the greater the dislike. And it's hard to imagine a greater service than saving someone's life. He may feel he owes you more than he could ever repay. And then if he sees—how shall I put this? Mary, you're very pretty and—well, graceful and sweet, you're obviously educated and gifted and living in a lovely place, won't that be a burden for him too? A poor, sick, deprived young man from what sounds like a council estate behind Euston Station?"

Mary looked at her. She felt stricken by a small panic. "I wish you hadn't been away," she said. "I wish we could have had this conversation before I asked for his address."

"And if I'd advised you, would you have taken my advice? Of course you wouldn't."

"It isn't too late," Mary said slowly. "I haven't been in touch with him. I just know his name and where he lives. What would your advice be?"

Frederica laughed. "Are you passing the buck? Laying the responsibility on me?"

"I don't know. Perhaps. I'm in the habit of doing that. Or I used to be. Advise me."

"Tear the letter up, give me the pieces, and on my way home I'll drop them in a litter bin."

"So that I couldn't get them out and piece them together again? It wouldn't be any use, I'm afraid. I know his name now. I have the address by heart. Wouldn't I always regret it if I didn't write to him? But perhaps he won't answer."

Frederica laughed. "He'll answer."

•   •   •

On the front doorstep in Albany Street, Edwina Goldsworthy gave Bean formal notice that she would be going away on holiday in ten days' time and McBride would be taking up residence in kennels.

Bean disapproved of kennels and his manner became chilly. But he had to go inside for the necessary paperwork, having first tied his dogs up to a lamppost, and this delayed him.

"Don't be surprised if he loses weight in there, madam," he said, and he cast a critical eye over Mrs. Goldsworthy's bulky form before adding, "Pining does more than diets, as I always say."

She was dependent on him, she couldn't say much, none of them could. They were in his power. Without him they would have to leave their beds an hour earlier, sacrifice their cocktail hour, get up off their arses and muddy their shoes. Bean smiled to himself. Power was not something he had personally experienced in his years as the late Anthony Maddox's and then the late Maurice Clitheroe's servant, but now he was making up for lost time. Absolute reliability, "sirs" and "madams" sprinkled among his remarks, a genuine love of dogs, punctilious punctuality, all this made him indispensable. He disliked being even five minutes late, for this detracted from his power, and he quickened his pace as he and the dogs made for Cumberland Terrace, home of Marietta, the chocolate poodle.

The actress Lisl Pring hadn't noticed the time. She kissed Marietta and had her makeup licked off. Bean had never seen anyone as thin as this woman, except in famine photos. They said telly made a person look fatter, which was no doubt the reason. He wondered how she did it, lived on salad, no doubt, or maybe she was like that model he'd read about who had nothing in her fridge but a lemon.

He reminded her of his seven-days-notice-of-holidays rule and she shrieked something about never having a moment to go anywhere, darling. If it wasn't shooting it was rehearsals from five A.M. till midnight, believe it or not. Bean nodded. He didn't really believe it. She must be rich. Up here in the hinterland of the terrace was like being in some Georgian spa, Leamington or Cheltenham, all mellow stone and ivy, blossom coming out and ferns uncurling, a smell like the country, green and sharp. Bean thought he wouldn't half mind living here himself, only he'd never afford it the way things were. He must put his power to wider use.

The bag lady with the green plastic bundles was meandering slowly up the Outer Circle as he came out of Cumberland Terrace. Her name, he knew, was Effie but in his mind Bean called her a horrible cow. Boris and Charlie and the rest of them always wanted to sniff her. This propensity of theirs, sometimes seeming to prefer people who smelled nasty to people who smelled nice, was his only objection to dogs. He tugged the leashes away with an artificial shudder. The bag lady told him to fuck off and gave him instructions about the kind of sexual activity he and his dogs might mutually engage in. Bean thought it a pity that the cleaning up of London, begun some three years before, had not included purging the streets of dossers, beggars, and foul-mouthed slags.

Before returning him to Mr. and Mrs. Barker-Pryce in St. Andrew's Place, Bean took a photograph of Charlie the golden retriever. He was a handsome dog and made quite a picture standing there, head raised, tail up, in the sunshine. Charlie's owner answered the door himself, cigar in hand. Mr. Barker-Pryce was a Member of Parliament for some London constituency and it was a wonder how he managed in the House of Commons chamber, having to go without his cigars for maybe a whole two hours. Bean and the borzoi proceeded on alone to Park Square. Here Bean used his key to let himself into the gardens in the center of the square.

These gardens, nothing to look at from the street, a wire fence, a scrubby (but impenetrable) hedge, the tops of trees, are a park themselves when you get inside. They might be the grounds of some great country house with their green lawns, curved flowerbeds, tall trees and flowering shrubs, lovely in their peace and tranquillity. Bean never noticed the beauty but he liked the exclusivity. He liked anything that put him among an elite, permitted privileges and pleasures few might enjoy. Here was an opportunity for another shot, a red blaze of flowering shrub that might serve for someone's Christmas card. The path to the Nursemaids' Tunnel descends in a shallow sloping curve between brick walls to the portico, which is the tunnel entrance. It gave Bean a bit of a shock to find himself not alone in the tunnel. There was someone in there, far up ahead. He would have thought nothing of this if the figure had been on the move, striding toward him or away from him, but whoever it was was leaning against the wall on the left-hand side at the Park Crescent end, holding a bottle to his lips. A street sleeper. Another of Effie's ilk. Like most people, Bean was afraid of the street people, and particularly afraid when with one in a confined space. He was a small man, far from young, and borzois, though large dogs, bred to hunt the wolf, are fine-boned and seldom aggressive.

Bean could have turned back. He could have gone back and crossed the Marylebone Road at the lights by Regent's Park tube station. But he didn't want the man with the bottle to see this happen, to see him turn tail and of course understand perfectly why he had retreated. For he, Bean, was a man of power and if he turned he would have yielded power into the hands of this dirty reject, this piece of flotsam fit for nothing but a city's sewers. He imagined broken drunken laughter echoing down the passage, reverberating off the damp walls.

He hadn't much money on him but he didn't want to lose his camera. It was a Pentax and, like so much in Bean's possession, had once belonged to Maurice Clitheroe. If he'd only thought of it five minutes before he could have slipped the camera inside his jacket.

How had the man got in here? They were careful with their keys, the Crown Estates. In order to obtain one you had to be a resident of the Square or the Crescent, or the adjacent terraces and mewses. He touched the camera like someone fingering an amulet, and quickly drew his hand away. He walked on, somewhat more slowly than he would have done if the man with the bottle hadn't been there, but not so slowly as to show his fear. The borzoi took its normal delicate steps, loping on tiptoe, but very steady in its progress.

The light at the end showed Bean a gaunt thin figure with long black hair and a beard stained blue. A momentary flashback took him sixty years into the past and a village school in Hampshire, the teacher telling them how in the distant past the inhabitants of these islands had painted their bodies with woad. Maybe the blue stuff on this roughneck's beard was woad. Bean determined not to look as he passed him, to walk past at a steady pace as if the man wasn't there or as if for some reason he hadn't *noticed* that he was there. He pulled the leash tight so that Boris was close up to him on his right side. This was the kind of thug that wouldn't think twice about kicking a dog.

The man turned his head to stare when Bean was about two yards from him. And Bean had to look, he had to return that stare for a single second before jerking his eyes away. In that second he received an impression of metal, of glitter, as of the man being covered in slivers of metal. It reminded him, unpleasantly but irresistibly, of Maurice Clitheroe's indulgence in S and M—Bean had no idea what those initials stood for, but he knew what it was all right—and of some of those who came to the flat in Mr. Clitheroe's time. Leather, zip fasteners, body piercing, there had been a lot of that, and a great deal of metal in many shapes and forms, most of it sharp.

Thinking of all this got Bean past the man, and the dog past the man, up the steps and out into the light. His mind had been distracted at exactly the right time. Safe, unmolested, his camera safe, he indulged himself in a spot of what the late Anthony Maddox called *l'esprit de l'escalier* and thought what he might, ought to, have said. Like, "What authority do you have to use this tunnel?" or "By whose permission are you in this private foot passage?"

James Barker-Pryce CMG, MP would have done that, so would Bertram Cornell. They had the right accent, they had been to the kind of school where they taught you to think of yourself as a king of the earth. Money did that for you too. As Bean walked out of the gardens and crossed the road to the Park Crescent pavement, he realized what those metal things were. They were keys. The man had keys hanging off him everywhere and no doubt one of them was the key to this garden. Something would have to be done.

Boris's home was not the house where the blue plaque testified to Marie Tempest's having once lived there, but a few doors along. The Cornells' housekeeper did what she always did and opened the basement door in the area. What was wrong with the front door? If she didn't know it, his days of being treated like a servant were over. Her attitude meant he had to go round the corner into Portland Place and all the way down the iron staircase.

The borzoi trotted in, ignoring the housekeeper, leaving Bean without the least sign of affection, without a backward glance. It pushed a door open with its long nose and disappeared into the room beyond, a cold dog with no feelings.

"It's Russian, you see," said the housekeeper as if that explained everything.

Bean nodded. "Mr. and Mrs. Cornell away, Valerie?"

The housekeeper said her employers were in France, coming back tomorrow. Even they called her Miss Conway. Apart from her friends, only Bean took upon himself the right to call her by her given name. She was getting up her nerve to tell him not to, but she hadn't got it up yet. Her revenge was to make him walk down those steps and necessarily, of course, up them again. She told him there had been another burglary in the Crescent, two in fact, one of them only next door.

"That must make you nervous being here on your own," said Bean.

It did. But she disliked being reminded of it. "I've got the dog."

Bean laughed lightly, shaking his head. "More of a pussy cat, that one," he said. "There are some rough characters about. I just saw something barely human in the tunnel, more like an alien. You don't want to open your front door to no one."

"Thanks a bunch," said Valerie.

She slammed the door. Bean winced a little to show his sensitivity for the benefit of any passersby who might be watching. He favored the statue with a passing glance, Queen Victoria's father, Prince Edward, Duke of Kent, standing on a plinth at the end of the gardens and looking down Portland Place. Someone had once told Bean he was the spitting image of the duke, and after that he had never passed the bronze figure without giving it a look.

He lived a little way away in York Terrace East. Normally, he would have gone back by way of the tunnel but he didn't want to encounter the key man again. Better brave the Marylebone Road, wait a good two minutes for those lights to change, then belt across before they changed back again. It was easier without dogs pulling him like in some chariot race.

He let himself into his flat. Neat as a pin, spotlessly clean, it was furnished exactly as it had been in the days of Maurice Clitheroe, its former owner, with heavy, highly polished late-nineteenth-century pieces, red and blue Turkey rugs, and in the living room a newish three-piece suite covered in tan-colored hide. This and the huge television and VCR reflected Bean's own taste. His kitchen was carefully geared for the freezer—microwave culture. There was no oven and there were no pans. The lot had gone on the day of Mr. Clitheroe's memorial service, along with the piano, the whip and gun collection, and the pictures of two saints undergoing particularly revolting forms of martyrdom.

Maurice Clitheroe had left Bean his duplex in recognition of services rendered. These had sometimes been onerous, particularly in the area of punishment, though here he had always been the executant, never the recipient. He had known where to draw the line, as for example in refusing to gratify Mr. Clitheroe's demand that both of them should wear spiked dog collars while at home alone. And in spite of this setting of limits, the flat had still been left to him according to a promise frequently made but never entirely taken seriously.

In relation to the flat he loved—he called it a maisonette—and in which he now settled down contentedly to microwave a Linda McCartney vegetarian platter, Bean had only one regret. He had no opportunity to impress his clients with his address, no chance of presenting them with invoices on paper headed York Terrace, NW1. For since the owners of his dogs were unable to claim income tax relief on what they paid him, every penny he received was black money, money in the back pocket, handed over in cash. His earnings from Mr. Clitheroe had never reached the tax floor, for all was found for him, his board, his lodging, even his clothes. The Inland Revenue probably thought he was dead or, more likely, had never been born.

He had a look at the camera and checked that there were three frames left on the film.

· · ·

In her third week at Charlotte Cottage, Mary was twice invited out to dinner. Her grandmother gave a rather grand dinner party for her. The nine guests and Frederica Jago sat down to deep-fried Crottin de Chavignol with cranberry sauce, roast guinea fowl, and French apple tart with clotted cream. A heavy meal suitable for old-fashioned old people. Everyone but Mary and one of the men she sat next to was very old, so it was plain that the young or youngish man had been invited for her sake.

Much the same thing happened at the other dinner party. This was given by Dorothea in Charles Lane, where she lived with her husband, Gordon, in the house next door to the Irene Adler Museum. Everyone among the eight guests was young, so they ate arugula and corn salad in an orange and walnut dressing, red mullet with couscous and deep-fried sage leaves, followed by cherimoya sorbet with a Sharon fruit coulis. Couples were either married or living together in long-term relationships, so it was apparent to Mary that the single (divorced) man she sat next to had been invited for her sake.

Of these two men, Frederica's protégé and Gordon's friend, the former rang Mary up the next day and asked if she would go to the cinema with him to see *The Madness of King George*. She said no. It was not only that she had seen the film, but that of all activities likely to improve two people's knowledge of each other, cinema-going must be the least effective. You met in the foyer, you sat side by side in the dark in silence, you had a drink afterward and said good night. Not that she wanted to improve her knowledge of him and nor apparently did he of her, for he suggested no alternative outing. The other man, Dorothea's, didn't get in touch at all.

"It's humiliating," Mary said to Dorothea the next day in the Irene Adler drawing room. "I wish you hadn't done it. I wish my grandmother hadn't done it."

"Oh, come on. I didn't do anything. The poor man's just getting over the trauma of his wife's running off with the VAT inspector. Gordon and I try to include him in as much as we can."

"And you thought this poor girl was just getting over the trauma of her boyfriend knocking her about, is that it? They'd be just right for each other? Well, he didn't think so. I haven't heard a word from him. And that is humiliating, Dorrie."

Nearly as humiliating as writing to Leo Nash and getting no reply. She had been so sure of a prompt answer to her letter. What a fool, to imagine the man longing to hear from her, desperate for a word, only waiting with bated breath for the chance to get in touch!

"You're overreacting," said Dorothea, and she stood back, trying to decide if the framed photograph of Irene Adler looked best displayed on the mantelpiece or semiconcealed behind the half-open secret panel. It was a question that had exercised her ever since the drawing room had been created in its present mode. "He's probably just too unhappy to even think of anyone else at the moment."

"Yes, I daresay. But to me it seems he must have gone home saying to himself, 'They needn't think they can catch me so easily. I know a trick worth two of that.' And then he forgot me."

As Leo Nash must have looked at the Charlotte Cottage address and the writing paper and wondered what form her patronage of him would take?

"Look, if you fancy him we can maybe manage . . ."

"I don't fancy him in the least. I'll just go on going to the cinema by myself."

She said nothing to Dorothea about being lonely. Dorothea would have asked her round to Charles Lane every evening, given a dinner party for her every week. School friends, college friends would have rallied round if she had got in touch. Her cousin in Surrey had invited her for the weekend, but she had said no because of Gushi. Being alone and minding it wasn't the best training for someone who was trying to be strong and independent.

The weekends were the worst. There had been only three of them but they were very bad. She got up late, she read, she walked Gushi until he was exhausted and had to be carried, she walked about the West End, went to the Wallace Collection and the Planetarium. In the evenings she worked on the new catalog and brochure she was compiling for the museum.

It was better on weekday evenings. She and Gushi watched television or played the Blackburn-Norrises' CDs. At bedtime she had stopped shutting Gushi up in the kitchen, where his basket was, and took him upstairs with her and let him sleep on her bed. During the night he edged closer and closer up toward the bedhead, and now when she woke in the mornings it was to find his frondy face on the pillow beside her and as often as not her arms embracing him.

For the first week, in the mornings, she had awaited the post, but nothing came except junk mail, hire car and taxi cards, fliers from a food delivery service. Her phone number was on the writing paper and when the phone rang she half expected a diffident, anxious male voice. But the only voice, and it wasn't diffident, was Alistair's.

After the early-morning call, he phoned three more times, the first to say he was coming to see her, he would be over the following evening to take her out to dinner. Her protests, her reminder that they were separated, had no effect. If not tomorrow, then the next day, he said. In the end she agreed to the second suggestion and went through agonies all next day and the next, wondering how to deal with him if he came back with her and wanted to stay the night.

Seven came and seven-thirty and at seven thirty-five he phoned to say he couldn't make it. She was relieved and at the same time angry. Angry with herself as much as with him for the two miserable days she had spent. That afternoon she had been so distracted that she had told an American tourist Irene Adler had lived in St. John's Wood Terrace and her royal lover had been the king of Serbia.

Alistair phoned for the third time to say he was worried about her health. He had made an appointment for their GP to see her.

"It's at eight-thirty on Thursday morning."

"Alistair, as you know I haven't got a car. Do you really think I'm coming to Willesden at that hour?"

"Of course you'd stay the night here."

"I'm perfectly well. I don't need a doctor." She tried to speak pleasantly to him, to be polite but firm, but when she said good-bye his furious shouting down the receiver made her tremble.

All of it made her ask herself if she had been right to take on this dog-sitting and house-minding at Charlotte Cottage. Of course she could not have stayed with Alistair, that was plain, but should she perhaps have gone first to her grandmother, and then found herself a place in a shared flat? To be with other people . . .

It was too late now. Outside it was sunny again, a warm still evening. Two people walked by, on their way out into Albany Street, their arms round each other. Loneliness was worse on fine evenings when the red sun went down over the horizon of a great city and the night sky grew purple, though with no chance of seeing the stars. She took Gushi on her lap and watched television.

The little dog was out with Bean and the others when the post came in the morning. A flier from a company selling exercise trampolines, another from Express Tikka and Pizza, and an envelope postmarked NW1. Her habitual hesitation at opening letters she told herself to abandon now, stop it once and for all. It was all part of the fearful temperament she had to learn to abandon. In a cool, controlled way she went into the living room, picked up the paper knife, and slit open the envelope.

She looked at the photograph first. A passport-size photograph taken in one of those station or supermarket kiosks of a man's pale thin face in front of a pleated curtain. To herself she was calling it anemic before she realized what she was saying. Of course he was anemic. Anemia had nearly killed him. . . . The eyes were light and clear, the hair so fair as to be almost white, the features regular, classical: thin lips, straight nose, very high smooth forehead.

A handwritten letter from the Plangent Road address.

> *Dear Mary Jago,*
>
> *I am the man whose life you saved with your more than generous donation. You not only saved it, you made it good again, worth living. I want you to know that I am well now, thanks to you.*
>
> *Since you wrote to me, I think you must want us to get in touch. I hope I am not being presumptuous in saying that you may want us to meet as much as I want it.*
>
> *I will not put you to the trouble of phoning me or writing back. In fact, I should make a confession and tell you I have no phone. Today, as I write, is Monday and you will get this letter by Wednesday at the latest. If I do not hear from you to tell me you would*

rather not meet me, I will be at an outside table at the Rose Garden restaurant in Regent's Park, the one north of the lake, from 5:30 till 6:00 on Friday.

I won't say, do come. But I hope you will come.

Yours sincerely,
Leo Nash

6

Most of the street sleepers, the dossers, the dropouts, the jacks men, were on the street because they had nowhere else to be. They were without roofs of their own, or roofs rented, to put over their heads. This was not true of Roman, who had had a roof, who had had his own home, but who was on the street because he had no more choice than those others, because the outside was the only option if he was to continue to live.

If he was to live. An alternative there had been, the alternative open to all. "Skipping out" on the canal bank, he had thought many times of sliding into the cold water one night, having first ripped his brain and his senses apart with the meths and water mixture, cloudy white fluid the jacks men called milk. The faith he no longer had stopped him. His Polish mother had brought him up a Catholic and if all of it was gone now, all dispelled by reason and science, vestigial fear remained, some absurd awe of the sin against the Holy Ghost.

So the street it had to be. Because home was unlivable in, a hollow place that howled at him, empty, empty, never to be filled again. A place so haunted that he had to hide his face from the staring walls and stuff bedding into his mouth to keep himself from crying out. And not just that house of his, but any house, flat, hotel, shelter he might move to.

It was as if claustrophobia of a kind never before experienced had come to him with loss. Just as an inability to work had come, to go about among ordinary people. He was obliged to avoid every aspect of life as he had known it, if he was to survive and not curl up somewhere into a fetus that screwed up its eyes and hid its face in its frog's paws. Only the outside was feasible to him, where those he encountered took it for granted that he was set apart, that he was to some degree mad. This was the point, that he should be the Wandering Jew, or Oedipus. And if he had not put out his own eyes, nor had he his daughter with him as companion.

It was possible to have been too happy. He knew that now and because, at first, after it first happened, he lamented that he had been as happy as that, wished his had been a bad or broken marriage, his children ugly and stupid, because of these indefensible thoughts he had cut himself off from everything, expelled his family from his mind, and then expelled everything else from his life. The idea was to have nothing to remind him, to make everything different; no roof over his head, no job, no friends, no social life, no familiar things around him. If he was going to run away, and he was, it had to be a proper running away, complete, absolute, the old life shed in every aspect.

Until the fair girl spoke to him and he spoke to her.

•   •   •

He had been up to Primrose Hill where nuns give out tea and bread and butter to the homeless at five in the afternoon. It was in some novel of Graham Greene's that he had come upon that phrase "a phony and a fake," and he applied it often to himself. For he had a home he had put into the hands of agents and sold. The money derived from that sale stopped him using the hostels and the day centers, to which others had a better right than he, it stopped him taking money passersby offered him, but he drew the line at the nuns' tea. He drank the tea and ate the bread and butter and left a pound coin on the table.

A lot of Irishmen were up there from the gloomy Victorian hostel in Camden Town. Their life expectancy, he had read somewhere in Talisman Press days, was forty-seven. The meths would do for

them, that and the cold and the poor diet. What you learn when you
drop out of life! Roman wandered down Regent's Park Road and
took St. Mark's Bridge over the canal. He counted seven houseboats
moored alongside each other in Cumberland Basin and one in front
of the Chinese teahouse. On its flat roof a woman lay sunbathing in a
green bikini.

The finger of the minaret pointed into a pale blue sky on which
the tiny clouds made a net. He thought of Omar Khayyám and the
sultan's turret caught in a noose of light. The sun made the mosque's
golden roof too bright to look at. He crossed the Outer Circle and
came into the Broad Walk. It was wild and thickly treed up here, no
flowerbeds, the neat lawns distant.

Roman sat down for a while on one of the seats by Sir Cowasjee
Jehangir's drinking fountain. An engraved legend told him it had
been put there from gratitude for a benevolent Raj's mercy to Parsis.
A man's face in stone looked out from the column above the inscrip-
tion. Since its foundation, how many thousands had drunk its water,
how many horses once refreshed themselves at its troughs? The Parsis placed their dead on towers of silence for the vultures to take, to
eat and pick their bones. He had been so placed, awaiting his fate.

From the zoo behind him came an animal sound, a loud grunt or
trumpeting. He and Sally had never brought their children to the
zoo but had taken them only to parkland where the big cats run free,
to Woburn and Longleat. Slipping into his meditative mood, his remembering time, he recalled the Longleat day, the glorious weather,
Elizabeth drawing pictures of a lioness and cubs on her sketch pad,
the whole of it rather marred for him by his ridiculous anxiety.

The car's windows opened automatically at the press of a switch,
they weren't the wind-down kind. He had heard of those windows
going wrong, of sticking either in the open or the shut position.
What if something should go wrong, one of the children open a window and the window refuse to close again? If lions surrounded the
car, if the car broke down . . . Later, when they were home again, he

discovered that Sally had been thinking in just the same way, with exactly the same fears. But it was often so. They had shared thoughts, fears, happiness, read each other's minds.

Strange then that he had never prevised what had actually happened to his children, to his wife. His fears had been no more than fantasies or sops to a providence in whom he had no belief. They were never actual anticipations of real disaster with the corollary of: What will I do if they are all taken from me? How will I feel? How will I survive? And when it happened he had been without fear for some time, had rid himself of all but normal anxiety now Elizabeth was nearly fifteen and Daniel eight.

Roman did not usually think of that day. He did not relive the moments in which the news had been brought to him. For one thing, he could hardly remember what his feelings had been. An amnesia had descended and left him with a memory of beforehand and—horribly, agonizingly—twelve hours afterward. The lost hours between he no longer tried to recapture. But he did think sometimes, and he thought now, as he got up again and walked away from the stone column, the tower of silence, of that later aftermath, of the awful recurring disbelief, of sleep that came so readily and so easily, sleep in which everything could be buried, but which had to be resisted, for when he woke the truth returned as fresh and new as when it was first told him. Sleep, which is supposed to be a blessing, the "balm of hurt minds," could be a curse too. Who would want a painkilling drug that when its effects wore off, brought worse suffering?

It was different now. Denial was past and forgetfulness never came. He lay down to sleep on some doorstep in the full acceptance of what had happened and his waking was to the naked knowledge of their doom and his fate. There was no longer room for illusion. But in those early days, before he took to the street, he would wake in the morning, turn to the pillow beside his, and wonder where Sally was, up so early. Then, like some slow rumbling explosion, growing in magnitude before the final roar, it had all returned to him and he groaned aloud his irrepressible pain. He whimpered and groaned and relived his homecoming that evening, the arrival of the police on his doorstep, their kindness and their total inability to soften what they called "the blow." That was when he had taken his decision to deny, expel, bury, pretend.

Now he had reached a point in the progression of his survival when he could control his memories. He was no longer at the mercy of these things bursting and breaking into the fabric of his general sadness. They were there, always there, the trigger of his madness, but he need not relive them or see what in reality he had never seen, the crash explode, metallic and black and red, on his inner eye. He could expel them and think instead of another happy time, of Daniel's last birthday, dinner at McDonald's for fifteen little kids and *Beauty and the Beast* at the cinema afterward. Elizabeth had come, a great concession, a considerable kindness, from a teenager to a small boy. . . .

Roman turned into Chester Road and entered the Inner Circle by the golden gates. Sally had always liked the rose garden, but later than this, a month later, while the roses were in bud and when their scent was still a delicate breath on the air. The precision of the garden had pleased her, its order, the considerable taste that had gone into its arrangement.

He left the gardens by the gate at the Open Air Theatre and walked on. As he crossed the long bridge over the northern arm of the lake he heard footsteps behind him and looked back. It was the fair girl. She was late, she was running, and he wondered if she was meeting someone.

It surprised him very much that she spoke to him. This was their third encounter and in any other circumstances that would have been enough to merit a greeting. But Roman had learned that street people merit nothing and those who see them every day still ignore them with averted eyes. Thousands never see them at all, any more than they notice the litter that lies everywhere. So when she smiled and said, "Hello," he was too astonished to reply. He could only stare at her.

"It's a lovely day," she said.

He found his lost voice. "Yes," he said. "Yes, it is. Lovely."

Instead of continuing to walk, he paused and leaned against the parapet of the bridge. He didn't want her to think he was following her and perhaps be frightened. For a moment she had made him feel like a man again, an insider, and he was not at all sure that he wanted that.

.   .   .

The Rose Garden Restaurant had a romantic sound. It turned out to be a building like a cluster of mushrooms, little domed roofs bunched together, and on a terrace little hexagonal tables. Mary took care to approach from the direction he wouldn't expect her to come from. She wanted to see him before he saw her. Not that there was any idea in her mind of turning tail if it should be someone who appeared uncongenial sitting there, but rather to prepare herself. Preparations were a commonplace in her life. She prepared herself before opening them for what might be inside envelopes, before answering the phone, before meeting someone new. She must make sure. She must compose her face, her smile. There might be several lone men sitting at tables, waiting for women. All she knew of him was from that photograph and that he was six years younger than herself.

He would expect her to come from the Inner Circle or perhaps up the path and past the kiosk on Holme Green. Instead, she came out of the gardens. Most of the tables outside the restaurant were occupied, couples, foursomes, two men together, three women together, one man alone, but he was forty at least. She was standing still now, her eyes traveling from table to table. Then she saw him. It was a boy she expected but this was a man, yet unmistakably the original of the photograph. Unexpected heat came up into her face and she felt it color her cheeks. As she had thought, he was watching for her to come from past the lake and across the road, but he turned his head as if that flush had communicated itself to him. She moved then and made her way to his table. He stood up and held out both his hands, a tall, very thin man.

"Mary Jago," she said.

"Leo Nash," he said, "or Oliver."

He had dropped his left arm as if he thought the act of taking both her hands, which he had evidently planned to do, was too forward. She put her hand into his and found it cold. He looked older than his age, a little worn, which was natural after so much illness and stress and surely fear. His features would have been handsome but for his pallor. Light gray eyes met her green eyes and she thought, with a little shock, that he and she were alike to look at, they might have been brother and sister.

"Now I'm here and you're here," he said, "I don't know what to say. And that's ridiculous because I've rehearsed things to say so many times. I've made speeches to myself, trying to express my gratitude, but I'm dumbstruck in your presence."

"Not quite." She tried a laugh but she was breathless. "I'd call you highly articulate."

"Only in a nothing-to-say kind of way. At least I can ask you if you'd like some tea. Would you? Or a drink? Or tea and cakes? What would you like?"

He hadn't a phone, which meant he was seriously poor. His clothes were just the young man's uniform, jeans, a T-shirt, a sweatshirt draped over his shoulders, giving nothing away.

"Tea would be fine," she said.

While he gave the order to a waitress, she sat looking at him in silence. Whatever she had expected, it was not this. His appearance, yes, but not her feelings. The knowledge that this fragile, thin, pale man's body contained the marrow from her own bones, a healing elixir that had restored his health, affected her so profoundly that she felt almost faint.

She hung forward in her chair and closed her eyes. It was as if she had slept with him the night before for the first time—no, it was more than that, almost as if she were in love with him. . . .

He spoke gently, "Are you all right?"

Her hands were over her eyes. She took them away and looked at him. His face was concerned, a little taken aback. "I'm sorry," she said. "You must think me an awful fool."

He shook his head. "You expected someone different?"

"Oddly enough, no. I can't say I expected you but you're not a surprise. I had your photograph." She made a great effort. "I mean, I'd prepared myself to see you and I had a good idea what you'd be like, but really seeing you, really sitting here with you—well, it's a strange sensation."

"Strange, but good. For me, at any rate."

"Would you—would you tell me how it's been for you. I mean, your recovery. Or is that an intrusion on your—well, your privacy?"

He laughed, but gently. She was finding it hard not to look directly into those clear gray eyes. The spell of them was broken by the arrival of tea. Cakes came for him, fruit tarts, a cream horn.

"I am supposed to eat a lot," he said. "Eat well, they're always saying to me. I expect they mean fruit and vegetables, not cream cakes."

This time she could smile. "Would you tell me about it?"

"The transplant, do you mean?"

"Yes, I think so. The whole thing. Your illness, the transplant, all of it. I want to hear. From you."

"Wouldn't that be very self-indulgent on my part?"

Her self-confidence was growing. "Think of it as indulging me."

"All right. That certainly makes it easier."

He hesitated. He was eating a cream slice with a child's enjoyment. It amused her to see him lick the cream from his fingers, look up, and give her a wide frank smile.

"I'd just finished university," he said. "I was looking for work, I was getting anxious I'd never find anything, and at first I thought the pain was—well, nerves. That's how it started, with this awful pain." He wrinkled up his eyes, remembering. "A sharp pain in my side. I thought it was nerves and then I thought it was appendicitis. I went to my GP and he said it was gastroenteritis. But I'd never had anything like it before, I couldn't believe what he said. Then the pain got intense, acute. Do you really want to hear this?"

"Of course I do."

"I've got an older brother. He's important to me—he's like a best friend. I told him and he rushed me to Emergency. The hospital found my spleen was three times its normal size. It had a lot to cope with. It had taken over the function of my white blood cells. They told my brother and then they told me."

"It must have been a great shock."

"Like being stunned by a totally unexpected blow. One minute I was a normal healthy man, or so I thought, a man with a pain in his stomach, and then—this. They operated and took out my spleen. They told me I had AML—acute myeloid leukemia. I thought it was a death sentence."

"But you went to the Harvest Trust?"

"Not at first. I'd been told I should have a bone marrow transplant. With siblings the chance of matching tissue is one in four, so I was hoping against hope my brother would match. He was willing." She saw him clench his hands. He spoke with intensity. "He was more than willing. He was longing for the chance to help me. We're very close."

"But his tissue didn't match?"

"As I said, I'd felt under sentence of death. When they told me about this one in four chance all that changed, I was so sure it would be all right. You know, if you were told you had to have surgery and there was a one in four chance of not coming out of the anesthetic you'd be sure you'd die, wouldn't you? I would. I was sure one in four meant my brother's tissue would match. I was so confident I didn't even think much about it. He was my brother, we had the same genes, the same coloring, the same sort of looks. I knew it would be all right.

"They tested him and he wasn't compatible. I couldn't believe it at first. I thought they must have made a mistake. But they hadn't." He sighed, then brightened. "Still, if my brother had been able to make the donation I wouldn't have met you."

"I doubt if that would have bothered you much," Mary said. "You wouldn't have known I existed."

He put his head a little on one side, as if considering what she had said.

"My brother tried to find a donor. He had leaflets printed and put them through a thousand doors. Can you imagine? Most people just ignored them but a lot came forward for tests. One of them was compatible, but he turned out not to be suitable. I knew I'd die unless a donor was found. That's a very unpleasant feeling, it throws you into a panic, knowing you've got something that can be cured, or at any rate arrested, and the drug, serum, whatever, is everywhere, maybe even quite common, but you can't find it, it's hidden away, it may be inside lots of people you see in the street but you can't get at it. Then the hospital told us about the trust."

"Go on."

He recalled the day the Harvest Trust told him there was someone prepared to make the donation and his happiness at this good news, his excitement, later on his realization of reprieve.

"I'd lived with the dread that I'd never see my next birthday. Now here was a bunch of people telling me the chances were I would. I'd tried to get used to despair, to my fate, and now I had to get used to hope."

There was a setback when they were afraid his condition had

deteriorated too far for him to be eligible for the transplant. But he seemed stable and they had gone ahead. While this was going on, he said, he thought of her all the time.

"I thought of 'Helen.' Maybe I'm a bit of a hero-worshiper. I worshiped my brother, still do, and now here was this woman for me to worship, this unknown woman. You were a savior to me, a sort of saint."

She disliked the ease with which she blushed. Never in her life before had she had such cause for blushing. Her face flooded with color.

"But it was *nothing*," she said, surprising herself by her own vehemence. "It was *nothing*."

"I'm not at all sure *I* would have done it," he said. "Getting over the transplant, I had a lot of leisure to think. I thought about that a lot, what would I have done if I could have made a donation, and I decided I wouldn't have. I'd have been afraid."

His eyes seemed filled with adoration. Embarrassed, awkward, but unable to stop looking at him, she tried to leave the subject, to deflect things.

"What about work? You couldn't have worked while all this was going on. How have you lived?" Again she had perhaps gone too far. "I'm sorry, I shouldn't ask. . . ."

"You can ask me anything."

The words fell calmly. His total openness was almost frightening. The sense of intimacy made her shiver a little, for although they had been there less than half an hour it was as if she had known him for a long, long time.

"No, I'm sorry," she said again, weak now with attempting she hardly knew what. "I have no right to pry like this."

"*You* can ask me anything. After all, I'm yours, aren't I?"

"What do you mean?" she said.

"Nothing to make you look so—so fearful. Don't you know that when you save a man's life he belongs to you? Like a servant. In the true sense of that word, I mean. Someone who will devotedly serve you." Her hands were on the table surface and he put his over them. The hands he had reached out to take hers and had withdrawn from shyness or some sense of decorum, he now placed over her hands and let them rest there with increasing pressure. The touch was extraordinarily comforting.

"My brother kept me," he said. "I have a job now. It's only part-time and it's not much. I work for him, my brother. It's not the kind of thing I had in mind. I'd been to a great university, I had high hopes of my future, but still—it's work, I was glad of anything once I knew I was going to live."

She waited for him to say what he did, what the work was, but he didn't say. The bill came. As he was taking it from the waitress's hand, Mary said, "No, let me."

This time he laughed. The girl was standing there listening, but he didn't seem to mind. "You're remembering I said I hadn't a phone. I only meant I hadn't a phone of my own. I've been sharing a flat with my brother since I got ill. I had to, I couldn't manage on my own."

Her hands felt cold now he had taken his away. She was aware that with the coming of evening it was no longer warm. She stood up. "I'll walk you to Park Village, shall I?" he asked. "Oh, don't look like that. I'm quite well. You've made me well, remember? I can walk long distances, Mary."

It was the first time he had used her name and she was unprepared for the rush of pleasure it brought her. They passed into the Broad Walk and made their way northward. The bearded man she had encountered earlier was once more on one of the seats, once more reading. She prepared to smile at him and say hello, but he kept his eyes on the page. Leo began to talk of the curious coincidence of their living so near to each other. He called her Mary again and managed to give the name a prettier sound than anyone else had.

She looked back once but the man on the seat had gone.

7

T here had not even been a period of wondering where they all were, of apprehensiveness, doubt, the tickle of specula- tion, fear growing from unexplained absence and the silent phone. He knew, or thought he knew. They were in Woodbridge, at his mother-in-law's. It was school holidays, the October half-term, and Sally had driven herself, Elizabeth, and Daniel up into Suffolk to see her mother, who had been ill. They were to stay overnight.

Afterward, in a kind of mad obsession with figures, dates, sums, he had tried to calculate how often she had made that journey in the previous fifteen years, how often she and he and all of them had made it. Two hundred times? More? Looking back over the years, consulting his diary, he eventually came to the precise figure of two hundred and twenty-three times, anything to distract his mind, keep it, if only for minutes, in the emotionless drought of measurements and number.

That number of times she had driven it without incident, without event almost, with nothing approaching a narrow escape. He hadn't been anxious. Of course he hadn't. Not once had he been tempted to pick up the phone and check. They were there with Sally's mother. Perhaps they would phone him and then again perhaps they wouldn't. When he had eaten he might phone Sally's mother and ask how she was. But he doubted later if he had thought those things at the time. He hadn't been thinking of them at all. His mind had been elsewhere, concerned with a manuscript purporting to be the diary of a runaway slave who had married a Havasupai woman that

Talisman might buy if it could be authenticated and the price wasn't too high. He had brought a copy of it home with him. It lay on the kitchen table, open at page four. Strange that now he couldn't even remember whether or not Tom Outram had bought that book.

He was pottering about, getting himself a meal. Not defrosted pizza but baked beans, because he preferred tins to the microwave. He read another paragraph while he was opening the tin. There was a bottle of Meursault in the fridge, half full (or half empty if you were a pessimist, though he never had been), its neck corked with one of those wine-saver stoppers. He had poured himself a glass of wine while he was heating up the beans. The slave's diary probably wasn't genuine, was fiction, but might be all the more publishable for that. . . .

The doorbell rang at one minute to seven. He thought it was someone collecting for a charity. He went to the door feeling for his wallet in his pocket.

The police officers gave him no details then. That came later. He learned all about it later. Then, at one minute to seven, his glass of wine half drunk, his baked beans burning on the stove till the police-woman turned off the plate, they asked him to sit down, they told him of an accident, then of serious consequences, then of fatality. He had stared at them. He remembered asking them to repeat what they had said, he was so certain his hearing was playing tricks, he *couldn't* have heard that, this *couldn't* be happening to him.

For a long time he associated the smell of burnt tomato sauce with the collapse of his life, the loss of all that made his happiness. Once he had smelled it in a workmen's café in Camden Town and felt as sick as if he had swallowed poison.

The day after the police came he learned that Sally had been driving carefully, prudently, obeying all the rules, within the speed limit. Elizabeth was beside her in the passenger seat, Daniel in the back. The car had come to a stop at a level crossing over the Eastern Region railway line somewhere near Ipswich. It was at the foot of a hill.

The lorry behind her, a twenty-ton container from the docks at Felixstowe with defective brakes, came down the hill too fast and slid into the back of the car, precipitating it through the closed crossing gates into the path of the oncoming train.

The three of them were killed instantly. The driver of the train was injured, but all the passengers were unhurt. As for the lorry driver, he had a bang on the head and badly bruised knuckles. Two hundred and twenty-three times it had been all right and all those times that two hundred and twenty-fourth time had been waiting to happen, coming nearer every time, with the force of destiny. If you believed that sort of thing. Roman didn't.

He didn't go to the inquest, but he went to the funeral. He *was* the funeral. Sally's dying mother was there and Sally's sister, but he hadn't wanted anyone else and had told people not to come. He slept heavily that night and woke in the belief that Sally had got up early, would appear in a minute with tea for him. The knowledge and the pain pouring back tore from him cries of violent protest.

Two weeks afterward, having resigned from the Talisman Press, he put his house on the market and took to the outdoors.

The funeral, that surreal occasion, was the event he thought had tipped him over the edge into insanity. Or whatever condition it was that he had developed and had lived with. The three coffins, carried up the aisle of that stark crematorium by men in black coats, made a picture Ernst might have painted, or perhaps Magritte. He saw the scene over and over as such a picture, stuck somewhere on the other side of reality in that world where bad dreams live, and drug-induced hallucinations.

Curiously, since he had admitted the past, it was liable to come back at all sorts of odd times and print itself in front of his eyes. Now was one of those times as he walked across Prince Albert Road, making for St. John's Wood churchyard, called "church gardens." Cars had stopped for him at the pedestrian crossing, but he hardly saw them. One of them hooted to hurry him along. Before his eyes the three coffins passed, carried by strong young men, the kind of young men only seen dressed like that at funerals, their fresh faces lugubrious, their eyes downcast.

There had been no flowers. Of course not. How could anyone suggest anything so ludicrous? Well, no one had suggested it. His whole life, his past, his present, and his future, lay in three wooden boxes. He sat, unresponsive, in a pew, looking at the boxes, while a very young man with an Adam's apple like a swallowed toffee going up and down in his throat, talked in a Potteries accent about the resurrection and the life.

The picture dimmed as he reached the opposite pavement. By now the light was fading as the cruel vision had faded. The churchyard would soon be closed. Police patrolled the park to clear it of vagrants before and after closing time, but Roman had found he could sometimes elude them in this shady place outside its gates and make himself a bed among the old tombs.

He blinked his eyes and saw only the green turf, the flowerbeds, and the trunks of plane trees, their bark like gray skin peeling here and there to show the lemon color beneath. The leaves of planes, the beeches, and the whitebeams looked very pale and tender in the fading light. All white things shone with a curious radiance.

Having walked many miles this fine day, Roman walked farther. He did as he always did in the church gardens and looked at the grave of John Sell Cotman, the watercolorist who had died a hundred and fifty years ago, and at Joanna Southcott's, the religious visionary, she of "the Box," dead before the Battle of Waterloo. On most of the gray gravestones the lettering was no longer decipherable, eroded by time and weather. The bluebells were nearly over, but the borage aped their color and the cow parsley shimmered as in a country lane.

He sat down on one of the seats, leaned back his head, and closed his eyes. Once he had been a man very conscious of comfort, one who chose a mattress with care, sparing no expense. Armchairs had to be

soft and have footrests. But in his wanderings he had lost all interest
in comfort and scarcely noticed whether he lay down to sleep on paving stones or on the comparative luxury of a lawn.

After a while he was aware of the presence of someone else in the
gardens. Not the police, that was not their tread. It was Effie's footsteps that he heard. He opened his eyes. She came up to the seat and
sat down on the other end of it, giving him a shy sideways glance,
looking away, saying nothing. Only another dosser sits on the seat
where a dosser already is.

She was quite a young woman, younger than he, though at first he
had taken her for old. Her stoop made him think so, that and her
wizened hands and thick bandaged legs. But when she took off the
old cap she wore and unwound the woolen scarf from her head, it
was a round unlined face he saw with a full vulnerable mouth and
the ox eyes the Greeks said Hera had.

It was in his own first winter that he first encountered her, for she
had been on the street a shorter time than he. A mild March had still
been March, damp and by night very cold. In this same churchyard,
though not on this same bench, she had sat beside him and as darkness came—it seemed like night, but it was only six—laid her hand
first on his knee, then shifted it to close the fingers between his legs.
Once he would have been shocked. He would have recoiled from
her and left in haste. But a mild interest was all he felt, that and curiosity and a wonder that after long celibacy, after five months of ban-
ishing sexual thoughts, his flesh responded to this tramp woman's
touch and it was a full erection she held in her warm, surprisingly
feminine hand.

Even then he had not shaken off his old, ingrained sense of superi-
ority, of belonging to an elite, and as he moved with her onto her
blanket spread on the grass, into the well of darkness between tomb-
stones, it was a favor he felt he was doing her. He was being kind.
He was enduring the earthy smell of her, the fishy smell, the burrowing of her hands, out of generosity. The unknown, dark, and

glutinous place into which he slid was honored by him; God knew what he risked, by this grace of his.

But when it was over and for the first time since he had known her he saw her smile, felt the arms that had gone round him squeeze in a hug, he understood in a blinding revelation that she believed *she* had been generous to *him*. Hers was a proud smile and the arms that held him almost maternal. Out of pity perhaps or empathy, she had given him the only thing she had to give. It was a lesson to him. He was ashamed. Only later, when she had left the churchyard, dragging her bundles, he recalled with a shiver of relief at whatever had reprieved him, how near he had been to paying her, to handing over a ten-pound note with a word of thanks.

Now, with Effie seated beside him again, he felt nothing of what he had once felt before he was married and encountered by chance and alone a woman with whom he had had a one-night stand: embarrassment, awkwardness, a threatening presence. The streets and the street people had changed him. Social graces and social inhibition had departed and with them the fear of what others might say or others might think. He would have no more sex with Effie, but it would cost him no embarrassment to tell her so or show her so. Turning his head, he smiled at her, and reaching into the bag in his barrow, said, "Do you want a drink? I've only got Coke."

She shook her head. She was one of those who had bad days and, less often, good days, and he could tell from the way she contemplated her hands, turning them palms uppermost, then onto the palms and back again, muttering softly, that this day was bad. What it was she saw on her hands, blood perhaps, or a rash, stigmata or ineradicable dirt, he could not tell. The hands looked like any woman's to him, but rough and prematurely aged. She turned them over and back, over and back, examining them more and more closely.

"I'm going to bed now," he said. "I'm going to sleep."

She turned her hands, looked at the dirty nails with the concentration of a woman who has just painted hers and admires them.

"Good night, Effie."

He would have been surprised if she had answered. She put her hands on her knees, then sat on them. She aimed a kick at one of her bundles as if it disgusted her, its weight, the need always to carry it, the ugly mud-green color of the plastic. The bundle rolled a few feet away along the path. Roman sometimes felt the streets were one vast sprawling psychiatric ward and he just as much an inmate as any of them.

He got up, walked for a little, and found himself a place to sleep between two flat granite slabs, from which the lettering had disappeared. The turf in there was composed of short grass and moss in equal proportions. Beyond the railings, lit now by the wash from yellow lamps, loomed the fronts of a huge block of flats, Byzantine, white and terra-cotta.

The traffic climbing up to Hampstead on the Lord's side sounded like the sea, the tide coming in over a shingle beach. But in here now it might have been a country churchyard, Stoke Poges perhaps, quiet, serene, with that indefinable air of resignation and rest and deep peace that prevails in all places where graves are. Roman spread his groundsheet, for he had experienced the results of doing without one, and over it his sleeping bag. Into this he climbed and lay relaxed, looking out at the red brickwork and the white stucco between the long slender stems of churchyard weeds. He had long foregone the use of a pillow. Because it was appropriate he recited what he could remember of Gray's Elegy.

> Perhaps in this neglected spot is laid
> Some heart once pregnant with celestial fire;
> Hands, that the rod of empire might have sway'd,
> Or waked to ecstasy the living lyre

Halfway through the next verse he fell asleep.

Darkness is not long enduring in May and dawn comes at five. It was growing light but not yet sunrise when Effie woke him, shaking his shoulders, her face close up to his face. At first he thought this was another overture she was making to him, though even by the standards of her world and his, it would have been a rough method.

"No, Effie," he said. "No." And because any excuse he might make or reason he might give would be false and a prevarication, he said, "That was just for once. No more of that."

For answer, she seized hold of a bunch of his clothes, T-shirt and pullover that covered his right shoulder, and with her other hand flung out, pointed northward toward Wellington Place. It was a gesture melodramatic, almost Gothic, in intensity. Her face worked. She always found speech difficult, from some natural impediment or later trauma, and now she managed only, "On the rails! See the rails!"

He made an immediate association with trains. She must mean the Jubilee Line that passed underneath them on its way to St. John's Wood station. He got to his feet, stretched his stiff legs, and flexed his arms. Sleeping outdoors sometimes felt good, but it left a dull numbness in the bones. One had a clear head but aching limbs and back. He rubbed his eyes. He followed Effie along the path where she preceded him with steps that flagged more and more until they stopped altogether.

"Where is it, Effie?"

She was shaking her head, not to deter him but as if the only hope for her was to deny what she had seen, what she wanted to show him.

"Where do you want me to go?"

She pointed. Her plump vulnerable face, turned to him with pleading in every feature, was full of grief. The finger she extended trembled. On an impulse he seized her hand and held it tightly in his own.

The sky was lightening, but here among the trees, in the dense boskiness, it was still dark, the shadows blacker than they ever are by day. She seemed to be leading him to the churchyard's northern boundary. There was no sound of traffic, no wind blowing, only a heavy silence. He seldom saw the early morning, for he slept most deeply in those hours just before and just after dawn. The sky astonished him. It was a clear jewellike unclouded blue.

Effie clutched his sleeve. She pulled him up the path toward the main gate in Wellington Place that faces Cochrane Street. There, on the railings to the left of the gates, he saw it. The rails, she had said, the rails. Now he saw what she meant.

The man's body seemed to be impaled on the spikes of the railing. The upper part of it hung head downward into Wellington Place and a single hand showed, half-clenched, clawlike. The lower part of the body was on this side, in the churchyard. Booted feet drooped and thin bony ankles showed below the ragged hems of dark dirty jeans. Effie began to make gibbering sounds, throwing her hands about. He hesitated, his heart beating fast. Then he went up to the railing, reached between the bars, and touched the dead man's cold hand. That was how he knew he was dead, because the hand was so cold.

He fancied he recognized the face but he couldn't be sure. The clothes that were nearer to rags showed him to be one of the street people. There was never any mistaking that.

When he saw the place where the spike had entered the body and the blood, now dry and black, encrusting spike, rags, and wound, he turned away from that tower of silence and looked instead up at the clear, blue, remorseless sky.

8

Most callers at the Irene Adler that day and the next and the next came to ask directions to the site of the murder. They bought entrance tickets but few of them lingered. It was the murder scene they wanted and to waste no time getting there.

"Turn left into St. John's Wood Terrace, left again into the High Street, and take the first turning on your right. You'll know it by the scene-of-crime tapes."

Mary and Dorothea could have recited that formula in their sleep, though neither of them had been to look at the site. If for nothing else, it was good for business. Apart from the direction seekers, there was a troop of tourists who had come on from Wellington Place, anxious to sample what else was on offer in the neighborhood, first the boutiques of St. John's Wood High Street, the cafés for a drink, then the Irene Adler, finally the murder site to round off a day's entertainment.

"I shall throw up," said Dorothea, "if anyone else tells me that poor devil died of knife wounds and the spike was just incidental decoration." Mary was squeamish and disliked hearing about it, even in reported speech, but it had not occurred to her to feel nervous about walking through the churchyard or the park. The visitors did their best to make her afraid.

"I wouldn't set foot in the park now," said a woman in the Hat Room. "Alone or accompanied. Not even with my Great Dane. You're asking for trouble if you take a shortcut that way."

"But it didn't happen in the park," said Mary.

"Not that one, no. But how do you know the next one won't?" The woman began closely examining a rose-colored hat swathed in pink ostrich feathers. "Women were safer in those days, weren't they? Not allowed out much, protected, respected by men, always in a carriage."

Mary wanted to say, not if you were working class and how about Jack the Ripper, but she didn't. It seemed unlikely that anyone who chose to kill one of the meths drinkers from the canal bank would single her out as his next victim. When she had first heard of the murder she had thought at once of the man she had met in the park, and then she remembered the morning she had found him waking up on the Irene Adler doorstep. It was absurd the way she found herself hoping quite desperately that the corpse on the railings was not him. A photograph in the evening paper was no help. One dark-haired bearded man looks very like another and this blurred print gave no more clues to identity than his name: John Dominic Cahill.

"Irish," said the woman, now studying a black hat with a white egret apparently flying from its crown. "I suppose one mustn't be prejudiced."

Mary wondered if it was she or some other visitor to the Irene Adler who had left behind, by accident or perhaps sinister design, a sheet of paper listing crimes reported in the park during the previous year and the year before that. Stacey found it on the counter, lying beside the guides.

"One grievous bodily harm, three actual bodily harms," read Dorothea aloud. "Two assaults on the police, two indecent assaults, four indecent exposures—why tell *us?*—nine cases of criminal damage, seven cases of misuse of drugs, sixteen burglaries. But last year there weren't any bodily harms or assaults on the police and only five criminal damages but *thirteen* misuses of drugs."

"It doesn't seem very much, any of it," Mary said. "Not in a year."

She walked home by her accustomed route. As on this evening

and the one before that, she was hoping to see the man that in her own mind she called Nikolai. She had read in the paper, among the many stories about vagrants and beggars that had appeared, that the street people all had nicknames. Whether this was true she didn't know, but she named the bearded man Nikolai from that moment because that was Gogol's name and he had been reading *Dead Souls*.

His voice interested her. Perhaps she was a snob, but she had not expected a man such as he to have a voice and an accent like his. Nor to have been reading what he was reading, come to that. She looked for him on her way home, hoping he was not John Dominic Cahill, whose nickname, the paper said, was Decker. She hoped very much that Decker and Nikolai were not one and the same.

But he was nowhere to be seen. She even took the long route, crossing the Long Bridge and entering the Inner Circle. It was dull and rather windy, therefore unlikely that he would be on one of the seats in the Broad Walk. She made a detour through the shady shrubberies in the southeast corner, but he was not there either. A waste of time, she told herself, and then that it would have been rather awkward if he had been there and they had suddenly come face to face along one of the dark paths.

Leo Nash was taking her out to dinner. He had phoned and asked her two evenings before. Mary was gratified because she had thought her behavior to him, her reticence, her caution, might have discouraged him. And now she hardly knew where that coolness had come from or what purpose it had served.

He had walked back to Park Village West with her, leaving the park by the Gloucester Gate. It all seemed familiar to him and when she asked he told her he had always lived near the park and always, since a small boy, loved the terraces, the villas, the lake, the glimpses of wild animals behind the zoo fencing.

"And you're called Nash!" she had said.

He looked at her, uncomprehending. "That's right."

"Nash," she said, "John Nash. He was the architect of the park."

"Ah. I've never thought of that before. I never made the connection."

"Perhaps he was an ancestor."

He laughed, but she thought he looked disconcerted. "There are an awful lot of us in the phone book."

They passed the Grotto and took the turn into the crescent of Park Village that was the longer way round. The lilac was past and it was too early for the roses. Crimson and gold wallflowers and the orange Siberian kind scented the air. Someone was cutting a lawn, the buzzing of the motor a country or suburban sound. It smelled like a florist's shop, he said, as if he had never been in a garden before and had only known cut flowers, forced flowers in pots and boxes. Mary stopped outside the gate of Charlotte Cottage. The rock garden was a mass of white and yellow and blue alpines and the first geraniums were coming out in the tubs.

"What a lovely garden," he said.

"The house is pretty nice too."

She fancied the look he gave her was a strange one, puzzled, as if he were suddenly adrift. She had been on the point of asking him in. For a drink, a cup of coffee. We have to have these excuses, she thought, or women do. But something stopped her, some sudden feeling of distance between them. The rapport she had felt up till then was gone, reminding her that he was a stranger. After all, she didn't know him. They had only just met. What did they have in common but shared marrow in their bones?

"It has been very good to meet you at last," she said, as if such warm words would soften her rejection of him. At once, in her own ears, they sounded like cold words. They sounded rigidly formal. She held out her hand, making things worse. "I hope we'll see each other again." She could see she had hurt him. He pursed his lips the way a man may do when he feels he has committed some solecism, when he has put a foot wrong but does not know where or how.

"I hope that too. May I phone you?"

"Of course."

"Then I will. Soon."

"Thank you for walking me home," she said, and she had gone quickly to let herself into the house, picking up Gushi and hugging him the moment she was inside.

After that it was a relief when he phoned. She could repair the damage, make all things well between them. She had waited for him to phone but wouldn't have been surprised if he hadn't, and then she would have had to get in touch with him. But he had phoned and surely at the earliest opportunity that he could have done so without seeming too eager. His voice had been warm and friendly and had evoked from her just such a warm response.

The call seemed to have released her to talk about him. When her cousin Judith phoned she spoke to her of the new friend she had made, the man who was the recipient of her transplant. She told Dorothea, who wanted to know if he was "personable," if he was "fanciable"—when was she seeing him again?

"That would be one in the eye for old Alistair."

"I've only met him once for half an hour, Dorrie."

She told her grandmother. Frederica Jago was going to Crete on the following day with some people called Tratton, old friends who had a house there.

"I know one shouldn't ever say I told you so, but I did tell you he'd reply, he just took a long time about it. And he's nice?"

"I think so. I think he's very nice."

"Not a—what do they call them?—not a yob? My darling Mary, you needn't look like that. We do judge people by the neighborhoods they come from."

"He's a clever, well-educated, quiet, and, I think, rather sensitive man."

"And you found that out in how long? An hour?"

Mary laughed. "A bit less. Perhaps you can meet him when you get back from Crete. I must go. I've been here much longer than I meant to." Frederica insisted on calling a taxi for her. She was not to wait out in the street. The murder had been too near for comfort.

"And take her right to the door, please," she said to the driver. "Into the crescent and right to the door, not just to the Albany Street corner."

Mary kissed her. Her grandmother smelled delicately of vanilla. She had looked back at the house and waved as the cab pulled away, at the great late Victorian pile, stucco, red shingles, red tiles, all gleaming in yellow lamplight, and Frederica's neat tiny figure on the steps under the big bulbous portico.

·   ·   ·

Leo was a little early. He had a taxi waiting, and though he came in, it was only to the hall while she shut Gushi into the drawing room. He wore a suit and this reminded her of Alistair, who dressed formally most of the time. She came back to find him studying a framed print of Christ Church in a series of Oxford college etchings on the hall wall.

"I was at the House," he said. "It looks just the same."

Did people still call Christ Church that? "Yes, you said you were taken ill just after you'd got your degree."

He smiled at her. The smile pulled his young face into a network of radiating lines. She thought he looked ill, suddenly aged, pale as a sick old man.

"Are you all right?"

"Yes. Why? I'm naturally a bit wan. It's the curse of the very fair-skinned."

He took her to an Italian restaurant in Paddington Street, off Marylebone High Street. It was a place recommended by a friend of his brother's. The distance could easily have been walked. But was he fit to walk half a mile? She very much wanted to ask him how he was now. Would he stay well? Was he, in fact, *cured*? She doubted if such a thing was possible.

As soon as they entered the simple little restaurant, Mary sensed that the food would be good, the service efficient and discreet. It was a pretty place, with wooden tables and comfortable seats instead of the rickety glass and wrought-iron kind, mirrors and paintings on the walls, flowers on every table and candles lit.

While they ate he talked of the first donor who had come along. Their tissue was compatible. In fact, it was a perfect match, as close as a brother or sister. But the man was chronically mildly ill himself and he was found medically unfit to donate marrow.

"It was the most appalling disappointment. I was sure I was going to die. I tried to teach myself to be resigned to it, I even wrote out instructions for the kind of funeral I wanted to have."

"Your mother wasn't compatible?"

His face was impassive. He no longer met her eyes. "My mother wasn't tested. She—well, she was afraid of the anesthetic, of going under. She's never had anesthesia. I can understand."

This had been her grandmother's fear. Perhaps it was common, this dread of loss of consciousness, loss of control, a brief experience of death. "There were no other relatives, then?"

"Cousins. Two were tested, but it was no use. Then you came along." He smiled. "In the nick of time."

"I'm sure there would have been others."

"No, I think not. You were the only one in the world."

There was an intensity in the way he said it and the look he gave her that made her glance away. He seemed to sense her embarrassment and began to talk of indifferent things, his brother's business, a vague merchandising that meant nothing to her, the place they lived in that he would like to leave when he could, but that had come to them when their mother moved out. A roof over one's head was not something to be lightly abandoned.

The bill came and she offered to go halves. His expression became stern, a little impatient. "No. Don't suggest it again, please."

She recoiled. His severity was unexpected and, gentle herself, she reacted painfully to brusqueness in others. It was almost like being struck and she put up her hand to her cheek, remembering Alistair, fearing verbal attack almost as much as physical. Leo's smile, warm and somehow conspiratorial, a small, sharing, intimate smile, restored them to where they had been before.

"The only one in the world," he said again. "You may not care for the idea, but I can't help feeling that makes for a special relationship."

She hesitated, then said quietly as they came out into the street, "Oh, no, I feel that too. I don't see how anyone in our situation could escape feeling that."

"Shall we walk back?"

It was not for her, she felt, to suggest he might be incapable of walking. But now the half mile she had first thought of as the distance between here and Park Village, in a more realistic estimate became at least a mile.

"If you like."

She tried to say it grudgingly. Her unwilling tone was assumed to give him the impression walking found no favor with her. If it did he chose to ignore it and they walked side by side up toward the Marylebone Road and the York Gate.

To her relief he had said nothing about the murder. He was the only person she had spoken to in the past three days who had not talked of the murder. Even her grandmother had touched on it with her injunction to the taxi driver. She asked Leo about his parents and he told her his father was dead and his mother lived in Scotland, had married again after his father's death. His brother Carl was ten years older than he, a clever gifted man, he said, and he added with a smile that he was nearly as much a lifesaver as she. Though Leo didn't say so, Mary had the impression Carl was gay. Leo only said that he was rather solitary, mysterious about his private life.

At the utterance of this last word, the word "life," Leo put out one hand to support himself against a shop front. In the artificial light it was hard to see, but Mary thought his pallor had intensified. He stood there, breathing carefully, then lowered himself to sit on a wall that reached to waist height.

"You shouldn't be walking," she said. "It's too far. It's too much for you."

He nodded. "I'm afraid it is. I'll be all right in a moment." The smile he managed reassured her. "This still happens. They warned me it would go on happening." He seemed to be considering whether what he wanted to say would be wise. The words came out in a rush. "I'm on low-dose chemotherapy. It's—" he sought for a word "—a bore."

"We'll get a taxi."

Quite a long time passed before one came. It was nearly eleven and Mary, who had been determined this time to ask Leo in, make coffee for him, explain to him how she came to be there and show him over the house, now saw that all this must be postponed. He opened the taxi door for her and she heard him tell the driver to take them first to Park Village West and then take him on alone to Plangent Road.

"May I see you again tomorrow?" he said. "To make up for making a fool of myself tonight? In a subtle sort of way you warned me not to try walking, didn't you?"

"I wanted to make you believe I was reluctant. I couldn't do more."

He turned away and said in a muffled voice, "You do everything quite perfectly."

She blushed in the dark. Her cheeks burned. She wanted to tell him how glad she was he hadn't mentioned the murder, but to say anything about it would defeat the purpose of the remark. As the taxi turned into Park Village West he took both her hands in his. His hands felt warmer tonight. They exerted a strong pressure on her, not the grip of a sick man.

"Tomorrow then."

"Tomorrow's Saturday," she said.

"All the better. May I come in the morning? May I come at ten?"

"Of course." Things seemed to be progressing very fast, but why not? What harm could it do? What had she to lose? "Look after yourself," she said. "Rest. Have a good night's sleep." She was aware of the chill of the night as she stood there for a moment. All the flowers were out, gleaming monotone in the pale cold light from street lamps. From a house nearby music was coming softly, but she heard a window close and then all was silent.

The inside of Charlotte Cottage felt warm and Gushi like a soft comforting muff. She buried her hands in his golden fur. The weekend ahead would be the first one she had spent there that would not be lonely and herself forlorn. She took Gushi up to bed with her and dreamed of Leo Nash, a dream in which she came upon him sitting in the park in front of an easel. He was making an architect's drawing of Sussex Place with its ten Oriental domes and array of Corinthian columns. As she approached he tore the sheet off a drawing block and handed it to her, saying, "You may like to see a compatible tissue-type."

The thin paper was icy in her hands and before she could look at the drawing it had melted like snow and dripped from her fingers.

·   ·   ·

A clock somewhere that she hadn't yet located was striking the last note of ten when he arrived. He put out his hand as if for a formal hand-shaking but, when he placed hers in it, covered it with the other in a warm intimate gesture. The little dog came running out and without hesitation he picked it up and held it in his arms.

"He is just the sort of dog I'd expect you to have."

"Why?"

"Small but strong, gentle and appealing, loving, childlike. Not *like* you but the sort of things you like. Am I right?"

"About the things I like or his being my dog?"

They had come into the living room and sat down. He had glanced at the work Mary had been doing on the Irene Adler brochure and she expected him to ask her about it, but instead he said, looking a little disconcerted, "Isn't he yours?"

Raised eyebrows, a half smile, his hands deep in the dog's fur. She had never seen such clear eyes, like glass, water in a smoked glass. He was in jeans this morning, a check shirt, a denim jacket. These boy's clothes restored his youth.

"I am beginning to wish he was," she said. "I've got very fond of him."

"You're looking after him for someone?"

"The owners of this house. Did you think this house was mine, Leo?"

He looked about the room, his eyes resting on a vase, a cabinet, then meeting hers again. "I suppose so. Isn't it yours?"

"I'm looking after it for an old couple who are friends of my grandmother."

He smiled. "The assumptions one makes!"

"They've gone on holiday to Central America and the United States. They've no children and no one to look after the house and the dog. My grandmother's away too, but only for a couple of weeks. She lives in Hampstead and she's not up to coming in here every day. She's over eighty."

"I'm glad you don't own this house."

"Why?"

He was serious now. A pair of frown lines appeared between his eyebrows. "You haven't seen where I live. I thought you must be rich. I'll tell you something. When I saw your address on the letter I almost didn't reply."

"Is that why it took you so long?"

It was a question, she now understood, that had bothered her for weeks. Why he had waited, why he had condemned her to waiting for the post, to rushing to the phone when it rang. She just stopped herself saying, "So that's why!"

"I wanted to reply, I wanted desperately to meet you. You still don't fully realize the depths of my gratitude. But when I saw that address I was—well, deeply disappointed. Taken aback, that may be a better way to put it. I came down here, you know. I came one evening and sneaked a look at the house."

"How devious," she said lightly.

"I concluded you were rich and privileged. It was a natural assumption to make. You were rich and therefore not for me, never for me."

"For *you?*" she said, the color flooding into her face.

"A figure of speech," he said. "I'm sorry. Already I—I think of us as close. I can't help it. You know what the Victorians used to say, flesh of my flesh and bone of my bone."

"That was husbands and wives. That was the one flesh of the old marriage service."

"They didn't have transplants then." His sidelong glance and half smile took away her discomfort. "It's a lovely day. Where shall we have lunch?"

"You must let me give you lunch."

"Why not? I will now I know you're not rich."

9

Roman's children had been fond of the British Museum. Elizabeth seemed to have passed her affection for it on to Daniel and several times they had accompanied him, both particularly attracted by Egyptian antiquities. It was the museum then that drew him when he felt the need to absent himself for a few days from his usual haunts, and he set up the nearest thing to a home he had on a doorstep in Russell Street.

The temperature had dropped and it was cold, but not cold like winter. He passed a lot of his time in Coram's Fields, reading Bunin's stories, which he bought in a secondhand shop in Theobald's Road. One day, after a visit to the baths and an attempt at smartening up, he went into the museum, and on another, unprecedentedly, to the cinema. His flight from Regent's Park had been brought about by the discovery of Decker's body, though he had not known it was Decker then.

For a few minutes he and Effie had stood there, not looking at it, but aware more than they were aware of anything, that it was there. In spite of himself and in spite of what he thought of as his new toughness, the result of true street wisdom, Roman had felt his throat rise and the awful black weakness that precedes vomiting take hold of him. But he had turned his eyes from that hand with the clawed fingers, from those booted feet and the blackened blood on the railing, and looked up at the cold purity of the morning sky. And slowly, while he held on to Effie and she clutched him, the nausea had passed. Whatever Effie felt, trembling and pale, looking up at him for help, also passed. He heard her sigh throatily.

The street was still deserted, the place still silent. Only now was the traffic beginning to swell in Wellington Road and its muted thunder to reach them. A van passed, its driver staring straight ahead.

"You go, Effie," he said. "Go into the park. Go back through the churchyard into the park. And say nothing. You haven't seen this. You haven't been here. Say nothing."

There was little fear of that. She could speak, but she seldom did more than mutter or curse passersby who cringed from her. He looked into her face. It was blank, snub-nosed, the eyes round and protuberant, the pink-brown skin smooth like a child's. The woolen scarf that wrapped her head smelled of old damp sheep.

So ingrained was his middle-classness, his education, his *gentility,* that it was impossible for him ever to feel the same toward a woman as he had before he made love to her. Strange term for what had passed between him and Effie, but what other to use that would not also revolt his middle-classness? He and Effie, though in grotesque circumstances, had performed that act that must make him forever feel some tenderness for her. He could never be otherwise than aware of a bond between them, though she hadn't spoken his name, was probably unaware of what it was.

He put his arms round her, hugged her tightly, and sent her off with a gentle push along the path. Then he too left the churchyard, uncertain what to do, uncertain whether to do anything. What he and Effie had seen on the railings back there he was very nearly sure no one else had seen before them. Except whoever had done this deed, always excepting him.

He tramped up St. John's Wood High Street—the meaning of the word "tramp" had been made manifest to him this past year and a half—until he came to a phone box. There he calculated his chances. All calls could be quickly traced, he was sure of that, but he had his voice to rely on. An anonymous call made in the accent of Westminster School and Cambridge would hardly lead police to the vagrant with his barrow.

He made his call. He reported a dead body impaled on the railings in Wellington Place. The second time they asked his name, he put the receiver back. Once, in the past, he had spent several nights asleep on the doorstep, under the Corinthian portico of the Connaught Chapel, once a church, now film studios—O times! O customs!—but it was too obvious, too open. Instead, in Ordnance Hill, in the garden of an empty house with uncurtained windows and a "sold" sign outside, he made his bed on concrete steps and rolled himself into his sleeping bag. Chilled and suddenly hungry, he was unable to sleep, and after a few minutes, perhaps ten, he heard the wail of sirens on police cars.

Later in the day, he crossed into the park by the Macclesfield Bridge. The canal walkways here were narrow lanes, for the embankments were so thickly overgrown as to be like woodland descending to the water. Planes and limes and hornbeams grew there, their trunks buried among the greenery and white fronds of cow parsley. Something less than two years ago he had brought the children here and told them how an earlier bridge had been destroyed when a gunpowder boat blew up underneath it in 1874. Now he stood on the center of the three segmental arches, looking down onto the narrow paving below him where police were questioning the jacks men. They were not in uniform, but he could tell they were police. Their denim jeans were pressed and their leather jackets glossy; they were well fed and they would not die at forty-seven.

Roman thought it foolish to mock or vilify the police, but he didn't love them either. His taking to the streets had removed him from that law-abiding company whose side they are on to another society that lies beyond the pale and where the police are enemies. He watched one of the jacks men, a thin gray-faced Ulsterman he had once or twice talked to, go sluggishly off with the two policemen to the car parked up in Albert Road. To help in their inquiries, no doubt, to be questioned until his meths-addled brain reached a point of incorrigible confusion.

The moment they spoke to him, Roman, they would know he was different. A crank, a dropout, therefore suspicious. His voice would alert them to his eccentricity while his clothes and barrow proclaimed his vagrant status. He walked on, going southward, through the park, out the other side into the Marylebone Road, across it and through what Dickens, he remembered, had called "the awful perspectives of Wimpole Street, Harley Street, and similar frowning districts." Four or five days should do and then he would go back. The sky was gray and the ramparts of these tall Georgian houses gray too, not a tree in sight, the traffic a river of shiny metal running down to Cavendish Square.

When Saturday came he returned. In the sunshine of early June he came back into the park by the York Gate, turning immediately to the left, to the water's edge and bobbing ducks, the tree-shaded lawns and the seats where Effie sometimes sat. But she was not there this morning. There was no one but the dog man with a borzoi, a beagle, and a golden retriever tugging on his leash.

• • •

They had gone out and had their lunch. He had let her pay for it, repeating his remark about its being all right because she wasn't rich. Afterward they walked down to Covent Garden in the sunshine and listened to a students' orchestra playing Mozart. The Flute and Harp Concerto, Leo said, the only one for these instruments Mozart wrote, composed for a rich patron and his daughter to play together. When the music stopped and the players began packing up their instruments, he had taken her hand. Not in a handshake but gently lifted as if he meant to bring it to his lips.

She looked at him, into his eyes, wondering with a small flutter of excitement, what next? What will he say next? What shall we do now?

He squeezed the hand he was holding, let it fall. "I'm going to leave you here."

She almost thought she had misheard.

"I must go," he said. "I have to meet my brother."

Did he mean her to come too? "We can get the tube if you like."

She fancied a note of impatience. "No, I thought I said. I have to meet my brother. Alone." Then, belatedly, "Will you be all right?"

"Of course."

Disappointment came later. At first she was only astonished at this sudden departure. A kiss on the cheek was to be expected, but he didn't kiss her. She watched him go off in the direction of Floral Street and the tube, that casual loose-limbed walk of his, his thinness so that his bones showed through whatever he wore, his bright fair hair. He didn't turn back to wave.

She was left to go home on her own at that worst time of the week to be alone, five on a Saturday afternoon. Walking back, at last getting into the tube herself, she reflected that he had said nothing about seeing her again, seeing her soon, phoning her. In an age when the merest business acquaintances kissed at a second meeting, he hadn't kissed her.

She tried to think what she had said, done, implied, how she might have offended. Nothing came to mind.

I didn't know it till now, she thought, but I want to see him again. I want to see him very much.

10

No man had ever brought her flowers before. She had believed it an outdated custom. Why did Alistair have to be the first? The flowers were carnations and that white stuff with myriad tiny blossoms whose name she could never remember.

Alistair had turned up without warning. There had been no more phone calls. She had even allowed herself to think there would be no more. He had given up, she had thought; perhaps he had met someone else.

"How absolutely over a man, sick and tired and done with him you must be," Dorothea said, "when you find yourself hoping he's met someone else."

"It would be simple relief. I don't think I'd have a moment's regret."

A fantasy she had while walking across the park involved a nice strong-minded woman for Alistair, handsome in a no-nonsense kind of way, someone who would laugh at him and stand up to him. The difficulty lay in imagining Alistair's response. Was the sad fact that he was a bully who needed not a worthy adversary but a victim?

She was thinking about him as she approached the house, so that seeing him on the doorstep, peering through the letter box as if he thought she was hiding from him, was like a thought miraculously and unpleasantly made real. Holding up the bunch of flowers, and looking constricted in his dark suit and with his black hair slick and short, he seemed like an illustration to P. G. Wodehouse. And in a Wooster-ish way he said, "Aren't you going to let us in?"

"Oh, Alistair . . ."

She was distracted, she hardly knew what to say.

It was Leo she had hoped would come this evening. She might have been thinking about Alistair, but it was Leo she wanted to see, Leo who had made no sign since the previous Saturday of wanting to see her. But in spite of his absolute silence, she half expected him and still half expected him. It was impossible that a man should have said the things he had said, looked as he had looked, and then quitted her life with a quick touch of the hand.

There was no question, though, but to let Alistair in. That fantasy woman might have shut the door in his face, but she was different. She took the flowers from him, standing aside to let him come in.

"I wished you'd phoned," she managed to say.

"Do people in our situation really need to phone and make appointments?"

She wanted to say, What situation? We are in no situation. We are separated, this is a separation that we are in, and that word "trial" was just a sop to both of us. But she said nothing. He was looking round him at the hall, up the stairs, into the living room, his eyebrows rising.

"Go in," she said. "I'll put the flowers in water."

Which vases were for use and which for decoration only? The Chinese ones looked valuable and frail. She opened cupboards, found a pottery jar and a glass vase, and tried to arrange the flowers. Irene Adler could probably have done it but now it was a lost art. She carried vase and jar into the living room.

Alistair was sitting on the sofa in the act of repelling Gushi's advances with the toe of his shoe. It was such a classic tableau, the former lover now cast as villain proving his worthlessness by kicking the dog, that she found it impossible not to laugh. Gushi had scarcely made contact with Alistair's shoe. She knew very well that he disliked dogs. But she laughed, thinking of Leo, who was already Gushi's best friend, and the scene briefly endeared Alistair to her.

"What's funny?" he said.

"Nothing. Poor Gushi. Shall I put him outside?"

He shrugged. "This is quite a place you've secured for yourself."

"Hardly for myself, Alistair. The owners will be back in September."

"Didn't you say they'd no children? No family at all?"

"So far as I know." The flicker of tenderness she had felt for him was dwindling. "Would you like a drink?"

"I thought I could take you out to dinner," he said rather peevishly.

She was in a dilemma. Having dinner with Alistair was not the way she would have chosen to spend the evening. On the other hand, she didn't much want Leo to phone while Alistair was in the house. If he phoned he might suggest coming over. It was not so much a matter of the men as rivals—Leo was a friend only, they had barely touched hands—as the awkwardness of introducing him to Alistair as "Oliver," the recipient of the transplant. What would Alistair do? Insult Leo? Abuse him? *Hit* him?

"I'll phone a restaurant and book a table," Alistair said. "Have you any ideas? You live here."

A quick decision must be made. She must not involve herself in prevarication, plotting, strategy, but tell herself the truth, that she had nothing to hide. Wouldn't it be wonderful if Leo came, whoever else might be here, whatever the consequences? And it was nonsense to think of Alistair hitting anyone. She had magnified a mild belligerence into a full-blown tendency to unprovoked violence.

"We'll stay here," she said. "I'll cook something."

He put the phone receiver down. "I hoped you'd say that. I mean that we could stay in. I don't care about food. Bread and cheese will do for me and we can have a bottle of wine. You do have wine?"

She nodded. Suddenly she had no idea what to say to him. No topic of conversation presented itself. The idea of spending a whole evening with him was dismaying, as if they were strangers, as if they hadn't lived together for nearly three years. What had they talked about? How had they passed a thousand evenings?

She found herself looking at him in despair, a misery not apparent, it seemed, from her expression for he said in a jovial way, "You don't know how I've missed you." He looked at her sideways. "That flat in Willesden," he said as if it were a place he had remotely heard of, not somewhere he and she had lived in for so long, "it's grim. It's a dump. I can't tell you how depressing I find it. And of course it's much worse now you're not there."

"If you dislike it so much you'll have to move." She heard her grandmother's briskness in her own tone and was glad of it.

"Yes," he said. "Yes, you're right. The fact is, darling, I want to do what I should have insisted on doing in the first place."

"I'll get that wine," she said. "I've got a salad made and there's some salmon. Will wine do, or do you want gin or something?"

"I should have insisted," he said as if she hadn't spoken, "on moving in here with you."

The confrontation she had hoped to avoid was approaching, was almost there. "I'd rather not talk about that. I'll get the wine."

She opened the bottle in the kitchen, so that he couldn't wrest it from her and demonstrate male skills. Leo came into her mind, Leo opening just such a bottle of wine for them to share before lunch that Saturday. He had raised his glass and said, "To you!" She tried to understand how so much warmth had changed abruptly to indifference, to an apparent need to get away quickly from her presence. How much of that was her imagination and how much real? Every time the phone rang she thought it must be him, but it rang seldom, and once or twice she had found herself willing it to ring into the oppressive silence.

She put the bottle and glasses on a tray, took the food out of the fridge, refilled Gushi's water bowl, washed her hands. Alistair was exploring the room, examining the Blackburn-Norrises' porcelain.

"What on earth have you been doing?" he said. "Been down the cellar, selecting a choice vintage?"

"I buy my own wine. I don't drink theirs."

He made her churlish. He brought out the worst in her. She handed him a glass with a forced smile. He raised it and said, "To us!"

There is no "us," she thought, but she said nothing, drinking in silence. Leo had said, "To you!" but, like Alistair's toast, it had meant nothing. . . .

"For one thing," he said, "I don't like you being alone here, not with people getting murdered in the vicinity."

"One person. A man. Some poor down-and-out. And St. John's Wood is hardly 'the vicinity.' " She must stop being tactful, discreet, cowardly. It was hard, but a beginning must be made somewhere. "Alistair, that's just an excuse. Why don't you say what you mean? You want to live with me again. Well, I'm afraid I don't want to live with you."

He was looking disbelieving. Not hurt or angry but simply incredulous. "Then why did you?"

"That was three years ago," she said. "People change. I've changed. I don't know if you have. I think you have, but it may be that I never really knew you. And you may never have known me."

His answer was cut off by the phone ringing.

Mary jumped, a reaction she knew she would have if the phone rang, but she was powerless to prevent the reaction. Her heart began to pound. It must be Leo. Leo, who had made no contact with her since Saturday, was phoning to ask her out or even to tell her he was on his way to Park Village. Alistair, on his feet again, put his hand out to lift the phone.

"No!" She had never, in all their time together, spoken to him with such force. She had hardly ever spoken to anyone so peremptorily. Astonishment stopped him in his tracks and he turned on her a shocked look.

She picked up the receiver, said a quiet "Hello," and gave the number.

The voice was not Leo's but a woman's, elderly, educated, gentle. Mary was aware at first only of a huge disappointment, a letdown that made her want to cry out in frustration. She had no idea who this was. The name Celia Tratton meant nothing.

"We have met, once, a few years ago. At Frederica's. At your grandmother's."

"Yes, of course." Enlightenment came quickly. "I do remember. I'm so sorry. My grandmother's staying with you, isn't she?"

"Mary, I have very bad news. I'm sorry."

"Bad news? She's ill?"

"Well, yes, she was ill. I suppose she was."

Mary said flatly, "She's dead."

"Yes. This afternoon. She can have known nothing about it. We were sitting out on the terrace, in the shade. One moment she was talking to us and the next she was dead. A stroke. It was so absolutely sudden, a terrible shock. . . ."

She had been as near as a mother. Mary spoke the necessary formal mechanical words. She replaced the receiver with slow deliberation, then shifted it, making sure it was correctly in its rest. Her mind had emptied and she felt cold. She was aware of Alistair's arm sliding round her shoulders and Alistair's hot cheek pressed against hers. Gushi came over and sat close up against her leg. Alistair tried to toe him away.

"Oh, stop doing that!" Mary cried. "Leave him alone. Why do you have to act so in character?" She began laughing and crying at the same time. She expected him to smack her face, but he didn't.

"I'm sorry," he said. "I didn't want him bothering you."

"My grandmother died. Did you realize that?"

"Of course."

She moved her face from his, took his arm away.

"Darling," he said, "she was old. She'd had her life. She was bound to die soon anyway."

Mary thought, I would like to get up and point to the door and tell him to go, to get out, I would like to have the power and the clout to do that. Instead, she leaned back, closing her eyes, and saw her grandmother quite vividly, her bright lined face, the sharp green eyes that were full of youth, and thought, she can't be dead, it can't be true, there must be a mistake.

"She must have been all of eighty-five," said Alistair, pursuing his technique of comforting. "She felt no pain. She was just snuffed out like a candle. We should all be so lucky when our time comes."

"Yes, all right."

"Imagine how it would have been if she'd lingered for months. Think what you'd have been through, seeing to all that, nursing her, you'd have had to, you were all she'd got."

"Yes, all right, Alistair. I know."

"She'd had a good life and a lot of people would say she'd made a fortunate end."

I am a poor meek thing, Mary thought, and I like quiet meek gentle people like myself. I liked, I *loved,* my grandmother, who treated men and women's feelings as if they were made of brittle glass and who handled them with fine dextrous fingers. I like people who go slowly and feel their way and are discreet and careful of their words, people who move delicately and tread on no one's dreams. "Civilized" is my favorite word. That being so, how could I have lived for years with this man? And why can't I tell him to go away?

Alistair brought her some wine and she sipped it. He told her she really should eat something and when she said she couldn't said that *he* would.

"I'm hungry and I don't mind admitting it. Life has to go on."

He brought himself a plate of salmon and salad with a hunk of granary bread. While he ate he talked about his day at work to "distract" her. Not listening to what he said, she put Leo in his place, wondering what Leo would be saying if he were here now, imagining sensitivity but not the form it would take.

After a while she excused herself and went upstairs. The door had a lock and a key, so she locked it in case Alistair came up. Then she unlocked it because locking it was absurd. She lay on the bed and thought, I would like Dorothea here or Judith, I would like someone just to be with me. I would like Leo. I hardly know him, I've only spent a few hours with him, but I would like him here now. Anyone but Alistair. Why does it have to be Alistair?

She *can't be dead.* But of course she can be. She was old, very old.

The age of the person who has died doesn't make any difference to those left behind. It's just as bad for them to lose someone of eighty-five as someone of forty-five or twenty-five. Leo would understand. He knew about death and she needed someone who knew about it. When she went downstairs again Alistair was watching television. He turned his head.

"Feeling a bit better?"

She nodded, though the nod meant nothing.

"There's nothing for you to do. I washed up my own plate and our glasses."

It was an effort to stop herself thanking him, but she made the effort and succeeded.

"I'm going to stay the night here with you, Mary. You shouldn't be alone."

"Really, that's not necessary, Alistair."

"I'm going to stay the night. I should never forgive myself if I abandoned you." In the tone of someone who expects to be told no spare room would be needed, he could sleep with her, he said archly, "Isn't there a spare bedroom going begging?"

She suddenly remembered telling her grandmother that she and Leo must meet when her holiday was over. Tears came into her eyes. She said good night, picked up Gushi, and took him upstairs to bed with her. She locked the door and this time it stayed locked. After a while she heard Alistair padding about, searching for an airing cupboard, then fumbling in it for bed linen.

The night was long but she slept at last.

11

I n the days when he lived in Bryanston Square as manservant to the late Anthony Maddox, Bean had come to hate his employer. Anthony Maddox had a dog, a spaniel, whom he never treated with much kindness, though it was an affectionate creature, and when one day during a bout of teasing it bit him, Maddox made Bean take it to the vet to be destroyed.

It was not in Bean's nature to feel self-disgust, but he many times reproached himself for obeying Maddox's order in this matter. He should have said no. He should have given in his notice rather than have Philidor put down. Meekly, though with sorrow in his heart, he had taken the spaniel to the veterinary surgery and asked for the deed to be done. But after that he took a slow, if largely concealed and invisible, revenge. In ways of which Maddox knew nothing until the day before his death, Bean made his life a misery.

He never guessed that into every bowl of soup Bean brought him, his manservant had first spat. Nor that a spoonful of Bean's urine went into every cup of tea and coffee. The caterpillars that Bean harvested from plants in the park (and in relation to which Maddox had a phobia) he did see, only to be told by Bean that increasing short-sightedness made cleansing lettuce of these creatures impossible. Maddox was very fond of salad but he stopped eating it. He was three times summoned for nonpayment of rates because, unbeknownst to him, Bean had appropriated the local authority's demands before they reached him.

He parked his car on the resident's parking to which he had a right in the City of Westminster, but many times, during the night, Bean moved it onto a double yellow line. Valuable books he borrowed from the London Library unaccountably disappeared. His electric blanket caught fire. Bean contaminated his goose liver pâté with a culture he had made out of a ham and cheese waffle removed from a park dustbin and gave him gastroenteritis. At first the doctor thought it was salmonella and this pulled Bean up short. He didn't want to kill the man and be done for murder.

Anthony Maddox had a stroke on his sixty-sixth birthday. It seriously affected his speech. Bean cared for him devotedly, but on the day before Maddox was due to be transferred permanently to a nursing home, he unburdened himself totally to his employer.

Maddox was having his lunch. That is, it was lunchtime and Bean was feeding him, or about to feed him, soup followed by peach yogurt. The soup was a delicate pale green, prepared by Bean from fresh Aideburgh asparagus, chicken stock, and cream. He was quite aware of the incongruity of these three ingredients with the fourth. It was from such anomalies that he derived his entertainment. He would have called it his sense of humor.

A damask napkin, washed, starched, and ironed by Bean, was spread across Anthony Maddox's shriveled throat, concave chest, and protuberant belly. The old man's mouth was drawn down to one side and his eyes bulged. They seemed to be, but probably were not, fixed upon the glorious prospect visible through the long Georgian window, of Sir Robert Smirke's church, St. Mary's, Wyndham Place, its pediment, its columns, and its Tower-of-the-winds capitals. The sun shone upon its cupola, turning the brownish stone to a rich coppery gold.

Lifting the spoon to his employer's parted lips—they were always parted these days—Bean said, "I spat in this soup while I was heating it up, sir. It's been a habit of mine to do that these fifteen years."

Maddox's eyes bulged farther and he recoiled from the spoon. His mouth worked.

"Some mornings I've brought up a lot of phlegm, sir, and that's gone into your soup too." Bean spoke in his customary deferential tone. "Smarmy" was the word applied to it by one of Maddox's friends. "I've pissed in your tea and coffee. Not every cup, probably every third cup. You drink rather a lot of those beverages, sir, and I couldn't keep pace."

Maddox vomited the soup he had already taken. His face was paper-white. Bean was very tender with him, giving him a blanket bath, making him comfortable, but Maddox had a heart attack and died in the night.

Few people kept a manservant in the eighties. Single men living on their own got in a team of cleaners once a fortnight, ate take-away or TV dinners from the microwave, had their washing done and delivered by the mobile laundry, and never needed to make their beds because they used duvets. Bean had his name on the agency's book for months. He was living on his savings in a rented room over a newsagent's in Lisson Grove. Anthony Maddox had left him nothing in his will, which made Bean even more pleased with himself for confessing about the spit and urine.

One day he got a job offer. The man who interviewed him was, in Bean's own words, "weird." He was plump and bald with a fringe of thin reddish hair growing round the naked pate and, although it was ten in the morning, wore a black silk suit over a shirt with a frilly jabot. The apartment—you couldn't call something on two floors a flat—had weapons hanging round the walls, mostly whips, but guns too with ornamental stocks. There was a picture of a nearly naked young man with a halo round his head and his body stuck full of arrows and an even larger one of another haloed man being grilled like a piece of steak. Not that Bean ever ate steak but he sometimes cooked it—and sometimes spat on it—for Anthony Maddox.

His interviewer was called Maurice Clitheroe, a stockbroker, though he told Bean nothing of this at their first meeting. His voice was high and fluting and his way of speaking rather puzzled Bean because it seemed that everything was "painful" to him and he "suffered" a lot.

"I am *painfully* aware of the need of someone to *look after* me," he said. "Of course I realize that you would *contribute* to my *sufferings* but that I could *endure* if not with equanimity, with *resignation*. I am afraid you may find me rather a *sore subject*."

Bean had no idea what all this meant but he took the job. Beggars can't be choosers and, living in Lisson Grove, he saw quite a lot of beggars. On bad days he imagined joining them, sitting in a porch, cap on the pavement, a dog maybe to keep him company and supply pathos. It was at first a matter of regret that Maurice Clitheroe had no dog, but later, when he understood about the whips, the visitors to the apartment, and the meaning of Clitheroe's funny talk, he was glad. God knows what might have become of a dog in all the excitement that was so often the order of the day in York Terrace.

The boys who came had been in the straightforward beating business and some of them hardly knew their own strength. Several times Bean had to put Clitheroe to bed with arnica on his bruises and cortisone cream on his weals. The young ladies were more refined, put saddle, bridle, and bit on Clitheroe and rode him up the stairs and through the bedrooms. Once or twice since his employer's timely death and his coming into his inheritance, Bean had happened to see one of those visitors in the street. He was out and about so much, it was inevitable.

She was soliciting in Baker Street and wearing very poor quality thigh boots and a miniskirt with a broken zip. Bean was in his new bomber jacket and baseball cap. Taking him for an American, she asked him in a mid-Atlantic accent if he would like to buy her a cocktail. For answer, he gave her one of his looks, a stare, and then a sudden swift baring of the teeth. She recoiled before telling him to sod off. That look of his always made people wince and few recovered as fast as this girl.

He went into Europa Foods, which stays open late, and bought himself some pot noodles, a jar of minced sun-dried tomatoes, button mushrooms in brine, a blueberry and almond practically fat-free yogurt, and a can of Sprite. The only other person of his acquaintance he met on the way home was the Cornells' housekeeper out with a man friend. They looked as if on their way to the Screen on Baker Street for the eight-fifteen showing. Remembering how she had sent him up and down those area stairs some four hours earlier and again some three hours earlier, Bean said loudly, "Good evening, Valerie. Lovely evening."

From the pavement newsstand in the Marylebone Road opposite the station he bought an *Evening Standard.* He wasn't a newspaper reader, or indeed much of a reader at all, but stuff whizzed past so quickly on the telly that sometimes you couldn't take in the details. The story about the impalement on the churchyard railings had by now been relegated to an inside page. An inquest had found that John Dominic Cahill, known as Decker, had died of stab wounds, principally of a stab wound that pierced the left ventricle of the heart. The body's being stuck on the railing spikes was merely an artistic touch, what the coroner described as evidence of the perpetrator's "evil and degraded sense of humor."

Bean read all about it while the microwave was heating up nis pot noodle, dried tomatoes, and button mushroom mixture. The verdict was of murder. No nonsense, Bean observed, about "unlawful killing" or manslaughter. He was a hundred percent in favor of the death penalty himself. If he had his way executions would be in public, not to mention putting lesser offenders in the stocks.

Drinking his Sprite, which had had five minutes in the freezer for a quick chill, he read an interview with Cahill's sister, a Bernadette Casey from County Offaly, who though admitting she hadn't set eyes on her brother or spoken to him for twenty-eight years, described him as a "lovely person" whose death had devastated her and all his other eight brothers and sisters. It was incredible to her that Johnny should have been living rough on the streets of London and she still hoped and prayed there was some mistake.

The police hadn't got very far with finding who had done it. You could read that between the lines. Of course, it was probable that, like him and any other law-abiding citizen, they didn't *care* who had done it. Wasn't this just another bit of human detritus swept up off the streets and thrown away like litter?

Bean switched on the television. It was news time, but the murder no longer merited space on the national news. He leaned back in his chair and gave himself up to dreams: the dog of his own he wanted and would one day have when he had decided on the breed and could afford a pedigree animal, sired by a Crufts champion; ways of augmenting his income; could he manage a third daily round of dog-walking?

At this point Bean's thoughts turned to his clientele, to the Barker-Pryces, the Blackburn-Norrises, Mrs. Goldsworthy, Lisl Pring, and the rest of them. He had hoped to discover, when he first began walking these people's dogs, secrets of their pasts, incidents they would not want known and might pay to keep secret. But they barely admitted him to their houses, they never confided in him, they presented to him only blank and blameless facades. He sometimes thought that living for eight years with Maurice Clitheroe had given him an exaggerated idea of what the average West End dweller's homelife was like. Perhaps they really were all innocent, happily married (or happily celibate), chaste, incorruptible, exemplary citizens.

As to the secrets he did know, if they were secrets, there was no use threatening with exposure the girl who had approached him in Baker Street, for she would very likely regard this as welcome publicity and in any case she had no money. He cheered up a bit when the notion came to him that Lisl Pring might well be bulimic. Now she was starring in a successful sitcom, she might not be thrilled to see *The Sun* running a story about how she binged and then stuffed her fingers down her throat.

Bean went out to the kitchen to fetch his yogurt. Next time he went to fetch Marietta he'd give the place a good sniff, checking for vomit.

.   .   .

The hamburger stall outside Madame Tussaud's smelled the same as human sweat. Very strong human sweat. Bean knew all about it. He had smelled plenty of it in Maurice Clitheroe days, especially when one of the young men came round. The hamburger stall was doubly offensive to him, for that reason, and because it emanated from meat. He wondered what had possessed him to come this way round instead of taking York Gate or Park Square, and as he passed the stall, pushing his way through the milling throng of adolescents from all over Europe, he held a tissue ostentatiously over his nose or mouth. Nobody noticed, or if they did they thought he was protecting himself from traffic emissions in the Marylebone Road.

Waxworks. Bean couldn't see the point. He had been in there once, into the Chamber of Horrors—where else?—with Maurice Clitheroe to look at someone hanging up on a hook and that French chap stabbed to death in his bath. Maurice Clitheroe liked that sort of thing and frequented Tussaud's. Bean fancied it had been less busy seven or eight years ago. These days it was almost impossible to make one's way along the pavement, but he refused to be driven into the road and used his elbows. A young woman with three rings in her left ear and two in her right tried to sell him a copy of the *Big Issue* but drew back at the glare she got and the bared teeth.

The beggar with the dog—that was how Bean thought of him— was sitting in his usual place, halfway between Tussaud's and York Gate. A plastic box that had once held a videocassette lay open on the pavement for the receipt of alms and the dog sat on the man's knees, sleeping, snuggled up with its nose in a jacket pocket. The dog Bean's expert eye identified as a beagle, lemon and white, a pedigree without a doubt.

He bared his teeth at this man too. It was a grimace that was always effective, due perhaps to its shock value. People always recoiled. Armed as usual with his camera, he stepped back to the pavement edge and took a photograph. The beggar put his arms up over his face but by that time it was too late.

Boris the borzoi was the first dog he picked up. As usual Valerie Conway made him walk all the way down the area steps. She had a message for him, she said, from Mr. and Mrs. Cornell, to keep his wits about him because there had been an epidemic of dog-stealing.

"Those dossers pinch dogs, you know," said Valerie. "They want them to keep them warm at night and then there's the pathos factor."

"The what?" said Bean.

"I mean, the British feel more sorry for a dog than a human, don't they?"

Bean stored up everything he learned on the chance it might come in useful and when he came to the flat in Devonshire Street to collect Ruby the beagle, he passed on this new information to Erna Morosini.

"Beagles are particularly in demand," he said. "For example, that down-and-out sits outside Tussaud's, he's got a beagle. You can see it's registered at the Kennel Club." His powers of invention came into play. "They drug them to keep them quiet all day. Valium's the favorite but Largactil runs it a close second."

"I wish you hadn't told me," said Mrs. Morosini.

"We all have to face facts, don't we, madam? I'll be taking some photos of Ruby in the coming week. If you're interested they'll be very reasonably priced."

The eyes of the Duke of Kent met his as he came back into Park Crescent, and Bean composed his features into a similar stern and haughty expression. He let himself into the gardens and he and the two dogs made their way down the sloping path to the Nursemaids' Tunnel. On this mild afternoon of hazy sunshine it was deserted as usual and there was no sign of the key man. The gardens of Park Square were equally empty but for pigeons and sparrows on the sunlit grass and a squirrel that ran down the trunk of one tall green tree and up the trunk of another. It being Saturday, the park itself would be crowded.

Bean told Mr. Barker-Pryce about the street people stealing dogs, in his version substituting golden retrievers for beagles. Barker-Pryce said nastily that since Charlie only went out twice a day and always with Bean, it was up to him to see that no such theft took place.

Bean said, "You're right, sir," but with rage in his heart. He didn't mention photographing Charlie and obviously the time wasn't right to say anything to Lisl Pring about pictures of Marietta. He'd told her poodles were currently the beggars' favorite prey and she'd reacted unexpectedly.

"They can have her. She's just shat all over my kilim."

"You don't mean that, Miss Pring."

Bean was shocked, by the sentiment and the language. Waiting in the hall while she went to fetch Marietta, sniffing like a hound, he opened a door that looked as if a cloakroom would be on the other side, but it was only a cupboard. A long embroidered dress on a dummy and a suit of armor, standing up as if it had a man inside it, startled him and he closed the door quickly. Remembering what Lisl Pring had said, he was deterred from saying anything to Mrs. Goldsworthy about scotties as dogs coveted for their pathos factor or bedwarming value.

The tall dosser with the beard and the Oxbridge accent passed him as he walked up Albany Street. This, at least, was one that didn't smell. Caught short one morning, Bean had tied his dogs up to the railings and popped into the public convenience just off the Broad Walk. The tall one had been in there, strip-washing himself and drying his hair under one of the hand dryers. Bean hadn't spoken to him and he didn't now. He looked the other way. These people were a health hazard. Who knew *why* he'd been washing?

The young lady that was house-sitting Charlotte Cottage looked a bit peaky this afternoon. She was wearing black, which meant little on its own, but she had someone in there Bean recognized as one of the undertakers from a firm in the Marylebone Road. His curiosity, always active, quickened.

As he took Gushi from her, he said in his most respectful tone, "No bad news of Sir Stewart and Lady Blackburn-Norris, I hope, miss?"

She wasn't the sort to pin your ears back and he despised her for her gentleness.

"Oh, no, no," she said in a sad abstracted way. "I'm sure they're fine. I had a card from Costa Rica."

Bean decided not to pursue it. He wasn't interested in her personal tragedies. He hustled the dogs up to the Gloucester Gate and let them off on the broad expanses beyond the Parsi's fountain. The park was as crowded as he had expected, young people lying about on the grass in various stages of undress, though the weather was far from hot and the sun kept going in. Charlie was the most friendly and uninhibited of the dogs and it brought Bean a good deal of amusement to see him bound up to some of those cuddling couples and poke his nose into their crotches and bottoms. They shrieked and cursed him. Gushi and Marietta found a picnic party and Marietta ran off into the bushes with half a Swiss roll. Usually, Bean preferred the park to be deserted, but this was the next best thing, a real crowd, most of whom seemed irritated and incommoded by the activities of dogs.

Even the sight of the woman walker with her orderly troop strolling the long path that bisects the park couldn't entirely dispel his mood of cheerfulness. It was payday. He would collect from everyone on the way back, as he always did on Saturdays.

The undertaker had left by the time he took Gushi back. The young lady's eyes were red. Either she'd been crying or it was conjunctivitis. He reminded her he needed paying, and she actually apologized to him when she handed over the notes. With one hand Mrs. Goldsworthy pulled McBride into the house and with the other thrust his money at him. It sounded as if she had a drinks party on the go, which Bean thought decadent at five-fifteen on a summer afternoon. He'd have bared his teeth at Lisl Pring if he hadn't relied on her custom, her goodwill, and the money she owed him. She came to the door in shorts and a halter top, skinny midriff bare as the day she was born, and a fellow behind her also in shorts with his arms round her waist.

Mr. Barker-Pryce stank of cigars so badly that even the dog flinched. He counted out Bean's money very slowly and then, like a bank cashier, did it all over again. Bean had to tug at the notes to extract them from the nicotine-stained fingers.

He said, "Thank you very much, sir," and the door was shut smartly in his face.

Digging out the key from under the new wads of money, he let himself into the gardens of Park Square. A squirrel ran across the path no more than three feet from him and Ruby the beagle gave a great tug on the leash in pursuit of it. She nearly pulled Bean over. The borzoi growled at her and curled back his lips in much the same way as Bean did when displeased by the sight of someone or something.

In spite of the number of keys to the gardens that must be in circulation, the lawns and walks were deserted and the seats were empty. The wind had dropped, or had dropped in here in the sunlit space between tall trees. Flowers, unidentifiable by Bean, scented the air and almost masked the stench of fumes from the Marylebone Road. A blackbird sang.

The grass was not worn away by many feet and there was no litter to disfigure the walks or overflow from bins.

A pity dogs were not allowed to run free in here. If they were he'd never go into the park again. He made his way down the steep walled path to the tunnel, Boris and Ruby padding side by side ahead of him.

He never came down this path without a frisson of tension. His muscles always flexed and he had to keep his hands from tightening into clenched fists. But there was no sign of the key man; the tunnel was empty as it almost always was. And it was never dark at this hour, even in the middle, but invariably quite adequately lit with natural light from both ends. A momentary nasty idea came then, that the key man might be waiting at the other end, outside, just round the corner, and would step out, glittering and clinking, to fill the tunnel mouth as he reached it.

But he gave no thought to what might be behind him and was almost at the other end, having heard no footfalls, no indrawn breath, when something struck him on the crown of his head. It was like hitting his head on the beams of a low ceiling or the lintel of a door. But rather worse, for he staggered and fell over, first to his knees, then sprawled on his back. There was a moment of darkness with dazzlement, a seeing of stars, tailed comets and satellites whizzing across a black sky, and in it he must have relinquished his hold on the leash.

Bean thought he felt a hand fumbling in the pocket of his bomber jacket. He groaned and made feeble movements. Then he did hear footsteps, running away, back into Park Square. He sat up. His baseball cap had fallen off, but it had been on his head when he was struck, and Bean had no doubt it had saved him from worse damage. Gingerly, he felt his scalp and looked at his fingers. There was no blood. He hated the idea of falling and wondered if he could have broken something. Osteoporosis was not confined to elderly ladies, he had read in a health magazine.

His camera! It was gone. For a moment he thought that perhaps for once he had left it at home, but he knew its strap had been round his neck when he took the money from Barker-Pryce. As for his keys . . . They had been in his jeans pocket, the key to York Terrace, the keys to Charlotte Cottage and Lisl Pring's and the one to these gardens. He ran his hand down the side of his leg, feeling for the ridges of metal, then thrust his hand inside. The keys were all there, but the pocket of his bomber jacket was empty. The wad of notes from four of his clients was gone and with it the best part of two weeks' retirement pension. Bean's stomach turned over. It was just as if his stomach had dropped onto the floor and done a somersault, turned itself over its heels.

At any rate he could get up. His legs were all in one piece. And he could see. The blow hadn't detached his retinas, which was another thing his extensive medical reading had told him could happen. The two dogs were gone. Bean told himself they couldn't get out of the gardens and dismissed wild imaginings of the two of them under the wheels of container lorries in the Marylebone Road. In vain he called them, his voice weak and reedy.

Of course he had to go looking for them himself. Boris he found rolling on the rotting corpse of a pigeon and Ruby, still attached to Boris by the leash, was running round in angry circles. Wearily he picked up the leash, his head throbbing.

One thing was for sure, he refused to go down the steps. When the Cornells' housekeeper appeared in the area he shouted at her that if she didn't open the front door he would leave Boris tied to the railings.

"What's got into you?" she said.

"I've been mugged, that's what's got into me. Open the front door, Valerie. I'm not feeling at all well. I've probably got concussion." After rather a long while the front door was opened. Bean saw white carpet, gilded furniture, and red lilies in a Venetian glass bowl. He unclipped the leash and Boris entered the house, as if he always went that way, padding silently, to push a door open with his long nose.

"I don't have to remind you my remuneration is due, do I, Valerie?"

It was appalling to think of the sum that had been taken from him. He would have to plunder his savings. And the camera. Why had he never thought to insure the camera? He put up one hand to massage the lump that was swelling up on his scalp. The housekeeper came back with his money in an envelope. She seemed to be keying herself up to say something unpleasant.

"I'll see you tomorrow morning," said Bean.

"And when you do, I'll thank you to call me Miss Conway!"

She had gone red in the face with the effort of it. Bean shrugged, pocketed the envelope, and walked home to York Terrace. If you lost consciousness, however briefly, it was concussion and you were supposed to go to the doctor. But had he lost consciousness? On the whole he thought not. As soon as he was inside he phoned the police and told them he had been assaulted and all his money stolen. An officer would call, they said. Meanwhile he should see a doctor.

"I know who my assailant is," said Bean.

"You saw him?"

"I didn't exactly see him but I know him. He's a vagrant, a down-and-out, goes about all covered with keys."

"Your own keys are missing?"

Bean admitted they were not, but he was tired of this officer sounding so bored and indifferent, and said he would come down to the police station himself.

12

Mary had thought people would take the loss of a grand-mother less seriously than, say, the death of a parent, but it had not turned out like that. Dorothea's husband had a week's holiday due to him and he took over her job. The Trattons in Crete saw to the arrangements for returning Frederica Jago's body. The undertakers were helpful if grimly lugubrious. Alistair arrived and shepherded her to the registering of the death, the ordering of flowers, the passing on of the news to solicitors.

"It's just the same as if you'd lost your mother," he said, his atti-tude quite changed from what it had been that evening the news came. "It's the same kind of grief. We do wrong when we judge the bereaved person's feelings by some level of kinship."

This man was the same one that only a week before had told her she should be thankful not to have had to nurse her grandmother through a lingering end. Alistair had not mentioned money or the disposal of the house in Belsize Park. He had not mentioned sex ei-ther, or staying overnight. And nothing had been said about the transplant or the Harvest Trust.

There had been nothing from Leo. She had met him only three times but she missed him. "Desperately" was the word that came to mind. She told herself not to be so extreme, hysterical almost. How could she feel an intense longing for the company of someone she hardly knew? She had begun to dream about him, once in an erotic and romantic scenario that shocked her awake.

Flesh of my flesh, she remembered, bone of my bone. Those

words of his had been the high point of an emotional moment when she had felt briefly that years of intimacy lay behind them. Was it unnatural or presumptuous to have believed then that years of closeness lay ahead of them?

He had disappeared into nothingness. The day after the dream in which he held her, kissed and caressed her, she had the strange feeling that if she never saw him again, if he had gone from her life as swiftly as he had entered it, those few hours they had spent together would remain with her always.

Sorrow at her grandmother's death competed with the emotions Leo had aroused, but it failed to drive him from her mind. If he had come to her she could have talked to him about Frederica Jago. He would have listened, would have wanted to hear. Alistair cut short her reminiscences. Memories and recollections weren't to his taste.

"I did know your grandmother, darling. I knew her a lot better than I know my own relations."

And Dorothea said dwelling on the past was upsetting. Once the funeral was over she should put all that behind her.

"I don't agree with all this talking things through. It just makes it worse. Look at all those people who talked things through and discovered they'd been abused as kids. Wouldn't they have been better off not knowing?"

"It isn't that kind of talking I mean. I don't want a therapist."

"You want to live in the present," said Dorothea.

Leo, Mary somehow guessed, would have listened and asked all the right questions, would have been patient with her, spent hours if necessary hearing about the grandmother who had been a mother and friend and a great consolation for the trials of life and whom no one could replace. But she was half-afraid now that she would never see Leo again.

She went back to work before the funeral. It was better to be at the Irene Adler than in Charlotte Cottage alone. An evening talking to Celia Tratton, who had come back from Crete the day before, made her feel calmer, more able to accept. The number of tourists visiting the museum had fallen off since the murder had ceased to be a talking point and no longer had its place in newspapers, and Mary used a half hour when no one came to try to phone Leo.

It had taken a good deal of self-persuasion to get her to this point. She had reminded herself of all the things he had said to her, the kind and flattering things, how almost everything he had said at that first meeting and on the Friday had indicated that he wanted them to be friends. His last words, tinged with impatience, she tried to put from her mind. She did her best to banish the picture she had of his abrupt departure. Something had happened to prevent his getting in touch, perhaps something to do with his brother. Or it might be that he had tried to phone her but had given up because the line had been so frequently engaged since her grandmother's death. Reminding herself of that, she had on the previous evening three times attempted to phone at his brother's number, but there had been no reply.

Had she ever told him precisely where she worked? He had told her only that he was employed by his brother and had a part-time job. Whether that was at home or in some office he hadn't said. There was no mystery about it, of that she was sure, there simply had been no occasion to go into details about the job.

By now she was beginning to ask herself what she would say if he did answer. Why haven't I heard from you? Can we meet? I would like to see you again? All were impossible for someone like her. She wanted an explanation but knew she was incapable of asking a man she had only met three times why he had dropped her. He could hardly be put into the category of an inconstant lover. Perhaps she could just ask him how he was, make some bland, empty inquiry. She dialed the number and again there was no reply.

It rained on the day of the funeral. Alistair took time off work and was there to hold an umbrella over her. The man she had met at Frederica's dinner and who had asked her to the cinema with him came to the church with a woman who was clearly a girlfriend. The elderly friends were there, all but the Blackburn-Norrises. Mary made a mental note to phone their hotel in Acapulco and break the news gently to them. Frederica's solicitor, who had also been at that dinner with his wife, sat in a front pew, and when it was all over, and the dismal gathering afterward in Belsize Park was all over, he stayed behind.

Mary wondered why, vaguely thinking that perhaps she had done something wrong in inviting mourners to a place that was not hers, or not yet legally hers. But she had supposed it would be even more heinous to hold any sort of party in Charlotte Cottage. However, Mr. Edwards had remained behind for a very different reason and one that Alistair, refilling his sherry glass, seemed to know all about. Suddenly a staginess took over from the funereal atmosphere. Mr. Edwards whispered something to Alistair and Alistair said, "I am sure my fiancée is quite up to hearing it now."

The two of them retired with measured tread to Frederica's dining room. Mary was so indignant at being called Alistair's fiancée that she hardly noticed the door had closed and they were in there together. It opened after a few seconds; Alistair put his head out and he asked Mary in a low, very serious voice if she would come in and join them.

Mr. Edwards had seated himself at the head of the table. Alistair sat at the foot. But when Mary came in he got up, held a chair out for her, and stood behind it. He went on standing behind it after she had sat down, like a husband in a Victorian wedding photograph, she thought.

"Mr. Edwards is going to tell you the contents of your grandmother's will, my dear."

"My dear" was another departure. The two of them were taking her over in a patronizing, paternalistic sort of way, and the idea came to her that if only Leo were there he would stop this happening. But she restrained herself, nodded to Mr. Edwards, and told him please to go ahead.

With a small deprecatory cough, he told her what she knew already, that this house was now hers, and told her too what she had never dreamed of, that her grandmother had left her everything she possessed, just under two million pounds.

. . .

If Mary had for a moment thought that somehow—she couldn't begin to guess how—Alistair had *known,* that he and the solicitor had been in cahoots, one look over her shoulder at his face dispelled that. It was like someone else's face, someone she had never known, for it had crumpled and grown soft, his eyes very wide open, his mouth slack. He pulled out the chair next to hers and sat down on it. She half expected him to throw his arms across the table and lay his head on them, but he remained quite still, staring at a picture on the opposite wall.

Mr. Edwards was talking about small bequests, little sums to little charities. She scarcely heard him. She was asking herself why it was she had never guessed her grandmother had had so much. He stopped talking quite suddenly and turned on her a bright, almost gleeful smile, as if he had not, some two hours before, attended the funeral of an old and valued friend and client.

"Thank you," Mary said.

Alistair took hold of her hand and held it hard. She saw Mr. Edwards looking at them benevolently, as at a young couple on the threshold of their married life, made happy by a windfall of gargantuan proportions. They could hardly realize it yet, he must be thinking, the joyful shock had half stunned them, but in a few moments . . .

Even the tone of his voice had changed as he began talking about probate, the law's delays. Mary nodded. Alistair found the tongue that she thought must have been cleaving to his palate and said, "Yes, absolutely. My fiancée is in no immediate need. And afterward—well, I am in banking as no doubt you know, and I can take care of all that."

The rain had begun again by the time Mr. Edwards left. He put up his umbrella and made his way at a half-run toward the street and a taxi. Alistair had phoned for one for them. They traveled back to Charlotte Cottage in silence. Having closed the front door, he turned to her and tried to take her in his arms. Worms turn, she thought, and I have not even been quite a worm, more of a trapped insect that can still sting. She held his hands, took them down from her shoulders, and stepped back.

"It's a strange thing," she said, "that while I was living with you I was your girlfriend and now I've left you I'm your fiancée. How do you account for that?"

"You're going to say it's the money, aren't you?"

"No, I'm not going to say that, Alistair. You've said it. You've said what I couldn't bring myself to say."

"Perhaps it's slipped your mind that I've been here seeing to things practically every day since your grandmother died. I didn't know what kind of money she'd left."

"You made an intelligent guess. You're a banker, as you told Mr. Edwards, you know about these things."

"Darling," he said, "darling, I want to marry you. All right, I didn't know that until you'd left me. Is that so bad? I didn't value you as you should be valued while you were with me, but when you'd gone I missed you so desperately."

" 'Darling' and 'my fiancée,' I think of them as expressions people use when they don't want to say someone's name."

He said angrily, "What's that got to do with it? I said I wanted to marry you, I told you why. You've no right to hold the past against me. Those things will never happen again, I've promised you that." He clenched his hands. "You haven't even noticed, have you?"

"Noticed what?"

"That I haven't once mentioned the transplant, that harvest thing, whatever you call it. I've put that behind me. I made myself a promise never to say any more about it and I've kept to that. What more do you want?"

It grew easier with every sentence. Her strength increased at an almost alarming rate. "I don't want anything, Alistair."

"What does that mean?"

"From you. I don't want anything. I thought I'd explained that."

"No, you've got everything, haven't you? What you've been waiting for. Independence. You don't *need* me is what you mean."

He made a kind of running jump at her, taking her by surprise. He seized her by the shoulders and began to shake her. His face had changed back to what it used to be, flushed dark red, the eyes very black. "You're mine, you can't get away from me like that, just because you're rich now, you think you don't need me, after everything I've done for you, after what we've been—"

The doorbell rang. His hands tightened, then faltered, and she twisted away from him. Her teeth were chattering. She put up her hand to cover her mouth as if its pressure would stop the shaking. The bell rang again and she went to answer it, speechless, trembling, unable to speak to Bean, who stood on the doorstep wearing his polite obsequious smile.

"Good afternoon, miss. Little fellow ready for his walkies, is he?"

The borzoi, the beagle, the golden retriever, the chocolate poodle, and the scottie were tied to the gatepost. A large sticking plaster covered most of the bald part of Bean's head. Mary looked at it in a dazed sort of way before fetching Gushi. Alistair followed her to the door, said a hearty "Good afternoon" to Bean and that it was far from ideal weather for dog-walking.

"Needs must, sir, when the devil drives," said Bean ambiguously.

Mary shut the door. Alistair was leaning against the wall.

"Look, I'm sorry about that. But you can be so exasperating I get carried away. I suppose I just have this feeling I can shake some sense into you."

"You ought to know by now that you can't."

She opened the door again. She was struggling hard not to cry and succeeded better with the door open, with Bean and the dogs still visible, with the man in the house opposite braving a shower to deadhead his roses.

"I'd like you to go. Please just go."

There was a moment, no more than a few seconds, in which it seemed he might wrench the door from her, slam it shut, and lean against it, confronting her. He must have thought of it, maybe postponed such action until a later date. Something had struck him as dumb as she had been with Bean, perhaps a too-late realization of what he had done, how he had reverted to the behavior he said he had put behind him. He took his raincoat from the hallstand and went out into the rain, walking very fast.

Alone, she could cry if she wanted to, but she no longer wanted to. She went into the living room, sat at Lady Blackburn-Norris's desk, and began writing a letter to Leo.

•   •   •

The nuns on Primrose Hill had dispensed tea to Pharaoh the key man at five on Saturday afternoon along with Racker and Dill and some of the jacks men and himself. Roman told the police all this and that he had spoken to Pharaoh, insofar as it was possible to have a conversation with anyone so distracted and strange and out of touch with reality as the key man was. He understood that he had supplied Pharaoh with an alibi for something that had occurred at five, though no one told him what.

When he asked what had happened, in his middle-class way, the way that expects explanation from authority, they said they were unable to tell him that. For a moment he thought the officer was going to call him "sir." Bewildered by his accent and perhaps by a very different manner from that of the jacks men, the young policeman was on the verge of calling him "sir" until he reminded himself this was a vagrant he was talking to.

Roman might have told the police something of Pharaoh's life but they hadn't asked him, and he had learned, while on the street, not to offer gratuitous information. There was no reason for them to suspect him of being the repository of Pharaoh's secrets, if indeed he was, if the story told him one night on the canal bank was even true. Roman believed it was. Francie Quin, who had recounted it, was no more drunk on "milk" than he normally was and he offered the story without bursting into the jacks men's mad laughter or their occasional growling belligerence. Everyone knew Pharaoh's real name was Jimmy Clancy, but only Quin had discovered where his sobriquet came from. Back in the seventies, when very young, when still in his teens, he had been attached to a religious cult that roamed the country in battered vans and trucks and, like strolling players of old, performed on the roadside or in a field its own version of miracle and mystery plays. In one such play, a dramatized "Moses in the Bulrushes," Clancy had played the King of Egypt, whose daughter finds Moses and brings him up. The title had stuck and he was Pharaoh thereafter.

It was in those days too that he had first, as was fashionable, put the blue tint on his hair. Or rather, his sister, a hairdresser, had done it for him. Quin fancied he had been schizophrenic since his teens, since before the time he joined the cult. Most of the members heard God talking to them, so there was nothing strange to be noted in Pharaoh's behavior.

"Though it was more Satan than God, if you ask me," said Quin. "An imp of Satan tormenting him. He was supposed to find the keys of the kingdom, whatever they might be."

"The keys of the Kingdom of Heaven, Christ is said to have given them to Peter," said Roman, and because he didn't want to seem a fount of knowledge, "or that's what I've heard. Something like that. The pope would have them now."

"They real then, are they? I mean, like what they lock up the park with?"

Roman said he didn't think so, more a symbol, or a way of speaking, but Quin seemed to know what he meant. In the dark canal a full moon was reflected, like a round white light under the water. Trees trailed thin branches across its surface as if to catch the moon in their net. It could have been some broad sluggish river they sat beside, with dense vegetation growing down to its banks, a mass of complex leafiness that might have stretched, for all that could be seen, back across the city for miles, covering buildings in a dark wilderness. Perhaps the Nile had been like that, where Moses floated in his rushy cradle.

A reddish London sky was all scudded over with wisps of black cloud. Distantly the tall Edwardian blocks, palely lit with sodium and neon, gleamed like palaces, the castles in the sleeping wood. The sounds of the city, as light as they ever became, thinned and rarefied, throbbed softly through the earth.

The rest of the jacks men had gone home to their hostel in Camden, a place Quin avoided if he could elude the police and sleep in the park. He had collected his DSS money that day, so had brown ale instead of meths and water, and he passed the bottle. Roman took a swig so as not to be standoffish. "When he got bad they sectioned him and he was in this bin for most of the eighties. He come out four or five years back to what they call care in the community." Quin gave a soft derisive laugh. "His mum gave him a bed for two nights. After that her and his stepfather changed the locks and he couldn't get back. He didn't know and he came back and tried his keys in the locks. Them was the keys he started with, the ones that wouldn't open her door."

"Where does he get them from? The rest of the keys, I mean?"

"Nicks them, God knows. He don't never *use* them. They're not the right ones, they don't open the doors he wants open."

"Lift up your heads, O ye gates," Roman muttered, wishing immediately afterward that he hadn't.

But Quin seemed gratified. "That's right. Say some more."

So Roman said, "Lift up your heads, O ye gates, and be ye lift up, ye everlasting doors, and the King of Glory shall come in . . ."

"You want to say that to Pharaoh," said Quin. "He'd like that, would Pharaoh."

But remembering the religious cult, Roman said, "I've no doubt he knows it already." Whether the police had actually spoken to Pharaoh he couldn't tell. He looked at newsboards, half-expecting to read of another murder, but there was nothing. Of Effie there had been no sign since the day they found John Dominic Cahill's body and he had told her to leave the gardens. But he sensed among the men and the occasional woman who slept rough on the borders of the park, a new tension, an awareness of danger and threat, as if nemesis had come to disturb their precarious peace.

The weather was mild, though still cold at night. He took his clothes and one of his blankets to the launderette in Baker Street. His old winter-worn trainers he threw away and bought a new pair. The best time of year was coming for the street sleepers. It was not until you slept on doorsteps that you realized real summer only comes to England after midsummer is past and in those short months perhaps a mere four or five nights will be warm.

On one of those, in the first week of June, he slept in the open on Primrose Hill, hoping to see the stars. But even up there the sky was overcast by some unnatural vapor and suffused from below by a reddish artificial light. He lay awake for a long time, remembering Elizabeth's interest in astronomy and how he had read it up to keep pace with her just as he had bought himself a book on pond life so that he might know what Daniel was talking about. But very little life of any kind remained in English ponds, fertilizers and insecticides had seen to that, and the stars were no longer visible from a West Hampstead garden.

He could conjure up their three faces as they had been when last he saw them, but now as he did so he thought how he had frozen them in the ice of his present. Had they lived they would no longer look like that. Sally would, but Elizabeth would be nearly seventeen now, a young woman, and as for Daniel—at perhaps no time once babyhood is past does the face change so much as it does between eight and ten, and Daniel would be ten now. So he, their father, was looking at a mirage, at outdated photographs, at lost lives gone beyond any real recall.

For the first time since he had taken to the street he thought of the future. Up until this moment there had only been the past and the present, for he supposed, though he had never put this into uttered or silent words, that he would not long survive, that life could not support so much pain. Men have died from time to time, he quoted to himself, and worms have eaten them, but not of love. Not of grief either, it seemed. The future stretched before him, the door to it had opened at last, and on the other side he saw, white and rolling uphill, an infinite street on which the homeless slept and he among them.

. . .

If Carl had said it once he had said it a hundred times, that he didn't want Hob coming upstairs. Well, he could come up for a social call if he wanted, but Hob never made social calls. He only wanted one thing and Carl was ready enough to supply it, but not at home, not in front of Leo.

Hob knew all that but he was desperate. He wasn't just in a state, this was the mother of all states. It was the worst he'd ever known since that time he'd spent all one night in a cell and they wouldn't give him anything, not even one of those new type antihistamines. They'd had a good laugh at his expense, it had been the funniest thing they'd seen in months.

He knew he was getting bad when he could hear the mice. According to Carl there was a mouse for every person in the British Isles, which made about fifty-eight million, and most of them lived in the walls of Redferry House. Or that was Hob's opinion. Another thing he'd heard was that no matter where you were, city or countryside, you were never more than six feet from a rat. His sister had told him you could be sitting somewhere really upmarket, like the bar of a classy hotel, and there'd be a rat lurking inside the wall behind you or outside the window with the velvet curtains. But it was mice he heard, running around and scratching behind the skirting board. Or, rather, he heard them when he was in a state. The rest of the time he didn't hear them or else he didn't care. He'd start feeling shaky, weak, and old, and his muscles would jump and then he'd hear the scratching.

It was hard to say what came first, the panic attack when everything frightened him—the air itself, the light, just having his eyes open, any sort of movement—or the mice scratching. There was very little furniture in his first-floor flat, only a brown vinyl couch with Mickey Mouse scatter cushions and the mattress he slept on and of course the TV, and there was never much food. He usually kept in a packet of Weetabix and one of cream crackers, for his health's sake. But the night before he'd drunk a lot of vodka in lieu of anything better, eaten a Weetabix to get something on his stomach, and fallen asleep in the middle of it.

When he woke up at dawn or something like that, light anyway, there'd been droves of mice round his feet eating crumbs. He'd yelled out and they'd fled, but he felt so bad that afterward he'd wondered if they were real mice or not and if they were real, could he have seen fifty of them, which was what he thought?

So what with the mice and nothing in the flat but the last of the vodka and six morphine tabs prescribed for his stepfather's ex-wife's cancer, he had to go upstairs and see Carl. The way he saw it he didn't have a choice. For once, the lift was working. If it hadn't been he reckoned he'd have lain down on the floor and died. His mother's nan, who was ninety-five, sang a song that went,

> I have no pain, dear Mother, now,
> But oh, I am so dry,
> Attach me to a brewery,
> And leave me there to die.

It wasn't a brewery he wanted, more like a chemistry lab, but the songwriter had the right idea. He growled the tune, going up in the lift, but had to stop because he was shrieking. Carl and Leo lived on the seventh floor. Carl had painted the front door quite a nice shade of yellow but someone had tried to break in, and though they hadn't succeeded they'd gouged a great slash out of the woodwork from the keyhole to the letter box.

A long time passed before the door was answered. Carl came at last. He looked Hob up and down. "I thought I told you not to come here."

"I'm in a state," Hob said.

"My home base is out of bounds, Hob," Carl said. "You know that."

"I'm in a state. I just want one rock to see me through the week-end." He pushed past Carl into the flat. "I got to have it, you know me."

"One rock wouldn't see you through a revolving door," said Carl sadly. "Say hello to Leo. He's not feeling too good."

"Him and me both. Hi. I got to have it, Carl, don't fuck me over."

Leo was lying on the sofa. He didn't look any worse than usual, or not in Hob's opinion. When Hob was in a state he hadn't much time for other people's ailments. Leo was reading a letter. He looked terrible when he laughed, his face more like a skull than usual.

"Now you're here you'd better sit down. Turn your visit into a social call, right? How about a cup of tea?"

Hob shook his head feebly. Sitting down in the brothers' flat, he could sometimes convince himself he was in a kindly rehab center. There was carpet on the floor and armchairs and if the rest of the furniture was of a slightly lower standard than the kind you see exposed for sale on the pavements of Kilburn High Road, it was furniture and it gave some semblance of home to the place. Carl kept it warm, too, for Leo's sake. Last year, just before Leo came home from the hospital, Carl had made an attempt to paint this room but had abandoned the task halfway through, so that two of the walls were green, one white, and one half green and half white.

Hob's mum, who'd known Leo all his life, said Carl was more like a father to him than a brother, thought the world of him, worshiped the ground he walked on, which wasn't much like Hob's experience of the paternal role. And Carl didn't have a very tender heart where others were concerned. Now he had Hob seated in a chair with a mug of tea in front of him, he was back conversing with Leo as if there wasn't anyone else there.

Hob didn't know who this woman was they were talking about and cared less. The tea tasted like mice piss, anyway. The woman had written to Leo, it sounded like, she was halfway to being his girlfriend, which was crazy on account of everyone knew Leo was on his way out. Carl wasn't going to talk about it in front of him anyway; Hob might be in a state but he didn't miss that tiny shake of the head Carl gave Leo. Maybe he'd mouthed something about walls having ears, only Hob couldn't see. His voice came out in a whine.

"I got to have something, Carl."

"The fountain then, the old drinking fountain. Ten. When it's dark. If it's not me it'll be Gupta."

"You not got nothing now? No shit?"

Carl said remotely, "Absolutely no shit, Hob, in all senses of the word."

"A couple of E's? Some cycles?"

"You're the expert, Hob. I don't even know what cycles are, but I bet they're on the controlled list."

"Some jellies?" Hob said hopefully.

"You're too scared of the needle, you know that," said Carl. "It's time I took payment in kind again, I think." He took the letter from Leo. "Nice handwriting she's got."

"She's got nice things to say."

Carl laughed. He put the letter in his pocket. "I've never done a violent act," he said conversationally. "Never drawn a drop of blood or caused a moment's pain in anger. The pain I caused gave infinite pleasure. How does it feel, Hob, doing what you do?"

"I don't know," said Hob. "I'm in a state. I'm fucked."

"I'll have a job for you one of these days. How would you like that, Hob? A job that was big enough to keep you in rocks or that elephant dope for the rest of your life?"

Hob said with as much eagerness as he could muster, "Have you got a job for me, Carl? I don't mind work, I'll work all the hours God gave."

Carl started laughing. "I bet you will. You're a scream, did you know that? You know that old dog man, the one in the baseball cap that walks the dogs?"

"I don't know him. Why would I?"

"I can't tell you why you would, Hob. Can't you stop that shaking? You're rocking the room and Leo's not a well man. The old dog man may have something for you if you're in the park around half four in the afternoon. Mind you, I'm only guessing but I reckon he'll have something. It's what I've heard. You'd better go now. I'll see you later, or Gupta will."

Leo was looking at him with those great glassy eyes in his skull face. Hob was beginning to feel very sick. He knew he wouldn't be sick because he hadn't eaten anything to bring up, but he needed to be out in the air.

"Say good-bye nicely to Leo," said Carl. "He's not feeling very bright."

Downstairs again, Hob forgot about the fresh air. He'd had an idea. There was just a chance, not much of one but a faint chance, that he'd left a tab or even some blow—who was he kidding?—in the pockets of his clothes.

Everything he possessed lay in heaps on the bedroom floor, some of it piled on the blankets on the end of his mattress to help keep him warm on cold nights. The best he had came from charity shops; the worst, which was his daily wear, out of litter bins or off skips. He started fumbling through the smelly welter of garments, the pockets of an old red cardigan, stiff with dirt and food stains, jeans with missing knees and ragged hems, a scuffed leather jacket that had been his grandfather's decades ago. The pockets yielded nothing but dead matches and old scratch cards.

His searching became manic and, frustrated, he flung stuff across the room, aged T-shirts that were grayish or blackish, sagging vests, a pair of striped pajama pants. The movement must have disturbed the mice, for the scraping noises began again, and a scurrying and a faint high-pitched squeaking.

Hob lay down on the mattress as the panic attack started and buried his face in the old clothes, uncertain now whether the sounds he heard were made by the mice or by himself. A huge empty loneliness isolated him and he whimpered. He pounded his fists on the floorboards and all the mice fled like an army in the full tilt of retreat.

13

Boris and Ruby lugged Bean across the Marylebone Road at the lights between Park Square and Park Crescent. They were never red for long enough to satisfy him and he bared his teeth and shook his fist at impatient drivers. But he wasn't going back through that tunnel while the key man was still at large.

He had given the police a precise description, from the long black hair and beard dyed a fierce cobalt blue to the feet in split and filthy leather boots. The keys, he believed, were fastened to his clothes with safety pins, and he described them as like an armor plating, a kind of chain mail worn for protection. Several times, because no arrest was made and nothing seemed to be done, Bean went back to the police and harried them. He wanted an identity parade so that he could pick the key man out. They told him they were working on his case and if anything developed they would get back to him. Bean had no faith in them.

Though he knew a large number of people, he had few friends, and those he had were acquaintances he met in the Globe on a Friday night, the only evening out he had. There was Freddie Lawson, who worked as odd-job man for the Crown Estates, and Peter Carrow, a park attendant, whose life had changed very much for the better when he was issued with a vacuum cleaner for sucking up the litter in the Broad Walk and round the pavilions. Lawson, a widower, and Carrow, whose wife had left him long ago, both drank far more than Bean did, drank away their wages in the Globe or the Allsop Arms every night, but it was on Friday that they met him in the

Globe and it was there that Bean recounted to them his experiences
with the key man. Carrow, who knew most of the dossers by sight at
least, immediately recognized Bean's description and was even able
to tell him the key man's name.

By now Bean had convinced himself he had seen Clancy when he
was mugged. He believed it. The two encounters had become
blurred in his mind and he told Lawson and Carrow that it was just
after he passed Clancy in the tunnel that the key man had stepped
away from the wall and struck him on the back of the head. A
number of other people, including the inevitable tourists, heard him
say this.

"And the Bill won't do nothing for you?" said Lawson.

Lawson always called the police the Bill. Carrow called them
the Filth.

"They're protecting him," said Bean, "for reasons of their own."

He tried to enlist the help of Valerie Conway. Since their confrontation over the matter of her given name, Bean had called her nothing. All kinds of styles and titles were in his repertoire, miss, miz,
madam, ma'am, as well as surnames preceded by miss or miz, but he
called her nothing now and she perceived that he had won that
round. Therefore she was on her guard when he asked her if it
wasn't a fact that he had described to her his encounter with Clancy,
calling him an "alien."

"That wasn't the same time as when you were mugged," said
Valerie.

"Oh, please," said Bean. "Don't give me that. I came here with the
dog and for once you opened the front door to me on account of me
being in such a state. I was on my knees, I couldn't hardly see
straight."

"Maybe, but you never said who'd done it to you. If you want my
opinion, you're confused. You can't expect me to make a fool of
myself going to the police with a story that's a figment of your imagination."

"Perhaps you'll fetch the dog," said Bean.

Victory to Valerie, she thought, shutting the area door behind them. Bean crossed the road and went to pick up Charlie the golden retriever in St. Andrew's Place. James Barker-Pryce, a wet dead cigar plugged into the left corner of his mouth, brought the dog to the door. Bean advised him to be careful if he was thinking of going out. There was a dangerous vagrant at large, identifiable by his blue-dyed hair and the keys pinned all over him. Barker-Pryce said he hoped Bean hadn't been drinking. He never gave credence to anything told him by a member of the working class, never had and never would, they had always been mentally subnormal and were now even more reduced by television and drugs.

Bean told his tale to Mrs. Goldsworthy and then to Lisl Pring.

"I wouldn't like anything to happen to Marietta," was all she said.

Incensed, Bean forgot his usual deference. "Thanks very much," he said. "Never mind me." He added, ridiculously, a belated "Miss."

Lisl Pring started laughing. When she laughed she sucked in her diaphragm and you could count her ribs. She wouldn't have cared what Bean said to her so long as the poodle got its walks.

"I shall be going on my holidays to my sister in Brighton the first week of August," he said and watched her face fall. "I'm telling you well in advance so as you can make other arrangements."

Up in Park Village, Miss Jago showed more sympathy. She asked him if he was fully recovered, if the police had found whoever was responsible. Bean wondered what she was after. He had no belief in altruism. Maybe she was running short of cash in the absence of Sir Stewart and Lady Blackburn-Norris and thought soft soap might secure her a discount.

"There's no doubt who was responsible, miss," he said darkly, shaking his head in the way people do when they wish to convey exasperation and disillusionment. "The kind of alien a lady like yourself would no more notice than you would a bit of muck on the pavement. I wouldn't even ask you if you'd come in contact with him."

She came back with the dog in her arms, cuddling him like a baby.

"Every penny I'd got on me he took. And my camera. Luckily, I used up the film with the shots on it of these lovely dogs. Would you be interested in acquiring a portrait of the little shih tzu?"

She said it wasn't her dog. That was a matter for Sir Stewart and Lady Blackburn-Norris. He had guessed she'd say that and didn't much care. Mrs. Goldsworthy had said she'd love a portrait of McBride or even an album of pictures.

It was common knowledge he was to be found in the park every day around eight-thirty in the morning and four-thirty in the afternoon, say a quarter of an hour on either side of those times. Bean thought afterward that this must account for it. But before the man came up to him he had set the dogs free and was walking the long exposed path toward the bridge and the new pond by the Hanover Gate. It was warm enough to do without his bomber jacket and he tied it round his middle by its sleeves the way the youth did. For the baseball cap, smart protection from the sun's heat on his poor head, he was starting to feel a greater affection than he had for any human being. It had probably saved his life when Clancy attacked him.

By the railings that enclosed the grounds of The Holme, the big house that overlooked the lake, the woman was walking her dozen dogs. Not one of them was on the lead and all walked sedately, the little ones at her heels, the bigger ones in as orderly a fashion as if they had all been to training classes. Perhaps they had. The woman wore jodhpurs and a check shirt and her long dark hair flowed down her back. She must have one of those whistles inaudible to the human ear, for when a labrador lagged behind, Bean saw her put something to her lips and the labrador came running obediently.

Three of his dogs were close at his heels and the other three at the lake's edge, Marietta barking at a red-headed duck, the shih tzu and the scottie drinking from the scummy brown water, as Bean stepped onto the bridge that here crosses a loop of the lake enclosing an island. It was shady and dim, a dusty place, overshadowed by tall trees. Birds thronged the nearly stagnant water, pochards, mandarins, swans, mallards, pintails, coots and divers. Even in the winter a sour smell rose from the water and now, in the mild humidity of June, there was a powerful stench of decaying vegetable matter. He was halfway across when a man approaching from the other end stopped in front of him and asked for a light.

Bean might have said, "Sorry" or "I'm afraid I don't carry one," but in fact he said, "I don't smoke," in such a way as to put smoking on a par with snorting cocaine.

Instead of passing on, the man looked him in the eye. He was young, skinny but with a jowly face, a round head, and a crew cut, too young and strong for Bean to push past him. He had the sort of eyes Bean had heard addicts had, dull and with pinhead pupils. A flicker of fear plucked at his chest. But he was not alone. He could see Sunday crowds on the sunlit grass by the Hanover pond, footsteps were approaching behind him, and two girls with linked arms had come onto the bridge ahead.

"My mate heard you shooting the shit," the man said. "Or it come over the grapevine."

"I done *what?*"

The man took no notice. "I'm not talking about wasting. If you want him attended to it'll cost you a Hawaii."

Bean managed a mental translation but the last bit escaped him.

"Fifty smackers."

"Chance'd be a fine thing," said Bean. "I haven't got it. It was three times that he took off of me. And my camera. Bastard with blue hair and all over keys." He tried to collect his thoughts. "Fifty—that's a lot of money."

"Suit yourself. If you change your mind I'll be here next Sunday. Same time, same place."

It wasn't true he hadn't got it, but he couldn't easily afford to part with it. Once again Bean thought how imperative it was to find ways of augmenting his income. He watched the round-headed man return the way he had come and head toward the Hanover Gate.

The idea that someone young and strong might "attend to," which presumably meant "beat up," the key man was very inviting. With recollections of certain episodes in the domestic life of Maurice Clitheroe—once he had spent three days in bed as the result of an encounter with a young giant from Salisbury Street—Bean thought longingly of Clancy in a similar state. And in Clitheroe's case it had been *play*. It was only the cost that stopped him running after the round-headed man. Of course it was cheap at the price, but only if parting with the price didn't hurt.

The golden dome of the mosque, heaving into view, was somehow reassuring. The man would be there again next Sunday.

•   •   •

It was a week since she had written to him but he hadn't even phoned. What had happened that first time she had written to him, disclosing her identity, giving her address, was happening again. Dorothea, in whom up to a point she confided, said that perhaps he was one of those men who only want women who are hard to get. Women who were forthcoming and made overtures frightened them away. That wasn't much comfort to Mary, who was remembering with some degree of shame the warm phrases in her own letter and how she had reminded him of the special friendship they had. It had been to some extent an appeal, her own loneliness cited and her bereavement.

When Saturday came she had given up. He had dropped her. She had said or done something to upset him or he had changed his mind about her. Alistair had phoned and asked her to have dinner with him; and though she had refused, putting the phone down after a quick good-bye, she had wondered if next time she would yield, if

Alistair, with his small violent acts, his petty aggression, and his overbearing ways wasn't better than no one at all. When she thought of those small violences the blood came up and heated the cheek he had slapped.

She was looking at herself in the mirror, at that phenomenon of the reddening cheek, watching the color die away, when the doorbell rang. For once she didn't speculate as to who it might be. She heard a taxi move off as she was opening the door.

Leo stood on the doorstep, paler than she had ever seen him, even his lips drained of color.

"I've been in the hospital," he said. "I didn't want you to know."

The explanation she should have thought of but hadn't. "But why not, Leo?"

He hesitated. "May I come in?"

"Of course. Of *course*." She remembered what Dorothea had said, but she couldn't help herself. "I'm so glad to see you."

He came in diffidently. She closed the door. Already she was wondering how she could have listened to Dorothea's reasoning, could have doubted her own judgment.

"I felt I'd failed you," he said. "I'd let you down. You've done so much for me and I'd reneged on you. I'd been overdoing things, apparently. I know I had, I'm well aware of it. But you must be able to guess why I had."

She shook her head.

"How shall I put it? I don't want to upset you, Mary." He paused and seemed to be thinking what to say that would not be hurtful. "I've been overexerting myself because I'd met you," he said. "There. I've said what I've been afraid to say. I so wanted to be a—a normal man for you."

"Leo . . ." She took both his hands in hers.

He let them lie passively. His eyes were bright, too bright, as with fever. "I was going to—well, to let things slide between us. Slip away out of your life, if you understand me. It means so much to me that

you should never see me as ungrateful or indifferent, but at the same
time, I'd rather you felt that than that—you—you saw your donation had been in vain."

"But you've said you're all right. You've said—I think you've
said—the leukemia hasn't come back."

"I didn't know that when they took me in." He turned his face
away. "I was so afraid, Mary."

She tightened her grip on his limp hands. This time he made her a
small return of pressure. "Then your letter came. You'd said very little, but I think I knew what your grandmother meant to you. I
couldn't any longer stay away."

Their faces were very close. He reached a little forward and kissed
her on the lips. It was just such a kiss as she might have given him in
the unimaginable situation of her making the first advance, light,
gentle, dry but lingering. He put his arms round her and held her
close to him in a brotherly hug. She felt his bones through the mea-
ger flesh, birdlike, fragile. A pulse in his neck was beating fast. Still
holding her shoulders, but feather-lightly, in a ghost's clasp, he
looked into her face.

"I am afraid to say too much, Mary. When you've been ill, like I
have, when you've been so near death and thought you were near
death again, your emotions get very—very febrile, very wild and
hot, you think and fancy all sorts of things. But you mustn't—*I*
mustn't—express them too soon. I have to keep telling myself, there
is time, I *have* got years ahead."

Leo went into the living room and sat on the sofa, perfectly still, as
if in a trance. Unusually for him, he put out no hand to fondle the
little dog as it pressed itself against his legs. He said in a curiously
intense tone, "Tell me about your grandmother. Tell me all about
her and your childhood and everything."

It was what she had wanted. She began talking to him of things
never previously aired. The idea of telling Alistair of the day when,
newly orphaned but not yet knowing it, she had been brought to her

grandparents, how she had felt, was unthinkable. But she could tell
Leo, who sat listening intently, his eyes sometimes meeting hers, his
lips sometimes parting in a smile. She spoke of those early days.
Frederica had seemed old, but when you are eight all grownups
seem old. Children are quickly won over and a devotion in them is
easily awakened. The oddest thing was that from the first Frederica
was nicer than her own mother had been.

"It seems disloyal. It's something people don't say, that their
adoptive parents were better than their natural parents. But mine
were. My parents were very young, my mother was only twenty-one
when I was born. They only married because I was going to be born.
And afterward they wanted to go on living the same sort of life they
always had. I think my mother must have resented me. I remember
her as indifferent and rather rejecting. Why am I telling you all
this?"

"Because I asked you."

"And that's enough? Maybe it is. My parents died when someone's private plane they were flying in from an airfield in Essex to
France came down in the Channel. I was unhappy at first, of course I
was. I think my grandparents were very unhappy, they'd lost their
only child, but they never showed it to me. She was called Helen, my
mother. That's why I took the name when I had to write that note
for you. Guilt, I expect it was, though, not love.

"I loved my grandparents. I adored my grandmother. And, you
know, the air crash, which was so terrible for them and supposed to
be for me—I once overheard a woman say to my grandmother that
it was the great tragedy that had blighted my childhood—it was romantic, it was something to have and almost to boast about, it set me
apart in a rather dashing way from the other girls at school. If some
power, some genie, had asked me if I would like my parents back,
I'd have said no. But I'd never have told anyone; I'd have been
ashamed."

"But you're not ashamed to tell me?"

150

"No. Strange, isn't it?"

He said, "I want you to think you can tell me anything. I want to be the person you can talk to." He stood up, a little unsteadily, she thought, and for a moment he put his hand on his forehead. "I must go now. May I come back tomorrow?"

"I've tired you," she said.

"No. You're the last person to tire me. You refresh me." He spoke like a child, a very young boy. "Can I have a proper kiss?"

She nodded. He put his arms round her and kissed her, but very softly, very gently. His mouth tasted of some scented spice, cinnamon perhaps or cardamom. Afterward she thought it had been like no other kiss she had ever known, and if she had had to explain what she meant she would have said it was nonphysical, like a kiss in the mind, or like kissing someone not of this world, a wraith, a spirit, a ghostly visitant.

"You will come back?" she said eagerly.

"I promise."

He looked less ill the next day, though his thinness was extreme. She had the illusion that she could see through him as he passed through the hall and came into the living room, could see the shapes of furniture and the colors of cloth through his transparent form. They drank wine and she made lunch for them. He told her about his feelings for his brother.

"I love him and he loves me," he said. "Does that sound terrible to you, coming from a man?"

"Of course it doesn't."

"He's done everything for me. Given up everything too. He was at drama school, he's a wonderful actor, but he gave that up to be with me every day when I was so ill, so that I'd never be alone. He's been more than a father to me."

"I'd like to meet him."

He didn't answer that but said rather abruptly, "I'm moving out, I'm getting a place of my own."

"But why, if you get on so well?"

"Because it's not fair on him, Mary. I drag him down. I spoil his privacy. Besides, it's his place but he gives up the bedroom to me and sleeps on the sofa."

He had found a flat in Primrose Hill, in Edis Street, no more than a room with kitchen area and shower really, but it would do. She searched her mind for ways of putting it, finally came out with, "Leo, I'm going to be quite rich. My grandmother left me a lot of money. If there is anything I could—"

He cut her short. It was like that first time when he had reacted so peremptorily to her offer of paying her share of the bill. "Absolutely not. Please don't even think of it."

They had left the table and were once more side by side on the sofa, Gushi at their feet.

"I very much dislike the idea of your being rich," Leo said. There was an unprecedented distaste in his voice, though rather than rising in volume it had sunk almost to a whisper. "You may say that it's none of my business but—but I want things about you to be my business, Mary."

He looked deep into her eyes. She felt her face flood with color. Seeing the flush, he put up one finger to touch her cheek. The other hand followed. He took her face in his hands and kissed her with the gentleness of a woman kissing a child. Then, when she was unresistant, he began a soft delicate kissing, his lips on hers, then brushing her cheek, the tip of her nose, her mouth once more. The gentleness of it, the slowness, aroused her. She expected every moment a crushing embrace, hard lips, a tongue that prized her mouth open and reached chokingly, like some surgical probe, for the back of her throat. Leo kissed her lips and stroked her cheek. Her body, which she now felt to have been stiff and tense for weeks, the muscles held rigidly, began to slacken and melt.

"There is something I would very much like to do," he whispered. "May I ask you? If you say no, we'll just go on sitting here, but if you say yes . . ."

"What is it, Leo?"

"I would like to lie down and hold you. That's all, just hold you."

She nodded.

"I mean just hold you," he said. "Not anything more." He gave a dry unhappy laugh. "That has to be all, I think."

They went upstairs. He seemed quite unselfconscious when he took off his outer clothes. She looked at a skeletal but still beautiful body, straight, smooth, as white as her own. It would have seemed ridiculous, in anticipation or retrospect, to go to bed with a man in her underclothes, he in underpants, she in bra and tights, but in the present, as a happening, it was natural. She wondered where he had received the transplant but could see no mark on him.

In bed he held her in his arms. She had always found this position a difficult one with Alistair, for if maintained for more than a few minutes, the arm under his body would "go to sleep," as would his under her, while the other possibility, that of embracing him with one arm and folding the other behind her, brought an intolerable ache to her shoulder. But Leo held her without demanding that she hold him. She laid one arm across his chest, the other on her own breasts. He held her firmly but not tightly, and if the arm under her body grew numb he gave no sign of it. He did not speak. She had to remind herself that he was six years younger than she, for he held her as an innocent father might hold his child.

Not since she was a child herself, not since those days when she was laid down for a rest in the afternoon—by that mother who was only too glad, if the truth were known, for an hour of peace—had Mary slept in the daytime. But she slept now and Leo slept. His, she thought, waking after the unbelievable period of two whole hours, was the heavy slumber of a man who has missed out on sleep for too long and has a hundred hours to make up. She raised herself on one elbow and looked at his face, the narrow lips relaxed in sleep, the pale skin in places prematurely lined, the veined lids over his closed eyes, membranes like purplish leaves. When he was a child his hair must have been white, for even now it was only faintly colored, the shade of sun-bleached straw.

Something told him she had moved away, for blindly in sleep he reached for her. But not in the way other men had done, not as Alistair had done, seizing her roughly and pulling her down into a hard embrace and bruising kisses that made her lips sore and her gums bleed. Without opening his eyes, Leo felt for her hand and, taking it in his, brought it to his mouth. He kissed her hand gently, the wrist, the back of it, the knuckles. She thought, what is happening to me? Am I falling in love with him? Is it the strangeness of him that fascinates me, or is it that I feel an ever and ever stronger need to look after him?

I do need that. I need to bring him here and care for him. It is as if I have begun the process of healing him and I must carry it through. Soon I must let him go, I must let him go home, but I am afraid that when he goes, when he is out of my sight and my care, he will fail and fall and become ill again. Oh, if only I could keep him here I know I could restore him and then, one day . . .

Bean was back. The bell rang once, then again insistently. She put on a dressing gown, picked Gushi up into her arms and went down to answer the door. Bean smiled his obsequious smile, his eyes cold and empty. He thrust a package into her hand.

"Photos of the little chap, Miss," he said. "Just to take a look. No obligation to purchase."

14

While in Maurice Clitheroe's employ Bean had drunk heavily. Sometimes he had drunk to excess. There was always a lot of liquor in the house and he had helped himself. If Clitheroe knew, and he must have known, he never said anything. Perhaps he understood that Bean couldn't do the job he did without a stimulant and a sedative. It was no joke, as Bean often said to himself, being the companion, servant, pimp, and nurse of a serious masochist.

Most of the young people who came to the house in York Terrace were in it only for the money. They took no more pleasure in beating a fat old man than Bean did in doing his shopping and cooking his tournedos. But one or two were different. Bean, admitting them to the house, could see it in their faces and in the fixed stare of their half-mesmerized eyes. They were sadists, and when the whip or the cane was in their hands there was no stopping their frenzy.

It was then, hearing Clitheroe's screams and unable to sort pain from pleasure—or were they the same?—that Bean took the brown ale chasers with glass after glass of cheap Spanish brandy. Sometimes he was almost too far gone to see the visitor off the premises, but he had to persevere, he had to keep as steady as he could, for afterward Clitheroe needed his ministrations.

Once he found him unconscious. On another occasion he wanted to take his employer to Emergency, but Clitheroe, gasping on the floor, open weals on his naked back that bled into the Turkey carpet—fortunately predominantly crimson already—forbade his phoning for an ambulance on pain of dismissal. Bean passed out himself later, on brandy and brown ale.

There was one young man, nameless but called by him The Beater, that he particularly remembered. If the eyes were the windows of the soul, as Anthony Maddox said they were, he had no soul, for looking into his eyes was like looking into empty holes. There was nothing beyond. The tip of his nose and his upper lip were pinkish as if he had rubbed them with sandpaper. He walked gracefully, his body straight and relaxed, his shoulders permanently lifted and his knees ever so slightly bent. After his visits Maurice Clitheroe was in a worse state than after any other beatings or being ridden up the stairs or having sharp objects threaded into soft parts of his body.

He was sixty-seven, Bean's own age. His body was covered with scars, as a constantly abused slave's must be. Bean had never seen anything like it. He advised Clitheroe not to let The Beater come again, but his employer took no notice. Bean was not fanciful, he admitted with some satisfaction that he had no imagination, yet he thought to himself that, peculiar though it was, Clitheroe was *in love* with The Beater. He was obsessed by him. He desperately needed him. And The Beater killed him.

Or that was Bean's view of it. The beating Clitheroe got that evening was the worst Bean had ever known. Of course he was not a witness to it, he never was, and when the screams began, he swigged brandy directly out of the bottle and hid himself in his bed with the quilt stuffed into his ears. The Beater let himself out and Bean never saw him again. Clitheroe had a hemorrhagic stroke.

His doctor, from Harley Street, just across the road, knew all about Clitheroe's proclivities. He didn't look at the old man's body below the neck. By the time Clitheroe died ten days later the worst of the evidence had faded, though Bean had sometimes wondered what the undertakers thought.

So long as no one blames *me*, was his philosophy, and no one did. He gradually stopped drinking once the funeral was over. He was

interested in getting fit before it was too late, and now it had come
down to one whiskey and two bottles of brown ale in the Globe on a
Friday night. Freddie Lawson called the Globe "a real pub, all spit
and sawdust and sausage sandwiches," and Bean's dinner on a Friday was not exactly a sausage but a veggie-burger sandwich with
Branston pickle and sometimes a plate of chips.

He wanted to find out the identity of the round-headed man who
had asked for a light on the bridge last Sunday. Freddie knew nothing about it and Peter Carrow refused to say anything until Bean
told him why he needed to know. The air in the Globe was blue
with smoke. It made Bean hoarse and he had to raise his voice. Several people stared at him.

"Who d'you think you're looking at?" Bean said belligerently.

An American tourist turned his face away. Bean glared at those
who kept on staring. One of them was maybe the mate of the round-
headed man.

"You been drinking before you come in here?" said Carrow.

"I'm not pissed, so don't make insinuations." Bean dipped a chip
in Branston pickle and popped it into his mouth. "There's a feller
I'm on the lookout for. Got a pal with a head like Mussolini."

"Who?" said Carrow, who was a mere forty-five, and without
waiting to hear, "What d'you want him for?"

Bean told him, not lowering his voice much. "It must be him
overheard me talking in here."

Freddie Lawson started laughing.

"A Hawaii! Where did he get that from? A Hawaii!"

"I can't afford it," said Bean. "Shame, because I reckon Mussolini'd do a good job."

"It's a terrible thing," said Carrow, "when a working man has to
do the Filth's dirty work for them."

The American tourist, on his way out, whispered to Bean, "Hawaii Five-O, right?"

"And you can keep your nose out of my business," said Bean.

The round-headed man's friend failed to declare himself and Bean had to go home unsatisfied. While he was out at the shops the next morning he considered walking over to the cash dispenser outside Barclay's in Baker Street. Perhaps Mussolini wouldn't want it all at once but would accept twenty-five before the assault on Clancy and twenty-five after the deed was done. He started to cross the Marylebone Road before the lights changed, but he was too late and retreated angrily when a van nearly mowed him down. The driver stuck up two fingers in response to Bean's raised fist.

A few years back, someone *had* been hit by a van just about here. Well, in Luxborough Street, same difference. A laundry and dry cleaner's van it was. The one who was in the way had only been one of those beggars, so it didn't matter much. After that the van had skidded and hit a wall and the driver, who wasn't wearing a seat belt, had been thrown out and found by the ambulance men draped over the spiked railings of the mansion flats. Bean remembered the case well and remembered Mr. Clitheroe reading it out of the paper to him as he often did; he liked reading aloud.

The beggar had been killed instantly, hadn't felt a thing, no doubt, but the driver, for all he'd three broken ribs, had been found guilty of manslaughter, not just careless driving, and he'd gone to prison. Not for all that long, though going to prison at all Bean thought a monstrous injustice. But it went to show how dangerous the streets were round here.

With Clancy incapacitated he would be able to use the tunnel again.

Mr. Cornell came to the door. In the time it had taken Bean to exercise Boris, Valerie Conway had gone away on her summer holidays. Cornell, at any rate, was a gentleman, coming to the front door, not expecting Bean to go down into the area. Bean told him about the photos he'd taken of Boris and Mr. Cornell seemed interested, said that if Bean would drop a selection in sometime he'd like to have a look.

With no Valerie to needle or be needled by and no stairs to climb, he got to Devonshire Street five minutes early and saw through a downstairs window Erna Morosini kissing a man. They were both in dressing gowns. The man wasn't her husband, Bean was sure of that, and maybe he could make something of it, maybe it would lead to an augmentation of his funds. The trouble was that Mrs. Morosini looked not at all disconcerted when she answered his ring, but was all smiles, happier than he'd ever seen her.

"I'd love to see photos of Ruby. Will you drop them in? Not naughty ones, mind!"

That made up his mind for him. He could afford it. He was going to increase his income, would buy a new camera and draw out fifty pounds for Mussolini. The beggar with the beagle was sitting outside the Screen on Baker Street when he got over there, and talking to him, or standing beside him and wearing a typically evil expression, was Clancy, the key man. His hair had the blue sheen of a peacock's feather; the sun shining on his keys made a breastplate of them and made Clancy look, in Bean's eyes, like some demon god in a Hammer film. Bean went into one of the Sherlock Holmes souvenir shops and bought the red baseball cap with a picture of Holmes in a white circle he'd seen in the window. It was summer weight, with a perforated crown.

On Sunday he felt quite excited. It started to rain as soon as he got into the park. He was wearing his heavier-weight cap, and over his jacket a raincoat of clear plastic, so he was all right. Just the same, he would have preferred to keep under the trees but that would mean staying in those parts of the park where dogs were not permitted to run loose, Queen Mary's Rose Garden or the surroundings of the lake. But once their pads touched grass, Charlie and the borzoi pulled so hard that Bean could scarcely keep his feet. He had to set them free and the others with them.

A veil of rain and low-hanging clouds half obscured the Mappin Terraces of the zoo, brown man-made mountains and the ranged blocks of flats of St. John's Wood, red and white and sixties gray rough-cast. The few high-rise buildings loomed out of the mist, and to the south the spaceship head on the stalk of the Post Office Tower stood out distinct, but grayer and uglier than on a sunny day. Bean stuffed his hands in his pockets, feeling the roll of notes. Water began to drip off the peak of his cap, so he turned it backward, the way he'd seen kids do in American TV programs.

He took pride in doing his job well, but there were limits. The rain had come on more heavily and now the Mappin Terraces and all the trees to the north had disappeared behind a gray-out. None of the dogs seemed to notice except for Gushi, who stood close to Bean's feet, shaking himself and whimpering. Bean began calling them. As was always the case with dogs—except the woman walker's—some were obedient and some were not. Experience told him Charlie wouldn't come. He whistled shrilly while clipping Gushi, Marietta, and McBride onto the leash. Ruby bounded up, throwing herself on top of the scottie in a simulated act of sexual intercourse, gender not much affecting role in dogs.

Bean shouted at her and resumed his whistling. All the dogs shook themselves, their loose skin rattling. Bean wished he had invested in waterproof trousers when he bought the plastic raincoat. There wasn't a sign of Charlie, though Boris suddenly appeared out of the gloom, like the Hound of the Baskervilles Bean had seen in a Sherlock Holmes film. He padded up with lowered head and dripping ears, growling unpleasantly when Bean grabbed his collar.

He thought he had allowed plenty of time, but he looked at his watch and saw that it was nearly twenty to five. With five dogs on the leash, he stood not knowing which direction to go in. Where would Charlie go? One of the refreshment places maybe, to root about in a bin or beg for food. Not that anyone would be eating out of doors in this weather.

Neither was in the direction Bean wanted to go. Right up till this moment, he had been in two minds about Mussolini, hoping to meet him and give him the go-ahead and fearing to meet him. But now doubt had fled and he desperately wanted to see the man again, to reach the bridge, carry out his negotiations, and set the process in motion. As he plodded along the path, tugged by his troop of dogs, he saw the key man once more in his mind's eye, the blue hair and beard, the cruel eyes, the clanking chain mail. He mustn't miss his chance of teaching the key man a lesson. . . .

Charlie was nowhere around the restaurant. Did that mean he had to traipse all the way back to the Broad Walk? Ahead of him the path led down to the Long Bridge, crossing a different arm of the lake from the one where Mussolini would soon arrive, where he might already be. . . . Bean had never lost a dog, never had a dog go missing for more than a minute or two. But Charlie had disappeared, had been absent now for a quarter of an hour. It was five to five.

To the north of the lake, where ducks disported on the sodden grass or bounced on the little waves, Bean stood and cursed. The dogs, taking advantage of a pause, shook themselves vigorously. Bean began whistling again. Whatever happened, whatever he must forgo, he couldn't go back to Mr. Barker-Pryce and his bristling eyes and cigar without Charlie.

There was a sound of scuffle and splashing, a quacking and honking, as three pink-footed geese and a white duck rose in a flurry of panic-stricken feathers from the water's edge. Charlie was behind them, joyously leaping, his paws muddied to the hocks, his appearance so changed by total immersion that he looked as thin as the borzoi and as dark as the poodle. Bean made a grab for him and the retriever, understanding that the game and the glories of liberty were over, drew his whole body together and relaxed it in a massive series of shakes. Bean and the other dogs were soaked in water and flying mud. Even Bean's face was spattered with mud, his hands red and wet, his feet squelching in inundated shoes.

But he ran. With all six dogs galloping ahead of him like a husky team—if only he had a sled!—he made for the bridge over the loop of the lake. The sky was lightening and the rain easing up. Under the trees that led to the bridge it was almost dry. Bean took a deep breath and clenched the fist that held the leash. But of course Mussolini wasn't there; even if he had been there he wouldn't be any longer, not at five past five, not half an hour after the appointed time.

He ran across the rest of the span. The rain had almost stopped and the sun was coming out through the drizzle. Bean took the path toward the mosque, whose golden dome the sun had set glittering like an old coin, like a coin when they still made them of precious metals. He fancied this was the way Mussolini had gone last time. But there was no sign of him, there was scarcely a soul about but for the man tying up the paddle boats to the island in the Hanover pond.

He was never late but he was going to be late getting his dogs back. Their owners would worry. They wouldn't listen to excuses about Charlie's truancy. Bean hurried to the path that runs parallel to the Outer Circle toward the Clarence Gate, and lifting his eyes to scan the green prospect and the lake edge, searching still for the round-headed man, saw a rainbow form itself in a brilliant arc, one end in Madame Tussaud's and the other far away in Camden Town.

15

I n a cold winter, on a Saturday, when Daniel was five and Elizabeth twelve, he had taken them to the Planetarium, for which
his son was a little too young but which his daughter had enjoyed. Afterward, after lunch at a place in Baker Street, the sun had
come out and they had walked to St. John's Wood tube station
through the park. Frost still lingered on the grass and there were
patches of snow in shady places.

The lake was frozen over. Elizabeth, who was a skater, who had
had a new pair of skates for Christmas, wanted to know why no one
was on the ice, and Roman had told them, not going into too many
details because Daniel was so young, of the disaster on the ice of Feb-
ruary 1867, since which time no one had been allowed to skate there.
Several hundred people had been on the ice when it began to break,
for they had persisted in spite of warnings from the man from the
Humane Society who cried to them, "For God's sake get off, or there
will be a great calamity!"

"Were they drowned?" Daniel asked.

"Some were." Roman didn't say how many, he didn't say forty.
He didn't say that a hundred and fifty people went into the water
and forty died. "The lake was deeper then, it was twelve feet deep
between the islands, and the ice was never thick enough. The Ty-
burn River flowed through it and a fast current stops thick ice
forming."

The children had looked across the lake to the great house called
The Holme and at the islands lying below it. Swans and geese and

ducks congregated on their banks. Elizabeth wanted to know how the people were got out of the water.

"They sent down divers. Afterward the lake was drained and remade and now it's no more than four feet deep anywhere."

"Are there ghosts?" said Daniel. "In the night do the ghosts of drowned people come out of the water?"

"Ghosts don't exist, Daniel," said Roman.

But now he wondered, for in his winter dreams, he had sometimes seen the people from the ice disaster rising from the black water and the ice floes, as in that Pre-Raphaelite painting of the sea giving up its dead, and once among the faces had been his children's, wan in death, and his wife's.

Often, while the children were still alive, he had regretted even the expurgated version of events he had given Daniel, for the boy would revert to it in cold weather and Roman thought he too had dreamed about it. The bombing of the bandstand, another horror, had taken place within Elizabeth's lifetime, though she had been only about three and had known nothing of the IRA bomb that killed and injured so many bandsmen. At least he had never told them that, they had never in their park walks passed the spot where the bandstand stood on the northern bank of the lake, flanked now by memorial willows.

Was this, what was happening now, another park tragedy? Yet he had noticed, and wondered if others had, that the two murders, very obviously linked, had both taken place outside the park, if on its perimeter.

It was on a newsboard opposite Baker Street station and outside the Globe that he first read of the second one. Typically, the news on it was couched in ambiguous terms. You had to buy the paper to know the true facts. "Second Homeless Man Horror," said the newsboard. "Horror" could mean many things. The ice disaster and the bandstand bombing were both horrors.

Roman should have bought the paper but he didn't, not then. He

was on his way to the launderette in Paddington Street to wash his
clothes, after which he would return to the men's toilets just off the
Broad Walk, wash himself all over, and put on clean T-shirt,
denims, and sweater. Forty minutes in front of the rotating machines, another ten in the secondhand bookshop swapping *Dead
Souls* for *Kim,* and he was resolved on buying the *Standard* on his
way back.

It was on sale outside the station. Roman bought a copy and sat
down on the low wall to read it. The dead man had not yet been
named. His body, like John Dominic Cahill's, was found impaled on
railings near Regent's Park, but as in Decker's case, death was not
thought to be due to impalement. He had been stabbed first by a
knife with a six-inch-long blade. He was found in the early hours of
the morning by a man returning to his home in Primrose Hill from
an eighteenth birthday party. This man wasn't named either.

Roman hoped the body wasn't Dill's. He folded up the paper, put
it in his pocket, and walked up past Madame Tussaud's under the
scaffolding. They had been refurbishing, decorating, renovating the
building for months. He found he had been holding his breath and
now he expelled it thankfully.

Dill was sitting on the pavement with his beagle beside him and a
paper bag of dog biscuits that the animal was busily eating. Roman
sat beside him and showed him the *Standard.* Dill said he'd seen it on
the telly. They had an old black and white television set in the hostel
where he sometimes slept.

"They never said railings," Dill said. "They said broken glass on
top of a wall."

"Where was it?"

"Primrose Hill somewhere. They never said. It scared me."

Dill had a thin pale face and eyes whose swollen lids seemed
pulled down by the epicanthic fold, but he was too white and his
sparse hair too fair to be Oriental. Roman had never known him to
drink. He often seemed afraid and now his fear had intensified to

the point of straining and shriveling the skin of his face. His age, Roman thought, was probably no more than twenty-five.

"I don't like the sound of that glass," he said. "Glass going into you, lace—, lacer—, lacernating you. That's what they said."

A woman dropped a fifty pee coin into the hat on the pavement. "Thank you very much," Dill said. The dog sniffed the coin and wagged his tail. "It's us he's after," said Dill. "Our sort."

He offered no definition, used none of the many descriptive words, but Roman understood. The newspaper had said much the same and as cagily. The two men, murdered within a month of each other, had both been homeless. . . .

"You go to St. Anthony's, don't you?" St. Anthony's was the hostel in Lisson Grove. "Better stay there every night. You'll be safe then. Till he's been caught."

Roman could see in Dill's wistful look that in the summer he preferred the open air. If it wasn't wet or too cold he would rather sleep under the stars, or what passed for them, the reddish milky way of reflected light. But he nodded, somewhat comforted, and he put out his arms to pull the dog onto his lap.

Making his way into the park by the York Gate, Roman turned to follow the southern shore of the lake. An old woman in a tracksuit was feeding a black swan and her cygnets with broken biscuits. A heron took flight from a tree on the island and flew westward, its wings wide, its neck in an S-bend. The sun had brought the people out. They strolled desultorily along the lakeshore or sat on the seats. No fear showed in faces. There was nothing to indicate the violent death that had taken place half a mile from here the night before.

It was warmer, hotter even, than it had been all year. Real summer had come, you would say if you were a visitor or a tourist and unaware that real summer may never come, nor real winter for that matter, and that the weather is fickle, arbitrary, hot today and cold tomorrow, dry now and wet later. The park was a pattern of green light and shade, not much other color. Men and women wear bright colors in hot climates, but blue and gray here, brown and black and gravel beige. The water of the lake was a gleaming gray, glassy and calm.

Roman asked himself if he shared Dill's fear. As vulnerable as Dill (or Pharaoh or Effie or the jacks men), was he afraid to die, stabbed through the heart and the lungs and the great vessels round the heart, then impaled on a fence? He found himself unable to answer. Once he could have answered, once he would have welcomed death meted out by someone else. Was he afraid to die? It frightened him that he had changed, that he could no longer give an unqualified no, that he must give half a yes.

Because surely the opposite of saying no was, "I want to live. . . ."

In the men's toilets he washed himself all over. He waited until the sun was setting and most of the visitors had gone and then he washed himself at a basin, the top half first, then, discreetly, the lower half, with his towel clean from the launderette wrapped round his waist. Two men came in but he knew from experience they would ignore him, they would *fear* him. He was a dosser who might beg from them, gibber and wave his arms or shout imprecations. When they had gone he washed his hair and part-dried it under the hand dryer.

Being clean brought an unprecedented sense of well-being. He emerged, dirty clothes rolled up in his barrow, and sat on a seat at the top of the Broad Walk by the Parsi's fountain, looking at the weathered carvings of birds and animals and at the worn pink marble pillars. He drank the pint of milk he had bought, wished it were wine, and read *Kim*.

The police came round and shooed him out at nine-thirty, by which time it was too dark to read. He had no idea where to sleep the night; he thought of but rejected the Irene Adler's porch as being too near the site of the first murder, and Regent's Park Road as being too near (presumably) the second. Leaving the park by the Gloucester Gate and the deserted children's playground, he paused as he always did on this spot to look at Joseph Durham's figure in bronze of a pretty young girl, winsome, sweet-faced, standing on an artistic arrangement of rocks. Shading her eyes with one hand, she seemed to be gazing at Gloucester Terrace. Hers was precisely the face of a girlfriend he had once had, long before he met Sally. To look at this girl, set upon her rocky perch a hundred and twenty years ago, was to see his girlfriend again, to remember and feel a trace of nostalgia. Once or twice, while looking, he had wondered what his reaction would have been if that were Sally's face or Elizabeth's. Would he linger in front of the statue or shun it, dreading to look it full in the eye?

He crossed the road and peered down into the leafy dale, once perhaps an ornamental garden, known as the Grotto. The low wall of the bridge over a defunct arm of the canal bore a bas-relief commemorating the martyrdom of St. Pancras, the saint with uplifted radiant face attacked by a lioness that looked mild and friendly and jumped up at him like a dog.

There were rocks down there and a stone-coped pool, figure-eight-shaped, its water brown and coated with a network of scum. Among the laurels and rhododendrons, litter lay or was caught on branches—shreds of plastic, newspaper soaked and dried and soaked again, beer bottles, torn dark rags. Tangles of barbed wire and chain-link fencing muddled together seemed to serve no purpose.

Roman looked about for a way in. He walked along past the fresco and turned a little way into Park Village East, where a big Victorian villa was in the process of renovation.

Builders' skips, ladders, a concrete mixer, and timber stood about. He pushed open a gate in the wall and made his way into the derelict garden that overlooked the Grotto.

From this direction it was possible to avoid most of the wire entanglements. He had long since discovered that barbed wire does a poor job of keeping out intruders if the intruders don't mind getting their clothes torn. It was a neglected, decaying, private place that he found himself in. He plucked a couple of drinking straws, or a drinking straw unaccountably cut in half, from between the leaves of a bush. His groundsheet spread out on leaf mold, he prepared his bed, sheltered from the bridge by rhododendrons and from the night sky by the branches of a taller tree. In the damp leafy shade it was cold and he pulled on a sweater before he climbed into his sleeping bag.

At this time of the year the dawn came before 4:30. He saw the brilliance of a sunrise between leaves, a white dazzlement behind a tracery of black, but the first thing he thought of was the death of one of "our sort," and it surprised him that he had been able to sleep so peacefully. It was as if he had only just lain down, had this minute closed his eyes, and the whole night had passed in seconds.

Often he had no morning meal, but today he went into one of the early-opening cafés in Camden Town and, like the condemned man he was, ate a hearty breakfast, eggs and bacon, sausages, and fried bread. A glass of something bitter and thin he had learned to call orange juice came with it, and strong henna-colored tea. He would have felt self-conscious in there once, but no longer. Most of the customers looked like him. At least he had had a wash and changed his clothes the afternoon before.

At the Talisman Press they had published a book about the old farmlands of North London. He remembered it now as he walked along Albert Road, recalling the engravings of Chalk Farm and Primrose Hill. The only thing that looked remotely the same was the hill itself, rising out of the level ground more like a man-made tumulus than a natural formation. Once he had looked up there and seen a figure standing on the summit, his hands upraised to the sky. Suddenly the figure flung itself down, waving its arms and kicking its legs, before rising again and once more seeming to implore help from heaven. Roman had guessed it was Pharaoh, but he was too far away to see the blue on his hair or the glint of his keys.

The old farmland trees must have gone sometime in the nine-teenth century. It was all planes now and a few hornbeams, orna-mental trees that looked incongruous to him with lush tall grass growing close to their trunks. He took the paths along the eastern side, recalling the account of a murder from that same book. Sir Ed-mund Godfrey's body had been found in a ditch on the south side of Primrose Hill one day at the end of the seventeenth century. Though his sword was thrust through his body, strangulation had caused his death. Nothing had been taken from him, his money was in his pocket, but he was all over bruises and his neck was broken. Medals were struck to commemorate his death, on one of which he was shown as walking with a broken neck and a sword running him through.

Roman thought he remembered reading of several people being executed for the murder, and reading too of duels fought on the hill. He told himself he had come in there to find somewhere pleasant and peaceful to sit and read his Kipling, but he knew he had another reason. That accounted for his dwelling on the violent deaths of the past.

There was no one on the summit today. It was windy, the planes' thready branches blowing and the hornbeams ruffled. He walked along the northern perimeter and saw the blue and white crime tape on the railings far ahead of him. Long before reaching the place he went out into Primrose Hill Road. A row of cars were parked, obvi-ous police cars and probable police cars. On the opposite side of the road a small crowd stood, waiting, watching, though there was noth-ing to watch.

The tape cordoned off several yards of pavement but the railing itself was swathed in sheeting. A bunch of flowers, wrapped in cello-phane, lay on the pavement outside the cordon. Someone, then, had cared for this derelict, and Roman wondered who. He looked about him and saw railings everywhere. There must be miles of it in the park's vicinity, the spiked kind like this and the kind with blunted spikes. Here railings separated gardens from pavements and gardens from other gardens, skirted churches, made confining barriers along paths. Where in other places fences might be or hedges or walls, here were iron railings, straight, plain, usually painted black, crossed with two horizontal bars at foot and top, crowned with spikes.

This murderer could have no difficulty in finding a site for a crime. Sites proliferated. If all he needed was a homeless man and a stretch of railings, his activities could be infinite. Roman stood with the crowd, watching faces. But these gave nothing away, they were blank, apathetic, patient. A policeman who had been doing something to the tape, adjusting it or shortening it or pulling it in some different direction, got into his car and drove away. The red and white van of Express Tikka and Pizza slowed a little as the driver passed the spot but quickly moved on. A woman in the crowd lit a cigarette.

Roman turned back onto the hill and sat on a seat that was sunny and sheltered from the wind. He tried to read but his concentration was poor and his thoughts wandered back to Sir Edmund Godfrey, whose murder seemed as pointless as these, whose apparent killers had protested their innocence to the last and whose ghost was believed to haunt the hill. That reminded him of his son, brought Daniel before him, Daniel who half believed in the ghosts of the drowned rising through the broken ice.

After a while he was on the move again, in quest as he had been on the previous day of a newspaper. It was not much after ten but the *Standard* was already on the streets. He bought a copy and, leaning against a long sweep of railings, read that the second victim of the man they were calling the Impaler had been identified.

He was James Victor Clancy, age thirty-six, of no fixed address, known to some as the key man and to others as Pharaoh.

16

The American tourist asked for a list of items to be shipped to Cincinnati for himself and his wife: Irene Adler's best tea service, the framed picture that looked like a Klimt, the photograph she had given to Holmes, two lace tablecloths, and a heap of wax fruit under a glass dome. Mary was making sure he understood they were all replicas, not antiques, all the kind of thing a woman such as Irene might have possessed in 1885, when Stacey came in to tell her a man had called for her.

"To take you home," Stacey said. "Well, it's gone five."

"What's his name? Didn't he give his name?"

"I never asked."

It must be Leo. He was taking two days off to settle into his new flat and, on a fine afternoon, might walk from Edis Street to Charles Lane without too much exertion. The color came up into her face and from the way the American smiled she thought he had noticed and drawn his own conclusions.

"I'll come as soon as I've finished here." She wrote the things down in the order book. The man from Cincinnati gave her his card. Just as he was leaving—he had taken a few steps toward the shop door—he asked her where she thought the next murder would be located. Someone on their tour favored the zoo and they were laying bets.

"I say in back of the theater, and my wife, she's all for those big kinda gates by the rose garden."

Mary didn't know what to say so she only smiled, or tried to.

Dorothea had already gone. Mary turned the notice on the shop door to "closed" and hoped Stacey had done the same for the museum. She and Leo might go out to eat this evening and perhaps he would stay overnight with her. He had never yet done this, he had never made love to her, but it would come soon. This slow approach tantalized her, yet in some ways she wanted to prolong it, for the enhancement of a mounting sexual excitement. Three times now they had lain side by side in her bed at Charlotte Cottage and at last he had begun to caress her very softly and gently, with an interest that seemed more like pleasure than patience. She had whispered to him not to stop, that all would be well, he had nothing to fear.

"Next time," he had said.

Next time was this time. She was a little aware of her seniority and more than a little of the gratitude he owed her, but she managed at least for the time to dismiss all that. She had looked in one of Irene Adler's mirrors, gilt-framed with cherubs and curlicues, and thought that she looked better, younger, prettier, than at any time since she heard of her grandmother's death. The sun had turned her hair from straw to gold. She came out into the hall to greet Leo with a smile and her hands outstretched.

The man waiting was Alistair.

The smile that was not for him encouraged him to throw his arms round her. He would have kissed her mouth if she hadn't turned it quickly away and presented her cheek. Stacey watched avidly.

"Surprise?" he said.

"I didn't expect you, Alistair."

"Until they catch this man I don't want you walking to and fro on your own."

She shrugged, could think of nothing to say that hadn't already been said.

"I'm thinking of you. Of your safety. While you're still coming here, if I can't be here you get a taxi, is that understood?"

Some women, presumably, were flattered by this sort of hectoring manner, by being told what to do and then asked if a simple command wasn't beyond their comprehension. No one, not her grandfather, or from what she could remember, her father, had ever talked to her like this. And it was impossible to imagine Leo capable of the words or the tone without breaking down into helpless laughter.

"Oddly enough, Alistair," she said, trying to keep her voice light, "I can look after myself."

"I wonder how many foolhardy women have said that before coming to grief? Now why wouldn't you dine with me last week, Mary? I think I deserve an explanation."

"I'm sorry," she said. "I haven't got one. I haven't got an explanation."

She walked ahead of him out of the museum, thinking fast, making up her mind how to handle his presence and the plans he had no doubt made for the evening to come. Go out with him to eat somewhere she would not, nor take him back with her to Charlotte Cottage. Somehow she must shake him off.

He was hastening to the corner of St. John's Wood Terrace, his right arm already upraised for a taxi.

He said over his shoulder, "We have to talk about this, but of course you'll give up the—" he was seeking a polite word "—the shop, museum, whatever you call it. You won't *need* to work."

"Alistair," she said.

There must have been something in her tone he had never heard before. She was aiming at that and it looked as if she had succeeded. He said, "Yes, what?"

"I'm not going in a taxi with you. I'm not going back to Park Village. I'm on my way to see a friend."

"What friend?" He spoke abstractedly, watching the departing taxi with disappointment.

She took a deep breath. "The man who had my transplant." She tried again, not looking at him. "The man who received my bone marrow donation."

"You are not serious." His voice was cold and smooth as water. It was a strange voice to emerge from those thick lips, that flushed hot face.

He can't shake me out here, she thought. He can't hit me in the street. "I am perfectly serious. I have met him and I—I like him and we are—" How to say it? What words to choose? "—seeing each other."

He came close up to her. She saw his hands move to take hold of her and fall again as his sense of the conventions inhibited him. He trembled with impotence.

"You're not fit to be left alone if that's what happens when you're alone."

"And you're not my judge, Alistair." She spoke bravely but her voice was small. "I don't want you to—to pronounce on what I do, who I see."

He was shrill with indignation. "Someone must. You're not fit to do it yourself."

She shook her head, trying to be dismissive. "I don't want to see you again, Alistair."

"I am not hearing this," he said.

"We said our good-byes before I left. We went through every-thing. We decided—we *both decided*—it was best. It was all over. Don't you remember? You were happy to see me go, you said. And then you came back. It wasn't my wish and it isn't now. I hope we can be friends one day, but it can't be yet. I don't want to see you— can't you understand that?"

"I think it's generally true of you, Mary, that you don't know what you want."

"We shouldn't be having this—this discussion out here, in public."

"Then why are we? You began it."

She hesitated. "I would be afraid to have it indoors, that's why. Do you understand? I'd be afraid of you."

He made an impatient gesture. "Where does he live?"

Again she shook her head.

"You said you were going to him, so I ask you, where does he live?"

Had his manner always been so hectoring? Not when he got his own way. Of course not then. And he had nearly always, then always, got his way when they were together. If he had never raised his hand to her she would be meekly married to him by now.

She felt a dread of being captured by him, forced into a cab, taken home, browbeaten there, perhaps struck. Turning away, she began to walk, rather aimlessly, down Charlbert Street toward the park. Alistair came after her, taking bold purposeful strides. He grabbed hold of her arm with a hard hand and started to march her along. It was the way she had sometimes seen, and deeply disliked seeing, a parent manhandle a child of perhaps eight years old that was misbehaving in a shopping center. Like that parent, Alistair jerked her arm while keeping it pressed by his own hand close against her side. His voice had become abrupt, clipped.

"Tell me where he lives, this con man of yours."

"Why do you call him that?"

"Please. Be your age. How long have you been here? Six weeks? Seven? And in that time Oliver hasn't just made himself known to you, he's got to the point of—what's your phrase?—'seeing you.' Does that mean sleeping with? I sincerely hope not, Mary, I sincerely do, for your sake and his. In that time your grandmother died and made you a rich woman. Doesn't that tell you what he's after?"

"It tells me what you are, Alistair," she said quietly. "Perhaps what you've always been after. Oliver—I don't want to tell you his name—would prefer me poor, only I'm not and he has to put up with me as I am. Now will you please let go of my arm?"

For a moment she stood frozen; then she pulled herself away from him and began to run. The gesture was so sudden that he was startled and briefly he remained, stunned by her unaccustomed decisiveness and rejection of him. She ran across the road and he was unable to follow her for the traffic from the park end, three cars coming along almost nose to tail. One of them started to double-park, holding the rest up.

Mary ran without aim westward along Allitsen Road. When she had told Alistair she was going to Leo, this had been no more than an escape ploy and, as she now saw, an unwise one. There had been no real intention of visiting Leo's new flat and there was none now. She wanted only to elude Alistair and somehow hide herself from him until he grew tired and went home. But as she ran across Avenue Road—he was pursuing her but once again had been held up and frustrated by traffic, this time a stream of rush-hour cars pouring toward the park and the Macclesfield Bridge—she asked herself why not go to Leo, why not shake off Alistair and go to Leo?

It was a long time since she and her grandmother had been to call for that friend in Primrose Hill and she had no clear idea how to find her way to Edis Street, only a notion that it might be a turning off Gloucester Avenue. Since the second murder the thought of the open greens of Primrose Hill frightened her, but it was light, the broadest daylight, and bright and sunny too. If she had ever been in there before, perhaps twenty years ago, she had forgotten the place.

The man with the beard that she had come upon reading *Dead Souls* was crossing the green toward the Ormonde Terrace Gate. He smiled at her, she said a breathless "Hello," wanted to tell him, if he saw Alistair, to send him off in the opposite direction. But of course she couldn't do that. There was no time to pause and read the map at the gate. She looked back once, then rushed into Primrose Hill and hid herself behind the plane trees in the long grass.

It was quite unlike Regent's Park, wilder, nearer to Hampstead Heath. The hill rose up, a pronounced green peak, out of green slopes and plains, and all around its borders were tall trees and grass and cow parsley gone to seed. The grass where she squatted smelled like the country. She could see a cricket on a dandelion leaf.

If Alistair had come onto the hill it wasn't through that gate. She gave him ten minutes and, when he still hadn't appeared, began to walk along the path that runs parallel to Albert Road. Her pale cream shoes were streaked with green smears and threads on the hem of her skirt had been pulled by brambles. It didn't seem important.

There must be no chance of meeting Alistair head-on, so Regent's Park Road should be avoided. She began to run again, lightly, not too fast, because running made her feel free. It came to her that she had actually told Alistair she didn't want to see him again, she had told him things were over between them and told him why, and this pleased her, she felt it had been brave of her. Lately she had been thinking a lot about her own passive gentle temperament, her inability to say no, her politeness and her acquiescence, and she had wondered if she was one of those said to be born to be victims. Those people were attracted to the strong and aggressive and they to the victims. But perhaps, to coincide with her meeting Leo, she was changing, asserting herself, leaving victimhood behind. It was frightening to think of oneself as doomed to be used and maltreated by others, not a free agent and master of one's fate.

Avoiding Regent's Park Road was impossible, but she crossed it quickly, into Fitzroy Road. Wherever Alistair might be, he wouldn't come into these streets; she was sure he was even more ignorant of the place than she. Slackening her pace, she slowed to a walk until she came to Chalcot Road, which forms the spine of Primrose Hill. She had read somewhere that there was once an old manor house of Chalcot here and that Chalk Farm itself was a corruption of the name. Alistair would be lost here, he would have turned back by now.

As Mary walked along the pretty, shabby, dusty street the thought came to her that perhaps it was unwise to visit Leo out of the blue. She did not know him well enough yet to drop in on him. The unkind and prejudiced things Alistair had said had given rise to these

misgivings. Surely she should discard them, forget them. Those allegations sprang from his jealousy and unaccountable hatred of "Oliver" that started long before she met him. But even so might she not
be doing a risky thing?

She imagined Leo not alone. Not necessarily with another girl,
not that, but with the brother he was so close to or even their mother
or some friend to whom he would be reluctant to introduce her, or
just—since he had only yesterday moved in—surrounded by dis-
order and chaos, in a panic of failure to cope.

The prospect of turning back, going back to Charlotte Cottage
and spending a lonely evening with Gushi, kept her walking on.
Suddenly she was at Edis Street. There it was, a left-hand turning of
mid-Victorian terraced villas, more stucco, plaster scrollwork, un-
tidy flowery front gardens, bicycles chained to fences. Three steps
led up to a dark green front door. But first, dividing the small front
garden from the pavement, black-painted, spiked, iron railings. She
shivered inwardly. Did everybody in North-west One see railings
where they had never noticed them before?

There was still time to turn back. In spite of herself, she imagined
walking into his room and seeing a woman her own age sitting
there, her shoes kicked off, a glass of wine in her hand. A dark
woman, she thought, quite unlike herself, with a tangled bush of
hair and a bright sparkling face. The idea of it brought her a wash of
real anguish. But she pressed the bell marked with a newly printed
card: L. Nash.

No voice came out of the grille. He must have seen her from a
window. The door trembled and growled, came open as she pushed
it. She started to walk up the stairs, more quickly when he called to
her from above.

"Come up. How wonderful of you to come!"

He was standing in the open doorway. She was learning that he
didn't want to kiss or even touch her when first they met. It was just

that they stood close together for an instant, looking into each other's faces. They did this now and she felt her own expression echoing his with a small conspiratorial smile.

It was an ordinary little room that he had, two open doors off it disclosing the whole of his small domain. A very tidy man might have been living there for six months, the kind of man with a place for everything and everything in that place. Roses from a garden, not a florist's, filled a blue vase on the windowsill. He had been hanging curtains. One was up and the other, half its rings inserted, lay draped across the back of his single armchair.

"I was about to phone you and ask you to come," he said, "but I didn't need to. You read my mind."

She looked about her and a warm joy flooded her, filling her body and her head, until it seemed it must break out of her in happy laughter. "I was afraid—well, a bit apprehensive about coming. I thought you might not be too pleased."

He put his arms round her and laid his cheek against hers. She was aware as he held her of that peculiar feeling she had when with him of twinship, of being uncannily like him, older certainly, but physically so similar and with the same tentativeness, caution, shyness, gentleness, and fingertip-feeling sensitivity.

"I will always be too pleased," he said. "I will be too pleased for words, for anything. I can't tell you how pleased." He saw her arm and frowned at the angry red marks. "Who has hurt you?"

"It doesn't matter," she said. "It really doesn't matter now, Leo."

17

From force of habit Bean had continued to take delivery of a newspaper after Maurice Clitheroe died, and one day he had come upon an article about sixteen homosexual men convicted of assault for practicing particularly violent sadomasochism. In spite of the participants' admitted consent all had been sent to prison.

Bean heartily agreed with this verdict. In his view, consent or no consent, people needed protection from others' perversions, and he, he told himself, should know. But he was disgusted to find this sort of thing in a newspaper, reminding him of what he hoped to have put behind him forever. Anyone might read it and get ideas that otherwise wouldn't have crossed their minds. That was the last time he was going to read that paper, or indeed any paper. What, after all, was the telly for but to provide a pleasanter and easier-on-the-eye alternative to all these *Times*es and *Daily* thises and thats?

Concentration wasn't required to nearly the same extent. You could get up and make yourself a cup of tea or fetch in a cress and Marmite sandwich and when you got back it was still merrily spilling out the news, same faces, same music, and if the pictures were different you hardly noticed, you couldn't remember what the last ones had been. Thus it was that, although Bean saw all about the murder on Primrose Hill, knew the victim was another vagrant, once again impaled on railing spikes, he had been out in the kitchen making a mug of Earl Grey when the man was identified. He hadn't been much interested. If he thought about it at all it was to reflect that the police hadn't caught Cahill's killer and that the chances were they didn't try all that hard, weren't bothered when the victim was one of those beggars.

He had breakfast television on while he ate his breakfast. It was orange juice, muesli, a Danish pastry, and a cup of tea, and in the mornings the news was the BBC's offering, all those teenagers and cartoon bears and dinosaurs being a bit too much to stomach at seven-fifteen A.M. Nothing on it about the second dead man on the railings, that had been a flash in the pan, and he only kept the set on because he hadn't quite finished his tea. Bean already had his new baseball cap on and his Marks and Spencer's bottle-green cardigan, for the early mornings were chilly. He was thinking about switching off and setting forth to Mrs. Morosini's, his first port of call, when the doorbell rang.

Nobody ever called at this hour. Mystified, on his way out with his key in his pocket, he went to answer the door. Two men were there, both young. Bean thought one of them looked only about seventeen. The older one had a hatchet face and pitted cheeks, the way it was quite fashionable to have if you were a pop star or in cowboy films. They didn't look to him like police officers, but they said they were, an inspector and a sergeant, and they flashed warrant cards at him while they told him names he didn't catch.

Bean always thought of sadomasochism, even now, after all this time. They had caught up with him, even though he had done nothing more than he was told.

"What d'you want?" he said, his voice squeaky.

"May we come in?"

"I was just going off to my work."

They seemed to know all about his work and for some reason it amused them. The older one said he could give his work a miss that morning because, on second thought, instead of coming in they'd like him to accompany them to the police station. Then the younger one said there would be no harm in his phoning a client—one phone call only, mind—to say he was canceling this morning's walk.

Bean hardly knew whom to phone, who would be the best bet. He had to make up his mind fast and settled on Valerie Conway, back from holiday the day before, and in his estimation the closest to him of all of them in class and calling. The two policemen stood there watching him in a very laid-back sort of way.

"I'm not well," he said when she answered. He didn't know what he would have done if Mr. or Mrs. Cornell had answered. "I was wondering if you'd give the others a ring and let them know."

"What, all five of them?"

"It wouldn't take a minute. There's Mrs. Morosini and her number is . . ."

"I'll phone her," said Valerie. "She can phone the others. What's wrong with you, anyway? Laryngitis? It sounds like you've lost your voice."

The policemen escorted Bean to their car. He told them he had never had anything to do with those perverts, only opened the door to them and looked after Mr. Clitheroe when he was hurt and handed over payment when he was unconscious. They were amused but seemed not to know what he was talking about. He was inside the station and in an interview room before he got an inkling and then it was slow in coming.

"You drew fifty pounds out of your bank account at the end of last week," said the inspector, now understood by Bean to be called Marnock.

How did they know? How could they know? He nodded and his head went on nodding like one of those toy dogs people used to have in the rear windows of cars.

"What would that have been for, then?"

A phrase came to Bean from out of somewhere. "Day-to-day general running expenses," he said and he tried to clear his throat.

"Got a cough, have you?" said the young one.

"Must be all that dog-walking in the damp," said Marnock.

"Funny you've never drawn anything before for these day-to-day running expenses. Not for, let's see—" he looked at a notebook on the table "—seven months. That's right, seven months since you last made a withdrawal from that account."

Now he was pretty sure none of it had anything to do with Clitheroe and his practices, Bean was gaining courage. He affected a final throat-clearing. "I don't know what right you've got to go poking about in my private bank account," he said. "What's all this about?"

"Now he asks," said the young one. "Who's Mussolini, Leslie? I can call you Leslie, can't I? Or do you prefer Les?"

If he hadn't been so shocked at hearing the name of Mussolini uttered like that, Bean would have reacted violently to being called by his given name. He had hated it ever since his schooldays in that Hampshire village and since then no one had used it. He was always Bean. Bean, as far as everyone knew, was what he might have been christened. But hearing himself called Leslie was nothing to hearing the name he personally, he alone, had given to the anonymous hit man encountered once on the Hanover Gate bridge.

He tried playing the innocent. "He was Italian, like the leader of Italy in the war. Like Hitler."

The change in Marnock was shocking. He seemed galvanized. He leapt to his feet and stood over Bean, shouting, "Don't give me that. Don't you play games with me. Who's the man you called Mussolini when you were shooting your mouth off in the Globe?"

"I don't know his name." Bean's voice was still strong, but he had started to shake. He tried to stop his knees knocking together. "I don't know what he's called. I called him Mussolini because he looks like him. The spitting image of him, only young like."

They had this nasty way of changing the subject, just when you thought you were getting somewhere. "You don't like homeless people, do you, Les?"

Bean picked what he thought was the politically correct thing to say. "It's not right for a great nation like ours to have beggars on its streets."

Marnock laughed. It was as if he couldn't help laughing, though he would have liked to. "So you'd solve the problem in Hitler's way, would you? Couldn't quite call it ethnic cleansing—the Final Solution, is that it?"

Maybe the young one could tell Bean hadn't the least idea what Marnock meant, for he reverted to an earlier tack.

"What did you draw the money out for, Les?"

"It was for Mussolini, wasn't it?" said Marnock. "What was he going to do for it?"

"Nothing. I don't know. I never saw him."

"You *what?*" Marnock was standing over him again.

"I mean, I saw him once, he never came back, I never saw him *again*. I went back but he never turned up. He never did, I swear it."

"What was he going to do," said Marnock, "for this princely sum?"

"I said, I never saw him again."

"Kill Clancy, that was it, wasn't it?"

"Not kill him," Bean protested. "Not that. I never wanted that. Rough him up a bit—and why not? He'd mugged me, he'd taken a good bit more than fifty quid off me, I can tell you. Mussolini, whatever his name is, him, he was going to do the same, that's all, he—" A gradual, awful realization was dawning. The railings, the second vagrant, the vital part of the news he'd missed to make his tea. "I want a lawyer," he said. "I can have a lawyer, can't I?"

"Of course you can, Leslie," said Marnock. "I think that's a very good idea."

• • •

Their natures and ways were uncannily the same. And this was wonderful to discover, each shared emotion, reaction, approach, a relief to find. It was not just that he kept his home precisely as she kept hers, clean, neat, airy, that he dressed simply, got up early, was as good-tempered and warm first thing in the morning as when they at last put out the lights, but that they seemed to like and need and want all the same things. She had only to mention a taste or preference for him to confess a similar leaning. He even had the same sort of food in his fridge as she had in hers. In his bathroom, when she went to take her shower, was the brand of soap she used.

It was almost as if he had set out to make himself the same kind of person. When his phone rang he answered it by giving the number, as she did; he said "good-bye," not "bye-bye"; and when someone downstairs slammed the front door he winced and smiled at his wincing, which would have been just her own reaction.

Their lovemaking, when it finally happened, was what she had wistfully envisaged but never before quite known. With Alistair, and with a boyfriend or two before Alistair, she had tried to achieve the ideal she had made for herself long before. But, reluctantly, she had faced what seemed a universal truth, that her particular wish and need were not acceptable to men. They might not be violent or aggressive, but they were urgent, demanding, determined to make the rules, certain of what was right. If they acceded to her—and from time to time they did—there was always a feeling she had that they were keeping her sweet, being "patient," giving in so that they might get their own way next time. She had been called frigid by each of them, when they lost their tempers. Until Leo, she had almost reached a point of seeing herself as wrong and the Alistairs of this world as right. She had almost resolved that next time, whenever that was and with whom, she would accept the male attitude and try somehow to teach herself to like it. No doubt, that, like anything else, could be learned. But with Leo there had been nothing to learn or unlearn or make decisions about. She needed to ask him nothing, nor direct his hands, nor resist his urgency, nor pull away from the hardness of lips and teeth. He was as gentle as she, as languid, and—until the end when she, for once, was imperative and demanding—as slow and delicate with his caresses. But at that end she had cried out as those others had always expected her to cry and had held him in an embrace she was fearful of afterward, in case her strength was greater than his.

That had been three nights earlier, the time of her flight from Alistair. The next evening Leo came to her and, though she worried that Alistair might arrive, might turn up on the doorstep at any moment, she forgot him after a while. Discovering Leo, she forgot everything, lying in his arms, talking to him, *caring* for him. For it was inescapable, that feeling she must look after him, that he needed her as much to watch over his health, his fragile body, as for a lover.

Side by side in the warm evening, they were each as white as a marble statue, not a mark, a flaw, a flush of color on their milky paleness. She could scarcely see in the dusk where the skin of his thigh ended and hers began. Only his face, in repose, the bluish eyelids closed, looked more tired than hers, looked, she fancied, older than hers. But that perhaps was the fantasy of a woman of thirty, wishing to be nearer her young lover's age.

Their hair was nearly the same color, hers of a slightly finer texture, a clearer gold. The down on her arms was the same thistledown stuff as his. Each had the same kind of freckle sprinkling, pale gold, sparse, on the bridges of their noses. If their features were quite different, it was only as a brother and a sister's may be, each taking genes from a different parent. Their skin was the same matte-fine white, skin that perhaps lined early, though hers, in spite of her seniority, had fewer lines than his. She looked at those lines tenderly, touching them with a warm fingertip.

They had talked, earlier, of this similarity and Leo had pointed out what should have occurred to her but for some reason had not, that in people whose blood and tissue types matched so perfectly, resemblance was more likely than not. Wouldn't it have been far stranger if one of them had been dark and the other fair or one heavy and big-boned and the other slight? She had searched among the trust's literature and found one of its leaflets, the one with a happy smiling photograph of two young men, donor and recipient, and yes, Leo was right, they were much the same height, with the same coloring, the same smile. "We may even be distantly related," she said.

"I'm your lover," Leo said. "I don't want to be your cousin."

He stayed all night with her. She slept better than she had since coming to Charlotte Cottage. Gushi came upstairs in the small hours and snuggled into the space between their feet. Leo didn't mind. He got up first and made her tea. It was gone eight and she was still in bed when the phone rang. He took the receiver off and handed it to her. The voice said it was Edwina Goldsworthy and Bean wouldn't be taking the dogs out. Maybe he wouldn't be taking them out for a couple of days. He was ill. Some sort of inflammation of the throat, Lisl Pring had said.

So she and Leo had taken Gushi into the park and in a way she had been glad of Bean's bad throat because it meant she could spend the next night with Leo, of course taking the dog with her. For the first time she was feeling the constriction imposed by becoming a house-sitter. She was bound to remain at Charlotte Cottage until September, and once Bean was back, remain there every night because of Gushi. Alistair, in Leo's place, would have told her not to be bound to the Blackburn-Norrises, there had been no formal contract, but Leo did not. In his eyes the agreement was just as binding as if it had been drawn up by a solicitor and witnessed. In short, he felt the same as she did. "And I don't think I could quite move in with you," he said.

She hadn't suggested it, they had known each other only a few weeks, but it was what she wanted.

"There would be something—not sordid exactly, but not what I want for us, if they were to come back and—well, find us. It will be better for us to be forced to wait until September." He spoke very seriously. "I would like everything to be aboveboard."

She said softly, "What is it that you want for us, Leo?"

"At the moment," he said, "I'm still teaching myself to believe what's happened. That you're who you are, the woman who saved my life, that I've met you, and that you're—" he hesitated and his face flushed the way hers did "—the other half of me."

"Yes," she said, "yes."

"I'm falling in love with you, of course I am, but it's almost as if I was in love with you before we met, I'd made an ideal image of you and by a kind of miracle you are that image come to life." He smiled at her, took her in his arms. "It's not easy getting used to that," he said. "I don't want us to have any secrets, Mary. May we tell each other everything about ourselves, tell our whole lives?"

So they had begun doing that. He told her about his childhood with ambitious failures for parents, a father whose career as an athlete had been ruined by a ruptured Achilles tendon while training to run in the Olympic team and a mother who had twice failed to acquire through correspondence courses and evening classes the degree she longed for.

The result had been for them to expect him and his brother to fulfill hopes that in their cases had been dashed. They must be great sportsmen or great scholars, preferably both. His brother, Carl, had gone to drama school, incurring their father's anger and disgust. Acting wasn't a man's job. The only work Carl could get for a long time was modeling, more cause for outrage. Their father had died. That was when he discovered that all these years his mother had had a lover. Once her husband was dead, she had gone to Scotland to join him, leaving her sons with scarcely a good-bye. It had hurt Leo, for she had seemed never to take his illness seriously and had refused outright to be tested for tissue compatibility. Without Carl's devotion, he hardly knew what would have become of him . . .

"And the rest is history. That was where you came in."

"Yes. That was where I came in."

"I'm afraid my mother never forgave me for failing to run a three-minute mile and get a double first. Leukemia's not hereditary, you see. That's known for sure now."

She looked at him. "I'm not sure that I understand."

"If it were, she might be able to blame herself and my father. I mean, it wouldn't be their fault if one of them carried a faulty gene, of course it wouldn't, but people blame themselves for handing on to their children a poor genetic inheritance. Conversely, as I've discovered, they like not having to blame themselves, not having the grounds for it." He spoke not bitterly, but with amused resignation. "There's always the suggestion there, it's not explicit but it's there, that somehow I must have caught it or done something I shouldn't have to bring it on. My mother actually said once that nothing like that had ever happened to Carl." His rueful laughter took the sting away. "Still, grown-up people shouldn't live at home with their parents, do you think?"

"It's not something I know much about," she said, "but, no, you're right."

She was appalled by what he had told her. The mother he had not much wanted her to meet, though not much discouraged her either, she now wanted to keep away from until the time came when she and Leo . . .

"As soon as your time is up at Charlotte Cottage," he said, "I'm going to want you to come and live with me. I'm giving you advance notice. Will you, in this tiny place?"

"But, Leo, we won't have to. I'm rich—had you forgotten?"

His face, so ardent and eager, changed. "I'm afraid I had," he said. "I wish I could."

In the post the next morning came two letters. One, she could see by the handwriting on the envelope, was from Alistair. She opened the other first. It was from Mr. Edwards, asking her if she was in need of "funds," as there would be no difficulty in advancing to her from her grandmother's estate any reasonable sum. Bean arrived while she was reading the letter. He looked tired and old. She could see he had been ill. For the first time—perhaps she had previously not taken much notice—it was apparent to her that he was an old man, vigorous, well-preserved, but old.

He launched into an involved apology. It was all due to circumstances beyond his control, it wouldn't happen again. Mary hardly understood how you could guarantee you wouldn't get a throat infection a second time, but Bean didn't mention his throat. He said, to her astonishment, that he hoped Sir Stewart and Lady Blackburn-Norris would "never have to know."

"What, that you were ill?"

"That I missed taking the little chap out, miss. I'd feel easier in my mind if they didn't know."

Pathetic, the sadness of age. "I shan't tell them," Mary said warmly. "I shall have forgotten it by the time they get back."

She told Leo and they laughed about it. He had stayed the night but waited until Bean was gone before coming downstairs. Formerly, she would have waited until she was alone before opening Alistair's letter, but no longer, not now that she and Leo were so close. She said, "Here," and held it up. He put his arm round her and read it over her shoulder.

Alistair wanted to know why she had run away from him earlier that week. What was she afraid of? He wondered if she should be undergoing therapy, she was so strange, so unbalanced. Did she realize that in a hysterical outburst she had actually said she didn't want to see him again? He was treating that with the indulgence he was sure she now wanted. In other words, he would forget it.

Could he arrange a therapist for her? He would be happy to do that. Meanwhile, they should meet and talk about money. Where did she want to live and what would she think a reasonable sum to spend on a flat or house, given their changed circumstances?

"I'd like to throw it away and not answer it."

"But you won't do that," he said. "You're too much like me. Too polite and reasonable. You'll answer it and be firm but nice and re-peat what you said about not seeing him again." His voice took on a stronger note. "You won't see him again, will you, Mary?"

"I won't if I can help it."

He held her. "Please, Mary. For me."

●   ●   ●

The police had given him the phone book to look up solicitors. He knew the names of the man who had acted for Anthony Maddox and the man who had acted for Maurice Clitheroe, but the last thing he wanted was Marnock's attention drawn to his late employers. He found a firm to phone in Melcombe Street and after a little while a young woman turned up. Bean began to feel a whole lot better when she started telling them they couldn't hold his client for more than twenty-four hours without arresting him. Did they intend to arrest him? She told them firmly that they had no evidence against him.

But even Bean could see that they had. By the time the solicitor came he had already told them everything they wanted to know, all about the mugging, about Mussolini and his offer, the money and his failed attempt to meet Mussolini again. He had admitted he wanted some injury done to Clancy and, when pressed, that he hadn't been particular as to whether this injury was serious or, indeed, fatal. He hadn't meant to say any of those things, but they fetched it all out of him, and once begun there seemed no point in holding any-thing back.

What saved him, he thought afterward, was that he still had the money. He actually had it on him. Of course they could hardly know that it was the same money, but possession of it helped his cause. He was with them for a total of fourteen hours and could, in fact, have taken the dogs out the next day, was prepared to do his afternoon's duty, only they came back for him. They had found Mussolini.

Another day passed, a day of questions, mockery, teasing, taunt-ing and, from Marnock, outbursts of serious anger. Mussolini had told them all sorts of things about Bean, they said, which Bean was sure was untrue, for Mussolini, real name Harvey Bennett, couldn't possibly have known them, could only have invented them. For instance, he had never said, never in his wildest dreams would have said, that he wanted Clancy killed. He had never boasted to Bennett that he had killed a man once but was now a bit past it at his age. When he was told this, the deathbed of Anthony Maddox flashed awfully across his mind, but he had never talked of it, had spoken no word of it to anyone, it was all in Bennett's imagination.

He had never, as they insinuated, offered Bennett fifty pounds to kill Clancy with another fifty to come when the deed was done. Nor had he sought Bennett out, inquiring indiscreetly in the Globe for someone to do a job for him. His solicitor came back and got nasty with Marnock, reminding him of something called Judges' Rules.

After he'd spent hours there in a cell they let him go. He never knew why. He wasn't going to ask, the relief of being free was enough for him, but he felt very shaken. Still, he had his fifty pounds and he knew what he was going to do with that. Buy a new camera.

The shop where the first one had come from, purchased by Maurice Clitheroe some ten years before, was in Spring Street, Paddington. It was still there. He found it in the new phone book, gave them a ring, asked what they'd got and their prices. The shop stayed open till all hours, being bang in the middle of tourist country, so he went over there on the tube after he'd walked his dogs, it was only two stops.

The camera, being secondhand, came to less than he'd thought. The shop manager threw in a film and Bean, doubly departing from custom, bought himself a bottle of whiskey and the evening paper. Even if it was only a piece about the release of a man who'd been "helping police with their inquiries," he wanted to read about himself. Paddington was a lot shabbier, dirtier, and more litter-strewn than the Marylebone Road and it gratified him that he didn't live there.

He was coming out of the wineshop when he saw the girl again, the one who used to come to the house in Maurice Clitheroe's time that he'd made a face at in Baker Street. She was standing in the doorway of a dingy-looking video shop. He nearly missed seeing what happened and would have missed it if for some reason he hadn't turned round from taking a photo of a Highland collie, a really smashing-looking dog, that an old woman had out with her on a lead.

A red Mercedes had pulled into the curb and the girl was bending down to talk to the driver. Her clothes were a whole lot more up-market than the previous time he'd seen her: red sequined top, tight white mini, white stilettos. Whore's gear but not cheap. Then Bean saw the driver. It was James Barker-Pryce MP and his red whiskery face, for once without the clamped-in cigar, was framed in the window. Bean took a photograph. He took two shots. The car door was pushed open from the inside and the girl got in.

Bean went home and read the paper. There was nothing in it about him, only a long piece by a psychiatrist the paper called famous, though Bean had never heard of him, about crazy street people and Clancy in particular. The psychiatrist said theories had been put forward as to why the dead man collected keys, some suggesting this was for the purposes of robbery, others that they constituted an armor against possible attack. The truth was that in Clancy's disturbed mind these were the keys to dream homes. Having no home, he had collected keys to the homes of others, keys being the symbol of home-ownership, of possession and of the privacy he could no longer enjoy.

Bean had never read such rubbish. While looking through his collection of dog photographs and selecting negatives for enlargement, he drank rather too much of his whiskey and woke with a hangover. Putting on his baseball cap and a T-shirt patterned all over with pictures of endangered species, he was on tenterhooks lest the police come back for him. After all, they had been two days running, why not today? But no one came and he got to Erna Morosini's five minutes ahead of time.

She was rather short with him, not asking if he was better but moaning about how exhausted she was, having to walk Ruby herself. It was easy to see the beagle hadn't been using up enough energy. Like a team of sprightly carriage horses, she pulled Bean up to Park Crescent, puffing and lunging. He exchanged a glance with the Duke of Kent, who didn't look the kind of man to be intimidated by policemen, before Ruby pulled him on. Valerie Conway appeared at the area door with Boris.

"A Mr. Barker-Something phoned me yesterday to ask what I thought you were playing at. He said he hadn't had a word out of you and not to put yourself out to come when you did get back. He's making other arrangements."

"What's that supposed to mean?"

"He says there's school-leavers round here panting to do the job for a fraction of what you charge. There was one girl said she'd take Charlie out for free, he's so lovely."

Boris padded up the steps, his claws making a patter like the sound of hailstones on the metal treads. Waiting at the top, tied to the railings, Ruby fell amorously upon him, not much deterred by Boris's low growl and lips peeled back to show yellow teeth. Pity there was no market for dog pornography, Bean thought. He took them into the gardens and through the tunnel under the Marylebone Road. Now Pharaoh was dead, he could do that, and never again feel that trepidation, that tightening of the muscles and tensing of nerves.

In the park Marietta was uneasy, missing Charlie, not inclined to run by herself, but wandering aimlessly and stopping for a scratch. Bean got a shot of her standing on the rings of cobblestones round the Parsi's fountain, looking soulful. It would be a good picture and it somewhat calmed him. He had been boiling with anger and the injustice of it ever since Valerie Conway told him of Barker-Pryce's decision. The nerve, after what he'd seen in Paddington!

Two can play at that game, thought Bean.

18

T he police coming took Hob by surprise. Not their coming, he expected that, but their reason. He must be getting soft in his old age. He'd had a birthday the day before, his thirty-second, or he thought it was his thirty-second, but he couldn't be sure, it might have been his thirty-third. He'd asked his mum and she didn't know either. All she'd said was that he was a few years younger than her but not all that many because she'd been just a kid when he was born.

But he was old enough to be losing his grip because he thought the police came on account of the riot. He thought they'd come to *apologize* for all his windows getting knocked out in the mini-riot of the night before. That came of living on the first floor, he'd have been safe higher up. He still didn't know the cause but there'd been these boys, kids of thirteen or fourteen, running up and down the walkways armed with car jacks and milk bottles, and then it had turned nasty, one of their dads coming out with a crossbow and someone else with what looked like a shotgun.

Hob watched from his window. He'd got some E's, the yellow tabs, from Lew but he knew he'd get so excited if he took one now he'd be down there with the rioters. They were shouting out something about a boy they said the police had beaten up in his cell, some mate of theirs accused of dropping a concrete block off the top floor onto an old man's head. Hob didn't want to get involved.

The first of his windows went while he was out in the kitchen getting himself a vodka as a starter before his main meal of the blow he'd got for the weekend. It was bricks they were throwing now. Hob picked the brick up off the floor and thought about throwing it back but didn't. It must have come off that pile the council builders left behind when they built a wall round that raised flowerbed at the entrance to the car park. Pointless really because all the flowers had been torn out overnight and someone had started dismantling the wall. He took a swig of his vodka and wandered toward the settee.

Before he'd even sat down he heard a brick or bottle go through the bedroom window. Someone must have dialed 999, for two police cars screamed in while he was pushing broken glass about with his toe and kicking it into the corner. The police had riot shields. Hob could hardly believe it. Riot shields for a crossbow and a few bricks! He wasn't in a state but the vodka made him a bit rocky. He smiled at his pun, his joke, and went to his jacket pocket for the red velvet bag.

There was a terrible noise going on out there now. All his windows at the front had gone—good thing the weather was getting so warm. He didn't care much. He set to work on his ritual, cutting the straw in half, crumbling up the jumbo, screwing on the Imperial Russian Court cap, drawing in at last the life-giving smoke.

It might have been an hour after that that the police came or a lot longer. He couldn't tell. He'd danced about the room a bit, done some Power Ranger exercises, air punching and karate kicks, and then he'd built a pyramid out of the three bricks that had come through the windows and the broken glass and cut himself in the process but not so's you'd notice. He must have gone to sleep at one point, for the scratching woke him up. Mice. He lay there listening to the mice and thinking it was a nice sound, nice and peaceful, not like rats, he'd never heard of any disease you could catch from mice, when there came a sound that wasn't nice at all, a great pounding on the front door.

He looked out of the broken window and saw their car down there. Unmarked, of course, but still recognizable to him as a police car. They knocked again and he let them in, all smiles, certain this was a routine visit, nothing to worry about, sir, all cleared up now, sorry you've been inconvenienced.

They didn't say any of that, but pushed past him into the flat, looking about them with their noses pinched as if it were a sewer they'd come into. They asked him if he was Harvey Owen Bennett and where had he been on June the something, the night Cahill was killed?

"Here," said Hob. "On me tod. Where else?"

They pressed him for more than that and he tried to think. A Thursday it was. It was years since he'd had much of a memory. Maybe that was the day he'd talked to his mum on Leo's phone and asked how old he was and she'd said that about him being younger than her and she'd have to go on account of her and his stepfather going down the boozer for this party they were having for her silver wedding. What silver wedding, he'd said, on account of her only being married for about five minutes, and she'd said, so what, it would have been her silver wedding if she'd not got divorced and the whole family was coming including his dad.

"No, I tell a lie," he said. "I was at my mum and dad's silver wedding."

He hadn't a scrap of faith in it as an alibi, but he had to say something. They weren't going to leave him alone to get to a phone, they took him with them. On the way out he saw that the flowerbed was entirely gone, not a brick left, not a handful of earth. Maybe they'd learn now.

It was like a miracle what happened. People who knocked families ought to think before they spoke. His family was one in a million, solid as a rock, supportive was the word he was looking for. He didn't have to ask them, he didn't have to say a word—well, he couldn't, he was in that police car with the driver glaring at him— they came out with it all without hesitation, his stepfather told him on the phone afterward. Of course Hob had been at the party, there from nine till they packed in when the extension ended at one-thirty and he slept the night at their place. Two of his half-brothers and his stepsister's ex and the ex's girlfriend, they all backed him up, and his stepsister's ex who had an imagination said he'd done a beautiful rendering of "I'll Be Your Sweetheart" while they were cutting the cake.

"Any time, Hob, you know that," his stepfather said. "You don't have to ask."

He saw that he didn't.

·   ·   ·

Effie was up on the hill, drinking the nuns' tea, and so were Dill and Teddy and the man called Nello. Last time Roman had been up there all the talk had been of Pharaoh and his terrible end, of Pharaoh and of Decker. Who would be next? Would it be one of them? No one talked of it anymore. They were as they had been before, or almost. Roman fancied they were more subdued than usual, more wary. They, who had never been afraid of what people with roofs over their heads feared, the streets, the dark, were afraid of them now.

He had taken to leaving his barrow under the arch at the Grotto. Sooner or later it would be stolen, he knew that, but he didn't much care. It was a relief not to have to lug it around with him. Every time he saw Nello, who had all the marks of the amiable natural, the village idiot, almost the holy fool, the man would remind him of the risks he ran.

"They'll nick it off you, Rome," he said. "They'll nick it off you. Don't you know not to leave it about? They'd have it if you chained it up, they would. Don't you know to keep it with you?"

And Effie grinned and nodded and pointed to the empty space, the area four feet in front of him, where she thought the barrow should be.

"You want to go back and fetch your barrow, Rome," said Nello.

"You'll be lucky if it's still there. There's plenty as'd pay good money for that barrow."

Someone was killing the street people but he was to worry about the possible loss of a gimcrack box barrow. Psychologists, he thought, called that displacement. They all walked down the hill together, Effie and he, Nello and Dill and the beagle. Dill had told him that when he got a new uncle, when the old one had left and his auntie had found a replacement, the new one had turned him out of the house—well, it was a flat at Woodberry Down, but it came to the same thing. He had given him twenty-four hours to go and told him to take the dog with him. It had been his auntie's dog but she'd seemed glad to see the back of it, so Dill and the beagle had set off together.

"Like Dick Whittington and his cat," Dill had said unexpectedly, crinkling up his Oriental eyes.

But the streets hadn't been paved with gold and the beagle didn't even have a name. They just called it Beagle. Instead of a lead, Dill had a length of rope, but he let the dog off when they were in the park. Roman saw the fair-haired girl in the distance, walking toward the Broad Walk, and a man with her, as fair and slight as she, not the dark burly one he had sent off in the wrong direction.

The memory made him smile. A couple of weeks ago it had been and just about this time of day. Then, too, he had been up on the hill partaking of the nuns' tea and wondering, he remembered, if those charitable sisters were connected in any way with a church he often passed that was dedicated to the Handmaidens of the Sacred Heart. It was a name he loved and that stuck in his memory and he was thinking of it and of those nuns who were handmaidens to the poor and dispossessed, when the fair girl came running along as if pursued and called out to him a breathless hello.

That set off another train of thought, this time Russell's contention—or Russell quoting some other philosopher's contention—that at certain times and in certain situations to lie is moral. If, for instance, one should see a man running as if in fear of his life, and within moments his pursuers arrive and ask which way he went, then it is permissible to lie and tell them the left-hand fork when in fact the man fled to the right. This reflection had come into his mind just as he came out at the bottom of Ormonde Terrace and the dark and burly chap appeared, running, red-faced, obviously as mad as hell.

Roman nearly laughed aloud at the opportunity that had been sent him or he, coincidentally, had found. Would the man have asked him? Probably not.

He pointed down the terrace toward Primrose Hill Bridge and the park. "She went that way."

"What?"

"The lady you are chasing went down there into the park."

The man stopped and stood, indecisive. He had gone even redder. "Fuck you," he said to Roman. "Mind your own bloody business."

But he turned and ran down the terrace just the same. Roman watched him, laughing. He hadn't laughed so much for ages, not since before it happened, not since his loss. For a moment or two he had awaited further developments, the man's reappearance perhaps, the fair girl herself to come creeping back, but nothing happened. And since that afternoon he had twice seen her with a new man, this straw-haired pale-eyed one, who looked nice enough, who held her hand and once put an arm tenderly about her shoulders.

This relieved him of a burden, for he had thought, after amusement at the incident gave place to reflectiveness, that she was in distress, and he had come close to constituting himself her guardian or protector. He saw her so often, their paths were always crossing, that he felt he could easily keep an eye on her, see that she was safe. But safe from what? If the railings murderer, the Impaler as the papers called him, sought out young women for his victims, Roman would have made himself at once her watchdog. But she could hardly be farther from the type that had so far been his victims. She had a home, probably a nice one, and she was female. Did her femaleness exclude her? He gave Effie a glance, Effie with her bandaged legs and the men's suit trousers she wore and her green bundles, and wondered.

When they came to the Inner Circle he told them that this area, this ring enclosing a few acres, had once been designated by Nash, who was the prince regent's architect, as the site for the prince's summer palace. He meant to say no more, for he had no wish to be their didact, but Nello said to go on, to tell them, and Dill said to sit on a seat and tell them a story. Effie only stared, her eyes as empty and as desperate as they always were.

So he told them how the prince who became George IV had laid out this park, or rather Nash had under his instructions, and how Nash and Decimus Burton had built the villas and the terraces for the prince's courtiers. He talked about the great road that was to be built all the way from this inner circle down to Trafalgar Square, that it had been begun and Portland Place was the start of it, but the plan had to be abandoned for lack of money. They could appreciate that, they knew about governments' thriftlessness and abandoned schemes. Dill put the beagle back on its lead, or tied the rope to its collar, and they made their way through the rose garden, which was in full bloom, at the glorious zenith of its blooming. The sun was hot and the air perfumed, Roman thought, like those famous gardens of the East, the Shalimar perhaps.

They were a rag, tag, and bobtail crew, shuffling along these immaculate paths, and people gave them glances but no stares. The respectable were afraid of the retorts or oaths stares might evoke. Though dogs were strictly not allowed, no one said a word even when the beagle lifted its leg against a rose called Sexy Rexy. But Effie knelt down by the finest rosebed of all and buried her face in the full brilliant blossoms of Royal William, inhaling and lifting her head and burrowing once more in the rich scented petals.

Roman couldn't think of much more to tell them, though they

asked. The summer palace had never been built—what would it have been like? The Pavilion at Brighton?—and the great road had been spoiled by intersections, Regent Street having later been quite destroyed and rebuilt. The Inner Circle had been the province for a while of the Royal Botanical Society before becoming Queen Mary's rose garden. He left them then, Effie and Nello seated side by side on a bench near the bandstand, Dill and the beagle on their way to their pitch outside Tussaud's. It was time to buy his supper, make his way back to the Grotto.

The evening sun awoke in him memories of warm London nights. They were few, it nearly always grew cold, but sometimes, when they had a sitter for the children, he and Sally had gone to a restaurant in Bayswater or Notting Hill and eaten their dinner at a table outside. He was no longer able, when he envisaged these events, to see Sally's face clearly. There were parts of it, a curve, a feature, that whatever constructed such things in his mind failed to build accurately. It was not that she or the children receded from him but rather that a mist or veil had come down between them and him.

A curious thing was happening: He was able to remember with less pain, with something more like a sweet nostalgia. Something he had believed would never come was coming, a kind of resignation. It was not exactly hope he had, certainly not recovery, but he could, in connection with what he had suffered, repeat to himself Winston Churchill's dictum, that this was not the end nor the beginning of the end, but it was the end of the beginning.

Had he set forth on his pilgrimage then with the aim of being cured? He thought not. It had been escape, not therapy, but perhaps therapy had come just the same. His fate he had begun to see not as something to be fought against with rage and anguish—Why me? Why me?—but as marking him out simply to be a member of that rare band of people, not so rare in many places, whose whole family has been destroyed at a stroke. He could see himself calmly now as one of them, as different from the rest of mankind as a dwarf is dif-

ferent or an amputee, destined to live with that difference forever
and to accept.

He went into a shop in Camden High Street, bought a sandwich,
an apple, and a banana, and because he had wanted it the other day
when he only had milk, a bottle of wine. There was a corkscrew in
his barrow if no one had come and stolen it and all it contained, as
Nello had forecast.

He stopped for his usual contemplation at Durham's figure in
bronze. She gazed toward Gloucester Terrace with his old girlfriend's eyes, making him ask himself where she was now, what had
become of her. Would he know her if they met? Did she still look
like this maiden drawing water from the spring? She was not in the
least like the fair girl he had fancied needed protection. He was not
ambitious to become one of those men who haunt and harass
women, following them, dogging their footsteps, but still he thought
as he climbed down into the Grotto, that he would try to watch over
her from a distance.

For all that, he was unable to tell himself why he felt she needed a
guardian angel. She had the man who looked so uncannily like her.
Her brother perhaps? The burly dark one was just a fool who surely
constituted no real threat. As he opened his wine, he began to make a
little scenario. Her brother had come back from abroad, expected to
share her home with her, but found the dark one in residence and
they had fallen out . . . He couldn't finish the story, couldn't see where
it might go next nor account for her being chased to the gates of Primrose Hill. But he thought he would "look out" for her, and begin in
the morning, for he was sure she always entered the park just here, at
the Gloucester Gate, and walked past that sculpted tower of silence.

•   •   •

There came back to Bean a conversation he had once had with Clitheroe. His employer was in bed recovering from a particularly serious
beating. When he dressed it Clitheroe's back reminded Bean of

James Fox's in the film *Performance,* which he had seen while working for Anthony Maddox—only Fox was an actor and the weals and
cuts on his back were makeup, while Clitheroe's were real. He had
said something like that, something about Chas in the film, and
Clitheroe said, talking of acting, he's a pretty good actor, that chap.

What did he mean, actor, Bean had asked. And Clitheroe said
The Beater's name, which Bean couldn't remember, and then he
said, he's made himself into what he thinks I want him to be, and
he's right, I do want him to be that, I want a savage, Bean, I want
someone who enjoys beating someone else more than anything in
this world. Who gets all his pleasure from it, who wants it better
than sex or drugs or money, because to him it is sex and drugs and
money. Do you understand?

"Sure," said Bean, "of course I understand." Understanding made
him feel sick but he didn't say that.

"I love his excitement, Bean. Do you know, I think I love *him,* and
why not? It's just what a crazy pervert like me would do. I'd like to
do something for him, set him up for life, show him after I'm gone
that I had real feelings for him."

"Turn over," Bean said, "and let me have a look." He had stopped
calling Clitheroe "sir" about the time The Beater first began coming.
"Christ," he said, "I just hope this lot's not turning septic."

"It'd better heal up because (the name again) is dropping in for a
drink and fifty lashes on Saturday."

"He'll kill you," said Bean, not knowing how near the truth
he was.

"I can see it in his eyes that he's acting," said Clitheroe, wrig-
gling—with pain or pleasure, or were they the same? "There's
something dead in his eyes. And I'm glad of it, Bean, because it
would be too much for me if it was real, it would be too beautiful to
bear." He shivered and goose pimples came up between the wounds.
"He could act anything. I wonder why he doesn't? Make his living at
it, I mean. Maybe he's never had the chance. Or maybe he only wants

to act in life, not on the stage. He wants to *be,* you could say, not to act."

That was all too deep for Bean. He hated that kind of high-flown meaningless speculation. The Beater *had* dropped in for the drink and whatever and again the following Saturday and it was after he had gone that Maurice Clitheroe had had his stroke. Sometimes Bean thought himself lucky to have got the apartment under Clitheroe's will, for he might easily have left it to The Beater.

It was satisfying to have remembered, but not much use. Every morning, about this time, Bean still expected the police to come back for him, though it was over a week now since they had hauled him in for a second going-over. While he dressed and had his breakfast he kept running to the front to look out of the window and check.

· · ·

"Testimonials? I've never heard of such a thing," said Bean, annoyed, when Valerie Conway told him Mrs. Sellers wanted two independent references on top of Valerie's own recommendation before she would surrender her dalmatian to his keeping.

"Suit yourself," said Valerie. "But don't expect me to put myself out another time."

Bean said he'd ask Mrs. Goldsworthy and Miss Pring but he wasn't promising anything. This Mrs. Sellers should realize she wasn't doing him any favors. A reliable dog-walker was like gold dust, never mind Barker-Pryce and his school-leavers.

"Oh, get a life!" said Valerie, slamming the area door.

Lisl Pring was off on location somewhere, so Bean had to use his key to pick up Marietta. He asked Mrs. Goldsworthy about the reference and she said, Oh, sure, no trouble, she'd do it later and to remind her again if she forgot. Bean knew she'd never do it, she was the sort who had so much money she never bothered to do anything. He tied the dogs to the gatepost at Charlotte Cottage and pretended to ignore what Ruby was trying to do to McBride. Let them get on with it. He asked Miss Jago for a reference. Something like that would have looked better coming from Sir Stewart Blackburn-Norris but it couldn't be helped. She said, Yes, of course, and she'd give it to him the next morning, and somehow he thought it likely she'd actually do it.

It was a warm sultry morning, the kind of July day that threatens a storm to come. Swarms of gnats rose and fell above the surface of the lake, and from the bridge over the island the water had a fetid smell. The grass in the open areas was worn and bleached by the sun. Bean walked the dogs over the bridge and almost to the Hanover Gate. This morning the roof of the mosque was dull as an old copper pot. Watching the gambols of Boris and Marietta, he asked himself if he really wanted another big dog, a dalmatian. Big dogs were unruly and easily got out of hand. Pity they couldn't all be like that little Gushi, who stuck close beside him and only occasionally ran off for some puppyish adventure with McBride.

A man was walking down the Broad Walk from the zoo end. Bean was quite a long way away from him. Flowerbeds and ornamental trees and fountains and urns spilling out more flowers separated them. But he would have known The Beater anywhere, at any distance, by his slouching walk, the lift of his chin, his body movements as elegant as a black man's, the way his arms hung loosely by his sides. Bean had all the dogs on their leash by now and he approached nearer. He had no objection to being seen by The Beater and in the daylight and the warmth had lost the fears of the night.

When their eyes met The Beater's showed not a flicker of recognition. But he was an actor, wasn't he? Bean stared at him before turning abruptly away. How old was he? That had always been a mystery, but he must be all of thirty-five now. He turned around when he was sure The Beater wasn't looking and took in the jeans, the denim jacket, the longish hair. Was it possible . . . ? He had seemed clean enough but some of them *were* clean. There were hostels now where they could get showers, wash their hair.

So could The Beater have come so low as to be on the street?

Bean had no real reason to think so except that *they* did come in here and loaf about and The Beater seemed to have been wandering aimlessly. Where, after all, could he have come from and be going to? If he really was one of them maybe the Impaler would find him and he'd end up murdered and stuck on railings somewhere. Things would have been very different for The Beater if he hadn't beaten Clitheroe quite so hard and Clitheroe had lived a little longer and changed his will. . . .

Marnock and the sergeant were waiting for him when he got back to York Terrace, sitting outside in their car on a double yellow line. They were a lot more polite than on previous occasions, which made Bean cocky and say in a testy tone, "What is it this time?"

They wanted him to tell them all about the man who had mugged him in the Nursemaids' Tunnel. There was no need to go down to the station if he'd be good enough to ask them in. Was he sure the mugger had been Clancy? Was there any room for doubt over the identity of his attacker?

Bean had to rethink the whole thing. Maybe it hadn't been Clancy. He wondered if he dare give them a description of The Beater, but he thought better of this as too dangerous and said he couldn't remember. They stayed for nearly two hours, their politeness unflagging, and when they left they said nothing about seeing him again.

He had a Birdseye Lean Cuisine for his lunch and watched *Emmerdale* on television. After that, feeling cheerful, he told himself that nothing ventured, nothing gained. All his clients' phone numbers were written down in the accounts book he kept. As he dialed Barker-Pryce's number he thought, if she answers or some secretary or whatever I'll just put the phone down. When he heard Barker-Pryce speak, his throat dried.

"Yes? Who is it?"

He managed to speak. "It's Bean, sir. The one who walks the dogs."

"What d'you want? Speak up."

"I was wondering," said Bean, his rising anger strengthening his voice, "if you'd like to see some really beautiful photographs I've taken of Charlie. They're smashing, sir, I think you'd like them."

He was well named Barker. The noise he made, a laugh presumably, was much the same sound as that coming from McBride when he put up a mandarin duck.

"That's rich. Coming from you. You walked the animal, right? When did I give you permission to use it as a model?"

Bean drew a deep breath, expelled it, said, "Talking of models, sir, I nearly mentioned these pix the other evening when I saw you in Paddington with the young lady."

Silence. Bean seemed to smell cigar smoke.

"I'd been buying a paper, Mr. Barker-Pryce. A newspaper. It was to read that article about the gentleman from the government and the lady in the hotel. I expect you know him, don't you, sir?"

The voice was quieter this time, the tone more polite. "What exactly do you want?"

"Among other things, a reference, if you please, sir. For a lady with a dalmatian. I wondered if I might drop in after I've taken my *other* dogs for their walk. Say about five-thirty?"

19

It took Roman a while to find out where she lived. He felt a natural aversion to spying on her. But one Saturday, he saw her in Primrose Hill and with the utmost discretion followed her home.

He had been in a secondhand bookshop in Regent's Park Road and there found an old work, published in 1840, called *Colburn's Calendar of Amusements*. The bookseller only wanted two pounds for it, for it was in a ragged battered state. Roman stood in the shop doorway, reading a passage from it that touched him, that seemed to parallel in a zany, awkward way his own state.

> *The lion in the collection of the Zoological gardens was brought, with his lioness, from Tunis, and as the keeper informed us, they lived most lovingly together. Their dens were separated only by an iron railing, sufficiently low to allow of their jumping over. One day, as the lioness was amusing herself leaping from one den to the other, while her lord looked on, apparently highly delighted with her gaiety, she unfortunately struck her foot against the top of the railing, and was precipitated backwards; the fall proved fatal, for, upon examination, it was found she had broken her spine. The grief of her partner was excessive, and, although it did not show itself with the same violence as in a previous instance, it proved equally fatal: a deep melancholy took possession of him, and he pined to death in a few weeks.*

Deep melancholy may kill lions, but not human beings. Not even the deepest grief kills them, for men have died from time to time but not of love. . . . He was remembering, incongruously, how when he was a boy the zoo's telephone exchange was called Primrose and remembering too a joke about dialing Primrose 1000 and asking for Mr. Lion, when he looked up and saw her pass by on the opposite pavement.

She might not have been walking home but somehow he fancied she was. He put the book in his pocket and began to walk in the direction she was going. If she looked back, he thought, he would abandon his pursuit of her. He would give it up at once, for she must on no account be made afraid of him. How much, how infinitely much, he would have liked to read that account of the poor lion's fate to Sally, for there seemed no one else in the world to whom he could read it or tell it and who would react with the same tender sympathy. But she was not in the world, she was nowhere, ageless, lost, with her dead children.

The fair-haired girl, the Irene Adler girl, crossed the road ahead of him and then Albert Road and made her way into the park by way of St. Mark's Bridge, over the Outer Circle and into the Broad Walk. She hadn't once looked back. But why would she? She wasn't Lot's wife, leaving the Cities of the Plain, or Orpheus hoping Eurydice followed on behind. The walk was shady here, much overhung by trees, chestnuts and planes in heavy leaf. The two wolves, penned behind double wire fences, explored and sniffed their territory like dogs. He saw her turn to look at them but not pause. She took the first of the two left-hand paths that led to the Gloucester Gate.

He had been making his nightly home in the Grotto for nearly three weeks now, the longest time he had spent in any one place. And all the while, it seemed, she had been quite near him, for she had crossed the Outer Circle and was leading him along Albany Street. Park Village West. If she went in there she must live there, for it was a crescent, leading nowhere but back to that northbound artery. It was quiet, a bower of trees and flowers, green, scented, but the leaves a little dusty, for this after all was near the heart of London.

She hadn't once looked back, but she did so at the gate of a pretty Italianate house, and seeing him, not knowing that he had been behind her all the way from Primrose Hill, lifted up her hand and waved.

Only a woman in a million, he thought, would say hello to me, smile at me, and when there had been some hellos and smiles, wave to me. And he wondered if he should stay a while to see if her brother came home, but it might be hours, the brother might be in there now, and he turned away, opening his book and reading it as he walked along.

.   .   .

Someone had come and boarded up his windows. Hob didn't know who because he had been out most of the day, trying to get what he wanted out of the bunch of stony-hearted people he knew or was related to. He got home late, spaced out and low on the pediatric Valium syrup, which was all he'd been able to get out of his half-sister. It didn't do much for him beyond making him sleepy so that at least he was too tired to feel all the intensity of a state.

He'd first gone for help to his half-sister's boyfriend. This man, the father of her youngest child, made crack himself by mixing cocaine and bicarbonate of soda and baking the resultant paste in a microwave. He offered it to Hob at ten percent less than its street value, or he said it was ten percent, Hob couldn't work it out. But Hob had already handed over all his giro money to Lew under the Chinese trees and he was skint. The boyfriend shrugged and said too bad. His half-sister took pity on him, or more likely wanted him out of the house, and said she'd got a bottle of the kids' Valium he could have. They were supposed to have it in their bottles but she and the boyfriend found whiskey more effective.

After that he proceeded to his cousin's place in one of the blocks off Lisson Grove. The cousin and two of his mates were sitting in front of a hard-core video smoking weed. They passed the joint to Hob more or less as a matter of course, but none of them would give him any money or even lend him any. The cousin said he knew a man he'd met in a pub that might want a job done and he told Hob where he might find this man, giving him a funny look when he saw him swigging out of a kid's medicine bottle.

The pediatric Valium tasted very sweet and of something that brought back Hob's childhood. He couldn't think what it was and he was too sleepy to think much anyway. He hung about the news-agent's the man used for a long while, bought a couple of scratch cards, getting nothing up of course but a couple of Walker's Crisps and two diet Cokes. Then he sat on a seat outside on the pavement, but no one came along who remotely fitted his cousin's description. Fruit drops, that was what it was. It came back to him suddenly as he was trudging home, fruit drops that syrup tasted of, what his mother's nan called boiled sugars. His first stepfather used to buy them for him after he'd given him a harder clout than usual.

He was looking up high, to the top of the next block, Blackwater House, to see where the kid had stood when he'd dropped the rock on the old man, which was why he didn't notice the windows till he was almost at the door. Raw planks of wood were nailed up over all his front windows, the two in the living room and the one in the bed-room. It was a warm night and inside the flat it was hot like an oven. He sat on the settee and laid his head on one of the Mickey Mouse scatter cushions.

When the lights in the flats opposite and the lights in the car park went out it would be black as pitch in here. As it was, only thin lines of light, orange-colored, slipped through the cracks between the boards. It would be as bad in the bedroom. Hob drank more Valium syrup to put himself out and he must have spilled some on the floor, for he was aware in his sleep and his half-sleep of the mice at his feet, licking it up.

· · ·

"We could live here," Mary said, "when the time comes for me to leave Charlotte Cottage."

She and Leo were in Frederica Jago's house, big, turreted, late-Victorian red brick, in an overgrown rather dark garden. Mary had not visited it since her grandmother's funeral and the meeting there with Alistair and Mr. Edwards. It was stuffy and airless; she felt she should go about opening windows, but as soon as she came through the front door she had been lethargic and reluctant to take any positive steps. The place was filled with her grandmother. It was not a new feeling, it was how everyone felt in her circumstances, but all the time she expected the dead woman to walk in, to smile, to speak, to hold out her arms.

"I grew up here. It seems forbidding now but it didn't then. I remember being proud of living in such a *distinguished* house and I think I used to boast about it at school. I must have been a horrid child."

Leo had been silent ever since they came through the front door. Normally, he would have reacted to that last statement of hers, refuted it at once, and she even wondered if she had said it for that reason: to hear him tell her she could never have been horrid. She was growing hungry for praise from him. But he said nothing, only shrugged lightly. She took him upstairs, going from room to room. In one she opened a dressing table drawer, but the scent that came from it, vanilla and roses, was so much the essence of her grandmother that she drew back with a little cry.

In the big bay window of the master bedroom she turned to him and laid her head against his shoulder. "Leo, what is it? What's wrong?"

"Nothing," he said. "There's nothing wrong."

"I'm sure there is. Do you hate the place? We don't have to live here. I don't even know that I want to. There's something retrograde about choosing to live in the house where one was brought up."

He screwed up his eyes. He said, as if with an effort, "Your wealth. I suppose it's only now that I'm realizing how rich you are. This place has brought it home to me."

"I told you."

"I know. Now I'm seeing for myself."

She had no heart for the rest of the house and led him downstairs and back into Frederica's drawing room. He was looking all the while warily about him. She saw his eyes take in the pictures, the glass, the porcelain, and linger on a tall French clock in a case of brass and glass that began at that moment to strike four.

"If you'd known," she said fearfully, "when first we'd met, would you have still wanted to know me? I mean, would you have pursued it? Or would you just have said thanks and maybe we'll run into each other again one day?"

He paused. It was a long pause. "I don't know," he said. "I can't answer that."

Her heart seemed to fall through her body, sliding down in a sluice of coldness. "But you thought at first Charlotte Cottage was mine. When you first heard from me you had my address as Charlotte Cottage."

"Yes, and I was mightily relieved, I can tell you, when I found out it wasn't yours."

"But what can I do? I can't give it all away. And, Leo, I don't want to. I want somewhere nice for us to live. I want us to live as we please and you not necessarily have to go on working for your brother—unless you want to, I mean. I want to buy a car, I haven't even got a car and nor have you." She found she was talking wildly. "I can buy us a smaller place, a flat, a little house."

She put out her hand to touch his but it remained unresponsive. The memory that came back to her was always there but usually suppressed, buried under layers of pleasanter things.

"Why did you leave me that day in Covent Garden?"

He turned uncomprehending eyes. "What?"

"We were out together. It was the second, the third, time we went out together, and you suddenly said you had to go, you had to meet your brother, and you said good-bye and walked away."

"I suppose I had to meet my brother."

Some inner cautious voice told her not to pursue it. She stood up. "Let's go."

Outside it was very dark. Clouds had been gathering all afternoon and now thunder rumbled from beyond Hampstead and Highgate like distant explosions. Coming here, he had held her hand, but now he walked apart from her, his head down, sullen as she had never seen him. After a moment or two he said lifelessly, almost regretfully, "I love you."

Until then he had never quite said it.

The words themselves were gratifying. Perhaps they always were, no matter who said them. Suddenly she was uncertain, she thought she loved him, she loved being with him, she loved their love-making, but could she answer him in the way he would want her to? What made her suddenly doubt? A certain sulky childishness because he had difficulty in coping with the difference in their incomes?

They were in a taxi, silent again, and home in Charlotte Cottage before he said another word. By then the storm was full-blown, the lightning splitting a sky of huge black thunderclouds, the rain beating down all the flowers in Park Village gardens. She had put the lights on, it was like a winter evening. Gushi, terrified, hid under the sofa, his cold nose pressed against her ankles. It was the kind of

weather when you could take it for granted Bean wasn't coming.
Leo said suddenly, in an uncharacteristic outburst, "I can't bear that
man, whatshisname, Alistair, writing to you that you're going to live
together, you're going to buy a place together."

"But we're not. I've told you, all that's over."

"He wants to marry you, doesn't he?"

"Perhaps. I don't want to marry him."

A thunder crash seemed to rock the house. Gushi whimpered.
She got down on her knees and did her best to stroke his chrysanthemum head, reaching under the sofa.

"Will you marry *me?*"

She turned her head. It was ridiculous to be on all fours.

"Did you really say that?"

"I really did." He looked almost shamefaced. His face was her
face when she was awkward or embarrassed.

"Leo, I'm older than you. We've known each other for less than
two months. And—" she couldn't resist "—I'm rich." She saw him
wince. "We can live together, we're going to do that. We can get to
know each other."

"We do know each other." He got down onto the floor beside her
and held her shoulders. His eyes were very near hers. "We are part
of each other's bodies, and not just in the way all lovers are, but in a
special way. You are my bones, Mary. You are my blood. Who else
could we marry? Don't you see that after what we've been to each
other, it would be wrong for us ever to marry anyone else?"

She felt a little faint. She shook her head, on and on.

"Marry me, Mary, before he can marry you. Marry me now."

"Leo, you know we see eye to eye in most things, but this is—isn't
it a bit ridiculous? I do want to be with you, I do want to live with
you as soon as I can leave here, but why does it have to be marriage?
One day, yes. Maybe in two or three years' time. When we know
what we both really want."

He said very quietly, "There may not be two or three years."

"What do you mean?"

"I don't think I'm going to live very long."

It was as if she had put out her hand, expecting to encounter warmth, and had felt, instead, ice. She had been practical, prudent, and she could see he was deadly serious.

"What do you mean?"

There was fear in his voice now. "Just what I say."

The ice was touching her spine, sliding down. "Have they told you that? Have they told you at the hospital?"

"Let's say," he said, "they won't answer when I ask. I had a checkup on Wednesday."

"You didn't tell me."

"I would have if there'd been a—a favorable outcome. I shall be all right for a while. They talked about a while."

She said breathlessly, "Another transplant?"

"You would do that for me a second time?"

"If necessary. Of course I would."

There was a wild look in his eyes she had never seen before.

"I never thought you'd do that. I never considered it." He seemed disproportionately distressed. It was as if she had said something that might change his life and his plans, as indeed this might, but not pleasurably, not in a way to be entirely desired. "I wish I'd known," he said, half to himself, and then, "You'd do that?"

"I've just said so. Leo, it's nothing to the donor, nothing but an anesthetic and that's quite safe if you're strong and healthy."

She put her arms round him. She felt a pulse drumming in his neck, his heart beating steadily but fast. Her mind wasn't made up but she knew she was about to act as if it were.

"If you need another transplant, who better to have it from than your wife?"

20

Befor going to St. Andrew's Place, Bean called in at the chemist and picked up the ten enlargements he had had made. Expensive but worth it. The dog photographs, Charlie sniffing noses with McBride, Charlie in pursuit of a goose, Charlie reclining elegantly on sunlit grass, he had in a cardboard folder and he slipped one of the enlargements in with them. The others he locked up in Maurice Clitheroe's safe.

His newfound power led him to ask James Barker-Pryce not to light another cigar while talking to him. It was bringing on the asthma he thought he had left behind him twenty years ago. They had gone into a small office or study with a view from its long window of the Royal College of Physicians. On the desk was a stack of writing paper with House of Commons printed on it in green and a picture of a gridiron thing that Bean thought meant it was the property of the government. The cigar was left behind, smoldering in an ashtray in the hall.

He opened the cardboard folder and displayed two photographs of Charlie and then the enlargement. Barker-Pryce snatched it up. "I have others, sir," Bean said.

Barker-Pryce didn't even look at the shots of Charlie. Some of these people weren't fit to keep a dog. He picked up his dark green Mont Blanc fountain pen in khaki-stained fingers and wrote a reference on that same crested writing paper. His handwriting was not what Bean would have expected, being small and clear and perfectly legible. Over his shoulder, Bean could read desirable words: "reliable," "a true animal-lover," "unfailingly punctual."

"I've made other arrangements for Charlie," Barker-Pryce said in almost the tone he would have used to a neighbor or an honorable friend in the Commons. "I can't see my way to revoking those, if you understand me. But I'd like these pictures of my retriever."

The money was there, all ready and prepared. It was placed in his hand, the notes lined up against the edges of the envelope with the reference in it. Bean didn't count them, he could tell it was a hundred pounds. With an awful attempt at a conspiratorial grin, a squeezing shut of the eyes, a lifting of that thick hairy upper lip to expose teeth of the same shade and shape as the mahogany beading on the desk, Barker-Pryce said, "Buy yourself a few videos instead of the newspaper, eh?"

Bean did speak then. "I'll call again in a week's time." He'd dropped the "sir." He left the pictures where they were, the one of Charlie and the goose uppermost. The expression on Barker-Pryce's face was frightening, so he stopped looking at it. What those girls went through! No wonder they'd never let a john kiss them.

Charlie burst out of one of the rooms at the back and came boisterously up to him in the hall. Poor innocent creature, thought Bean. He touched the retriever perfunctorily on the head the way Queen Victoria's dad might have patted one of the dogs at Sidmouth. Barker-Pryce didn't say another word but stood in the study doorway, looking at him. Bean pulled the front door closed.

Mrs. Sellers and her dalmatian lived in Park Square, which would be convenient, being more or less on the way from the Cornells' to Lisl Pring's. The dalmatian (called Spots, "not Spot, please," said Mrs. Sellers) was obedient and docile and she took a fancy to Bean from the moment he entered the flat. The interview went well and it looked as if Bean would soon add another dog to his charges. The reference on House of Commons paper made an awesome impression on her but didn't stop her asking for a second one.

Miss Jago at Charlotte Cottage was the sort who when she said she'd do a thing, did it. Except that she hadn't. And he'd already twice reminded her of her promise. He noticed most things about his clients and it didn't escape him that Miss Jago had an engagement ring on her left hand. Not much of a ring, Victorian rubbish of nine-carat gold and tourmalines you could pick up for forty quid at Camden Lock. One of the numerous men she entertained was presumably going to make an honest woman of her. He wondered—for he was always on the lookout for a means of money-making—if Sir Stewart and Lady Blackburn-Norris knew, if they would mind, if she had told them. Would she be marrying soon? Would she bring hubby to live *here*? Was there anything in it for him?

More pressing was the matter of his reference. Having hesitated as to whether or not he wanted another dog and a big dog at that, he now desperately wanted Spots. He told himself he needed the increase to his income walking Spots would bring. Besides, it irked him, Mrs. Sellers doubtless believing by this time that no one else was willing to vouch for him.

Twenty-three days had elapsed between the first murder and the second and now it was just twenty-three days since the second murder. Bean expected a third at any minute. He believed in psychopaths ruled by the phases of the moon, cycles of madness, blood lust regulated by multiples of seven, give or take a little. So there should be another one at any time.

He was sure the police believed in it too. That was why they were so jumpy and so polite. He had stopped reading the papers, but the television had a program about fixated killers, killers with a mission or an obsession, and there was a psychiatrist on it—probably the one who analyzed Pharaoh's madness—talking about murderers who killed prostitutes or nuns or almost anyone so long as they could be put into a category.

The twenty-third day went by and the twenty-fourth and none of the homeless or the jacks men or the beggars got killed. Whoever it was doing it had probably gone off somewhere else, Bean thought, gone up north, they always went up north for some reason. He often speculated about The Beater and wondered if he ought to say something to the police next time they paid him a visit. They had been back twice since asking him about the mugger in the tunnel and he had begun seriously thinking of himself as their adviser, as genuinely helping them with their inquiries. But what could he say? That The Beater could act anything, pretend to be anything he wanted? A sadist or, doubtless, a respectable citizen?

Instead of leaving wet weather in its wake, the storm had just made things hot. Summer had come at last. All the rain had made the grass in the park very green and fed the roses so that they grew lush with dark shiny foliage. The sun shone on velvet lawns and sparkling dewdrops. By noon the temperature had climbed to eighty degrees, and in the evenings people watched performances at the Open Air Theatre in sleeveless dresses and T-shirts.

Calling for Gushi on the first really hot morning, the sky cloudless, the air clear, he asked Miss Jago for the third time about that reference. She looked genuinely aghast, he had to give her that.

"I *am* sorry. I'm so sorry. I'll have it done for you by this afternoon."

"I don't see you in the afternoons, Miss," Bean said in his most respectful tone.

"I'll try to be home by the time you bring the dogs back. Or else you can be sure it will be here when you come in the morning."

The woman who walked ten dogs was out with her troop. It was all right for her, she wasn't a day over thirty-five. She had given up waving at Bean since the day he returned her greeting with one of his looks. But nothing could stop their dogs fraternizing. Ruby made the Cavalier King Charles spaniel her prey. It was a lot smaller than she was and those dogs always had poor sight. Bean had to rescue it from gang rape, for McBride and Boris had followed Ruby's lead.

The woman watched his efforts without offering to help. Then McBride found a heap of horse dung—How did a horse get in here?

Under a mounted policeman?—and rolled his fat wet body in it, shaking smelly brown liquid all over Bean's trousers. It was no way to make a living, he told himself, he'd be seventy-one in September. But he had to have an income, he couldn't live on the pension, especially in a luxury maisonette designed for a fifty-thousand-a-year man.

Valerie Conway was waiting in the area doorway, well out of the rain of course. Boris would never go down the stairs alone, Bean had to take him, otherwise the borzoi would lie down on the top step and refuse to budge.

"You got the dalmatian on your books yet?" Valerie said as he descended.

"Why do you ask?"

"Just being friendly. As a matter of fact I'd like to think business was good because Mr. Cornell has given me a message for you."

"What message?"

"He's giving you two weeks' notice. Your services won't be required after the twenty-eighth."

Bean stared at her. He took his hand slowly from Boris's collar and the dog slunk through the doorway, drawing its body to one side so as not to touch Valerie as it passed her.

"What's brought this on?"

Valerie could hardly contain her pleasure and triumph, he could tell that. "They're going to live permanently at their place in the country. And I'm moving in with my boyfriend."

"Well, thanks very much. Thanks very much for the courtesy of *two* weeks' notice."

"I consider I've done very well by you, Leslie Bean or whatever your name is. Why d'you think I found you a new customer? You ought to be down on your bended knees thanking me."

He looked hard at her. He would have liked to say she could keep her two weeks' notice and she needn't think he'd ever have another thing to do with that foul-tempered dog, that cold-hearted, evil Russian, the animal that hadn't even attempted to defend him when he'd been mugged. But he couldn't, he needed the money.

"Thank you, Valerie," he said, and was about to add that he'd see her later, but she had slammed the door.

The sun grew almost unpleasantly hot by three-thirty. Bean never thought he'd be complaining about the heat, but he would gladly have missed out on the afternoon walk. Marietta, always the least controllable of the dogs, the liveliest, the bounciest, went too near a family of cygnets and got a peck on the chest from the swan. She screamed as if she'd been stabbed with a knife, but Bean couldn't see a mark. Little Gushi was too hot under his thick shaggy coat, puffing and whimpering until at last Bean picked him up and carried him. The dog was heavy for his size and he panted, his tongue hanging out.

All this made Bean late getting back to Charlotte Cottage. He rang the bell, hoping Miss Jago was home as she had said she would be. But there was no answer, so he let himself and Gushi in with his key. She kept it very clean, he always noticed. What he would really have liked was to have taken Marietta in there and left her to run about shaking and splashing the pale walls and silk chair covers with muddy water. But, thinking of his reference, he left the other dogs at the gate, carried Gushi into the kitchen, and refilled his water bowl.

Taken all in all, it had not been a pleasant day. Bean had still not been back to the Globe. It was not that he was any longer afraid to go there, or that he believed the police would watch him go there, but he saw himself as punishing the place by ostracizing it. All the trouble he had been in was due to the Globe and the Globe's clientele telling tales. Bean had an obscure feeling that a well-run pub wouldn't have those sorts of customers.

So, for the past three Fridays, he had been going to the Queen's Head and Artichoke. He knew no one there but that bothered him very little. He went there to drink and this evening he felt particularly in need.

Someone in the pub the previous week had buttonholed him and started giving him a history of the place, how the original house that had stood here had been built by one of Elizabeth I's gardeners, hence its name. Bean wasn't interested and he looked cautiously about him now so that he could give the historian a wide berth, but the man wasn't there this evening. He asked for a double whiskey, Bell's, and ginger ale, and took it to a table in the corner.

Without the whiskey he would probably never have thought of going up to Park Village. A second double emboldened him. After all, he was already in Albany Street, and it was a beautiful evening. At just after nine-thirty, the sky was clear and cloudless, violet-colored and still stained red in the west. So near the park, the air smelled of the scents distilled by the sun from grass and leaves and roses.

Twenty to ten, which was the time he would get there, was not too late to pay an evening call. He remembered Anthony Maddox's rules about that—he was talking of the phone but it came to the same thing—"nothing before nine A.M. or after ten P.M." Besides, she couldn't complain, she had promised him that reference over and over again. On the spot, he could stand over her till it was done. Well, stand there and perhaps be offered a drink while she wrote it.

·   ·   ·

When she said she was going to be married, Dorothea assumed it was Alistair.

"It's Leo I'm marrying."

Dorothea had to think who that was. "How awfully romantic," she said.

"It is, isn't it? But I'm so glad you think so, I'd thought you'd disapprove. We haven't known each other very long."

"Knowing the person very long isn't necessarily important. You can have an instinct about someone being right for you."

"That's exactly it. I have an instinct about it. But I do wish my grandmother were alive to see us, to see *him*."

"You thought I wouldn't approve but she would?"

"Oh, maybe it's that her generation expected marriage, they thought in the terms of marriage, whereas ours doesn't. I suppose I'm getting married to make, as they say, a public commitment." And, she thought, but didn't say, because he may not live long. "I'm older than he is. Why should I wait?"

"Do you know what I'd really like, Mary? I'd love you to wear one of Irene's dresses. Why not *the* wedding dress?"

They looked at it in its glass case. Irene Adler had never existed, nor had Godfrey Norton; she had never been married to him, so never had had a wedding dress. This one had been worn by some Edwardian bride, long dead. It was white lace with a high boned collar and long embroidered train. Mary laughed.

"I'm getting married at Camden Register Office. Can you imagine *this*? I shan't even have anything new for it. We don't care about things like that, he doesn't any more than I do. And we shan't have a honeymoon. We can't, I have to stay at Charlotte Cottage for another five weeks. He'll go back to his place and I to mine, I expect—and then, I don't know. But I think we'll be happy, Dorrie."

"And what about Alistair?" said Dorothea.

Since she had run away from him and hidden herself among the trees on Primrose Hill she had seen and heard nothing of him, apart from the letter. She had not yet been able to face replying to it.

"He wants me to let him invest my grandmother's money. He says I'll never find anyone more competent and more cautious. But I haven't got the money yet and shan't have it for ages."

"You sound as if you don't much want it."

"That would be silly, wouldn't it? We all want money. Now that I'm going to marry Leo I want somewhere nice to live."

She said good-bye to Dorothea and took the path straight across the park, but their talk had delayed her and it was only when she reached the gate of Charlotte Cottage that she remembered telling

Bean she would be home early, that she would be home before he came back and would give him his reference. He couldn't have been gone long. Gushi, with fresh water brimming his bowl, was lying exhausted on the kitchen floor.

Mary sat down to write Bean's reference, the little dog on her lap. It took her a long time because she had never done it before and had no idea what was requisite to say. And to whom did you address it? She had written *To whom it may concern* and "Mr. Bean"—should she try to find out his first name?—when Leo arrived. He looked white and tired and said he had had a hard day, he would have to lie down for a while.

The reference finished, she decided to write to Alistair. She would tell him she was getting married in three weeks' time to Leo, and she had begun, had rejected "My dear Alistair" for plain "Dear Alistair," when Leo called her from upstairs. She came into the bedroom and he started to say rather peevishly that she had promised to look after him, to care for him, but although she knew he was exhausted she had virtually ignored him since he got home. . . . And then, suddenly, he was laughing at himself, apologizing, saying how absurd he was, he was only making excuses for wanting her.

So she went into his arms and after a while he began his gentle delicate lovemaking, his fingers with the soft gossamer touch of a moth's wing, his lips as cool as petals, so that it was like being in bed with a phantom. She closed her eyes and thought, when I open them there will be no one there but a shadow. And then his movements strengthened and his body grew real and seemed infused with a sudden great heat. The sound wrenched out of him was like a groan of pain.

They slept and woke to see a red sunset behind the trees of the village and the double spires of St. Katharine's. The red dimmed and the sky was blue covered with tiny pink feathers. Mary got up, had a shower, put on loose cotton trousers and a T-shirt, and began

to make their supper. But Leo came down while she was tearing lettuce for a salad and gently shepherded her away: He would do it, he
was fine now, he wasn't ill.

He laid the table, opened the bottle of wine he had brought. She
finished her letter to Alistair. Everything she wanted to say had presented itself clearly, she had had no difficulties with it, and what had
seemed an insurmountable problem resolved itself into a simple telling of the plain facts, kindly, precisely, without emotion.

It was nine before they sat down to eat, his pasta dish with black
olives having taken detailed preparation. She ate and was glad to see
him eating so heartily, a second helping and another slice of *ciabatta*.
Remembering Alistair's suggestion, she asked him if they should
start house-hunting this weekend. They would be bound to like the
same things, they always did, so it should be a delightful exercise. If
he agreed, she had quite decided to sell the house in Belsize Park.

The idea seemed to appeal to him and he speculated about houses.
Buying a house, buying any property, had never come in his way
before, he confessed, it was something that the grown-ups did. And
she laughed because she felt just the same. It was not for them, they
were children to whom such businesslike adult stuff had never occurred, but now they must, they must be serious, they must realize
that, give or take a little, they could have whatever they wanted.
He had got up and come round the table, had put his arms round
her, and was holding her close in a bear hug, when the front doorbell rang.

Mary said, "It's Alistair."

"Yes, I expect it is." Leo hesitated only infinitesimally. "I'll go. It's
time we met."

She jumped up. "I don't want him to hit you!"

Leo laughed. "He won't hit me."

She wondered how they would look together, side by side, the
one so slight and fair and with the unearthly pallor, the other dark

and heavy-set and choleric. Leo came back. The man with him was Bean.

"Not wanting to put pressure on you, miss, but I shall be going on my holidays in a couple of weeks' time . . ."

"Your reference," Mary said, stammering. "Your—yes, I—yes, I have it here. I'll just get an envelope."

When she came back into the room Bean was sitting on a chair at one end of it and Leo at the table facing him. She handed over the reference.

"It's for a dalmatian," Bean said.

That made Leo laugh. He laughed almost crazily, throwing back his head, and when Bean had gone, he shouted the words, still laughing. "It's for a dalmatian! A dalmatian! A reference for a dalmatian! What'll it do with it, d'you think? Eat it? Bury it?"

She had never known him so noisy, so wild. She laid her hand on his shoulder but he still shouted, his face convulsed, "A dalmation? Can you imagine it reading it? Does it wear glasses? A dalmatian!" And then, suddenly, he was weeping, the tears streaming down his face. He clutched her, pulled her down to him and knelt with her on the floor. His arms held her so tightly she wanted to cry out.

"Mary, Mary, I don't want to die. I want to live, I want to live with you. Why can't I live to be old like others will? I don't want to die!"

· · ·

At some point in his pilgrimage Roman had made up his mind to settle nowhere for more than a few nights at a time, to be always on the move so as to distance himself as far as he could from an approximation to domestic life. And now he had been at the Grotto for three weeks, had even turned it into a kind of home, storing his barrow under the lee of the archway, sleeping there on his groundsheet, keeping, in a cave of bushes, a store of food. The litter had irritated him and he had gradually tidied the place up, picking drinking straws out of branches, stuffing broken bottles and packaging into the carriers they gave him at the grocery. And the rain had washed the place clean, scouring the coped edges of the little pool, filling it with fresher water.

When the sun came out, a hot sun at seven in the morning, he sat with his back to the ironwork of the bridge, looking at his garden, the rhododendrons, the elder trees. The water in the nearer pool was now so clear that he could see his thin bearded face and gaunt figure reflected in its glassy surface and use it as a washbasin for splashing face and hands. He could wash the mug he used for drinking milk and wine and the knife that was his only utensil. But this domesticity brought home to him an unwelcome thought. Homelessness could not be artificially contrived but must come about through real need and real deprivation. And again he called himself a phony and a fake, one who had partaken of others' misery because it was *there* and available.

He should go now. He should move on. His reluctance to leave the home he had made—he would be rigging up curtains next, building partitions from cardboard boxes—brought him a wry amusement and taught him that he could be amused, he could even laugh. Hadn't he laughed with pure glee at the plight of the man, *her* boyfriend, he had sent off in the wrong direction?

If he left he could less easily keep an eye on her. She had her brother now, he had several times seen them together, her brother would protect her from the dark, red-faced pursuer. Perhaps, then, he would stay just a week longer. He knew where she lived and where she worked, that she had a little dog the old man in the baseball cap took out with the rest, that her brother visited her every day, that she was harassed by a dark-haired man with, to say the least, an aggressive manner. His daughter, he sometimes thought, might have grown up to look rather like her. Elizabeth had that same very slender fairness, the fairy face, that look of being often startled by events.

He remembered a camping holiday they had once had, he and Sally and Elizabeth. Daniel was not yet born. It had been in the Highlands, a place not in the least like this Grotto, this spoiled London garden, yet there had been a cave there and a little pool. Mountains soared beyond and there was a beach of silver sand on the loch. Elizabeth, with a child's passion for place, had wanted to stay there forever. It was impossible to make her understand that they had to go back, that livings had to be earned, the house maintained, she had to return to school. One night he had let her have her heart's desire and sleep, not in their tent or hired trailer, but in the cave itself. But anxious parent that he had been, he had worried and, unable to sleep, had moved himself into the mouth of this hole in the mountainside and mounted guard there all night.

Now he was doing the same thing in another place, for someone else. He closed his eyes and saw his daughter, his wife, his son, and though their faces were less clear than they had been, their identities remained, his eternal companions. And he thought, in a paraphrase, *forever wilt thou love and they be fair.* Time could not change them or take them away again and however he became reconciled, however able to find a kind of contentment—for he could feel contentment coming, closing in on him, like fate—they would never be lost or farther from him than now, nor would their lives be forgotten.

He wept for himself and them, sitting by the pool, his head on his knees, quiet accepting tears. Then he got up and stationed himself below the wall to see her when she came up the street and entered the park.

21

Y our father was a doctor," Leo said.
"And yours was a civil servant."
They were reading each other's birth certificates, sitting
in the registrar's drab foyer.

"That's a polite way of saying he worked behind the counter at
what was then the Labor Exchange."

"Mine was a GP, nothing grand." Mary found herself often reassuring him. She was bent on establishing an equality between them.
Leo, she saw, had been born in 1971 and she pointed out to him
bravely her own birth date of 1965. "You were only a baby when my
parents died."

The date of their own marriage was fixed for August 17, a Thursday. After the formalities were completed Mary asked Leo if his
brother would come to their wedding.

"I don't think so. He's not much of a one for weddings."

"We shall have to have two witnesses and he's an obvious one. I
thought I'd ask my cousin Judith and my friend Anne, and Dorothea and Gordon will come. Will you ask your brother?"

"If you want me to."

"And I should like to meet him first, Leo. Can I meet him?"

They sat down at a table outside a café in Marylebone High Street
and ordered coffee. Leo looked as if the long walk had been too
much for him and Mary made up her mind to take a taxi home. He
had rested his head back against the chair and now he closed his eyes
momentarily.

"Can I meet your brother, Leo?"

"Why do you want to?"

"Because he is your brother. I've hardly any relatives of my own."
He said nothing. She watched him ruefully, his tired face, his spent
look.

"Am I nagging you?" she said.

He touched her hand. "You couldn't nag anyone."

"It's just that you're so fond of your brother, you're always talking
about him. If he's such an important person in your life, won't he be
important in mine?"

The coffee came, black for her, a cappuccino for him. "When I'm
married I shall break with my brother," he said, and he looked away.
"I don't want you to meet him. There, I've said it. I don't want that."

"But you love him so much. He's done so much for you. I don't
understand, Leo."

Leo said stonily, "I loved him once. That's all in the past. He
won't come to our wedding."

.   .   .

On one of the hills of Kemptown in Brighton, Bean's sister owned a
small two-bedroom terrace house. From the back garden, if you
stood on a chair, you could see between two high-rise buildings a
segment of sea. Every August she went to stay with her ex-husband's
sister-in-law in the Peak District, and while she was away Bean
stayed in her house. Most years they didn't even meet. Not since
Maurice Clitheroe died had he spoken to her except, briefly, on the
phone. He made careful arrangements for his holiday. His clients
were assured, not once, but again and again, that he would be back
one week from his departure.

"I shall be in harness again on Friday the eleventh," he told them,
one after another.

Erna Morosini said she had seen a young woman exercising a
bunch of dogs. The woman always wore jodhpurs and had long

dark hair. She looked young and strong. Her name was Walker. Didn't Bean think that was funny, her being called Walker and walking dogs? Did Bean know anything about her? Did he think she would take on Ruby while he was away?

"Would you really entrust your much-loved beagle to her, madam?" Bean asked. "She obviously takes charge of far too many dogs. You can see they're out of control."

"Well, if you put it like that . . ."

Mrs. Goldsworthy caused him even more disquiet by telling him that the school-leaver who had taken on Barker-Pryce's Charlie would be exercising McBride "as a temporary measure."

"I can't do it. Not with my knee."

It was the first Bean had heard of Mrs. Goldsworthy's knee. Giggling and showing off her ribcage, Lisl Pring said she had made the perfect arrangement. She didn't need the exercise but her boyfriend did and he was going to ride his bicycle round the Outer Circle, dragging Marietta behind him.

Bean was shocked. "That's against the law, miss."

"The cops are going to bother about that, are they? When they've got this murderer to catch?"

Mrs. Sellers said she would simply go back to what she had been doing before Bean was engaged, walking the dalmatian herself. But she looked aggrieved. Perhaps she thought there should have been something in the references about him having holidays.

Lunchtime or late morning were good times to catch Barker-Pryce, before he went down to the House. Bean encountered the school-leaver on the doorstep, about to exercise Charlie. He had a low opinion of anyone who didn't take a dog out before noon and he gave the tall sixteen-year-old one of his looks, baring his teeth.

This time Barker-Pryce said absolutely nothing. He opened the door, stood aside to let Bean in, closed the front door, opened the door to the study, stood aside to let Bean in, closed the door. Where was his wife? His servant? The cleaner?

Bean had brought more photographs, but when offered them, Barker-Pryce shook his head in silence. He had the money ready, five twenty-pound notes in a stack on the desk next to the headed paper. Bean held out his hand and Barker-Pryce put the money into it, saying not a word. He opened the study door, stood back for Bean to go through, and left him to let himself out of the house. As he closed the front door Bean heard the rasp of a lighter struck by a thumb and the leap of a flame as a cigar was lit.

Dealing with The Beater would be less straightforward. Or so he believed. He had no knowledge of where The Beater lived nor of his real name and it was no use seeking him out where they had previously met, for that would defeat the purpose of his enterprise. He could of course wait for him in a likely place and make his demand, but as he walked back to York Terrace he asked himself whether it was necessary at this stage to do anything at all.

They had looked at each other and they had done so speechlessly. The silence, though, had been eloquent and Bean was certain each had read the other's mind. The Beater would know that he had taken in the whole situation and appreciated exactly what the position was. The Beater would need nothing put into words. He would be more silent than Barker-Pryce. Even now, at this moment, he would be thinking of everything Bean knew and just how disastrously Bean could ruin his life and his prospects if he chose.

Bean went home and opened all the windows. In weather like this he wished Maurice Clitheroe had installed air-conditioning before he died. He put a pack of frozen Bombay potatoes and another of pilau rice into the microwave and, tucking Barker-Pryce's hundred pounds into the suitcase he'd be taking away with him, thought that if he went on at this rate he'd soon be able to send out for stuff from Express Tikka and Pizza.

With BBC 1's *News at One* turned on, sipping at a can of diet Sprite, he started wondering about The Beater once more. It was becoming clear to him that he need do nothing. The Beater would seek him out. He knew where he lived, for he might well have expected to inherit Maurice Clitheroe's house himself and would have watched closely to see who would occupy it after Clitheroe's death.

The Beater might come at any time.

This thought was vaguely unpleasant. Seated in the very room where so many unsavory happenings had taken place, Bean seemed to hear again his employer's screams, the swish of the switch and slap of the cane. The Beater was not only an accomplished actor but strong, too. Thinness didn't mean much, it was the muscles that counted. Bean fancied he would be quite ruthless. It might be wise not to let him into the house but to suggest, for instance, that they meet in a pub or even talk in the street.

He would do that. When The Beater surfaced—and Bean was sure now that this would happen before his departure for Brighton on Saturday—he would be prepared, leave nothing to chance, above all, never be alone with The Beater where there were no other people, no lights, no life.

He set off as usual at a quarter to four. Ruby didn't want to be walked and dragged her feet all the way up Portland Place, only showing some interest in life when they came to the parking meter with which she conducted a desultory love affair. Passing the Cornells' former home, Bean saw that the Venetian blinds were pulled down at all the windows and three black plastic bags of rubbish had been left in the area. A stink of something spicy and decaying wafted up to the pavement.

The afternoon was hot and he was wearing his red baseball cap with the perforated crown, his jeans, and a short-sleeved T-shirt with a herd of elephants marching across it, but he was sweating. When he was in Brighton he might invest in a pair of shorts. More and more people were wearing them, even men of his age. Into the gardens of Park Crescent where the lawns, green and springy the previous week, were fast drying and turning yellow. Ideally, he ought to find another dog in this area so that he didn't have to walk the solitary one on her own all the way from Devonshire Street to Park Square. That prompted him to ask Mrs. Sellers if she knew of anyone, but she stared vaguely at him as if she didn't know what he was talking about. Spots started panting as soon as they were out in the street.

A hot wind blew the trees and raised litter on dust clouds. McBride came sleepily out of the house in Albany Street, disinclined to walk, stopping every thirty seconds to scratch himself, but Marietta was quite sprightly, her chocolate skin looking as if it had been shaved, and perhaps it had. He didn't even have to ask Lisl Pring.

She seemed to have forgotten his reproof or never to have taken it in. She said she'd just had a phone call from a friend who'd been ill. The friend had a lively young spaniel and was at her wits' end to know how to get it exercised.

"Where would she be living, miss, this friend of yours?" Bean said. "Not too far away, I hope."

"I'll have to think. I mean, I've never been to her place. Gloucester Avenue? Or was it Gloucester Place? Same difference, you know what I mean."

Bean didn't. He thought there was all the difference in the world, about half a mile's difference.

"I don't mind asking her to give you a ring."

"Thank you very much indeed, miss," said Bean, but she didn't notice the sarcasm. She wouldn't.

Miss Jago was out at work. He let himself into Charlotte Cottage and, with Gushi running about him, jumping up his legs, had a quick look round. A postcard from Lady Blackburn-Norris, all about the weather in some far-off place and saying nothing of interest, a bunch of junk mail, fliers from a dry cleaner. Bean tucked Gushi under his arm and went out, back to the other dogs.

Once in the park, he took a photograph of Spots and McBride, looking sweet side by side. A beggar materialized from nowhere, the way they did, an oldish man with brown teeth and stubble on his face. He held out a hand that was more like one of those toadstools that grow on tree trunks than part of a human being.

"Change for a cup of tea, guv?"

"Bugger off," said Bean. He'd have liked to kill them all. Whatever they said about that Impaler, his was a mentality he could understand.

. . .

It was the hottest day of the year. No one would have chosen to walk across the open center of the park, treeless and exposed to the heat of that sun. Walking home, she kept to the shady Outer Circle. Two men were running on the oval track by the Primrose Hill Bridge but they were dark-skinned and perhaps interpreted the heat as pleasant warmth. She crossed the Circle at the Gloucester Gate and glanced down over the low wall. The man with the beard was lying asleep on a groundsheet spread between the two round shallow pools, a book open and face-down beside him, a bottle of something standing in the water to keep it cool.

Next time they encountered each other, should she give him money? She had always given to beggars, but since her accession of wealth she had carried five- and ten-pound notes to distribute. Was he the kind of man who would welcome alms? He seemed to be sleeping in total peace, as if he had no cares, or had discovered some secret of life. She walked home and she must have been early, for Gushi was still out.

He trotted in, clearly affected by the heat, five minutes afterward. Bean's face was glistening and beaded with sweat. He was an old man to be walking so far in temperatures in the upper eighties. She paid him for his week's dog-walking. Gushi in the kitchen noisily lapped water. Mary went with Bean to the gate and was introduced to the dalmatian, a docile dog who licked her hand.

"A member of the company due to your good offices, miss," said

Bean. "Your reference went down a treat with Mrs. Sellers."

His obsequious manner always embarrassed her. But now it was accompanied by the kind of leer only to be expected from a much younger man. He looked her up and down, as if making some kind of assessment or calculation. She went quickly into the house.

It was too hot to eat, or too hot for human beings. Gushi had recovered enough to wolf down a can of Cesar and she picked at bread and cheese and salad. When the time came to leave she would miss the little dog. Perhaps she and Leo could have a shih tzu of their own. She wrote a letter to Judith in Guildford, inviting her to the wedding, and another to Anne Symonds, who had been at college with her; and then with Gushi on the lead she went out to post her letters.

The pillar box on the corner was out of use, the two slots sealed up. The only other one she knew of was under the main arch of Cumberland Terrace. It was still very warm at nearly nine, the kind of evening that comes only after a day of exceptional heat. A few days before, in a sudden high wind, there had been a premature falling of leaves, plane leaves turning yellow and dropping onto the pavements. Or perhaps it was not premature but a normal happening that occurred always at this time of the year, an early warning of autumn. The leaves, dried and shriveled, crackled under her feet. She walked through the passage at the Cumberland Terrace.

A haze hung over the park, soft and mysterious. The trees had become purplish-gray shapes, utterly still. The air smelled of diesel and lavender, a curious combination. Few people were about. They would all be at café tables on pavements, in the gardens of pubs. She posted her letters, watched the locking of the park gates. The park police went in, it was said, and rounded up the dossers who tried to spend the night in the shelter of the restaurants and pavilions, but some always escaped their vigilance, sleeping among the bushes or under the lee of the zoo. That reminded her of the man she had seen asleep that afternoon, and carrying Gushi now—"You are just a baby," she murmured into his fur—she made her way back into Albany Street at the Gloucester Bridge.

Mosquitos danced in swarms above the water of the pools. The air was crowded with wheeling insects, moths with dusty wings, gnats, blue flies. They seemed not to bother him. He sat among the rocks, resting on a rolled-up sleeping bag, reading his book. It came back to her that once, to herself, she had called him Nikolai, because she had seen him reading Gogol. When he saw her he got up, just as a man might when a woman comes into the room.

"Good evening," she said.

He smiled. "Good evening."

It was an opportunity. He had come a little way up the slope and was looking at her with what she interpreted as concern, though it couldn't be. She could go down there and sit with him and talk. But what about and why? It was an absurd idea. Besides, Leo was coming, would be there in ten minutes. Even more absurd was what she said, in the light of what she had just said.

"Good night."

He nodded, as if confirming something he had suspected. He had very blue eyes, intelligent and kind.

"Good night," he said.

She remembered as she walked away that she had intended to give him money, but she had had none on her and now, anyway, it seemed an absurd idea, insensitive and wrong.

•   •   •

It was a man's voice on the phone and somehow he had expected a woman. Well, he hadn't really expected ever to hear another word about it. Not from that Lisl Pring, that butterfly brain. The funny thing was that he'd been watching her on television. *Eastenders* was a favorite program of his and he never missed an episode. Lisl Pring had been doing her stuff, looking quite different from in the flesh, if that was the term for someone as bony as she, looking fatter for one thing, quite well-covered and shapely, and the credit titles were coming up, when the phone rang. If the program hadn't been more or less over he wouldn't have answered it.

The voice said what its owner was called, or he supposed it did, and then something about a dog.

"Are you a friend of Miss Pring?" he had said because he hadn't caught the name.

"I just said. It's really urgent. I'd like to see you as soon as possible."

Bean hadn't cared for the tone. "I shall want to see *you,*" he had said, "and the dog. I'm not sure I'm prepared to take on a lively young spaniel. It *is* a spaniel, right, and a puppy?"

"Not a puppy. He's two years old and he's been to dog-training with me."

"Well, I'll see," Bean said grudgingly. "She said Gloucester Avenue." Or had she said Gloucester Terrace? "That's seriously out of my way, you know."

"As a matter of fact, it's Gloucester Place, the top end."

Maybe the top end wouldn't be so bad. He was starting to say so, not sounding too enthusiastic, when the voice said, "But I'm moving. I'm moving to Upper Harley Street in a month's time."

Just exactly where he wanted another dog, halfway between Ruby and Spots.

"I could look in tomorrow," Bean said. "About this time tomorrow?"

"Make it half an hour later."

He'd enjoy himself all the more in Brighton if he knew he'd got six dogs to come back to. Six was a good round number, a number he should make a point of sticking with.

"Say nine o'clock then?"

"Nine will do very well."

Bean switched off the television and went back to his packing. He always packed a little bit every night for a week before he went away and so made sure of not forgetting anything. But he left out the red baseball cap and the elephant T-shirt. He'd travel in those.

nother job for the old dog man. Putting it like that made
Hob laugh. It didn't take much to make him laugh these
days. And this would be the biggest job ever. The money
on offer made him feel dizzy just to contemplate it. He saw it as putting an end forever to all states, with such a huge sum states could be
kept at bay indefinitely, he would always be as he had until now
hardly ever been, the happy dancing joker, the Power Ranger, the
laid-back man, the laughing man.

He'd come down very low, waited outside the women's toilet at
Chester Road and when he'd seen a woman go in and had made sure
she was alone in there, gone after her, found her washing her hands.
While she screamed he'd taken her handbag. Seventy pounds in
cash. Everything else he'd left in the bag, and he'd left the bag on one
of the seats so she'd be sure to find it. Coming home, the cash con-
verted into crack, he'd unlocked his front door and stumbled into
the hot darkness. Strips of light lay across the floorboards looking as
if someone had drawn on them with orange chalk. At first he hadn't
seen the note. It was a folded piece of paper, lying on the floor just
inside the front door. An envelope was with it. Hob wasn't much
good at reading. Somehow he'd never got the hang of it and he was
worse when in a state, as now. The note and the envelope on the
floor beside him, he crumbled up one of his rocks and dropped it
through the mouth of the watering can rose, then came the cap, the
straws, the tin lid, finally the lighter applied to the perforations. He
breathed in, a long hauling breath, as if his lungs were engines for

dragging and tugging. The smoke in his windpipe felt like the first time he'd tasted ice cream.

Happy as the day is long, he was at his reading best. The envelope had a letter in it from the council, something about putting new windows in at nine A.M. on the fifteenth and to be sure to be in to admit the operatives. Or that's what he thought it said. The note was from Carl, harder to read because it was in handwriting. He was to go up that evening and Carl might have something for him.

It was a long time since Hob had seen either Carl or Leo. He thought Leo had left and he wouldn't have been surprised if Carl had gone too, though where he couldn't begin to guess. No doubt he came back from time to time. Leo was going to die, you didn't have to be a doctor or have Carl's brains to know that. Hob got up and did a little dance, punched the air, sang one of his mum's nan's funny old songs, and then he sang "I'll Be Your Sweetheart" and "Night Train to Memphis" because he wasn't going to die, whatever might happen to Leo. The mice must sleep in the daytime. He pictured them asleep behind the skirting board, looking like Jerry in the Tom and Jerry cartoon, or Mickey Mouse on his cushions, but furry and soft too. Maybe there were hundreds of them, curled up and cuddling each other. All that boarding up made the place airless, but the kitchen smelled fresher than the rest of the flat. He took two Weetabix out of the packet and crumbled them up on the living room floor in front of the telly. The crumbling made him giggle because maybe the Weetabix was for the mice like crack was for him. Then he went upstairs.

It would have been too much to expect the lift to be working still. It wasn't. The stairs were nothing to him when he was well and he pranced lightly up the seven flights, making a noise about it presumably, because Carl must have heard him. He was standing there, holding the door open, looking as miserable as sin and his face as pale as Leo's.

"How's Leo doing, then?" Hob said, which he never would have if he hadn't been fit and raring to go.

Carl didn't answer, just shrugged and looked away. "I'm going out," he said. "This won't take long. You can make two K out of it, which is the entire extent of my resources, all I've got till the week after next, rather."

"Two *K*? You mean, two *grand*?"

"It's no use haggling because, as I said, it's all I've got."

"I'm not haggling," said Hob.

"And five hundred grams of E, so long as you'll take the yellows."

"That's fine by me, Carl."

. . .

Sweat was pouring off him. The medical book he'd been reading told him your sweat didn't smell so much when you got older, but Bean wasn't taking any chances. He'd had a horror of it all his life, but his repugnance had increased after those beating sessions and the house was filled with the meaty, oniony stench, the result of wildly expended energy.

He had a shower, his second of the day, sprayed himself with deodorant, and put on clean clothes, nicely pressed jeans, the elephant T-shirt, and his red baseball cap. The T-shirt he'd give a quick rinse to when he got back and it would be dry by the morning, ready for the train.

They closed the park at nine in August. That would just about allow him to walk to the top of Gloucester Place by way of the lake and the Kent Gate. He left home at eight-thirty. It was as warm and as humid as Florida, thought Bean, who had never been there.

The other route would have been shorter but there would have been all those roads to cross and all that traffic. The park was peaceful and quiet, the lake glassy and the air thickening. When he looked up, the darkening blue of the sky was fading under a veil of mist. A moon had risen, a pale oval, blurred and fuzzy, like the corpse of something that had long lain in muddy water.

All the birds had gone to roost. From a distance a black swan, sleeping on one leg with the other and its neck tucked into the plumage of its back, looked like a monstrous mushroom. Green- and chestnut-feathered ducks curled themselves up into silk cushions at the water's edge. But the coming dusk was robbing everything of color, the grass turning gray, the water like black glass, the trees shapes and shadows rather than living things.

A beggar wandered toward him. He fancied it was the one who had asked him for money the day before, but now that there was no one else about, they were alone, passing each other on the lake path, Bean looked the other way, pretending not to see him. You could never tell these days who would turn out violent. Most vehicles were banned from the park, but a Royal Parks Constabulary police car went slowly past, the kind they called a lettuce sandwich because it was white with a dark green and light green stripe along its side.

To the left of him the Turkish domes of Sussex Place gleamed like an encampment of tents at dawn. The boats were all tied up to the island in the middle of the Hanover pond, bobbing gently on the water. He glanced up that way because he could never pass it without remembering Mussolini, so when he turned back and began to cross the grass toward the gate and saw Mussolini approaching him under the trees, he refused to believe his eyes. He actually rubbed his eyes, as if stimulating them to see straight.

It was as if Mussolini had been waiting for him. He wasn't going anywhere, he'd just been standing there, what the police called loitering. Bean could see the street lamps in the Outer Circle. There were people walking up there, traffic heading up to the Macclesfield Bridge. He turned his eyes on Mussolini, making out his pudgy features, skinny body, and filthy old clothes in the warm gloom.

"You took your time," Bean said.

Mussolini was wrapped up for such a hot night, wearing the sort of layers, dark matted rags, favored by the beggars. He was chewing something and Bean didn't think it was gum.

Whatever it was, he eased it into the corner of his mouth, pushing it with his tongue.

"You was late," he said. "You dropped me in the shit."

"That may be, but it's you that's too late now. The job I wanted, someone else did it. And a bit more thoroughly than what I bargained for."

"Could be another job," said Mussolini. "There's always jobs folks want doing."

Bean shrugged. He had lingered for a moment, but now he began walking on toward the gate, a wide gate with maybe twenty-five spikes on its railings. Mussolini had got into step beside him and Bean was quickly aware of his smell. Not the cooking smell of fresh sweat but of dirt ingrained, unwashed clothes, the excrement of vermin, the acrid coldness of chemicals. He tried to draw himself aside, but Mussolini was close now, his head bent down to Bean's lesser height, peering at Bean's chest.

"Dig your elephants," he said, and then he said, "Jumbo, jumbo," and started laughing. "Jumbo, jumbo."

His laughter made an eerie manic sound in the silence of the park.

23

Park Road runs northward on the western side of the park from the top of Baker Street to the junction of St. John's Wood Road and Prince Albert Road and communicates with the Outer Circle by means of the Hanover Gate and Kent Passage. The London Mosque is in Park Road. So are the Rudolph Steiner House, a defunct pub called the Windsor Castle, Dillon's Business Bookshop, and a number of Indian restaurants. There are sandwich bars and a wine bar and a fur shop where no one ever seems to buy anything.

The bookshop is so situated for its proximity to the London School of Business Studies, a graduate school housed in Decimus Burton's most spectacular of all the park terraces, at Sussex Place. This is on the Outer Circle, an amazing range of Corinthian columns, polygonal bays, and cuboid domes, so light and airy that they might be tents of silk rather than towers of stone. Graduate students in need of books need not walk all the way down to Baker Street and up Park Road to reach the shop but may turn left out of the terrace and find the opening to an alley called Kent Passage.

The passage is narrow and long and absolutely straight, tree-shaded and confined by high hedges behind chain-link fencing, not railings. On the southern side it is overshadowed by the pale brick walls of the Royal College of Obstetricians and Gynecologists. The trees and shrubs that grow along its length are planes and sumacs, snowberries and the rose of Sharon. Near the Park Road end the passage opens out into an oval shape, closes again, and the pavement of the wider thoroughfare is reached. The bookshop is a few paces to the left while on the right lies the Kent Terrace.

This is the only terrace not to face onto the Outer Circle, a plain range of buildings with Ionic columns. Anthony Maddox once told Bean that the terrace had been built in 1827 and named for George IV's brother, the Duke of Kent, but the duke, as well as being the parent of the heir presumptive to the throne, was long dead by then, so there was no need for too much grandeur or originality. Bean thought this was said spitefully, for his resemblance to the duke's statue had already been pointed out, but he never passed the terrace without thinking of what had been said and wondering if malice was intended.

Kent Terrace, however, has one peculiarity. As well as the usual black iron railings, a feature of the place is the spikes adorning the top of the pillars in its grounds.

A pair of these pillars flanks the gate that leads into Kent Passage and the steps down into Kent Passage. These are man-height, cuboid and very solid, and from the tops of both sprout five iron branches in a cluster, each one terminating in five spikes. They look rather like bunches of thorn twigs, but ugly and menacing too, and it would be hard to say what purpose they were intended for or what was in the designer's mind.

A man's body was impaled on these iron thorns.

It was so arranged as to be invisible from Kent Passage unless you happened to be looking at the sky, and visible from the terrace only if you peered behind the pillar. Besides, a heavy mist had hung over the park and its environs since dawn, obscuring even those objects that were near at hand in swathes of white vapor.

The body was supported in its position by the splayed spikes penetrating its chest, head lolling forward, arms dangling, legs hanging. Barefoot, dressed in jeans with ragged hems and missing knees, torn gray T-shirt with washed-out black logo and a dark red cardigan that was stiff with foodstains and blood, it had once been a smallish man. The legs and arms were thin, the white feet pathetic. No doubt its total weight amounted to no more than 130 pounds. Even so, to lift it up so high must have taken considerable strength.

A great many people passed it during the morning. None of them looked up to the height of the pillar. Even after the mist had gone and the sun came out, the body was not discovered until noon. A police officer on the beat entered the passage from the Outer Circle. First he had walked round the pond where the pleasure boats were moored, crossed the yellowing balding grass, and had left the park by the Hanover Gate. His eye had been on a dosser in camouflage pants and gray vest who was fumbling in a litter bin suspiciously close to a parked car whose windows had been left open.

The policeman lingered, watching until the dosser, having found the remains of a take-away in the bin, shambled off northward toward the Macclesfield Bridge. Then he stepped into the passage and strolled slowly along it. Someone shook a duster out of one of the high windows in the building on the left. The passage was in deep shade for three-quarters of its length and there the sun came through the leaves, making a dappled pattern, before there were no more leaves but only a sunlit space.

Onto this space fell a shadow.

It was like a crab or part of a crab or perhaps it was like a paw, the extended limb of a frog. He looked up. The body hung like a sack in clothes or a guy, limp and slack, and its hanging hand had a trail of blood dried between the fingers.

24

Dill and the beagle were sitting on one of the seats on the southwest side of the lake, watching an old woman in a tracksuit feeding the geese. There were not so many geese as a year ago and the story was that the street sleepers were catching them to kill and roast over fires on the canal bank. Dill always talked to the beagle as if it were a person. He said that much as he'd like to taste roast goose, for he never had tasted it, he wouldn't know how to go about catching a goose, let alone killing it. And how would you get the feathers out? And the innards? He was talking like this about a goose to stop himself shaking with fear about the dead man.

The beagle's tail started to wag, thumping on the slats of the seat. Roman patted its head, stroked it, sat down next to Dill and Dill told him the goose story just as he had told it to the beagle a moment before. But it no longer had the power to stop Dill shivering.

"What's wrong?" Roman said. "There's been another, hasn't there? Is that it?"

"The fuzz had me in, mate. They had me look at him."

"To identify him?"

Dill nodded. He held on to the beagle's collar to steady his hands. "They said they'd seen me with him but they never had." He looked up, turning his head in a crooked cautious way. His Oriental eyes were puffy as if he had been crying.

"They was okay," he said. "They didn't hurt me."

"What happened?"

"I went in this place." He wrinkled up his nose. "There was this geezer lifted up a sheet and showed me what was under. It was just a dead face, mate, you couldn't see no cuts. I didn't know him, I'd never seen him before. They said was I sure and then the geezer put the sheet back. They was okay. There was one geezer give the beagle a bun."

"Maybe it was one of the jacks men," said Roman.

"I don't reckon. I don't know what to think, mate. I reckoned I knew every geezer up here. You ever seen a dead person, Rome?"

"My mother." Sally and his children, but he didn't mention them. Daniel's face had been cut to pieces. "I saw my mother."

"Do they always look like they're made of wax? Like they've never been alive?"

"I don't know. You're sleeping at St. Anthony's, aren't you, Dill?"

"They won't let me take the beagle. What am I supposed to do about the beagle?"

Roman walked on toward the Clarence Gate. The flowerbeds and the grass here were covered in a soft gray quilt of goose down. Goose feathers floated onto the petals of flowers. He bought a paper at a newsagent's at the top of Baker Street. The front page and four inside pages were devoted to the murder and the two previous murders. On the front page was a four-column-spread photograph of a stretch of railings, purporting to be but perhaps not those on which the body had been found, black spiked railings with grass behind and trees shapeless in the thinning mist. Inside were more photographs, Cahill's and Clancy's, more pictures of park railings, and one of a group of jacks men sitting or standing about on the canal bank.

The body was understood to be that of a man in "late middle age," whatever that meant, of no fixed address. He had not yet been identified. The pockets of his jeans and cardigan were empty. His feet had been bare. The police wanted help from the public in their inquiries. . . .

Roman decided not to go away this time. He would stay and sooner or later they would question him. They would question every dosser in the vicinity of the park, in the whole of London probably. He would stay, do his best to answer their questions, be a good citizen. It was all part of the way his life was changing, turning back on itself, turning him back into something like what he once was.

. . .

Blue and white tape printed with the words "Police Do Not Cross" made a flimsy but deterrent boundary around the sturdy column and its crest of spikes. Kent Terrace looked livelier than usual, most of its windows wide open and from time to time heads poking out. But if there had ever been a crowd waiting and hoping for new sights as when Pharaoh's body was found, there was none here. A uniformed policeman strolled about on the forecourt.

In Park Road the traffic kept up its customary steady roar. Veiled women, men in pairs, snowy-shirted, chatting animatedly to each other, never to the women, made their way up to the mosque. Roman had come up there because he was interested by descriptions of the column he kept hearing about but which he had never yet seen.

A dark trickle, the color of burnt umber, ran tearlike down the cream stucco from the roots of the spikes.

"It's not what you're thinking," the policeman said. "It's rust."

"Some strength was needed to hoist a body up there. Was he on the top?"

"It's all been in the papers, mate," said the policeman, and he turned away, discreet or perhaps only bored.

The next day, by chance, they asked him to come to the police station and talked to him exhaustively about the inhabitants of the park environs, growing more and more mystified, he thought, by his manner and his accent.

When they asked him if he would accompany them to the mortuary and attempt to identify the latest murder victim, he said, "Certainly. If you wish it."

The sergeant—he didn't merit an officer of higher rank—gave him a look and the detective constable with him a look, and if he didn't quite cast up his eyes he sketched the gesture. Roman was taken to the mortuary by car. He could tell the two policemen expected him to smell, were all prepared to go through pantomimes of flinching, shifting their seats and opening windows, and when they found him inoffensive were almost disappointed.

The body was in a sort of drawer with a green sheet covering it. Roman remembered what Dill had said about waxiness. He thought of carvings he had seen out of soapstone or white jade. The face could have belonged to a man of any age over, say, forty. It was somewhat Hanoverian with small mouth and full cheeks, and although he could not identify it, he thought he had seen this man somewhere before.

That was all he could tell the sergeant.

"You know him but you don't know who he is?"

"I wouldn't say I knew him, but I've seen him before."

"Where would that be?"

"In the park, I expect. I spend my life in the park."

The sergeant finally asked him what a man like him was doing on the street.

"I prefer it," Roman said, not wanting to go into the events of his private life. "It suits me."

"Some sort of eccentric, are you?"

"Perhaps."

He resisted asking permission to go but sat in the open-plan office waiting while the sergeant fiddled with papers, giving him from time to time meaningful looks. Once, in such a place, Roman would have been tense and self-conscious, searching his mind for minor motoring offenses he might have committed, but now he felt nothing beyond a mild boredom.

The sergeant said, "That's it, then. You can go," and he added, perhaps unable to resist, "You want to get yourself together, pull your socks up, put a roof over your head. The street's no place for your sort, as you must know."

Roman nodded. He walked out and no one tried to stop him. The Grotto, where he returned, had been scoured clean of litter by the police. They had done a better job than he had ever been able to do, taking away every scrap of paper and shred of rag in their search for evidence. His barrow had gone, stolen probably, not taken by them.

It was hot and close, the abode of flying insects. They swarmed above the pool in which the water was no longer clear and fresh but coated in scum. He sat down on the dry ground in the dusty shade. Soon he would have to go out, up into Camden Town, and replace the contents of the barrow. Buy secondhand clothes, another groundsheet, more blankets, a water bottle, and a host of other things. It seemed to him a foolish exercise, absurd, because he *could* buy them, he could within reason buy anything he wanted.

The sergeant's comments only reiterated what he had himself been thinking. What he had done had served its purpose but had now become artificial, a quixotic slumming, and to continue it was self-indulgence.

The real courage would lie in returning to the world.

. . .

Leo spent every evening with her but not the nights. He gave as his reason the one they had used before, that Charlotte Cottage was the Blackburn-Norrises' home. So in the mornings she was alone and she took Gushi out alone. He missed his companions and, spoiled baby that he was, often plumped down on the grass like a cushion of chrysanthemums and refused to move. She carried him home, a furry muff in the August heat.

But in the evenings, when Leo came, they walked him together. Leo's mood alternated between a kind of sorrowful brooding and an almost manic brightness. He was going to turn these obligatory walks into adventures, he said, and announced his intention of running to earth Mrs. Sellers and Spots.

He even went up to one woman exercising a spotted dog of dubious provenance. "Did my fiancée give your dalmatian a reference?" he asked her.

She looked panic-stricken and backed away. Another dog owner, faced with the same inquiry, pointed toward the Inner Circle and asked Leo if he knew there was a police station down there. Mary was amused, then embarrassed. On their way back to Park Village she again asked him what was wrong. "Are you worried about getting married?"

"That's the last thing I'm worried about. Marrying you is what I want more than anything in the world."

"Then what is the first thing you're worried about?" she asked him gently.

"Death," he said and burst into shrill laughter.

Once they were inside the house he began kissing her. He kissed her mouth and her throat and, drawing open her shirt, kissed her breasts. She was not used to passion from Leo, rather to something more controlled and gentle, but she responded eagerly. It was as if this was what had always been missing between them.

He whispered, "Not upstairs, in here," and pulling her into the living room, kicked the door shut behind him.

Once before, in here, he had held her, both of them kneeling, and asked her to marry him. Now he began to make love to her as if it were the first time. Her whole body seemed to melt into a warm languid liquefaction. He was no longer light and phantomlike but strong and urgent, his mouth holding hers and his arms wound tightly round her. The phone ringing made her cry out in protest at a cruel interruption.

Leo cursed. "Leave it. Don't answer it."

She simply shook her head, unable to speak. The ringing went on interminably. They listened to it, stilled and motionless. When it stopped, Leo stroked her hair, her shoulders, turned her on her side, and entered her like that, a hand clasping each breast. She gave a clear cry of pleasure, arching her back as he let out a long sigh.

A little before ten he left her to go home to Primrose Hill. They had sat for the rest of the evening with their arms round each other, talking about the future, where they would live. His earlier wildness had been displaced by calm and, she thought, hope. After he had gone she took Gushi onto her lap and fondled him, doing her best not to resent the little dog whose presence stopped her returning with Leo. Bean would be back from his holiday and in the morning would be at the door as usual at eight-fifteen.

The phone rang again as she was watching ITN's ten-o'clock news. She turned off the television and picked up the receiver. Alistair's baritone sounded deeper and smoother than usual. The sound of it made her brace herself, her body tensing after the long relaxation of the evening.

"I phoned you earlier," he said and his tone was accusing, admonitory.

She and Leo had sometimes laughed together about those people who apparently expect you to be sitting close by the phone all day, waiting for their call. She decided not to placate him.

"Yes, I heard it ring. I didn't answer it. I was—occupied."

"Don't you think it rather irresponsible not to answer the phone? It could be something serious. It could be an accident to someone close to you."

"Now that my grandmother is dead," she said quietly, "I have no one close to me except Leo, and he was with me." It was true and her solitariness struck her forcibly as she said it. Dorothea and her cousin she was fond of, but really there was only Leo. She breathed in. "You got my letter, Alistair?"

"That, of course, is why I am phoning. At last, you might say. I've taken my time, haven't I? It was a blow, Mary, it was a heavy blow."

What could she say? Not that she was sorry, certainly not that. "Sooner or later there was bound to be someone. There will be for you."

He didn't like that. "In your case it was rather sooner than later, wasn't it? As to someone for me, as you put it in your romantic way, don't imagine I've been celibate since you left. I'm hardly that kind of man."

She didn't believe him. She didn't care. He made it impossible to resist some kind of apology. "I'm sorry if I've hurt you."

It was as if she hadn't spoken. "I had better get to my reason for phoning. You've rather distracted me from the point. As a civilized man, I wanted to congratulate you. I hope you'll be very happy."

"Thank you. That's very nice of you, Alistair."

"And to tell you that I've got something for you. A wedding present."

She was astonished. "You're giving me a wedding present?"

"Is that so strange? Didn't you say to me a few weeks ago before you so inexplicably ran away from me that in the time-honored cliché you hoped we could be friends?"

"Of course I hope that. I didn't think you wanted it."

"Mary," he said, "I have a wedding present for you. Don't tell me to send it, please. I want to put it into your hands."

She found herself passionately not wanting to see him, to have him come there, spoil her weekend with Leo. Just waiting for his arrival, fearing what he might do, would make her apprehensive for hours. She remembered that evening when Bean had arrived unexpectedly and before Leo answered the door she had assumed it was Alistair.

"Monday," she said reluctantly. "Would Monday be all right?" Not here, though. "Would you come to the museum on your way home from work? We could have tea or a drink."

"You won't run away from me again, will you?"

It was chilling the amount of venom he could put into those innocuous words. Her usual urge to be conciliatory came, departed, driven away by rising anger.

"I've said I'll meet you, Alistair. It will be the last time."

. . .

His barrow gone, the Grotto trampled by police and no longer a desirable home, Roman set off to find another place in which to spend the night. All his possessions were in a rucksack he had bought, blue plastic, very cheap, but still plainly new and costing money. Every step he now took seemed to be leading him inexorably back into the world.

Some people were having a party on one of the houseboats in Cumberland Basin. He paused on the bridge and looked down at them. They were young, one of the men was naked to the waist, a woman was holding up a frothing bottle of champagne, another had a guitar from which she plucked dull reverberating notes. A young girl, holding her glass out to be filled, saw him and waved. Nothing could have made him so certain that his shedding of the street was apparent.

St. Mark's Church in Albert Road on the fringe of Primrose Hill was a grim neo-Gothic place, the kind of building that made him wonder why the Victorians wanted to revive in their places of worship the creepy and sinister elements of medieval architecture. Its gate and its doors were painted sky blue, an incongruous color perhaps used to soften the grim effect. A garden rather than a graveyard surrounded it, a place of late-summer-blooming shrubs and fluff-headed thistles. He crossed the road over the water, for here the canal turned northward in its passage up to Camden Lock. The place where he stood was called the Water Meeting Bridge.

A green rectangle on the bridge contained a gold shield bearing the legend, WITH WISDOM AND COURAGE. These were qualities he needed and would have liked to have. And perhaps he had more of them now than ever in the past. On the parapet he looked along the

canal to the next bridge. Between the two bridges grass and weeds
reached to the edge of the towpath and the churchyard trees overhung it.

He turned into St. Mark's Square, then into Regent's Park Road
where the other bridge was. It was with a little thrill of dismay that
he noted the row of spiked railings at the chancel end of the church,
another set serving as balusters up the steps to what was perhaps a
vestry door. Someone had tied a bunch of colored balloons to one of
the spikes. There must have been a children's party. Thinking of
Daniel, who had liked balloons but hated the noise they made when
burst, he opened the gate into the garden and walked along the path.

White Japanese anemones gleamed in the dusk. The place was
alive with mosquitos and all those cousins of mosquitos that are
smaller but sometimes fiercer, midges, gnats. They danced on the
warm air. A bat swooped, then another. He remembered Sally's fear
of bats, her curious superstition, the only one she had, that bats had a
predilection to get in women's hair and bite their scalps. He didn't
mind bats but the mosquitos in their dense concentration would be
unbearable.

There were no gravestones. He wondered why not. Where they
might have been were green garden seats, enough to seat a dozen
people. Nothing lay below him but the trees and snowberry bushes
and long grass descending to meet the path and the dark yellow
water. Chain-link fencing made a formidable barrier between the
fringes of the garden and the canal bank, but it was climbable. He
scrambled over, his sights set on the other bridge, a sheltered place.
Street sleepers traditionally made their beds under bridges—wasn't
there a song about it? A Merle Haggard song about making a kingdom under the bridges?

He dropped down onto the path. It was starting to get dark, a
light up on the bridge reflected in the oily water. A tubular metal rail
offered some sort of security to those going too near the edge under
the bridge. The light gleamed on its silvery surfaces. He was only a

few yards away when he saw that the area under the brown brickwork already had an occupant. Street people, no matter what they
wear, or what they started off wearing, always seem to be dressed in
darkness. They are blackened, everything muted by time and dirt to
the color of shadows, so that when seen from a distance a group of
them look like figures in bronze.

In his early days on the street, Roman had been no different, and
this man was no different. He was an incarnation of dirt, a bundling
and layering on this warm night of dark greasy rags, string-tied, his
skin much the same color as the shred of cloth round his neck, as his
cracked boots. His face peered out from between the knotted neck-
cloth and his battered hat, a face dark as a black man's but sickle-
shaped in profile, with a long hooked nose and rough pitted skin.

He might have spoken when he saw Roman, he might have recognized him as belonging to the same kind, but he didn't. Roman
was very aware in that moment of his own cleanness, his washed
clothes, some replaced and new, his new backpack. He wanted to
laugh when the man under the bridge scowled at him and made a
gesture of dismissal, shaking his fist. What did he think he was?
Some tourist who had lost his way? But he understood. He looked
like that tourist, he had indeed lost his way, and now had only the
tourist's recourse.

"Okay," he said. "I won't disturb you. Good night."

It was the final sign. He climbed up the bank again, over the fence
into the churchyard, left by the blue gate, and set off to walk up to
Camden Town where, in his new respectable guise, one of the cheap
hotels would give him a bed for the night.

25

When it was eight-thirty and still Bean hadn't come, she took Gushi into the park herself. It was already very warm. The grass was soaked and beaded with dew. Not a breath of wind stirred the trees, their foliage pendulous and dripping off the branches as if composed of some thick viscous fluid. The sun that was turning lawns and flowerbeds and greensward into a desert laid a burning skin on her arms and face.

She walked across the Broad Walk, past the restaurant and over the Long Bridge. Gnats had begun their dance above the scummy brown water. Once, when she first came here, the uneven juxtaposition of the Outer and Inner Circles had confused her and she had been inclined to lose herself in the flower gardens. But now she could have drawn a plan of the park with her eyes shut. She turned left along the path opposite the back of the theater, meeting and passing a woman she had never seen before but whose dog Gushi evidently knew well.

The scottie and he encountered each other nose to nose, tails wagging, then noses were inserted under tails. The two of them began a play fight, growling, rolling over in the grass. The woman turned back, smiling tentatively. Mary remembered that she had seen this jaunty little black dog among the others tied to the gatepost of Charlotte Cottage.

The woman didn't introduce herself even when Mary said who she was. "That bloody Bean has let us all down again."

"I thought perhaps I'd got the date wrong," Mary said.

"Oh, no. He was due this morning. Too nice down by the seaside, I expect. He'll be back tomorrow with his tail between his legs."

The metaphor was so unconsciously appropriate that Mary wanted to giggle, but she controlled herself. She called Gushi, eventually had to drag him away, and passed on along the path without learning McBride's owner's name. Back in the park, on her way to the Irene Adler, it was far hotter. The blue sky was already whitening and the air was thick with humidity. The zoo animals she passed seemed to feel the heat no more than the cold but to lumber and munch placidly, bent solely on the getting of food. Up in Albert Road there was a smell of diesel and exhaust, a hot bitter stench. She could see a bevy of street people stretched out on the grass in the church gardens. They could have been taken for sunbathers except for the rags that still covered every inch of them but for stricken faces and coarsened hands.

Dorothea said to take the whole of next week off—why not? Gordon would take over. She should have a whole free week for her wedding. But Mary remembered that Alistair was coming on Monday to bring his mysterious wedding present and she could see that changing this arrangement might lead to terrible difficulties. And she didn't exactly have a lot of preparation to make for the wedding anyway. So she said she would take from Wednesday morning off if that was all right with Dorothea and Gordon.

"Go home early this afternoon then," Dorothea said. "Nobody's going to come looking at corsets and crinolines on a day like this."

And remarkably few did. Mary was home again by four, in time for Bean's arrival at a quarter past. But again Bean didn't come. She waited for half an hour and then she dialed his number in York Terrace. No reply. Leo arrived just after five and they sat outside in the shade, drinking tea and then sharing a bottle of wine. The garden was full of brown and orange butterflies and little coppery-winged moths. Gushi lay under a lilac bush, puffing showily, his tongue hanging out.

Leo remembered the name of Spots's owner and they found her in the phone book. But Mrs. Sellers hadn't seen Bean for a week or heard from him. Mary and Leo took Gushi out themselves when it was cooler, though it was not very cool. As they walked back, arms round each other's waists, he asked her to come back to Edis Street with him for the night. But if she did that she wouldn't be here for Bean in the morning, and she was sure Bean would be here in the morning. Leo didn't argue. He kissed her and said he would be back in Charlotte Cottage before she woke up. He would come quietly into the house and if she would like that, to bed with her.

"I'd like that," she said, smiling.

She overslept. She was lying sleepily in Leo's arms, having made leisurely, half-awake love with him, their bodies naked and damp, cooled by sweat, when at last she looked at the clock. It was almost nine.

Bean hadn't come. He had a way of thrusting his fist at the bell and pushing with all his body weight behind it, keeping it there until someone answered. She would have heard. He would have seen to it that she had heard.

She put on a robe and went downstairs. Leo had picked the post up from the doormat when he came in and left it on the hall table for her. The letter postmarked Cape Cod was from the Blackburn-Norrises and announced their return rather earlier than expected. They would arrive back in London on August 19.

She made Leo tea, took it up, and showed him the letter.

"The order of release."

"I thought it might be," Leo said. "You can come and live with your husband a mere two days after we're married."

For an hour or so it distracted her from the problem of Bean. But at ten-thirty she phoned Mrs. Sellers, who hadn't seen him, and then,

using the number Mrs. Sellers gave her, she phoned the actress Lisl
Pring. Lisl wasn't just annoyed, she was worried. The chocolate poodle Marietta was all right, Lisl's boyfriend took her out twice a day
trotting behind his bicycle. It was doing wonders for his figure and
he didn't mind how long it went on. But what had happened to
Bean? He would never absent himself like this unless he was at
death's door. She gave Mary the names of Bean's other clients.

Mary and Leo took Gushi out. It was too hot to go far. Gushi
drank nearly a pint of water when he got back and returned to lie
under the lilac bush. After she had called Express Tikka and ordered a thali each for their lunch with pickles and naan, she phoned
Erna Morosini.

No, it wasn't she that Mary had encountered in the park the previous morning. Her dog wasn't a scottie.

"Mine's the sexy beagle," said Mrs. Morosini. "You must know
the one. My partner says I ought to have her doctored but I'm still
hoping for pups one day."

"Bean—" Mary began, but Mrs Morosini cut her short.

"Oh, yes, he's disappeared, hasn't he? He left me his Brighton
number, I insisted, and I've called it and talked to his sister. She
hasn't seen hair nor hide of him. Well, she only came back herself
yesterday, but there's not a sniff of him in the place."

As if Bean were a terrier that had turned himself into a stray, as if
he had run off and would turn up without his collar and with his ear
bleeding.

Their lunch came just before one, brought in the red and white
van by the man who had removed his chef's hat and was wearing
nothing but shorts and a red and white vest. Their thalis were eaten
outside in the shade of the laburnam and the Japanese cherry and all
was peaceful until Leo produced their dessert of raspberries and nec-
tarines. Then wasps drove them indoors. They put Gushi in the
coolest place, on a windowseat in the north-facing bedroom. Mary
hadn't asked how they should spend the afternoon but Leo antici-

pated the question. He pulled her down onto the bed.

"Let's not go downstairs again."

. . .

When the gates had been open only for an hour and before the heat mounted, they took the dog into the park. A marathon was being run. Round the Outer Circle, in at Chester Road, round a segment of the Inner Circle, out at York Bridge, and round the Outer Circle again. Then repeat—twice? Three times? The runners were all male, all thin, their faces contorted with effort or agony. Their T-shirts, clinging to bony chests, were as wet as when taken dripping from the wash.

Leo said they made him feel tired. They made him feel ill.

She looked anxiously into his face. "You're all right, aren't you? All this walking isn't too much for you?"

"It's vicarious," he laughed. "I'm feeling it for *them*."

But as they walked back, arms round each other, hip to hip, she thought back to the transplant and had the strange feeling that it was ongoing, continuous, that when they were together like this or in bed side by side, the flow of strength from her still proceeded into him, like an injection of some serum into a permanently open vein. She leaned across and kissed his cheek and felt the arm around her tighten and his hand caress her waist.

"If Bean comes now we shall have to send him away empty-handed," Leo said when they were back in the house and Gushi was stretched out exhausted on the kitchen floor. "But I don't think he will come, do you?"

"No, I don't. You know, Leo, he could be in that house of his, collapsed, dead. I don't suppose anyone has gone to see. He's an old man, older than he looks."

"He's a bit over seventy."

Mary stared at him. "How do you know?"

"How do I know? Let's see—he must have told me that night he came here for the reference. Look at me, Mary. Do you like Bean?"

"Like him? I haven't thought about it. No, as a matter of fact I don't. I don't like him a bit."

"That's all right then. You can stop worrying about him. Forget him."

Leo went out to buy the Sunday papers. They looked through the property pages for likely houses in St. John's Wood and Hampstead and Leo even called one of the numbers given in the small ads, but no one answered the phone. Bean hadn't come. Just before lunch Lisl Pring phoned, enthusing about a new dog-walker she had found. A woman called Amelia Walker—Walker the walker, wasn't that hilarious? Mary thanked her but said she could hardly entrust Gushi to the care of someone unknown to his owners. For the time being she would go on taking him out herself. Leo said it was too hot to do anything but rest and the bed was more comfortable than the Blackburn-Norrises' sofa. The temperature climbed to ninety degrees.

"Why do they always give shade temperatures?" he wanted to know. "It's so cautious and petty. Why not what it is in the sun? It'll be a hundred and five in the sun."

"I suppose because the sun isn't always shining."

"My love, you sound so sad—don't be sad."

"All right," she said. "All right, I won't."

They made slippery love, their bodies closing together and withdrawing from each other with soft sucking sounds. Sweat became another amorous secretion, thinner and colder, strongly saline. She tasted his salt on her tongue and the faint sting of it in her eyes. They fell lightly asleep, wet palms clasped against the wet skin of belly and shoulder. A river flowed between her breasts.

The windows were wide open but no wind moved the heavily hanging drawn curtains. A bumblebee's throbbing buzz, alternately terrified and reassured, woke her. She lay watching it until at last it found a way to freedom through where the curtains met. Leo slept on. She got up, had a shower, and came back into the bedroom wrapped in a bathtowel. What she saw made her gasp. Tears were running down Leo's sleeping face. They were not perspiration but real tears. He was crying in his sleep.

She knew she must tell him about this, must ask him, but she postponed asking him. He seemed so happy when he got up, suggesting they go out to eat somewhere when it was late, when the warm dusk was giving way to dark. What about that little Italian restaurant they had gone to the first time, the day after they first met?

In the meantime Gushi must be walked. It was too hot to go far. The people in the park were mostly prone, sprawled on the yellowed grass.

"They look dead," said Leo. "They look like bodies after the battle is over."

It was an opportunity. She spoke gently, lovingly. "Why do you cry in your sleep, Leo? Your face was wet with tears."

"Wet with sweat," he said lightly and quickly.

If he had been a frightened child her voice could hardly have been more tender. "It was tears, my love. You were crying. Really."

"I had a bad dream. We all do sometimes."

"It must have been a very unhappy dream."

He refused to say any more but began instead to talk about people who lay in the sun, about sunbathing being a mid-twentieth-century fad that would disappear as fast as it had become fashionable. They put Gushi on the lead and walked back, past the children's playground to the Gloucester Gate.

A police car was parked outside Charlotte Cottage. The officers had left the car and sought the shade of the porch. When Mary and Leo came up to the door the elder of them produced a warrant card.

"Detective Inspector Marnock."

The other man, the sergeant, muttered a name Mary couldn't catch. "May we come in?"

It was Leo who said, "What's this about?"

"And you are, sir?"

"Leo Nash."

"Well, Mr. Nash, it's about Leslie Bean. You know a man called Leslie Bean?"

Mary's hand tightened on Leo's arm. "What's happened to him?"

They were all in the living room. Gushi, a hot bundle of fur, jumped for the sergeant's lap and lay there, gazing into a not very prepossessing face with slavish worship.

"Can you tell us what's happened to him?" Leo said.

"Perhaps. With your help. And yours, Miss Jago. I understand you knew him. He walked your dog. You saw him frequently?"

"Yes. Every day."

"So you would recognize him?"

"Of course I would."

She had the feeling that Marnock was struggling with an inhibition on saying too much to the public. It would be ingrained in him to say, "That I am not at liberty to tell you" or "We can't answer that," but he was plainly making up his mind how much he could reveal without total indiscretion, and how much he must reveal in order to gain their compliance.

"A Miss Bean has contacted us to report her brother as a missing person. He has not been seen since the evening of Friday the fourth."

"And?" Leo said sharply.

"On Saturday the fifth the body of an unidentified man was found in the vicinity of the Kent Terrace. . . ."

"But that was one of the street people," Mary said.

"We thought so at first. We haven't for some days. You don't want to believe everything you read in the papers. Nor do we think this was the work of the man the tabloid press calls The Impaler."

"But why not?"

"That," said the sergeant when Marnock hesitated, "we are not at liberty to tell you." Evidently a dog lover, he fondled Gushi's ears.

"The clothes on the body weren't his own. They were put on him after he was dead."

"As some sort of joke, no doubt," said Marnock. "Psychopaths can have an unfortunate sense of humor. Now, Miss Jago, Mr. Nash, we've been unprecedentedly frank and open with you. For a reason, of course. We want you to do us a favor. Mr. Bean's other lady clients feel a natural distaste . . ."

"For what?" said Leo.

"For identifying the body, sir."

Horrified, Mary said, "Surely his sister could do that!"

"She's eighty years old," said the sergeant. "Besides, she hasn't seen him in twenty-five years." Suddenly more confiding, he gave a little laugh. "Oh, yes, we know it's peculiar, it's that all right. He stopped in her house while she was away and left before she got back. Every year. Year in and year out. They'd not set eyes on each other for as you might say a quarter of a century."

· · ·

They both went.

Inside the mortuary it was cold and there was a strong icy smell. Mary thought it must be the smell of death, of decomposition impossible to mask, but Leo told her it was formaldehyde.

She was there to identify, if she could, the body, Leo to support and comfort her. He had only once seen Bean, and that briefly, in the evening, by artificial light.

The bodies were in drawers, green metal, like filing cabinets. It seemed to her a dreadful depository of a man's life, even though it was not a final resting place. One of the drawers was pulled open and a plastic sheet lifted.

She had expected to feel violent shock and revulsion and had tried to prepare herself all the way here, but when she looked on the face it was calmly and with no particular feeling. The dead man was Bean, there could be no doubt, but it looked more like a waxwork of

Bean from Madame Tussaud's. This sculpted head and rigid face seemed as if they had never been alive but had been cast in this shape and turned out of a mold.

"Yes," she said. "That is—is Mr. Bean."

"Quite sure, Miss Jago?"

Had she sounded dubious? Impossible to explain to this policeman the awe death induced in this pitiful place, the wonder she felt at what man came to at the last, an effigy in a metal drawer.

"I am quite sure," she said.

It had shaken them both. She and Leo were subdued, refusing the policeman's offer of a lift home, needing to be away from the police and talk of dead Bean. They would make their own way back. All ideas of revisiting that little Italian restaurant were abandoned, for Mary didn't feel like eating. They walked, hand in hand, sometimes giving each other rueful glances until Leo said, "Smile. Please. For me. You were wonderful in there. Cool as a cucumber. Why are cucumbers cool, anyway? They are. We all know that. But why are they, when marrows aren't and melons aren't?"

"You'll have to ask a botanist or a vegetable gardener."

"The tiresome thing about all this for me is that I have to go to a funeral tomorrow."

She turned to him, distracted by this flat statement where none of his attempts at distraction could succeed. "You didn't tell me."

"No. It's an old friend of my family's. A bore—I mean the funeral is, not the friend was."

He said no more until they were in the house. She noticed that his eyes were puffy as if he had been suppressing tears. His voice had a ragged sound.

"The funeral is in the afternoon. My mother will be there and I'll have to go back with her afterward. I probably won't see you all day."

"Leo, if your mother is in London, can't I meet her? And wouldn't she come to our wedding?"

He beckoned her to him, took her face gently in his hands.

"You're so beautiful. I shall never tire of looking at your face. Never a day goes by when I don't want to gaze and gaze at you."

She smiled. "I asked you about your mother."

"I'm leaving my family behind after tomorrow. I'll say good-bye to them tomorrow. They won't know it's for the last time, but it will be." She knelt down in front of his chair and he bent forward to put his arms round her. "So I'm not going home tonight. Wild horses couldn't drag me home."

"We won't let the wild horses try," she said.

26

T hat night he again cried in his sleep. He made no sound, but when he turned his face to meet hers the wetness touched her cheek. It was dawn and she could just see. The tears glistened.

In the morning he was up before her, bringing her tea in bed and the post, the newspaper, more fliers, a tax demand for Sir Stewart Blackburn-Norris, hire car cards. He was so cheerful, pulling rueful faces but making light of the ordeal ahead, that she decided to say nothing. His intention to wear a dark suit for the funeral pleased her, for it was in accordance with her own ideas of what was decorous and civilized.

Still he was unwilling to talk about the funeral, who this family friend was, why his mother would be there. It made her wonder if it was for this dead friend that Leo's nightly tears were shed. She felt she couldn't ask. Perhaps one day he would tell her. He held her hand at the breakfast table. Together they took Gushi into the park and there, by the Parsi's fountain, Leo left her and went off toward St. Mark's Bridge and Primrose Hill.

His parting from her brought back that afternoon in Covent Garden. She watched his receding figure as she had on that previous occasion. He had never satisfactorily explained why he had gone after apparently intending to spend the day with her. Did it any longer matter? This time he had kissed her tenderly, held her in his arms, and whispered that he loved her.

. . .

A party of eleven children came into the museum at four. They were Scots from Lanark on a school trip to London who, having done the Sherlock Holmes house, had come up here in their minibus. Mary showed them round and gave them the guided tour because their harassed teacher preferred that to a Walkman and a tape for each child.

It was the kind of day when she longed for air-conditioning, wholly impractical for this little house of small rooms in a climate where the heat would endure for only a short time. The street door and the window in the shop stood open, but it was still almost insufferably hot. The sun blazed and the air was motionless. In the shop, where the children, like so many visitors, showed more interest in the artifacts for sale than in the museum exhibits, papers and prints on the counters had begun to curl in the heat.

By five it was no cooler and Alistair still hadn't come. Mary supposed she would just have to wait. Running away from him was something she was now ashamed of. There was a childishness about it she wanted to eradicate from her character but knew that Alistair, though censorious, rather liked. Weakness and folly in women made him feel more powerful and in control, more able to justify a superior stance.

Once Stacey had gone home, Mary went outside and sat in the shade on the low wall that bounded the courtyard. On such warm summer evenings London acquired a pavement life. Restaurateurs were putting out tables and chairs and striped umbrellas in preparation for those who preferred to dine outdoors. Shopkeepers, in the half hour before their shops closed, sat on their doorsteps. Every sunblind was down and at the café opposite in St. John's Wood Terrace someone was casting bucketfuls of water over the flagstones.

She watched steam rise from the wet pavement. Her thoughts were full of Leo as they had been for most of the day. She sensed that being in the company of his mother and brother might be as troublesome and painful as the funeral itself. The relationship he had with his brother became each day more mysterious. If he loved him so much why break with him? She was resolving never again to ask Leo if she might meet his mother or brother when she looked up and saw Alistair coming down Ordnance Hill from the direction of the tube station. The present must be very small. He wore no jacket and carried only the thin flat briefcase she had once given him but had thought even at the time too small to accommodate more than a few sheets of paper and a diary.

He waved when he saw her but did not quicken his pace. It was too hot to rush. She couldn't fail to remember how once, seeing him approach from a distance, her heart had leapt and a thrill run through her body. She felt nothing for him now, no faint lingering regret. He looked uncomfortably hot, his face red and beaded with sweat, his hair wet with it and sticking to his scalp. His hot hand felt wet through the thin stuff of her blouse as he laid it on her shoulder. She freed herself and began walking back toward the museum. Then she thought, as she had not thought before, this may be the last time we shall ever meet, we shall very likely never see each other again. We were lovers, we once thought we loved each other, perhaps truly did, though impermanently—how sad and awful to terminate it like this. . . .

"Alistair, let's go over to the café and have a drink."

His eyebrows went up. She hadn't noticed till then, but now she saw how unpleasant his expression was, how grim. "Sure," he said, "and while I'm inside ordering two Perriers you'll do another of your famous flits."

"No. I promise I won't."

They had turned back and were crossing the road, he somewhat reluctantly. "I don't think we ought to part," she said, "without some . . ."

"Ceremony?"

"I was going to say, without saying good-bye properly, and without saying perhaps that we have no hard feelings for each other."

He laughed. A waitress came up and he ordered without asking Mary what she wanted. "You seem to think," he said carefully, "that I still feel for you what I used to. I suppose it pleases your vanity. Well, I don't. I'm over you. As for hard feelings, I've plenty of those. You could say, those are all I have. And now I want, frankly, to get shut of you."

She could find nothing to say. Perrier came, a large bottle of it, with ice and lemon in two glasses. He poured their drinks. She had a sudden dreadful feeling he would fill another glass with water and throw it in her face. She even edged her chair back a little. Her life, she realized, had been shot through for a long time with imaginings of what Alistair might do, fantasies far exceeding what he actually ever did. He drank the last drops in his glass, reached down, opened the briefcase, and took out a small flat parcel. It was about the size of a videocassette, rectangular, less than an inch thick. The gift-wrapping, pink and silver paper, narrow silver ribbon falling from its knot in curlicues, looked nevertheless as if he had done it himself. The corners were clumsily folded, the ribbon twisted. On a card he had printed her name in rather large but uneven capital letters.

"Thank you," she said faintly.

"I want to say something, one last thing. It's this. Don't think you can come back to me. When things go wrong, I mean."

She said, with a spark of spirit she didn't feel but forced to flash out, "Don't you mean, *if* things go wrong?"

"No, Mary, that's what *you* mean. As long as you know. I won't be available. I won't be carrying any torches. I shall have found someone else."

Thinking of this meeting, she had planned all kinds of things to say, charitable wishes for his future, even the expression of some impossible hope that they might go on knowing each other. But now she had no words, she simply felt a kind of despair in his presence that she knew would disappear entirely once he had gone. He was the kind of man, she thought, that she would always run away from and she wondered that she had not done so before, long ago.

He paid the bill. He jumped up and struck an attitude. She watched him, appalled, already nervous.

"And whether we shall meet again I know not," he declaimed. "Therefore let us our everlasting farewells take. Forever and forever farewell, Mary!"

A group of tourists approaching the next table turned and stared. He said it again.

"Forever and forever farewell, Mary!"

He pushed back his chair and sent it skidding across the pavement where it toppled and fell over. Then he walked rapidly away. Someone laughed. Mary was embarrassed and rather shaken. She picked up the parcel but it was too big to go into the small bag she was carrying. She would have to carry it in her hand. It was too hot to walk far but she would walk, she would keep to the shady side of the street, and hope it was true what they said about endorphins being released by exercise to calm you down, to create a sense of well-being.

More than endorphins, she wanted someone to comfort her. Leo, of course. But she knew she really wanted her grandmother. Her grandmother would hold her as she had done when she was a little girl, hug her in warm silence, but her grandmother was dead, was ash, was dust. Leo would be there, eventually he would, though he was spending the evening with his family. When Leo came in at the front door she would go quietly up to him and he would take her in his arms.

The man she called Nikolai came into her mind and she thought, strangely, that he was one of the few people she could think of who she would like to talk to, to have listen to her, to receive from her confidences whose nature she hardly understood. But when she came to the Gloucester Gate and, crossing the road by the bronze maiden, looked down into the Grotto, there was no one there and no evidence of his occupancy. A cigarette packet, discarded over the wall, floated on the surface of the pool. Otherwise the place was as neat as a suburban garden.

She put the parcel down on the hall table. Gushi was too hot to run out to meet her. He lay panting on the cold kitchen floor, his tongue hanging out. There was no point in taking him out for hours yet, perhaps she would wait until Leo came home and they would walk him together. She stroked Gushi's head, gave him fresh water, then went upstairs to shower and put on trousers and a T-shirt.

It was at this point that the telephone rang. It was Leo. Once, several years before, she had spoken on the phone to Dorothea's husband Gordon just after he had come round from an anesthetic. Leo's voice sounded like Gordon's had then, thick, throaty, half-choked, aged by many years.

"I can't get away this evening," he said. "I don't know when I will. Things haven't been too—too good. I'll see you tomorrow." There was a pause in which she fancied she heard sounds like sobs suppressed. "Is that all right?"

"Leo, of course it is. But can't I . . . ?"

"No, I don't know what you were going to say but you can't do anything. No one can. I shall be fine. Did you see Alistair?"

"For the last time, I'm sure. He's given us a wedding present."

"What is it?"

"I don't know. I haven't opened it yet."

"Perhaps you'd better not open it. Perhaps there's a bomb inside." There was a hysterical edge to his voice. Had she imagined a sob? "Mary, I'm sorry I can't come back tonight."

"It doesn't matter," she said. "I understand."

But she was not at all sure that she did. She was aware of bitter disappointment. Why is it worse to be alone on fine summer evenings than when it is cold or wet? The food in the fridge looked uninviting. She drank some sparkling water, ate a peach, and settled down to put the final touches to the Irene Adler brochure. It was due to go to the printer by the end of the week. By the time it came out she would no longer be Mary Jago but Mary Nash.

Did she want that or would she keep her maiden name? She hadn't thought of that before. Somewhere on the brochure there should be a line saying, "Designed by Mary Jago" or "Designed by Mary Nash." She wrote the new name to see how it looked, how it felt. Many people would say it was unlucky for a woman to write her new name before it was hers, before she was married. She tried her new signature, disliked it, and almost decided to keep the name Jago.

From the hall Gushi gave a sharp yap. She went out to see what had alarmed him and found another flier from Express Tikka and Pizza on the doormat. Alistair's present was on the hall table where she had left it, pink and silver paper, curlicues of ribbon, clumsily bunched corners. She took it back into the living room. Gushi jumped onto her lap and curled up like a cat.

Sticky tape held the parcel together under the ribbon. It was surprisingly hard to get off. She had to disturb the dog to fetch scissors. Leo's words came back to her then, about the present being a bomb. That was absurd, of course, he hadn't been serious, but she held the package up to her ear as if to hear something ticking. She shook it. There was nothing loose inside, nothing to rattle.

She cut the sticky tape, then the corners. Inside the paper was a flat silver box, the kind you can buy from the gift wrapping section in stationery shops. The lid was taped to the base. More cutting and the lid came off. Bubble-wrap, cotton wool, a handful of tissues for padding, and a card in an envelope.

It was a strange choice for Alistair to have made. That was her first thought as she looked at the picture of a bride and groom, doll-like figures, the man in a top hat and morning coat, the woman in white crinoline and bridal veil, the pair of them standing on the carved and scrolled icing of a beribboned cake. Underneath the legend read: *Wishing You Joy on Your Wedding Day*

Was this his present? Was this all? Inside the card was an enclosure; evidently a letter, the paper folded twice. He had written noth-ing on the card, not even his name. For a moment she thought of not reading the letter, of throwing it away unread, apprehensive of his insults and reproaches. But it was cowardly not to read it. It could do her no harm, it was only words and from someone who now meant nothing to her. She was holding it between thumb and forefinger, still unfolded, when the phone rang again, and as she picked up the re-ceiver it was still with her, just a standard sheet of paper, folded twice.

Leo's voice said, "I'm sorry. I'm sorry for that—that display just now. I'm at my brother's, but he's gone out for a moment and I'm ringing back as soon as I could. Forgive?"

"Nothing to forgive. Are you all right?"

"I'm fine."

She said wistfully, "I wish you could come home now."

"Mary, my mother wants me to stay the night. She's here. I may not see her again for years, if ever. You know what I said about that. That this was the final meeting ."

"That's all right," she said. "Of course you must stay. Don't worry about it. I shall be fine." Afterward she didn't know why she had told him. "I've opened the present. It wasn't a bomb. Just a card and a letter and a lot of padding."

"I love you," he said. "I just wanted to ring you and say that. On Thursday you'll be my wife. It's too good to be true."

"It's true," she said.

His brother must have come back into the room. He said good-bye, he would see her on the following evening, and put the receiver down. That reminder that he was with his family for the last time was disquieting. It suddenly seemed unnatural, unnecessary. She wished she had asked his reasons, simply asked to know more about it. Anyway, it wasn't too late. Tomorrow she would ask him.

She unfolded the sheet of paper she was still holding in her hand.

•   •   •

The logo of the Harvest Trust, the scarlet mushroom shape, the Battersea address, and opposite this the direction to her, Ms. Mary Jago in Chatsworth Road, NW10. Below it was a line that this was from Deborah Cox, Donor Welfare Officer. The date was six days earlier.

Her first thought was that the letter shouldn't have gone to her old address. Then she remembered she had never given the trust a firm change of address, only asked for one letter, the last she thought she would receive from them, to be sent to her care of her grandmother. She read:

> *Dear Ms. Jago,*
>
> *It is probable I am bringing you news you know already since I believe you have been in correspondence with Mr. Nash and have met him. This is confirmed by our receiving no replies from you to our recent letters informing you of his decline and illness.*
>
> *Therefore I hope it will not be a shock to you, though certainly giving distress, to know that Mr. Nash died yesterday. He passed away quite peacefully in the night at the hospice where he had been for the previous two weeks. His mother and brother were with him.*
>
> *While this must be a cause of great sadness to you, you will know that by your generous donation you succeeded in giving him a longer life, and of higher quality, than he would otherwise. . . .*

Mary laid the letter down in her lap. She was simply confused. How could Leo's death be a shock when she had spoken to him five minutes before? They had made a mistake. They were confusing her with someone else and Leo with someone else, they had their files mixed.

She picked it up and read it again. *This is confirmed by our receiving no replies from you to our recent letters. . . .* What recent letters? Transplant updates that Alistair had received and opened? She was suddenly very cold and she moved into the sunshine of the open windows, feeling the heat touch her. *Mr. Nash died yesterday . . .*

Now, at seven, it was too late to phone them and ask for an explanation. Anger and indignation started to replace the initial shock. Alistair was as much to blame as the trust in perpetuating their mistake, and surely out of malice. He had sent her this letter as a wedding present, the most vindictive act he had ever committed against her.

The phone rang and rang. At last he picked it up and said, "Alistair Winter."

"Alistair, Mary. You must know why I'm phoning—"

He put the phone down. The dial tone began. She looked at the receiver in disbelief. Blood rose into her cheek where he had struck her and she put up a cold finger to feel the heat. After a moment or two she poured herself a measure of brandy and drank it down neat. The brandy made her choke but filled her with warmth as if some heating agent had got inside her and sent its rays to travel outward to her skin. She told herself to take deep breaths. Alistair's malice had shaken her profoundly. She fancied that in his silence at the other end of the phone she had heard satisfaction and glee.

But she reminded herself that it wasn't he who had written that letter. He had only sent it on. It was a real letter, from a real place, not something Alistair had forged. He had only been the instrument that ensured she received it.

This was no time for those old hesitations. Avoiding thought, she dialed Leo's brother's number at Redferry House. It rang and rang, there was going to be no answer. Leo had said he would be there, but he wasn't there. That meant very little. He and his brother might have gone out for a drink or he gone back with their mother to wherever she was staying. It just seemed strange, she felt it suddenly as suspicious and odd, that he should have talked to her about breaking with his brother, never seeing his mother again, yet be going out with them, staying the night with them.

Mary needed someone to be with her, to bring to this letter, to these events, a detached and dispassionate mind. After a while she phoned Dorothea, but instead of coming out with all of it, she found herself asking if it would be all right not to come in tomorrow. She had arranged to take a week off from Wednesday but could she start her holiday tomorrow instead?

"Sure. Why not?" Dorothea said. "Gordon will cope. Are you okay? You sound a bit shaky. Pre-wedding nerves?"

"I expect so," Mary said, and for some reason tried to smile into the receiver as if Dorothea could see her. "Thanks, Dorrie."

"It's your wedding, not your funeral."

"Yes."

It had been impossible, would have been grotesque, to have read or quoted the letter to Dorothea. To anyone? She picked it up again, read it again, and this time saw something that she had not previously noticed. Under the Harvest Trust address was Deborah Cox's own home number. Mary had begun to feel sick. The brandy perhaps or not having eaten for so long. She wondered why she had told Dorothea she wouldn't go to the museum tomorrow. What was she anticipating? What specter awaited her?

The fear of knowing was starting to overcome the fear of not knowing. Suppose she were to destroy the letter now, tear it into pieces and burn the pieces in an ashtray? Or make a little bonfire outside? Then she could pretend it had never come, that Alistair's parcel had contained only a card, say nothing of it to Leo. . . . She dialed Deborah Cox's number.

It was answered after the second ring. Scarcely waiting for Mary to say what she wanted, Deborah Cox asked her if she wanted counseling. The trust would be happy to provide counseling. She would advise it, particularly as Mary had written to Leo Nash, had even got to know him.

"You did actually meet?"

Mary hesitated. She had begun to tremble, her knees shaking. How she could tell so blatant a lie she didn't know. "No," she said. "No, we never met."

"But you had contact? By letter?"

"Yes. We had contact." Mary had to clear her throat. "What did he look like?"

"I'm sorry?"

"What did he look like? Leo Nash." Her voice was hoarse, but the lying got easier. "I asked him for a photograph but he didn't send one."

"Fair, short, about five feet six, dark eyes. It's probably just as well you didn't meet. A donor can get emotionally involved with a recipient. It's to do with the nature of the transplant, and that makes it all the worse when the recipient dies."

"You said he had a brother . . ."

"That's right. Ten years older. They shared a flat. But I wouldn't advise contact, if that's what you're asking. Now, as to arranging counseling . . ."

Mary said no, thank you, and that wouldn't be necessary. She put the phone down very quietly.

27

H ob was well.
For more than a week now there had been no states. He was fast forgetting what being in a state was like, or even what feeling low was like, for he never let himself decline far enough from being well to find out. He was rich enough to stay well for months, maybe a year, nor did he need to work. The irony was that more work came in than had done for years beforehand, and with it, necessarily, more money to keep him well.

He wondered why this should be and one day he asked Lew. There was no one else he dared ask since Carl had disappeared. Lew was old and weird and had been into all that stuff when he was young in the seventies and he said it was because of Hob's positive attitude. He was positive and in touch with his inner self. People sensed this and came looking for him when they wanted a job done. He'd done three jobs just since the big one—the biggest of all big ones—and one of them, funnily enough, had been a second roughing up of that git who hadn't the sense he was born with, the one who lived in St. Mark's Crescent.

Hob hadn't stayed at home much. Home was a dump, anyway. For all their promises, the council hadn't come to mend the windows. Maybe he hadn't read the letter right, so maybe they'd never said they were coming. Whatever the way of it, he couldn't live in a boarded-up box no different from being inside a microwave, not in this heat he couldn't. So he'd more or less taken to the outdoors and it had been lovely, like a holiday, better than Corfu really, he'd never been much for going in water.

He wandered the park and Primrose Hill and St. John's Church Gardens, sitting on the seats, lying on the grass. By day he'd sit at a table outside one of the refreshment places and he'd drink, but he seldom ate more than a Magnum or a packet of kettle chips. When he was well he never much fancied food. Mostly he drank vodka or sometimes tequila for a change. After the first few days he bought a bottle of each and carried them with him, but in a proper rucksack, not plastic carriers like those beggars. The rucksack also held his gear, the watering can rose, the lighter, a batch of drinking straws—he helped himself from the counter when he paid for his drink—and reserve supplies. He never let himself get low, let alone run out. The thought of a state even looming on the horizon made him shudder.

Drinking straws ended up all over the park. Sometimes he wondered, giggling to himself, if anyone noticed, remarked on it, wondered what the hell was going on: straws caught up on rosebushes, littering flowerbeds, floating on the scummy water under the bridges. Because he was a joker he stuck one in the mouth of the bronze maiden and made a woven crown of six others for Sir Cowasjee Jehangir's drinking fountain. He was happy. One day he bought a postcard of the lake with boats on it and sent it to himself. He had to go home sometimes, for a change of clothes and to catch a bit of the athletics from Trent Bridge on telly, and when he crept into that furnace of a flat he found his postcard on the mat with "Great wether, wish you was heer" on it and "luv from Hob."

That made him laugh a lot. It was the funniest thing he could think of, getting a postcard from himself, wishing he was somewhere else. He fell about laughing and got so excited he needed a shot of vodka to calm him down. He had started to lose weight. Not on his head or face, those bits of him were as big and heavy as ever, but his body was thin and the skin sagged round his middle like an old sock when the leg has been pulled out of it. Leo had once told him about a girl he knew who'd been fat, obese he called it, and for some reason she turned anorexic. Her skin hung on her skeleton like draped material and they'd operated on her, cut bits out and stitched her up, and all on the National Health Service. He'd started wondering if he could have the same thing, only he couldn't because in a hospital he'd never be well but would get into a state the first day.

Now that he was rich he'd been buying all the rocks he wanted and E too and angel dust when there was any about. Big H was no use to him because he couldn't face needles, which was why the coming of crack had been such a godsend. The only time he'd tried the needle he'd fainted dead away. God knows what had happened when he was a kid and they'd tried giving him those shots for polio and whatever, he'd never asked his mother, but the answer probably was she was too shellacked to take him or too bone idle.

He never cared to think about the time, a year or two back, when he'd been reduced to sniffing ozone-unfriendly aerosol stain remover. He thought instead about the other two jobs, breaking a geyser's leg in Chalk Farm and a straightforward beating up round the back of Lisson Grove. He got a Hawaii for each of those, though he reckoned he was underpaid for his Chalk Farm effort, as fracturing a leg wasn't the simple task it was cracked up to be. He enjoyed the pun he'd made and had another good laugh.

Most evenings he went through his ritual by the pond in the Grotto. The beggar with the fancy voice had moved out. The people who owned the house the builders were doing up—and months they'd been at it—had put up more barbed wire and more fencing in their inexplicable efforts to keep intruders out. He couldn't understand it, it wouldn't keep him out or any streetwise person. He sat on the coping of the pool in the insect-infested half dark, dropped his rock into the watering can rose, screwed on the top, inserted two fresh straws, applied the lighter to the rock, and set the apparatus in the tin lid.

The crystalline lump fizzed and crackled. Far from a state though he'd been in, his condition took a dizzying upturn when the smooth sweet smoke drew into his lungs. Later on he'd take a tablet of E or maybe smoke some PCP and if he got too excited bring himself down with a couple of cycles—cyclobarbitone calcium to you ignorant buggers, he thought. It takes an alcoholic to be an expert on alcoholism and a junkie to understand the journey to oblivion.

He began giggling uncontrollably. The laughter he allowed full rein, he let it rip, and he lay down there rolling on the flagstones and the dusty earth among the dry crackling leaves. A face looked over the parapet of the bridge. He could just make it out in the dusk, a thin face with pitted skin that watched him for a long moment, fascinated by the sight of this man rolling on his back like a dog in a pile of shit.

When he was ready to stop laughing and rolling he stopped. He was in perfect control. He started putting his gear back into the rucksack, took a swallow of vodka, noticed what he'd been carrying about with him for more than a week now: a red baseball cap and a T-shirt with elephants marching across it. The funniest thing in the world, it seemed to him, would be to take them up to the Oxfam shop in Camden High Street tomorrow, hand them in, and make sure they put them on show in the window.

As he clambered out of the Grotto and crossed on the lights at the top of Albany Street he began giggling again at the thought of that. Making sure he was unobserved, but still giggling, he climbed over the spiked railings of the Gloucester Gate and disappeared into the soft still darkness of the park.

·   ·   ·

Her loneliness left her exposed and vulnerable. She was like someone put ashore on a desert island who watches the boat recede across an empty sea; there is no one left in the world who knows or cares where one is or what has happened.

She held Gushi. Afterward, long afterward, she sometimes said that the little dog, snuggling in her arms, licking her fingers, had saved her sanity. Holding him, his warmth necessary in spite of the heat of the day, she understood that some monstrous fraud had been perpetrated against her but not how or why. Even who it was that had done what had been done she didn't know, for she had no means of knowing Leo's identity. Trying to solve this enigma brought on fits of shivering as if it were cold out there, as if snow covered the park.

She must have sat there for more than an hour, still, scarcely thinking, in a state of shock, for when next she looked at the clock it was nine and dark outside. She switched on a table lamp and a flock of moths came in, brown and yellow and a black and white one, spotted like a dalmatian. They made for the light, circling the lampshade. She thought of his laughter, of "A reference for a dalmatian," and gave a little cry of pain. The light off, the room in darkness to let the moths escape, she dialed the Redferry House number again, her throat dry and constricted. There was no reply. She wouldn't phone again. She was resolved on that. For one thing, absurdly, she had no idea what she would say.

The idea of the night was horrible. It would be so long, so lonely, and the small hours unbearable. She went upstairs and in the medicine cabinet in the Blackburn-Norrises' bathroom found a phial of capsules with *Lady Blackburn-Norris* printed on its label, *For the sleeplessness,* and the name of the drug with instructions to take one or two at bedtime.

She put Gushi out into the garden. The night was warm and soft and above her in a velvety violet sky a few stars were visible, a rare thing in London. Gushi started yapping at the bats that swooped overhead, so she brought him in again. When she had locked up and settled him on the foot of her bed, she opened the bedroom windows wide, took her clothes off, fetched a glass of water, and swallowed one capsule, then a second. She scarcely had time to lie down. Sleep came at her like a black walking specter, cloaked and hooded, seizing and absorbing her into itself and its wide winglike arms.

In the early hours, five or six, she awoke, ponderously limp and weak from the drug, but remembering him beside her and making love to him. Over and over, he whoever he was had made love to her, with sweet gentle touches and strong unstoppable passion and murmured loving words. She got up and just made it to the bathroom. She was sick, the retching painful, tearing at her throat. On and on she vomited until she had collapsed onto the floor, drained dry.

After a while she slept again and slept until Gushi came asking to be let out, his nose like an ice cube against her naked shoulder. She got up off the floor, put a robe round her. Another splendid day was out there, blue sky, sunshine unhindered but the sun itself an invisible fire.

The phone started ringing just as she had come in from the garden. No one knew this number but for Leo, the man who said he was Leo. Alistair knew it, but she was certain, as if it were a law of nature, that Alistair would never phone her again, that she and Alistair would never speak to each other again. She let it ring and ring, watching the instrument. She picked up the receiver.

It was Deborah Cox.

The question of least importance was the one she asked. "How did you know this number? I didn't give it to you."

"I dialed the number that gets you the voice to tell you who made the last phone call."

"Yes. Oh, yes. Of course. What was it you wanted?" She had never before spoken so rudely to anyone. "I'm sorry. I mean, what can I do for you?"

"There's something I wanted to tell you. You seemed so interested in Leo Nash, the sort of person he was, what he looked like and all that. I'm not sure I ought to tell you, it's just between you and me, but I know you're discreet."

The woman knew virtually nothing about her. . . . "What is it then?"

"Leo," Deborah Cox said, "when he began to get ill again refused to ask you to make a second donation. You were the only possible donor but he expressly forbade us to ask you."

Mary said stonily, "I don't understand."

"He said he wouldn't put you through the process again, going into the hospital, having a general anesthetic, which is always a risk, the convalescence afterward, all that. He wouldn't. We did everything in our power to persuade him but it was no use. I thought you'd like to know."

"You mean he was a hero," said Mary. "A knight in shining armor, a selfless saint—is that what you're saying? Someone who laid down his life so that I shouldn't have a week's discomfort?"

There was a silence in which, somehow, outrage was apparent.

"Frankly, Mary," Deborah Cox said at last, "I didn't realize you were quite so disturbed. You're undoubtedly in need of therapy, so about that counseling—"

Asking herself if all this would turn her from a well-mannered courteous woman into a rude one, Mary quietly replaced the receiver in its rest.

·   ·   ·

The man, whoever he was, the con man, the man who had deceived her, would come to the house as he always came when he had been away for the night. Already the heat was closing in as if a giant lid were held over the steam from a pan. From the comparative cool of Charlotte Cottage, Mary came out into a heat that enveloped her like a blanket. She left Gushi behind. It was too hot for him to walk and he must be content with escape into the garden twice a day. She was leaving the house to avoid the man who had been her lover but whom she dared not think of in those terms in case she was sick again.

It was a matter for regret now that she had asked Dorothea for the day off. The museum would at least have sheltered her, given her a place to be where he wouldn't find her. There seemed nowhere to go but the park, but even as she entered it, going in by the Chester

Gate—farther north, nearer the zoo, she might meet him—she told herself this running away couldn't be prolonged. They would meet, they were bound to, he couldn't know Alistair had exposed him and she had found him out. Probably today, sometime today, they must encounter each other. She began to shake again. She felt weak, enfeebled, the sleeping capsules still taking effect, and she sat down on a seat under the trees in the Broad Walk.

The day after tomorrow was to have been her wedding day. He would have married her, of course he would, that had been the purpose of the project, to marry her for her money and that vast barrack of a house up in Belsize Park. Tears came into her eyes and ran down her cheeks. He had been so plausible, so *nice,* so gentle, a wonderful actor. But who was he that he could show the registrar Leo Nash's birth certificate and have Carl Nash for a brother and receive her bone marrow and *die,* yet be alive?

The man she had once named Nikolai had come to sit on the other end of the bench. She hadn't heard his arrival; he might have been there for five minutes, ten. Her tears, her thoughts, had cut her off from the external world.

"Don't cry," he said, and then, "What is it?"

She lifted her head, turned her eyes. Her sight was blurred by tears, but still she was sure he looked different. The change was subtle, not definable, for he still had his beard, he still wore his jeans, his denim jacket, the threadbare T-shirt, the battered trainers. But he was a man now, not a dosser. Whatever it was must be in those blue eyes or in the more confident set of his shoulders.

The classic response, but what else could she say to a stranger? "It's nothing."

"You're very unhappy," he said. "Shall I go away? I expect you'd like me to go away."

Her newfound rudeness had its limits. "No. No, of course not." She turned her face away. "I am unhappy. No one can do anything about that."

He was very hesitant. "Do you want to tell me? I mean, just to tell someone?" It came to him then how he had told no one about his wife and children. He had talked of them only to that other self inside his head. If the other street people knew it was only that a tragedy figured in his life just as tragedies figured in all their separate lives. "The cliché is true," he said. "Sometimes it's best to talk to a stranger."

She shook her head. She got up and when he protested, he would go, the last thing he meant was to drive her away, shook her head again, made a gesture with her right hand indicating he should stay where he was.

"I can't talk," she said. "It's not just—well, inhibition. I wouldn't know what to say. I don't *know,* you see, I don't *know.*"

He looked at her neutrally, trying not to encourage or discourage.

"I don't know what's been done to me, only that it's bad and cruel, I think."

"Sometimes," he said, "it helps to get angry. You could try anger."

She nodded abstractedly. He watched her walk away. He was convinced that something terrible had happened to her and with that thought came a sense of failure. By his presence, near her, he had absurdly thought he could save her from suffering, protect her from life. Who did he think he was? He hadn't been able to save himself, so how could he hope to save another?

But now, while she was out of doors, he would never let her out of his sight.

28

Walking down from St. Barbara's House in Camden High Street, the women's hostel where she sometimes slept, Effie turned her eyes to the window of the Oxfam shop. She looked at it as another woman might look at the windows of Selfridges or D. H. Evans. Oxfam prices were usually beyond Effie but they were a possibility, they weren't ludicrous, they weren't that other woman's Harrod's. She needed a T-shirt, it was so bloody hot. The only one in the window had elephants on it, a married couple of elephants they were supposed to be with a couple of babies. Vanity had gone out of Effie's life ages ago—but her with a family of elephants on her front?

Do me a favor. Anyway, it was about sixteen sizes too small.

A baseball cap she could live without. A pimple on an egg that would be on her Humpty-Dumpty face. Maybe she'd try the Sue Ryder place for her T-shirt if she could remember where it was. She wandered on, shifting the heavier bundles she carried from her left to her right hand, heading for the Gloucester Gate.

Dill went up there later to cash his giro, but he didn't look in the Oxfam window because he never bought clothes. The nuns who had a soup and bun stall in Eversholt Street five nights a week handed out cast-off clothing for free. He was more interested in food for the beagle, which he'd run out of, so he tied the dog up to a parking meter and went into the Indian mini-market where he bought five cans of Cesar, gourmet stuff but light to carry in those little foil cans. The beagle would wolf it down.

Roman passed that by on his way from the Hawley Hotel to Lisson Grove where the Benefit Office and Job Center is, a long walk but nothing much to one who had walked miles every day for the best part of two years. A slight embarrassment stopped him looking at the Oxfam shop as he passed it. He consciously kept his eyes averted. The previous day he had handed over to them all the clothes—those that had survived and were in a reasonably decent condition—he had worn while on the street, having washed them first and worked on them with the hotel's ancient iron. They would very likely be in the window. He had taken no money for them, but it troubled him vaguely that there were people out there prepared to pay for and wear his castoffs. So he didn't look.

Nor did Nello, also on his way to cash his giro and spend half of it in the Red Lion. The school-leaver who had inherited most of Bean's dogs dragged all his charges past the window, heading for the pharmacy where his mother's repeat prescription for barbs was regularly dispensed. As often as not, the dogs never saw the grass of the park these days; the school-leaver was too busy shopping or playing the fruit machines.

It had taken him only two days to time the early walk for two hours later. Outside the pharmacy he tied the dogs up so tightly that Ruby couldn't get her leg over or Spots catch a sniff of Charlie's chuff. Another hundred chlorme-something or others, please, and this prescription for his baby brother who never gave any of them a wink of sleep. It was for pediatric Valium in syrup form. The school-leaver was going to divide it up and sell it in forty-milliliter phials, there was a good market among the buffs for coming down from a speed hangup. Cough mixture would go into the Vallergon bottle and his brother no doubt would keep on screaming half the night.

It had to be one of Bean's regulars who spotted the T-shirt and the baseball cap, but few of them ever looked in charity shop windows, let alone went inside. In any case, Camden High Street was too down-market or just bohemian for the Barker-Pryces, Erna

Morosini, Mrs. Sellers, and Edwina Goldsworthy, and not sufficiently recherché for Lisl Pring. Just as well for the school-leaver or
they might have seen their dogs lashed to lampposts outside the pin-
ball arcade. The one who looked but saw no need to go inside was
Valerie Conway.

She was living with her boyfriend just off Camden High Street
and was walking down to her new job as receptionist in the Peugeot
showrooms. The neighbors in Jamestown Road had been all agog
when they found out she'd known Bean quite well, seen him every
day and talked to him. It was a wonder it wasn't she the police had
hauled in to identify his body.

"I was like Bo-Peep's sheep," Valerie said. "They didn't know
where to find me."

But she wasn't without public spirit. And she wasn't too posh for
Oxfam shops. Her sister had bought a really nice boob tube from one
of them and worn it on her honeymoon in Bodrum. Valerie was on
the lookout for a halter top. A red one was in the very center of the
window and the idea apparently was that you wore it with the red
baseball cap they'd stuck on the plaster model's head. Valerie went
inside, her heart thudding uncomfortably.

"D'you know where you got that from?"

"If you mean who brought it in," said the sour-faced middle-aged
volunteer, "I do remember the the man, but we're not in the habit of
divulging the names of donors."

"Suit yourself," said Valerie. "I'll have the red halter. I just
wanted to know about the baseball cap because the last time I saw it
it was on the head of one of those blokes that got themselves impaled
on railings."

•   •   •

The day came and went. The wedding day. He hadn't come, so
Mary understood that he must somehow know he was discovered.
The scam was over. If he was close to the real Leo Nash, and he must

have been, perhaps the Harvest Trust had let him know they had informed her. After all, she would have received that letter much sooner if Alistair hadn't delayed sending it on.

His failure to come was at the same time a relief and a disappointment. A relief because of her shame at the things she had said, her confidings in him, her confessions of love, the relative speed with which she had let him make love to her and later, her reveling in that lovemaking. The disappointment was because she was angry. Although she had appeared indifferent to it at the time, she had taken to heart Nikolai's advice. *You could try anger.* She had tried, perhaps for the first time in her life.

Anger had come and begun to grow and as it grew brought with it a kind of liberation. Why hadn't she previously let herself be angry? With Alistair, for instance? But the anger she now nourished needed expression and it could only express itself to *him*. And he didn't come, would never come.

The police came instead.

They wanted more identification, this time to tell them if a red baseball cap and T-shirt with elephants on it had belonged to Bean. Had she ever seen Bean wearing them?

"Many times," she said. "He wore the hat every day in hot weather. I only saw the T-shirt once, but it was his."

There must have been a new firmness about her, a decisiveness, which she fancied made Marnock give her one or two surprised glances. Had she ever seen Bean with anyone? Had he, for instance, ever been accompanied when he came to fetch or return Gushi? She answered no without hesitation to both questions and the policemen thanked her and left.

Dorothea was coming round in the evening. Mary had phoned her the night before to tell her the wedding was off but giving no further explanation. She had phoned her cousin in Guildford. After all, if she didn't understand herself, how could she explain? She found a bottle of wine, the Chardonnay Leo had been so fond of, and dialed Express Tikka and Pizza for chicken korma with pilau rice and Bombay potatoes for eight o'clock.

One of the qualities for which she liked Dorothea was her willingness to accept a refusal to explain, her submission without protest to silence on a particular subject. She was discreet, could keep a secret, and understood about other people having private places they wanted to keep inviolate.

"Don't ask," Mary said. "I say that because I don't really know why myself. Perhaps I'll have an explanation one day and then I'll tell you. And then maybe you won't want to know, you won't care."

Dorothea had brought a basket of peaches and a carton of clotted cream. "Better put this in your fridge till it's time to eat it." In the same tone she said, "Are you very unhappy?"

"I don't know. That's a peculiar answer, but I really don't know. I'm angry. I've never been so angry with anyone and it feels so strange and new. But I can't be angry *with* him because I don't know where he is."

They sat on the terrace and drank Campari with ice and orange juice and lime slices. Gushi lay half under the lilac bush and half on the grass, snapping at any moth that came his way. The sky was very pale blue, as if long exposure to the fierce sun had faded it. There was a smell of smoke. Not illegal smoke from an illicit bonfire, Mary thought, but a fire somewhere, perhaps on the embankment of the railway line coming out of Euston. Fires kept breaking out from cigarette ends tossed onto tinder-dry grass. "I brought you a paper," Dorothea said, "for distraction. Well, a rag, a tabloid. Have you ever heard of an MP called Barker-Pryce?"

"I don't think so."

"That man Bean that was murdered used to take his dog out. The dog must have gone out with Gushi. A golden retriever called Charlie."

"I remember the dog."

Dorothea passed her the front page. There was not much text. It was mostly photographs and headline: THE MP AND HIS TOY, with beneath it, WHAT WAS THE LINK WITH MURDERED MAN? One photograph was of a choleric-looking elderly man with bristly whiskers and badly cut hair, sitting at a table in what looked like a drinking club but might have been in a private house, next to a young heavily made-up girl with waist-length hair. A cigar with a pendulous head of ash pulled down one corner of his mouth. Fingers fat as sausages could be seen gripping the girl's shoulder from behind. Her head rested on his shoulder. The caption read, *A Toy is only a toy but a good cigar is a smoke. James Barker-Pryce, Conservative Member for Somers Town and South Hampstead, parties with a friend.* The other photograph, snapped on a beach somewhere, was of Bean.

It was hard for Mary to take much in. Distraction does not always distract. She seemed to have no concentration. The lines of print danced.

"Here, you read it to me."

"All right. I like reading aloud. *The missing link. The time has come for the public to be told. What was the connection between James Barker-Pryce MP and Leslie Arthur Bean, the murdered dog-walker?*

"*It is several days since the police revealed that Bean was not The Impaler's latest victim but that this was a copycat killing. Leslie Bean was well known to Mr. Barker-Pryce's friend Miss Toy Townsende, 23, who has told police, 'I knew Les when he was a butler. That was three or four years ago at my friend Mr. Maurice Clitheroe's home. Les was employed by my friend James Barker-Pryce to walk his beautiful retriever dog Charlie, but I think there must have been some disagreement between them as the dog-walking ceased, though Les still paid visits to Mr. Barker-Pryce's Regent's Park home. . . .'*

"Can you imagine anyone actually talking like that?"

"It sounds libelous to me. How do they hope to get away with it?"

"Perhaps they don't care. *On the phone today Mr. Barker-Pryce, 68, said he had no memory of any photograph of himself and Miss Townsende. It was possible she was the young lady who made a suggestion to*

*him while he was parking his Mercedes in Paddington Street, London
W1, two months ago. Mrs. Julia Barker-Pryce, 62, Mr. Barker-Pryce's
wife of 33 years, was not available for comment. She and her husband
are . . . Turn to page two.*

"Here's a shot of the girl in a G-string. She can't really be called
Toy, can she? *She and her husband are spending the weekend at their
country retreat at Upper Slaughter, Gloucestershire . . .* Upper Slaughter? I don't believe it."

"There really is a place called that. Dorrie, did you hear the front
doorbell?"

"I don't think so. Listen. It goes on, *Mr. Barker-Pryce later told our
reporter*—I suppose they're all barracking him outside his country
house—'*There was no quarrel between me and Mr. Bean. That would
be impossible. He was a working man and I believe former servant. I dismissed him for incompetence and there is no truth in rumors that he visited my house or that I continued to pay him a remuneration . . .*' Oh,
that must have been the bell!"

The tikka man had come round the side of the house in search of
them. He was wearing his red and white T-shirt with red jeans and
carrying a tray laden with covered dishes, fastened to his torso with
straps like a rucksack.

"I'm so sorry," Mary said. "We weren't sure if we heard the bell."

"Shall I put it in the kitchen for you?"

"Thank you."

He went indoors. When he came back, he gave Dorothea a doubt-
ful look, then a smile and a, "I'm not mistaken, am I, madam?"

"No, no. You used to drive the dry cleaner's van, didn't you? Oh,
it must be five years back."

"That's right. Spot on. And you live in Charles Lane up in St.
John's Wood."

They began reminiscing. Mary went indoors, turned the oven on
low, and put the korma, rice, and vegetables inside. Leo's engagement ring that he had bought her in a shop in Camden Passage was

still on her finger. She took it off and wondered what would happen to it if she put it down the waste disposal unit and pressed the switch. It might break the unit. Better give it to some poor dosser to sell. She took it off and dropped it inside the cutlery drawer. Then she peeled two peaches, sliced them, and looked for a liqueur to pour over them. The Amaretto Leo had brought the previous week . . .

Even in her mind she had better stop calling him that. Leo wasn't his name. He wasn't Oliver either, he couldn't even be called by the pseudonym under which she had so long known the recipient of her donation, for he wasn't that recipient, it wasn't into his bones that her marrow had been induced, but an unknown dead man's.

She took the wine out of the refrigerator, found a corkscrew, and put it with two glasses on a tray. Dorothea was lying back in the lounging chair, gazing up at the pale sky, now covered with a network of vapor trails. Gushi had climbed onto her lap. The tikka man had gone.

"That poor man," Dorothea said, sitting up. "He went to prison for running someone over when he was driving a laundry van. Of course I didn't mention any of that. But I remembered. I don't think you ought to go to prison if you didn't *mean* to kill someone, do you?"

"Sometimes I think no one ought to go to prison for anything," said Mary. "But that's not very practical. Was he on drugs or drunk or what?"

"He'd been drinking," said Dorothea. "Talking of which, do you want me to open that for you?"

• • •

The traffic in the Marylebone Road speeds up at the weekends. There is less of it, less to slow it down or bring it to frequent stops. On the Sundays of mid-August less traffic uses the road than perhaps on any other days of the year and it seems like some highway in the fifties or sixties when driving was pleasurable and the air relatively pure.

But on mid-August Saturdays, with so many people away on holiday and so many tourists car-less pedestrians, the traffic speeds along, three lanes of it, roaring up to Euston and the underpass or tearing down to Chapel Street, the Marylebone Flyover and the M40. Sometimes brakes shriek when a stop is enforced at Baker Street lights or those at Park Crescent. In the week it is a slow lumbering battering ram that plods at fifteen miles an hour, but on a late summer Saturday it becomes a swift juggernaut and therefore far more dangerous.

Mary thought all these things as she came back from buying bread in Marylebone High Street on Saturday morning. Gushi was tucked under her arm. She had brought him with her on a supernumerary walk but he was frightened by the traffic noise and buried his face in the palm of her hand. They crossed quickly and she brought him into the friendly green of the park. He ran down the bank and drank thirstily from the lake. Already a hot vapor hung over the broad expanses of grass, bleached yellow and in places entirely bared by the drought. The water with which the flowerbeds were sprayed first thing each morning had dried by now and some plants hung their heads. She kept to the shady side of the park.

A man on a seat was reading a paperback of *The Catcher in the Rye,* the woman at the other end of the bench a broadsheet newspaper with the front page headline: MP TO SUE OVER MURDER AND SEX ALLEGATIONS. Mary tried to think about her future, where she would live, what she would do. Leo, Oliver, that man whoever he was, had said, *Two days after we're married my wife will be able to come and live with me....*

She remembered then. Today the Blackburn-Norrises were coming home. He had said that because the Blackburn-Norrises were coming home and she would be free. She looked round for Gushi. He was making friends with a Jack Russell, touching noses, wagging tails. She went back for him, put him on the lead, gently shooed the other dog away.

"They're coming home today," she said to him. "Your master and mistress, your people, owners, whatever you call them. Come on, let's get back fast."

So that's what I've come to, she thought, talking aloud to a dog in public. Gushi licked her fingers. No, he's not sorry for you, he doesn't understand, she said to herself, he's a nice dog but he's just a dog.

They went out into Albany Street by the Cumberland Gate and Cumberland Terrace. As they came into Park Village West the Blackburn-Norrises' taxi was just pulling away from the gates of Charlotte Cottage.

. . .

He had slept that Friday night in his own flat for the sake of seeing the horror movie, *How to Make a Monster*. The boards, of raw beech that gave off a strong resinous smell, encased the broken windows and made of the interior a dusty kiln. There was no way of ventilating the place except by leaving the front door open and no one did that, no one dared. He'd gone through his ritual and used two rocks before the film started, then gone on to vodka, neat but with a spot of Tabasco sauce and a sprinkling of mustard. He didn't need excuses but if he did he'd have said it was to take his mind off the stink in the flat and the heat. For his health's sake, he nibbled at a Duchy Original biscuit, the gingered sort, with his drink.

The telly was still on when he woke up. His watch had stopped and he didn't know what time it was. Dark or light, it was all the same in here, or almost. A strong sun high in the sky penetrated the cracks in the beech boards and laid bright bars across the bit of filthy carpet on the floor. The smell, he realized now, was himself. He smelled like the hamburger stall outside Madame Tussaud's that the people in the mewses between the waxworks and the park complained filled their places with the reek of onions and fatty beef. He wondered if it mattered or if he should do something about it. In the pitch dark something ran over his foot.

Hob yelled. He jumped up, smashed the light on with the flat of his hand, and saw the mice flee, scurrying for the honeycombed skirting board. It was only mice, that was all it was. They had been feasting on Duchy Original crumbs. He staggered to the bathroom and urinated copiously. His half-brother had told him blow made you pee a lot and he was right. The bath was full of dirty dishes, the washing up of weeks. He had long used up every piece of crockery he had, and it lay piled there, dusty by this time, coated with the little waxy white pellets like seeds that were fly eggs. Hob thought he saw things moving between a plate and a glass and he turned away. That was funny because he'd never hallucinated, he'd never been interested in acid, microdot, shrooms, or any of that stuff.

He decided against a bath. Where would he put the dishes? He went back and turned the telly off. He turned the light off too and lay on the settee. For some reason he started thinking about his brother-in-law that used to be before his sister divorced him. Hob had rather liked him, had felt sorry for him because when he was a teenager he'd done acid, just the once, and he'd been left years later with these visions of rats. They'd come at any time and crawl all over him. Hob's ex-brother-in-law had been dead scared of rats, had a phobia about them, so it was a miserable existence he led. Shame, Hob thought. But he never thought about anything or anyone for long. Like alcoholics with drink, he thought about, talked to himself about, considered, wondered at, the substances he used. He would have talked to others about them, only there was no one to talk to.

The mice were back. He could hear them scuttering. Someone on the floor below had told him she'd woken up in the night and heard this trundling noise and when she shone her torch under the bed she'd seen this mouse rolling a Smartie she'd dropped toward a hole in the wall, pushing it with its nose. You had to laugh. He saw a thread of light appear on the floor, then another. It must be morning.

Sometime today he was due to work over a bloke up in Agar Grove who'd done something that got up Lew's nose—though not what he liked up there. Promised to take a bag of smack along with his dope and had reneged (Lew's word) on the deal. Hob was getting a hundred for putting the shyster out of action for a couple of weeks and four rocks over the odds. His thoughts drifted to those rocks but he'd only got two left in the flat, so when thinking instead of *using* got too much, he wandered off looking for what he'd brought in the evening before. The red velvet bag, the stuff was with the bag, maybe in the kitchen.

He found it and poured the powder into a foil bag that had once held some adjunct, sensitive to light, of a photocopier. Like much of his paraphernalia, Hob had found it in a wastebin in one of the more prosperous parts. He slit open the bottom of the bag and held it over the powder in one of the saucers from the bath, screwed up the open top, and put his mouth over the resulting aperture. It wasn't as clever or as satisfying as his watering can rose but it would do for now. Better than one of your ordinary stems, anyway. He lit the powder with a match.

It was angel dust, or phencyclidine, out of fashion and therefore relatively cheap. Hob had seen on telly that it was basically the stuff they shot into rhinos and elephants on darts to put them under when they moved them away from ivory hunters or whatever. PCP was a change and, anyway, he liked it because it made him feel unreal, like he was a person in that *How to Make a Monster* movie, living inside the telly and watched by millions, or else invisible and not watched at all. Both sensations were pleasant enough.

Sweat began to break out all over him. That was the effect of the dust, as was this floating sensation. He got up and walked about, took a few dancing steps, feeling suddenly like a tall thin man with a small head and a ballet dancer's feet. Maybe he'd get out of here and go and do the shyster over before the day had really begun.

He could feel his heart beating. The idea that you couldn't always feel your heart beating amused him and he laughed as he danced about the flat, picking up what he needed. Unthinkable to go out without the red velvet bag, without something to keep him well, without something else to bring him down if the heartbeat got so strong it was painful. All ideas of having a bath or changing his clothes had receded. Who needed that shit?

His heart had stopped. For a moment he was transfixed with terror, for he had forgotten what had just made him laugh, that a beating heart cannot normally be felt. He pranced again, punching the air, and into his ears, squeezing up through his body, came the tick-tick-tick of his heart. Laughing again, he thumped himself on the chest, on the place where, under the skin and ribs, the ticking clock pumped.

With the red velvet bag in his jacket pocket, he left the flat and came out onto the concrete walkway. A cannibalized van stood tireless on what was left of the grass and broken glass littered the empty aisles of the car park, thick as flints on a beach. Around here they used spray paint for the graffiti and the kind they used was red, like blood. For all that, the morning was beautiful, the sky translucent like a blue pearl, the air as yet cool and almost fresh, as if some breath of it had wafted this way from the park in the night. Hob noticed only the emptiness, the absence of anyone. This was only so in the very early hours and his watch told him it was not quite half past six.

He went down the concrete stairs and tried to think about getting to Agar Grove, but for some reason his inner eye could only see the railway line running across the Euston wasteland, the visual part of his mind throwing up bridges and flyovers and cranes with necks like Meccano dinosaurs. He'd have to come down, he needed something to bring him down. Yellow Jackets or V's—what had he got?

He palmed two Nembutal, swallowing them in his own saliva.

The place still had an appearance of emptiness when the police came looking for him half an hour later. It was still only seven. The police car crunched over the broken glass and stopped by the mutilated van. Marnock had a sergeant with him and a man in uniform, the one who was driving. They saw the boarded-up windows, looked at each other and shrugged. There was no doorbell. The sergeant banged on the knocker. He did that twice, then shouted through the letter box, "Police, open up!"

No one did, so they broke the door down, no difficult task. It yielded after two shoulder charges and a thump from the driver's boot. The smell that came out to meet them was so bad that at first they thought there must be a dead body inside.

29

I t was Marnock himself who found Hob.

They had been searching for him since morning in all his known haunts. The latest sighting came from a man in Agar Grove who, from his hospital bed, was able to name his assailant. He had lost four teeth, had two cracked ribs and a broken collarbone, but he was anxious to talk about Harvey Owen Bennett.

It was his opinion that Bennett was the Impaler, Bennett was guilty of the street people killings. Marnock disagreed but didn't say so. He thought the Agar Grove man entitled to sling mud and make wild accusations. For the time being. He was no angel, had a string of convictions as long as the Broad Walk, which Marnock would later make longer. It was his belief the Agar Grove man was responsible for the mugging of Bean in the Nursemaids' Tunnel.

He was always made happy by villains gassing. It gave him hope for the future. Harvey Owen Bennett, for instance. Bennett had killed Bean and stuck him on that five-pointed iron tree, but someone had paid him to do it and Marnock now hoped Bennett would tell him who. The Agar Grove man had created a happy precedent.

Marnock called that day on every member of Bennett's extended family. They weren't truthful people, but this time, with misgivings, he believed them when they said they hadn't seen him. His mother said she hadn't seen him for six months and this amused Marnock in the light of what she had told him back in June—that at the time of Pharaoh's murder Hob had been among guests at an all-night silver wedding party in the Holloway Road.

They scoured the park for him. Marnock thought of the Grotto as the abode, more or less reserved, of the toffee-nosed dosser with the Oxbridge accent, and he nearly didn't look. It was a drinking straw, spiraled with red like a barber's pole and stuck up in the branches of a tree, that caught his eye from his seat in the back of the car. The ritual that served Harvey Bennett's habit required drinking straws. . . .

He was lying half in, half out of the dirty little pond. They heard his breathing long before they reached him and that was how they knew he was alive. Marnock's sergeant was on his mobile calling an ambulance before they had laid a finger on Hob.

"He's young," Marnock's sergeant said. "Well, youngish. But I reckon he's had a stroke."

The ambulance man, getting Hob onto a stretcher, said superfluously that he wasn't a doctor. Then he said that in his opinion Hob had had a stroke.

"Or several," said Marnock. "I once knew a bloke, only a year or two older than him, same taste for substances, had twenty strokes in quick succession."

"Bloody hell," said the ambulance driver. "Did it kill him?"

"In a manner of speaking," said Marnock. "After a couple of weeks they switched off the machine."

.   .   .

Be angry, Mary said to herself, you must be angry. You must walk on past him, pretend he's not there. Or stand your ground and tell him what you think of him. She held her fists tightly clenched. He was in front of her now.

"I've been here since eight this morning," he said, "waiting for you."

"I didn't come into the park this morning," she said.

"It was so hot. I brought a bottle of water, but it got warm. I tried to keep awake but I fell asleep and when I woke up I thought I'd missed you."

"What do you want?" She knew he had never heard that note in her voice before.

"I suppose that's how you think of me, as always wanting something, as doing everything I do for what I can get out of it."

"Wouldn't that be a true picture?"

"Not entirely."

She walked into the shade of the trees, put her hands against the rough cool bark of a tree, and bowed her head. "I thought I'd never see you again. I hoped not. I know what you did, I've thought about it these past days, I haven't had anything else to think about, and there can't be anything you can say to me in extenuation." She turned to look at him, half look at him, and remembered then what she hadn't thought of for perhaps an hour or two: their lovemaking. It came back and brought hot angry blood into her face. He must see that burning color and know. "It won't mean anything to you if I say it was the worst betrayal I've ever known."

Alistair's small misdemeanors, what were they compared with his offense?

"Would you—could we—is it possible to ask you if we could go back to the house?"

"The Blackburn-Norrises have come home."

"Then will you sit down here with me or on a seat or somewhere and talk to me?"

Her head bowed again. She found she was shaking it from side to side. The words came out hoarsely.

"What is your name?"

"What?"

"I asked you what your name is. I can't call you Leo. You aren't called Leo."

"My name is Carl," he said. "Carl Nash. Leo was my brother."

She sat down. He dropped onto the grass beside her but moved when she indicated by a pushing movement with her hands that he was too close. She looked at him properly for the first time, a gaze of deepest scorn, and saw that his eyes were full of tears.

. . .

"I brought Leo up. He was more than ten years younger than I. Oh, yes, of course I'm not twenty-four, I'm older than you, Mary, not younger, I'm thirty-five."

"We believe what people tell us," Mary said. "Or I do. I believed what you told me. And I saw your birth certificate."

"You saw his. When the leukemia was diagnosed and they said he needed a transplant I thought there wouldn't be a problem. There was our mother—not that she'd taken a scrap of notice of Leo since he was ten, she'd left that to me—and there was myself, a couple of half-sisters somewhere about. None of us was compatible. Can you imagine that?"

"You've already told me. Except that you suggested it was you and not your brother who needed the transplant. If you're going to explain you should . . ."

"Tell you why I posed as Leo?"

"It was for my money," she said bitterly.

He lifted his shoulders, not denying. "I was an actor once. Only there was no work. Then I was a schoolteacher. Funny, isn't it? Then I made a bit of money," he said. "Dealing, mostly."

She knew she was innocent but not what she was innocent of. The look in his eyes told her he wasn't talking about scrap metal or antiques.

"Drugs," he said impatiently. "I'd needed funds to find a donor for Leo. That was before the Harvest Trust. I thought maybe I'd have to go to some Third World country and buy a donor. Then you came along."

"I wasn't rich then," she said. "I'd been living in a one-bedroom flat in Willesden and earning twelve thousand a year. What made you think I was rich?"

He said simply, "The heading on your writing paper. The address. Charlotte Cottage, Park Village West."

Briefly she closed her eyes. Unseeing, she sensed he had come closer to her and she drew away. She looked at him.

"And when you found out I didn't live there you dropped me, you meant never to see me again. That was what happened. You weren't ill, you were never ill."

"True," he said. "It was a bitter disappointment." She looked incredulously at his wry smile. He had aged in the past few minutes. He might be forty, forty-five. The smile creased his pale face into lines and ridges. "I did need money, you see. I knew Leo would get ill again, I could see the signs, I'd made myself an expert in his illness." All the ironic amusement died out of his face. "I loved him so much. Believe me, if you can believe anything I say, believe me, I'm not trying for your sympathy, your compassion, but I'd like you not to think me a total monster. I loved him as if he were my own child. Or I think so, I've never had a child."

"So that was all right? Using me was all right because you loved your brother?"

"No, Mary, it wasn't all right. But it was all I could think of. Your grandmother died and when I heard that I came back. You told me what she'd left you and it was more than I'd imagined in my wildest dreams."

She had become curious in spite of herself. The sheer suicidal nerve of it compelled a question.

"I might have found out at any time. The trust might have told me Leo—your brother—they might have told me he was becoming ill again. What would you have done?"

"What I did when they did," he said. "Disappeared. But I used to scrutinize your post. I was—I was usually up first." He had turned away his eyes.

"So that's why you stayed with me," she said bitterly, unable to bring herself to use the words. "That's why you stayed those nights, so that you could get to the post in the morning." The words were hard for her because she had never used them before. "That's why you screwed me, *fucked* me."

He said with a simplicity she had to believe at last was honest, "It was at first. I came to love you. Couldn't you tell?"

.   .   .

For half an hour she had been unaware of anyone else in the park but themselves. A child's shriek, a blue and white lightweight ball bouncing across the grass, coming to rest at their feet, reminded her they were not alone. She stood up, brushed dried shreds of grass off her jeans, and lobbed the ball back. He watched her, anxiously waiting.

"What do you want me to say?" she asked him wearily.

"Only that you believe me."

She supposed that she had noticed. It was when the lovemaking changed from a sick man's effete attempts to enthusiasm, when acquiescence became passion, that she had been aware of it without asking why. He had been ill and now he was getting better, that was all.

"I believe you."

She said it dully, for it was a few moments before relief came and she understood that she need no longer feel humiliation and shame. He had wanted her, he had not had to force himself.

"I wanted to marry you by then," he said. "I'd never wanted that before." He squeezed his eyes shut and sprang to his feet. "Will you do one last thing for me? Will you walk a little way with me?"

"I don't know." She nearly called him Leo. "I don't know, Carl."

He flushed at the sound of his own name. It seemed to confirm him as its true possessor. "Do you remember that place we went to for dinner? That first time? The Italian place?"

"When you pretended to be ill?"

He winced at that. "I'm sorry. I had to. I thought I had to. Mary, I've done worse things than that to get money."

"I don't want to hear," she said.

"I thought—I wondered—if you'd let me take you there now, tonight. If we could—it would be the last time, wouldn't it?"

She nodded. She still wanted answers. "I'll walk with you."

"And you'll come to the restaurant?"

"Perhaps."

He got to his feet and held out a hand to help her, but she shook her head. They walked across the grass in silence, across Chester Road and down the Broad Walk.

"Leo knew all about it," he said. "He thought it was funny at first. We both thought it was funny at first. He used to want all the details but I—I stopped telling him things after a while."

"Just as a matter of interest—" Mary knew she was no good at the ironic tone, she found it hard to be scathing, but she tried "—just as a matter of interest, why didn't Leo meet me himself, or isn't there anything amusing about being honest?"

"Oh, Mary, he was just a boy, undersized, not educated, never quite well. I loved him and perhaps you'd have come to love him if you'd known him, but not like that, not in that way. You'd never have said you'd marry the real Leo."

Suddenly, as they came down the path and reached the lake, she stopped thinking about herself and reluctantly, almost fearfully, began to think about him. The anger had evaporated. It had never been thriving. She put her hand on his arm and looked into his face.

"You must be very unhappy."

"Thank you for that," he said.

"Oh, Carl. It was like losing your own child."

"I suppose so. But it was worse. I killed him, you see."

"*What?*"

"Oh, I don't mean that. Not actually. Not like that Impaler kills people. I mean I killed him by taking away his only chance of getting well."

"I don't understand."

"You would have given another donation, wouldn't you? If it had been asked for you'd have done it?"

"Yes, but . . ."

"You said so. When we'd been to your grandmother's house, the day I asked you to marry me. You'd have given it to me, to your husband, but it wasn't I that wanted it, it was the real Leo Nash.

"Leo was dying by then. Perhaps you could have saved him, but I couldn't ask, could I? I couldn't let the Harvest Trust ask. I thought maybe if once we were married and I said I had to have money, I had to have, say, fifty thousand, you'd have given it to me and I'd have gone to India and bought the right sort of bone marrow for Leo. But Leo died."

She thought about it. She had withdrawn her hand from his arm when he spoke of killing his brother, but now she replaced it and let it lie there lightly. They had come out of the park at the York Gate and the clock on Marylebone Church ahead of them began to chime the hour. Perhaps because of the VJ Day commemorations the traffic was dense and swift.

"It was a monstrous irony," he said. "That I, who loved Leo, who would have done anything for Leo, who did do anything, spoiled his chances of life by what I did. By choosing this way to make a fortune for Leo, I blew it. So I killed him. If by killing someone we mean that but for us he'd be alive. But for me, Leo would be alive."

They had come to the pavement edge and begun to walk toward the lights at Harley Street. The traffic noise was so loud that he had to shout.

"The old dog man," he began.

"Bean," she said. "Bean—what about him?"

"He tried to blackmail me. He was going to tell you—things about me." He smiled. "Not the things I've told you. Other things you'd have liked even less. I couldn't allow that."

"I can't hear you," she said. "I can't hear you for the traffic."

"Just as well," Carl said, softly now and half to himself. "I know you won't forgive me, anyway, but you'd never have overlooked paying someone to—deal with Bean." He turned to look at her, seized her by the shoulders. "Mary!" It was very nearly a shout. "Can you hear me now? I've blown it with you too, I know that. Just for the record, how did you get the Harvest Trust's letter?"

She also had to raise her voice. "Alistair sent it to me. As a wedding present."

"The bastard."

.   .   .

She never once looked behind her. Roman saw her put her hand on her brother's arm and for a moment he thought things were all right, and then he knew they were far from that. He knew too that it wasn't her brother. A sense of foreboding filled him. He had been about to turn back, but now he wouldn't, he would stick with it.

The charge of emotion between them was so powerful it tensed their bodies. He marveled at it, walking a dozen yards behind them. She withdrew her hand, recoiled, spoke a name, "Carl . . . ," loud enough for him to hear. So it was Carl. But what was her name? Strange that after so long, so many brief chance encounters, he still didn't know.

"What?" he heard her cry.

Carl was explaining something. She shook her head vehemently, but after a moment or two the hand was back, resting on Carl's arm but distantly somehow as if placed there out of pity rather than affection. You are imagining too much, Roman told himself, and you are spying too much, they can take care of themselves. It's no more than a lovers' quarrel being made up.

But he followed them down York Gate. The clock on St. Marylebone was chiming seven. The pavement of the Marylebone Road was choked with crowds, the traffic pouring fast down toward the Euston underpass. He was very close behind them now, so close that if she turned round and saw him he would have had to make an excuse for his presence and he had no explanation. But she didn't turn round. She was looking into Carl's face, not with love, not with passion, but still as if no one else in the world existed.

Her voice she kept low, drowned by the traffic's roar, but the man called Carl shouted above it. He shouted as if he didn't care who heard him.

"I don't want to live without him, you see. I can't face life without him."

For a brief while Roman had been so near her that by putting out his hand he could have touched her; then, as happens in crowds, two people pushed in front of him, squeezing between him and her and forcing him to step back. They were part of the group at the pavement edge, waiting to cross when the lights changed. You could wait ages here for the lights to change, they were red almost too short a time to allow for crossing. Seven or eight people stood poised to cross and she and Carl were at the head of them, waiting while the traffic pounded down its three lanes.

Things happened very quickly then. Roman, craning his neck, but taller than those in front of him, saw Carl give her a little push back from the curb. A little saving, protecting push into those waiting behind. He put his head down and plunged into the road, threw out his arms, and ran into the traffic, in front of a car, a taxi, into the path of a container, running at bonnets, under wheels.

A woman was screaming from the moment he leapt from the curb. Roman heard his own rough gasp as he clenched his hands.

Brakes screamed and horns brayed. Carl was flung into the air, his body describing an arc in the blue air against the setting sun, splintered by flashes of light from sun-glinting chrome, the sudden full beam of a headlight blazing on him as he fell under wheels and was ground between tangling metal.

There was blood somewhere. Roman thought he saw a long splash of it fly against white enamel. He was struggling to reach her, catch her as she fell, but the crowd made a wall around her, leaning over her, kneeling beside her. He stepped aside, let it go, and stood holding his bowed head in his hands in the suddenly emptied street.

Sirens were already wailing.

30

F or quite a long time Marnock or his sergeant sat by Harvey Owen Bennett's bed, hoping for a name, hoping he would come round sufficiently to tell them who had paid him to kill Bean. One or another member of his large extended family was usually there, a half-brother or sister, a stepsister, his mother, stepfathers and men who said they were his uncles. Some of them touched his lifeless hand.

He never moved. He was fed intravenously and a machine kept his heart beating and his lungs breathing. Sweat occasionally broke out on his large forehead and slablike cheeks.

Three weeks after he had been brought in, the doctor in charge of his case told Marnock that Harvey Bennett would never speak again. His eyes were open and he would never close them. It was unlikely he could think or remember or speculate or even suffer. Large areas of his brain had been destroyed.

• • •

James Barker-Pryce sued the tabloid newspaper and was awarded substantial damages. These were not on account of their allegations that he had been consorting with a known prostitute; he had admitted that and there was some question whether his constituency party would readopt him at the next General Election. He had brought the action because the journalist alleged he had been involved in a conspiracy to murder.

The school-leaver went back to school, or rather to a sixth form college to take some A Levels, and all Bean's dogs except for Gushi were walked by Amelia Walker, who seemed to find no difficulty in handling seventeen animals at once.

Mary Jago had always meant to sell her grandmother's house and buy another, but having gone there to live after Carl Nash's death, there she remained. She had builders in to convert the upper floors into self-contained flats and her friend Anne Symonds had moved into one of them. The Harvest Trust asked her if she would be willing to remain on their books and in December she gave another bone marrow donation, this time to a girl of sixteen she knew as "Susan" and who knew her as "Barbara."

Roman Ashton rented two rooms in a house in Princess Road, Primrose Hill, where he was not particularly comfortable. All the money derived from the sale of his house he had sunk into a precarious venture with Tom Outram, the Talisman Press having been taken over and absorbed into a massive conglomerate. With some American backing they had started a publishing house that produced only historical novels in paperback originals. So far it had been startlingly successful, but how long would such success last?

Their headquarters were in the Marylebone Road and when it wasn't raining Roman walked to work through the park. He never saw the fair-haired girl. She no longer walked through the Gloucester Gate and south of the zoo to the Charlbert Bridge. She no longer crossed Chester Road or ran through the rose garden.

And then one day he saw her. He was going to work, crossing the Outer Circle, and she and her little dog were getting out of a car she had just parked by the Monkey Gate.

"Hello," she said.

"Hello."

"Do you know, I've often looked for you in here, but I've never seen you. I thought you must have—well, moved away."

"I've looked for you too," he said.

They passed through the gateway into the Broad Walk and across onto the grass. She unclipped the lead from the dog's collar, let him go, stood up, and held out her hand.

"Mary Jago," she said.

"Roman Ashton."

"I was house-sitting for some people when I last saw you. They gave me their dog. They didn't like him much, you see, and I did. I live in Belsize Park now and I've got a car so I can still bring him into the park, but I'm rather late today."

"That's why we've never met," he said.

"You stopped being a street person?"

"Last August." He saw her wince at those words and said quickly, "I did it to get over something. It's something I'll never get over and I don't really want to, but I'm glad of the two years I spent sleeping rough. It gave me—something else to think about. I've got a job now and I'm looking for a place to live."

"When we last met," she said, "you advised me to be angry."

"Did I? I don't remember that. And were you?"

"There was no one to be angry with," she said, and she looked down at her shoes. "Except myself. I think I've got a bit stronger. I don't placate people so much. I'm not so trusting. Oh, I don't know why I'm telling you all this. You can't want to know." She started calling the dog. "Gushi, Gushi, where are you?"

"I'll tell you something," he said. "When you lived in Park Village I appointed myself your guardian. I thought I could watch over you. I told myself you needed protecting. Once when there was a man running after you I sent him the other way."

She was looking at him, incredulously at first, then with a smile dawning.

"But I didn't do much, did I? I didn't do a thing. I couldn't save you from whatever it was."

Her face suddenly grave again, she said, "You couldn't save me from that. I fell into something because I was lonely, something awful. It's over now."

I know, he thought. I saw. The shih tzu came running up, sat at her feet quivering, looking up into her face.

"He always wants to be carried. He's such a baby." She picked up the dog. "You said—you said something about looking for a place to live. Only—well, I've got this big house and I've had some conversions done, and I thought if it was a flat you were—but perhaps . . ." She hesitated, as if putting a restraint upon herself, reminding herself of past indiscretion. "Perhaps we ought to get to know each other a bit better first."

"That seems a very good idea," Roman said.

.   .   .

The man on the canal bank had been there for weeks, months, ever since high summer. Not all the time, he had his occupation, but by night, three nights a week at least, watching and waiting. He had been there since before the body of David George Kneller, whom they called Nello, had been found on the railings outside the zoo.

He blamed himself for that. If he had been more vigilant, done what he had started doing in August two months before, Nello would be alive now. No use asking whether the life he lived had been worth living, the life he now lived, for that wasn't the point.

The first evening he had come down here the man with the beard they called Rome had also come down, looking for a place to kip. But he had got him to leave with a shake of his fist and a scowl on his ugly face. It *was* ugly—so what? There were things they could do for acne now, drugs and whatever, medication was a *cleaner* word, but there hadn't been when he was fourteen. The scars hadn't stopped him getting a wife and promotion or the right to do what he was doing.

For the fiftieth time, or maybe not quite so many as that, he scrambled down through the churchyard and the brambles and stinging nettles onto the canal bank. The clothes he wore, black, ancient, stained rags, were dead men's clothes from the rotting boots to the greasy cloth cap. Sometimes he wondered what he would do if he found someone else on his pitch, settling down for the night. But he never had and he didn't now. Once he'd sat down he always listened to the traffic passing overhead, fancying but doubtless mistaken that he'd know the sound of the van, the diesel noise that was somehow bigger and more of a gargle than that made by a taxi.

The bridge throbbed when cars went over it, boom-boomed when it was something bigger like a truck. It had been dark for hours, since five in the afternoon, but it wasn't cold. Under the bridge it was always damp, the brickwork oozing moisture, the ground sticky, the canal waters dark, more shiny than he ever expected and with rainbow streaks of oil. There was something uncanny about a river that didn't flow but where the water was stagnant, just water put into a ditch really, and the ditch had been dug by men. He'd never thought of any of that until he came to sit nightly by the canal.

He always tried not to fall asleep, but often he couldn't help himself. If what he was waiting for happened that would wake him up all right. When he woke, usually a bit before dawn, his legs ached and his back ached from lying on damp concrete and he felt filthy, as if some sticky substance had been pasted on him in the night, to make a coat between his skin and his clothes.

Tonight he thought it unlikely he'd sleep. It had been his day off and he'd slept away the afternoon. Since that first evening when he'd forgotten, he'd never come down here without food, plenty of it. A pizza—ironical that, really—a couple of mini pork pies or a samosa, cold sausages, a bag of crisps, bananas. His wife called bananas the junk food of fruit and he saw what she meant, not that they weren't good for you but that they were so easy to eat. He ate one. He drank some coffee out of the flask he'd brought.

The barrow he had with him he'd found dumped in the Grotto. God knows who had put it there or had used it. It was his now and he filled it up with groundsheet, sleeping bag, cushions, a torch, the cigarettes he shouldn't smoke but probably would before the night was out, food, the coffee flask, a bottle of water, *Today,* the latest Stephen King—when was Stephen King going to write about canals, the horrible way they just lay there, not moving, just waiting, still or lightly rocking? Maybe he already had.

Up in Camden Town a dog started barking. It barked for a bit, then began howling like a wolf. The wolves in the zoo never seemed to howl. He tore the pizza in half and each half in half and started eating. You couldn't tell from the state of the darkness but it was after eleven, it was nearly midnight. Overhead the traffic was a lot lighter. For a long while there wasn't any traffic and then the bridge would thump and rattle.

It was too dark to read his book or his paper and he wasn't keen enough on either to bother with his torch. He contemplated the slightly rocking black water with the skins of light lying on patches of it. He started counting the seconds between one rattle of the bridge and the next, calculating that enumeration at a medium-fast rate was counting seconds. A hundred and ten, next time a hundred and eighty. It was when he was counting for the third time, reaching two hundred and seventeen, that he had this crawling sensation that someone was looking at him from the parapet of the bridge.

He couldn't see the parapet from where he sat, only the underside of the arch, greenish with lichen, a single drop of water falling from between two redder bricks. Grubbing with his fingers in the grassy earth, he picked out a flat pebble and, first holding it parallel to the ground, sent it skimming across the surface of the water. It made a trail of spray as a toy speedboat might. He thought he heard footfalls on the bridge above his head.

He belonged to a profession whose members are not supposed to feel afraid. It was the same with the armed forces. But these days it is no longer necessary to pretend you don't feel fear, only not to show it. He was afraid and he knew all the ways of not showing it. At least, the hand didn't shake that reached for the cigarette packet, took out a cigarette, and brought it to his mouth. He struck a match and watched the blaze of light under the bridge, the glitter on the tubular rail, the black shadows fleeing into the water.

Which way would the man come?

He listened, heard something crushed underfoot, a piece of litter, plastic and hard. It cracked under the pressure of a shoe descending. He looked toward the sound, preparing to act his part, raising a fist to ward off an intruder, the way he had when the Oxbridge dosser came down.

It was over now. For good or ill, for himself or the Impaler, this must be the end. No more waiting and watching. Before he saw anything else he saw the glint of the knife.

He started to get up. Act naturally. The dosser on the canal bank would get to his feet, would start back, drop his cigarette into the dark water. He had his back to the underside of the bridge. It struck cold through the padding of his clothes. The man came down, revealed himself in the dark that is never quite darkness, tall, youngish, a dark combat jacket over that red and white vest, camouflage pants over the red jeans. His lips curled back like a dog's.

The way he hurled himself onto the dosser with his back against the wall was sudden, a violent reflex, but not unexpected. The knife sank into something soft and thick, but not into flesh. There was no blood. It was pulled out to strike again but never reached its target. The poised arm was seized, brought up at an unnatural angle; a leg came out from the bundle of black rags and kicked with practiced aim, and the man in the combat jacket gave a soft groan. His upraised hand trembled, opened, and the knife fell clattering onto the concrete.

It was then that the kick came again, harder, more assured. Arms went up and for a moment the figure was poised on the coping, just a foot away from the guard rail, mouth open to scream. The booted foot slammed in just below the ribcage, a flat ram, and he went in backward, the scream released, making a huge splash as he struck the water. The spray flew up to the height of the bridge and drenched the man on the bank, who cursed and shook himself.

He lay down flat in the wet. He was checking if his quarry could swim. Not well, but enough, enough to flounder down there in a doggy paddle, treading cold water, spluttering and coughing.

One of the other objects in the barrow was a mobile phone. He fished it out and made his call. As he was speaking, telling them where he was, where to find him, he thought how everyone had speculated as to why the Impaler avoided the park. What was sacred about the park, or dangerous about it? What placed an embargo on the park? But it was simple. The answer was simple. There was no traffic in the park, it was closed to all but park police and park administration vehicles—closed to a red and white take-away van.

The man in the water could hold out for five minutes and that was all it would take. They would be here to help him in five minutes, less than that now. He watched the struggles, the inefficient battling toward the canal rim and feeble grasping of the stone.

His eye on his watch, he waited another two minutes. Then he scrambled up the bank, searching till he found a six-foot-long stick, a branch with dead leaves still clinging to it. Down onto the puddled path again, the branch extended for its life-saving purpose. White, water-bleached hands grasped the wood. He pulled, bracing his feet against the place where the brickwork met the concrete path. He spoke the form of the caution and the man's name and said, "I'm arresting you for the murders of Dominic John Cahill, James Victor Clancy, and David George Kneller, and the attempted murder of Detective Inspector William Marnock . . ."